I0787944

James R. Hugunin

Elder Physics

The Wrong of Time:
Stories from an Elder Home

ISBN 1-884097-52-9
ISBN-13 978-1-884097-52-2

ISSN 1084-547X

Elder Physics

$$i\hbar\frac{\partial}{\partial t}e^{\frac{i}{\hbar}(px-Et)} = \frac{-\hbar^2}{2m}\frac{\partial^2}{\partial x^2}e^{\frac{i}{\hbar}(px-Et)} + V(x,t)e^{\frac{i}{\hbar}(px-Et)}$$

The Wrong of Time: Stories from an Elder Home

by

James R. Hugunin

Journal of Experimental Fiction 52

Journal of Experimental Fiction Books
Depth Charge Publishing
Geneva, Illinois

Elder Physics

$$i\hbar \frac{\partial}{\partial t} e^{\frac{i}{\hbar}(px-Et)} = \frac{-\hbar^2}{2m} \frac{\partial^2}{\partial x^2} e^{\frac{i}{\hbar}(px-Et)} + V(x,t)e^{\frac{i}{\hbar}(px-Et)}$$

The Wrong of Time:
Stories from an Elder Home

by
James R. Hugunin

. . . how beautiful are the old when they are doing a snow job!
— Saul Bellow, *Seize the Day*

Nothing in this life that I've been trying can equal or surpass the art of dying.
— George Harrison

Nobody disobeys a ukase, said the Dead Father. He chuckled.
— Donald Bartheleme, *The Dead Father*

When the subject calls upon the Father . . . he encounters only an echo
in a void that triggers a cascade of delusional metaphors.
— Jacques Lacan, *Érits*

I am quite content to go down to posterity as a scissors and paste man. . . .
— James Joyce

True aesthetic innovation can only come from reworking and transforming existing
imagery, ripping it from its original context and feeding it into new circuits of analogy.
—Andrew V. Uroskie, "Beyond the Black Box"

Self-Portrait in a Mirror (pencil on paper, 2004) Gerald Hugunin

Although this is largely a work of fiction, and any resemblance to actual people or places is purely coincidental, much of the material was inspired by actual events in my father's life.

Dedicated to my father, Gerald (1922 - 2008)

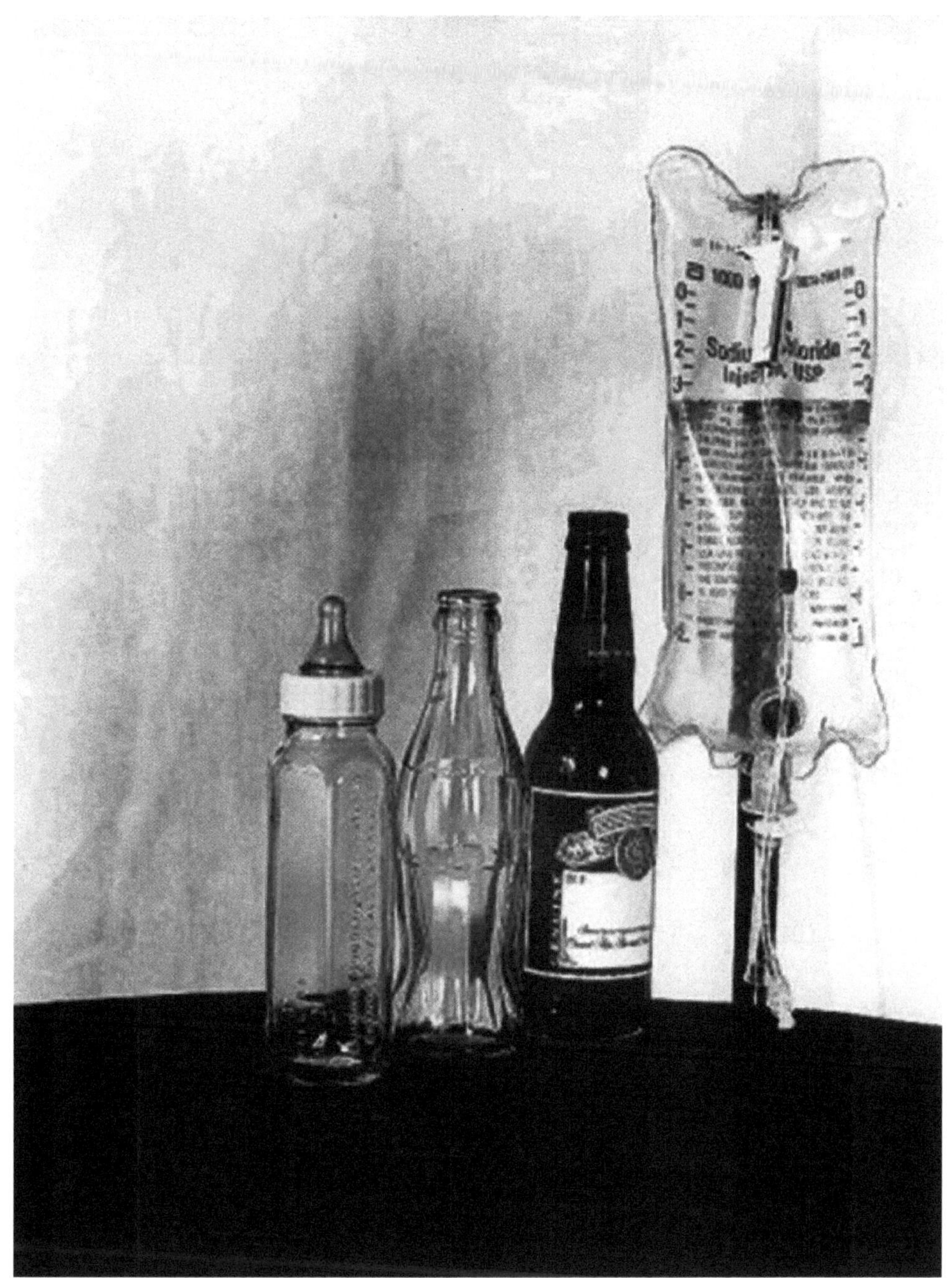

The Four Stages of Life (pencil on paper, 11 x14, 2005) Melanie Mercaptan

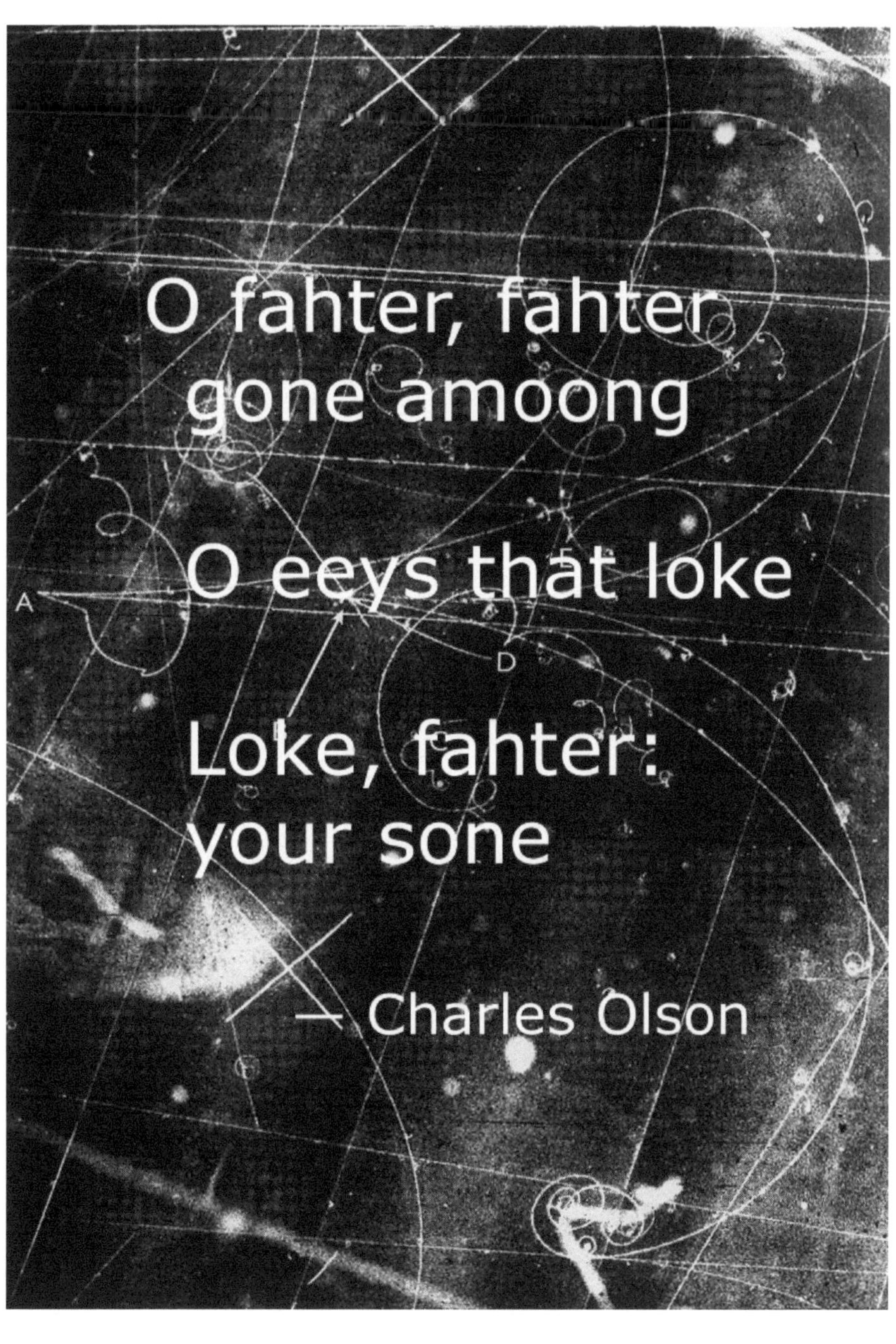

O fahter, fahter
gone amoong

O eeys that loke

Loke, fahter:
your sone

— Charles Olson

Part I

Independent Living

My Life Broken Down into Segments

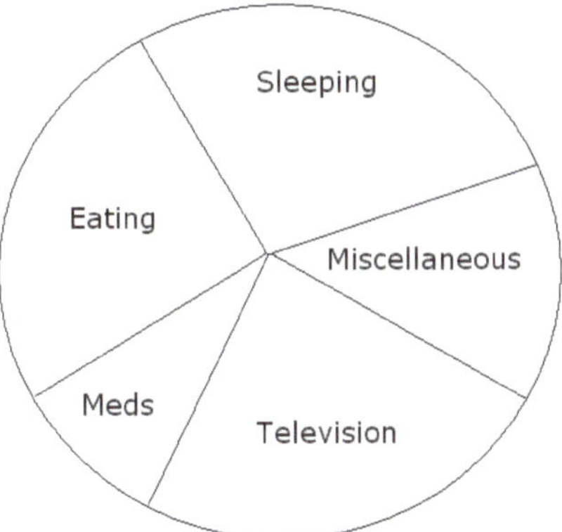

El'-der Home, *n.* a simulated environment, a universe of ceilings, constrained by known elder physical principles — a turbulent field in which various and variable materialities collide, congeal, morph, de-evolve, and disintegrate; significant inconsistencies in the noetic density of the underlying fabric of this region of existence weakens the gravitational pull of memory, and movement is defined from the place of arrival and the end toward which the object is directed by a sort of "appetite" — but which still permits the occurrence of multifarious event anomalies. Within elder physics, mass will be a permanent property of things, while energy will express itself through sweat, grunts, groans, and curses. The contingent aspects of the mathematical models peculiar to elder physics lend themselves to be used to reach cosmological conclusions. A universe where "Star Trek: The Next Generation's" Deanna Troy advises "just take that memory and put it aside for a moment." Or as Gerald Hugunin frames it within his *interpretive armamentarium*: "It all Depends. Today rules are ambiguous, adversary concealed in aliases, and the oracles broadcast a babble of contradictions; it's all wheels-within-wheels, like in ancient cosmology."

Gerald in his flight jacket with squadron insignia (2005)

The Situation

In the Beginning Was the Situation: An extended mood with and without joy and sadness. Sobs and laughs, black humor and white seriousness — events in the Elsewhere of Elder Physics where the wrong of time rules and where escape velocity seems impossible to reach. Where every day is a patchwork of small battles and myself a brochure of needs. Where Lorentz contractions and time dilations are common and everyone feels like the dummy-hand in Bridge. Where once I am a will within a world of wills, now I am a weed in a wall of indifference; where I now *sit* as many risks as I *run*. Great context for a personal narrative delivered healthy (if not the narrator) and full of beans, where I can *play* at being exactly what I am, a suspicious fellow in a melancholy year littered with psycho-inquisitorial sessions within a society best described as organized crime working within a general larval conformism.

Yep, my body has grown a tale in which I will try to isolate the look from the eye, the action from the verb, and extricate the twitter from the machine. This little tale will wag a *have pity on us all and don't get mad at me for writing it*. If you have tears to shed, prepare to shed them now! And excuse me if sometimes I tend to speak *vatically*. I'm Gerald, Catholic, wary, tight-lipped, and tough-minded in my beliefs. I have my strong opinions. And Jim, my son? Well, he has his soft opinions. I look at stars and see sparks from a train of God's thought, but "Jimmer" merely sees loopholes into 256 dimensions. "If God existed, he'd be a library," says my bibliophile offspring. When he defiantly asks, "If God is good, why does he permit evil?" I trump him with, "To thicken the plot." For instance, every day I manage more and more finely terrific internal turmoil, driving off a flood of black crows in the fibers of my inner tree while it seeks the torrid truth of a two o'clock sun.

Today, the sky skys, the blue clouds cloud and blue as I sit in my tiny room where the pressure of reality has put me. I swear I see a fly escape from a cheap print of a Dutch flower painting parked on my abode's south wall and start to explore the human comedy therein until being dismissed in my missal, slammed twixt hallowed pages. Fingers are on my Smith Corona typewriter using a blue ribbon gotten *gratis* in cartons from Sunny "Storm" Atkins's brother, Butch, a night warehouse watchman in Stickney, Illinois. I'm banging out my memoir, *By the Seat of my Pants,* by machine. It's what us old farts do, it's what I'm doing right now. But, be forewarned, light of head, I play moon to my pedantic son's assistance. So here goes!

Here is the imperfect human. Here he is. The imperfect human. You will see the imperfect human function. How does such a number function? Waiting. What kind of thing is it? To be waiting, only waiting, for Ticktockman. Or as engineers (like me) phrase it: *the negative entropy in the ordered organization of life has now become balanced by the positive entropy of disorder and death.*

My head's stuffed with dried memories in place of quick thoughts, the YesterNow of elder physics. My experience of myself is like it's shot at 100,000 frames-per-second and projected back at 24 frames, dragging out time toward my end endlessly.

Mirroring my mood inside, outside my window Illinois's black clouds stall, darken the view of my street below, and threaten to make known their views. My gaze, wandering outside, segues to old memories, curious stories, only to have them at some point suddenly stop, disintegrate, blow away. In my Brave New World — more Huxley's use of the term than Shakespeare's — the days harden with cold and boredom like last year's loaves of bread and I cut them with blunt knives, without appetite, in lazy indifference. Typical self-reflection: *Where did I put my shoe, did I have a shoe? I did, and the lost one seems now in the right place, but then where are the Benicar pills and where am I?* See? No surprise, I oft fantasize a kindly beckoning large neon sign reading: THIS WAY TO THE EGRESS.

But my son — who prefers the adjectives: "new," "revolutionary," "exciting" — tries to keep my interest up. Last week, a trip to the famous Art Institute of Chicago Museum where I drink in a Bellini, a Carpaccio, a Monet. I am shaken with my "museum disease," an exalted sentiment full of adjectives like "immutable," "noble," "ideal" which such art enkindles within me and imprints upon my bodily appearance an expression which, when compared with my well-behaved surroundings, must seem awkward if not comic: smile alternating with seriousness, a too-fast gait followed by sudden stops 'n starts, a close gaze followed by a far gaze, arm around Jimmer, then my hands entwining nervously.Then yesterday, a trip up to the observation deck on our home's top floor to see the fog lift from about the skirts of Chicago in the eastern distance, a coy disclosure, a kind of coquetting.

Another kind of revealing, I'm going through the carbons of my past stories and journal sketches at Jimmer's urging, like this old entry: *My childhood illness began so strangely with so many profound and intractable trans-formations.* Makes me feel at once ghoulish as if it were tissue of my own skin I was peeling back to see in. I'm caught in between my past and my dubious future. Once, in a more comfortable time, I believed in a past leading inexor-ably to the future in simple strides, looking straight ahead. But that was the past. Some days, looking at the deepening reds of the going-down sun, I feel lumpish; a lumbering lubbard loitering slow, but prone to go — BOOM — flat on the carpet in front of not amused staff. Once in front of The Presence, a shitter of filthy flocks of words erupt-ing like Popocatepetl. We call him "Ill-Phil." When his lips are silent, he still chatters on with his finger-tips. Today I saw him holding a homemade sign announcing in black felt-tip marker: 'ENGLISH' IS AN ANAGRAM OF 'SHINGLE'. He's alternately thorny, bossy, bristly, and can writhe into every form of nervous entanglement, all the while slinging verbal vile annoyance. "To what purpose do you spend?" he oft yells at eldsters returning with parcels.

One day when my mood was more Storm Cloud than Sea of Tranquility, Phil yelled at *moi*: "You will die slowly, your blood growing cold, your flesh petrifying, your heart beating its last as a rusted group of iron valves as your life fades from you and sinks into the earth." So I got physical, kicked him right in his coordinator, and followed up with a verbal riposte, an I-know-every-syllable litany of Biblical references: 32nd of Deuteronomy, the 119th Psalm, the 15th of 1st Corinthians, the Sermon on the Mount, and most of the Apocalypse. I then silently sent a perplexed question up to Heaven: *Oh Lord, must I love* this *neighbor of mine? Do you allow exceptions?*

Did I mention Phil calls me "The Berg"? It's 'cause I can give him a dead, cold undersea eye and I'm big 'n slow 'n hard to negotiate around in the narrow halls here. He groks that most of *moi* lies submerged deep under what people see on top. First thing Phil said to me when I arrived here was: "Odor rockets over oily lagoons . . . silver flakes fall through a maze of dirty pictures." First thing *I* said when I was dumped here was: "Orientate me! Locate me, put me in the picture, draw me a map." Had to find the latitude-longitude of this slow-sailing Berg. First thing I smelled here was urine . . . first thing I remember smelling when in my teen glory days playing high school football was moldy jockstraps mixed with a whiff of pool chlorine.

Thinking of glory days, I remember Jimmer and I camping at Yosemite when he was a (much to my athletic disappointment) sophomore-in-high-school-who-didn't-play-football. Ah, the squeak 'n rubble of mountain wind contrasting with the stale patter of commerce at the Valley's many concessions (one sold my favorite snack, Squeakers, deep fried cheese curds with a soft, white cheese interior). Our fingers light 'n cold as we Spring rustle through heavy packs for trail mix, mountain shadow touching hiking boots, Coleman lamp spattering light on faces. Whispers of my Air Corps adventures over reconstituted freeze-dried camp chow, while suffering the tempting smell emanating from a big iron pot of salt pork 'n beans at an adjoining campsite stocked full of laughing Park Rangers, laughing until someone ran in yelling, "Klinker's dead!" Then silence. We assume the doom-news referred to someone's beloved canine. A prefiguring of the day when a nurse tells Jimmer: "Gerald's dead!"

It was during that father-son camping trip that Jimmer and I first jousted over religion and politics (as we continue to do). It hurt me to hear him confess that religion seems to him discreditable — discredited — putting forth its authority in a cowardly way, watching how far it might be tolerated, continually shrinking, disclaiming, fencing, finessing; divided against itself, not by stormy rents, but by thin fissures and splittings of plaster from the walls. Not to be obeyed. Only to be scorned. I try appealing to Nature, like a present-day Emerson, to birdsong and the welling of bell-toned streamlet by its shadowy rock, and recount the pride of purple rocks and river pools of blue and the tender wilderness of glittering trees and the misty light of evening on immeasurable hills. All things that God has given by Intelligent Design. Nothing works though. Moreover, he's anarchist-suspicious of government. Sees visible governments as the toys of some nations, the disease of others, the harness of some, the burdens of more.

These writings, to which you are listening (by now) to the dead with your eyes, are a sea-journal of my last and final voyage. Nature's original intention with the human organism was that it live 130 years, but my drafty tenement of soul suggests much less. I have limited time to *pro-prose* a world-past and a world anew birthed from my portable typewriter (I passed my penchant to pun to Jimmer).

Appropriate that I, a Wisconsin boy, have returned east to the Plains, the fulcrum of America where people have to fasten themselves like tent stakes to survive. The Plains — half sea half land, a high sun as metal and obdurate as the iron horizon — where the world pulled and pulled and pulled, and the world ached and pulled so hard it hurt and I was born. Where BIG America spreads like a pancake. (Jimmer copped this from Charlie Olson, 'cause Olson railed against plagiarists, was a Catholic like me and, like my son, was obsessed with his daddy.)

It was Jimmer who offered me the phrase "the cold equations of elder physics," encouraging me: "Dad, stretch your typing fingers. Get ready to astound your writing club. You can observe Potential and Velocity separately, have to, to measure The Thing, the Elder Home. You'll get approximate results, but they will be useable enough if you're okay with the Heisenberg Uncertainty Principle. . . . 'Hub-a-hubba, get crackin''," he says, citing our health-nut resident Bondo McCracken's repeated attempts to get our old bones moving, believing his enthusiasms, his terrific zest for life, can be our steroids.

Finger bones willing, but I can only *concentrate* to write so many minutes per day. Then I sleep, either chair-snoring — fighting a Sitskrieg for one of the limited number of chairs in the dayroom — or in bed wherein I fight against the covers like a bather swimming against the current, kneading it and molding it with my body like an enormous bowl of dough, waking up in sweat, panting. I smell of sleep. The delights of yawning only leads to a painful cramp of my palate, almost to nausea. Dull imprisoned suffering, I reek of unmade bed, of unwashed hair. My room is decorated in Medieval monastic-sparsity (as Wordsworth said, "Nuns fret not at their convent's narrow room"). Bed with cockroach-colored headboard. Armoire. Bureau. The aluminum walker — a recent addition to my Situation — I often refuse, despite the fact it is politely propellant. A bitter smell of illness has settled into my room's rug from past residents. A large sketch pad with a drawing I just did of myself in a mirror propped against the wall and used as a defense against the day when my face will dissolve into a worried net of wrinkles and harden into an old plank full of knots and veins, from which all memories will have been planed away. Jimmer says that the disturbing thing about mirrors is that, like the act of copulation, they multiply the number of human beings.

Now that mirror sees my eighty-six-year-old face which, thank God, looks more like seventy or less. Except my eyes — once braziers of delight — are now dull and rinsed out. That increasing dullness these last few months that suggests a mind on some complicated matter known only to someone who is not fully present any longer, absorbed by *dementia,* they say. Always trying to prove it too, they are, such that my gray matter often clicks over and over like a car hood opened and closed in the pit stops of the Indy 500. Knot by knot, I feel myself being loosened from the ties joining me to humanity. I put up my barriers and guard the perimeter. Watchful for *wheels-within-wheels*. No coincidences, only conspiracies, in my elder world. Before retiring I open my a door slit and yell,

"I know who your are!" close it, peep through the peep-hole, put a wooden chair up against the door handle. Don't want unexpected visitors.

Waking, I often open my mouth, smacking my lips with distaste, a dry tongue, bitter. An oiling body like an overheated factory. I look around helplessly, as if searching for something. Slowly I come alert to any conspiracy of winking hidden eyes, of tuned-in ears, of suspicious gestures. Sound. Sound destroys the possibility of distinguishing between subject and environment, between interior and exterior. Can't always tell who's talking from where. They say I hear voices that don't have a body, like off-screen voices in a film. Yes. Unhappy is the pappy-me. Me the pap, he the son. Me his "para*papa*noid" — as Jim calls me — but my real name is Gerald. And when I speak, it is only to issue commands. I can grow instantly into prophetic anger, choking with brash words that are emitted like a machine gun. I'm incapable of imagining that others wouldn't want to do whatever I think is best. The words *obey* and *obligation* conclude every *no* that issues from my mouth. The father's role is to rule and provide, the son's role is to obey and prepare for his father's dotage. Oh, the din of battle over these rules and my grump 'n groans can send my son running for cover at my aggression in the guise of faith from this former sanctimonious Altar Boy. Son says he's suffered burns from my glares. Often we don't have the vocabulary to explain each other. We then need a *treuga dei*, a divine truce, to limit the violence between us.

In my elder home monastic snuggery — where the radiator whines and sneezes and I imitate its sounds out of boredom— I dress with care, without haste, with long pauses between separate manipulations. When I get about my room, I try to move on tiptoe, afraid to arouse noisy and excessive echoes that would give away my position to monitoring ears. I try to ignore the furniture and the blind walls with their prying, silent stare (silent so far, that is). Things don't like me. When not listening in, my furniture tries to trip me up. Once a sharp corner of some polished thing literally bit me. My relations with my blanket are always complicated. A pair of large scissors sits on top my toilet (for fecal emergencies). How pleasant my life was *ante-scissors*, when my bowels were elastic . . . ra-ta-ta-ta-ra-ree . . . my juices then did flow within me . . . ra-tee-ta-doo-da-ta . . . contract, guts, contract . . . tram-ba-ba-boom! See, I know how to do things with words! And so does my son. His vital juices are so thoroughly absorbed by his writing and his nose-in-the-theory-book mentality that impulses of ordinary men only act on him indirectly, the way a billiard ball caroms off another (i.e., he's a *pedant*: one of his academic tomes is 250 pages long with another 250 pages of endnotes). With his still boyish fingers, he thumbs through my written material. Eventually, with additions and deletions rooted in his vast database of literary citations, which prove invaluable, he approves my blue inked ms. as a ripe 'n ready record of "Elder Blues." See? We're literary *pards*, if ya know what I mean, destined to be *on the same page*.

Today, the rain turns into a fraudulent snow — huge wet flakes from a sentimental flick starring Jimmy Stewart. Could hear thunder out over the lake, rumbling distantly like doom, propelled by a westward wind. I, the doomed-me propelled by something else. A riddle: Propellers are with me all my life, what am I? I'm smart. Made eyes smart. Made smart remarks, too. Too smart. And paranoid (they say). Inside my head, a black outline of a man in a coat, ready suspicious eyes, shoulder hunched, moving toward conflict, always overrating his centrality, forever rehearsing a traumatic delight in reaction, attachment, and causality, *in*

roads *out* from the Rome-of-Self. As fussy as an old house-
keeper, suspicious as a C. I. A. operative who listens with
the attention of a blind man listening to fireworks. Aware
that particular corner windows, archways, and street lamps
know a great deal about me and use the knowledge threaten-
ingly.

 Question: Who has a birthmark, the sort by which
mothers recognize their kidnapped children decades later?
Moi! Or "Big Guy" to my son, whom I affectionately dub
"Jimmer" or, unaffectionately, "Jammer" (code for "obstacle-
boy") when he screws me or insists that my concept of the
boundary between the relevant and irrelevant needs policing.
Either way, I'm his jester, angle jokes off him like a
handball off a low wall. And he returns my serve. Not so
with Jeane, my former wife. When I'd slip into my paranoid
vernacular, stirring things up, propelling myself into her
world, she'd maintain a brittle pose, delicately draw out a
premium-length cigarette from its pack with fingers stained
the color of fumed oak, and reprimand me in a frightened
reedy, emphysema-inflected voice that sounded like someone
had squeezed her windpipe partially shut,"You think God made
trees to keep the sun off your head!" I'd reply that, unlike
her photographer-lover (more on this later), I didn't sub-
stitute cologne for character. Poor Jeane, destined for
pain, trouble and dishwater, for bathrooms with special
little toilet-seat and toilet-paper covers on. But she does
love our son and he her, their hearts pulsing in unison,
skulls vibrating in sync. A boy's best friend is his mother.

 Unlike Jeane, I had a future. In aerospace. I read it
in the North Woods's stars. As a kid, I'd put my knuckles up
in between those stars to see how much space between them
and I could tell I was meant to be. The stars knew who I
was. Winked at me — some people call it twinkling.

Before The Weakness came upon me, I would propel myself, albeit
slowly, for miles around what was home before this home, Oceanside, California.
My modern suburban environs had almost succeeded in excising the casual walker
from society. Roads, no sidewalks. All motored hither-thither, foot to pedal, not
to concrete. Nice to soldier on here, unimpeded, on my own pegs. I saunter down
to my art supply store for exotic papers and pens, or up to the small, local park
to chat up the strays slumped on benches. I make my way three blocks north to
my Church for early Mass. Or haunt the new snazzy postmodern village library to
either feed my autodidacticism (my mind doing that race-condition thing where
every time I try to concentrate on something I think about how I was trying to
concentrate on something and should stop thinking about how I was concentrating
and just concentrate), or try to trace the dim trails of my Huguenot genealogy
(I'm somewhat computer literate), or wipe spots of rain 'n dust from my past to
add to my writing project (our "Happy Scribblers" writing club meets in two days).

 Jimmer, Heavy Culture Man, in a drop of think, advises me: "Literature
is the intelligibility of mind transferred to the most alien medium," and encourages
me to, as he does in his own writing, "include a flotsam of literary tags imbedded
in an indescribable jelly of content." From his own observations, he gives me
clues. A woman on the Assisted floor in a wheelchair, he describes as, "wearing

a cravat of drool hanging from a rusting ivory tooth as her green algae eyes blankly gaze our way." Of Ill-Phil: "He's the difference that makes the difference. The thing's impervious to the negative beta ray! Got the unique phenomenon of being in-your-face, however distant he may be." Jimmer urges me to develop prose as straightforward as a spear, with stories that include learned dogs and voracious jackals, psychotic moles, worldly-wise apes and vainglorious mice. "Oh, you mean, of course, a good-natured romp about this place in company with my fellow inmates?" That got a laugh. "Go get it, Big Guy. It's all good pickin's here."

      In the long horror film of history, this is where I came in. I cannot paint what then I was. But I was born as beast 'n monk of hearty Huguenot Wisconsin peasant stock. Of Rose and Richard. The two R's (they are). Rose met Richard : Richard met Roseanne (we called her Rose). She was flipping griddle-cakes for lumberjacks. He was cutting wood. Those disappearing North Woods. As a flight of wild geese went across a Wisconsin violet sky, I flapped my little boy hands before my stern daddy — whose face already sported a dim jerky faraway smile, hands constantly working pickpocket fingers — and cried out, "I can fly father," making it understood in my mind as a pun on *flay father* and *fly farther*. For my much kinder mother's benefit I cried, "Hahtch me mommy, hahtch me do big beuwy-sop" (my infantese for belly-flop). In memories of mother, I am returned to the childhood happiness of pure noun, remembering words spoken to her, a Rose on a bleak winter hillside with my little sled when I was four. Was my sled named "Rosebud"?

      Mother married dad after The Great War — which he'd not have done if he'd known we'd end up with a sleazomania culture — months after he was gassed in the Argonne. Took to painting houses and schools in the Wausau, Wisconsin en-virons in working-class irons. Had the passion of the hunts-man and artist rolled into one; painted Northwoodscapes with indigenous game prominent. I inherited his black metal box of Windsor & Newton paints. Inside were little tin tubes (Chrome Yellow, Chrome Green, Zinc White, Terre Vert, and Viridian) all twisted like corpses in their narrow compart-ments, frequently stuck down with linseed oil that had split from the pigment, several caked with color that bled from the ruptured tubes. I also inherited his painter's passion, excelling in seascapes, harbor scenes, and sunset or dawn over mountain vistas. (Jimmer prefers the abstracted pig-ments splayed on my palette *as is*.) Rarely did I see my penny-pinching pater shaken with spasms of laughterly delight. "Should've been named "'Sternickle,'not Richard," said my son after I hinted at child abuse while we lived on Hudson Street in Antigo (a Native American word). A wee house too tiny for me and my two sisters: one who liked me, one who didn't. The one who didn't, didn't 'cause I heartily disapproved of her marrying a suave non-Catholic twenty years her senior. Her marriage flourished. Ironically, I also married a Protestant, but my wife finally opened our wedlock 'n tossed the key.

      Like / dislike. Laugh / bluster. A founding dichotomy working its way through my life. Bipolar seasons in Northern

Elder Physics

Wisconsin: summer and winter. How appropriate. I'm a bipolar kind of guy. Kind and cruel. Warm and cold. Extreme intimacy and sudden, violent retreat. I can approach a dog as though it holds the secrets of the universe, then turn on a loved one as if they had a communicable disease. My fluctuations are perfectly timed: quick to emerge and slow to dissolve. Accompanied by a wide variety of mannerisms, flourishes, and poses. Up 'n down, down 'n up. "A broken jack-in-the-box," as my wife described me. Helped my father paint houses. Up ladders. Down ladders. My work-life just like my emotional-life (I try to be honest about it now). Admired a drunk painter who fell off a ladder and (without missing a beat) got back up to brush-and-brush after brush with death.

My main claim to fame in those days? Up early and at 'em altar boy at St. Joseph's. The only altar boy in the history of the parish to wear different colored gym shoes so they would match the priest's vestments: red for martyrs, white for feast days, black for requiems. I remain a clear-cut committed Catholic. Attending Mass, where the words slide into the slots ordained by ordained priests and glitter as with heavenly dust. Even when, under an unkempt sky, the enormous elms around my hometown church stood with their arms upraised, like witnesses of terrifying visions, during the funeral of my high school sweetheart, Margaret Kuss, a heat-shimmer that once came off her now gone cold in a wintry car accident.

In high school didn't like my dates (never blondes) dating other guys who'd give them "soap opera kisses" behind the gym. Jealousy. Liked to kill roaches in the houses my dad and I were painting. Played football. Straight-armed player later to play as "Crazylegs" Hirsch for the L.A. Rams. After my Margaret died, dated Jeane who smelled of coffee and cigarettes; became my steady and, finally, my wife, who protested my bottomless anger and noisy demands. Beat out my close competitor, "Chuck-the-Shmuck," who recently kicked from an infarction. Ah, the joy of outliving competitors. My son picked up on this revenge-by-longevity bit. He made a heap o' enemies when he claimed that the Establishment selects the avant-garde. Says he wants his last conceptual art project to be a photobook, like California artist, Ed Ruscha, is known for, depicting himself pissing on the graves of all his unfavored dead, titled *Various Small Dribbles and Graves*. Being an academic and art critic, he's got a lot of the unfavored to piss on.

Was a tall guy, thin, back then. (Still am cubits of tragic stature, but not thin.) At aeronautical school in Glendale, California, after graduating high school in 1940. Danced. Studied. Got into a few fights. Wrote Jeane, she wrote me. Saw a P-38 crash. On my way to Mass one Sunday, the Japs attack Pearl. Almost got into the Royal Air Force (Cherrio-pip-pip-'n-all-that-sort-o'-rot) but nixed by my daddy's expert backhand. Later signed papers to fly U.S. Army Air Force all the way, but washed out of pilot training over a fluke. So reassigned as a bombardier in the clear plastic nose of "St. Christopher," our four-engine B-17 war-bird flying out of East Anglia, England. Then, 1944, it seemed the sky would forever and forever, to the crack of

ack-ack, insult and murder men. We'd make bad gallows humor,
"plane puns", telling our wet-behind-the-ears waist-gunners,
"If you B-17 now, you ain't gonna C-47 later." (Besides the
ago reference, the C-47 was the plane you flew back to
London on to catch the boat home.) Jimmer began punning at
five. By maturity, he could pun in Tzotzil, Yoruba, French,
Japanese, and Pitjantjatjara! I'd praise him, playing off
one of his Air Force duty stations: "Ya got the Wright
Patter son."

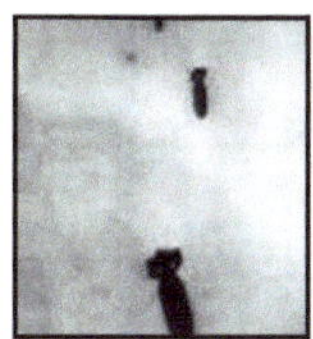

On that day, D-Day, plane after plane
sped overhead heating the sky with raw noise as
propellers bit into the sky. Over my heavy
flight-gloved left index finger I affixed a
rosary-ring of silver so I could thumb its tabs
and say my "Hail Marys" as we dropped lethal
ordinance on the Hun. In those war-days, we
lived lives that played with death as if life
were checkers played in a kitchen. In those days, Jeane and
I, engaged, sent each other letters longer than patience and
often linked together daily like barges behind a tow.

After the war, my son tried to steer me clear of
German restaurants because I'd end up asking the waitress
where she was from and if she mentioned a German city, I'd
exclaim, "Oh, I bombed it!" So then I'd have to leave an
exorbitant tip to gloss over my *faux pa* (pun intended).

Best moment? Thirty-five missions done and not a
fucking scratch (still have a chunk of shrapnel BIG-AS-MY-
THUMB that parted my hair, stuck in a bulkhead behind) and
so become member of The Lucky Bastards Club. Certificate to
prove it. Worst moment? Watched buddy-filled bomber burst
over Holland. Most embarrassing moment? Had to crap in an
ammunition box on our plane. November '44. Home. Breathed in
the sugar of pure morning. Heard the long phrases of the
birds. No enemy wanting my life. Married. Jeane and I honey-
mooned in Los Angeles. Driving a '41 Chevy.

Later back to live there with our two kids: Jimmer
and Leslie. Driving a '55 Ford. Airframe designer at Lockheed's famous (and Top Secret) Skunk Works where being a
little paranoid is a work benefit aspect. I astound my
supervisor on the first day on the job by proving to him his
Marlboro cigarette container is proportioned according to
the Golden Section. My last design project? The Stealth
Fighter. I saw a UFO once. But I digress. Before designing
aircraft, I put very slow Westinghouse elevators in Roosevelt University's Louis Sullivan Auditorium Building. Spent
a lot of time goose-necking, thrilled by Sullivan's famous
ornament. Always had an artistic penchant. Kept my hand in
as an amateur painter, oils and watercolor. Turned my son
onto the Impressionist painters when he was a teenager.
Discovered the Cubists during a high school field trip. Then
conceptual art as an Air Force photographer. Mixed up words
and images into a heady scripto-visual cocktail too strong
for the local photo-aficionados.

Milwaukee in '46. The place got much more snow then.
Studying aeronautical and mechanical engineering at Marquette University because priests who taught there quoted
from a nineteenth-century essay, "The Mental and Moral

Influence of an Engineering Training," The best corrector of
human depravity is the engineer. Commonsense (do what it
will) can't avoid being surprised occasionally. The object
of engineering is to spare it this emotion and create mental
habits which shall be in such close accord with the habits
and cold equations of the world as to secure that nothing
shall be unexpected. Like my use of "shall"? That's a
Catholic education for you. Spiffy English and handwriting,
too. Hell, my son's cursive is godawful. The Catholic engineer's mantra: *All facts lead eventually to mysteries*. I
could mesh my penchant for engineering (facts) with my
Catholic eschatology (beliefs) with the ease of an automatic
transmission shifting gears.

So got this thing for priests, as in "total belief
in." So you can understand my ire when my son would arrive
home from parochial school and yell, "Send the nuns abroad
and the priests to the moon." Had a high school bud, Jerry,
who became one. Died in a Beer-Town car crash under mysterious circumstances. I took his name as my nickname. His
seminary was all hush-hush about it, like security at the
Skunk Works. I pressed the rector for details: Was he drunk
at the wheel? Caught in a sexual indiscretion? Distracted by
reading his breviary? The old priest looked at me like I was
delivering news from alien places and mysteriously pro-
claims: "A flaw can be an entertaining thing to discuss, but
it can also be a good way of forgetting pleasure." I've been
meditating on that one for fifty years. Suppose somewhere in
the Vatican there's a file . . .

Jimmer's born in '47. He calls me "Big Guy." (If I
already mentioned this, I'm sorry, my memory sometimes ...)
Ironic that he'll one day get a part-time teaching gig at
Roosevelt U. and squawk about those slow elevators I put in
there. He also squawked once, bouncing in my lap; turned
unexpectedly and my drafting pen harpooned his head. Indelible tattoo just hidden by hairline. Later, as my son's
hair recedes like glaciers suffering global warming, he'll
notice it. A blue dot. Like those on Sylvania Blue Dot flash
bulbs my son will later use in his photography.

In college, in the early fifties — when my young
family is ashine with an innocent Eisenhowerian light — I'm
praised by my English professor for the stories I pen, confessing, "I'm itching with sentences, I am." Here's an
excerpt: On the other side of the fence, behind that jungle
of summer in which the stupidity of weeds reigned unchecked,
there was a rubbish heap on which thistles grew in wild
profusion; from where in my sexual confusion, I'd whistle.

I rise to conversation; great sense of humor. Handy
in the bars. My kids inherit this. Just as they will always
dig Milwaukee. Near aunt and uncle and lake shore. Prospect
Street, our first home. Railroad tracks behind and below.
Always proud to show them it and my Alma Mater when vaca-
tioning. I take my brat-lovin' brats to Mader's world famous
German restaurant for hearty Sauerbraten or Rouladen, where
my dinner-stories about our early years in Beer-Town gain
new vivacity as I can actually show them the sites of said
events. Thirty years later, my son — a doctor of philosophy
at a time when philosophy is sick — will have as his under-

grad student the stunning Aryan-blond daughter of Mader's owner and get a dinner-on-the-house, twice. One semester, his theory class befuddles a direct descendant of famed WW II cartoonist, Bill Mauldin. The next — a contrary possible unlikelihood — G. Gordon Liddy's daughter shows up on his class roster. God's truth! What happened after that is fodder for a long short story or a short long story.

See! Although all our aging minds are a Swiss cheese of forgetfulness, my long-term memory shows no battle damage. It's still air-worthy, frame relatively intact. Trim OK. Props turning in perfect pitch, on course. It's just those short-haul passengers that I misplace. I mean, just watch this.

As I sit on my small bed, playing the spokes of my one wooden chair's back like a noiseless harp, I recall some of the categories in a life-long pedagogical pet project of mine, a personal encyclopedia of aircraft (titled *The Heavenly Emporium of Benevolent and Not-so Benevolent Aircraft*) which I'm compiling. Here goes: gliders, single-prop planes, twin-prop planes, pusher-prop planes, turbo-prop planes, biplanes, triplanes, gull-winged planes, high-winged monoplanes, V-tail planes, seaplanes, straight-winged jets, Earhart's Electra, swept-wing jets, delta-wing jets, stealth planes, fixed-gear planes, retractable-wheeled planes, bomb-capable planes, supersonic jets, spy-planes, JATO-planes, twin-boom planes, planes-with-skis, experimental planes, planes-snatched-by-UFOs, planes-celebrities-died-in, planes-lost-never-to-return, planes-with-joy-sticks, planes-with-steering-wheels, planes-that-never-got-airborne, suicide-planes, flying-wings, tricycle geared planes, flying-bombs, armed drones, cargo planes, the Flying Guppy, the Bee-Gee racing plane, Hughes's Spruce Goose, VTOL planes, STOL planes, planes-prone-to-making-widows, planes-I-designed, noisy planes, quiet planes, cool-planes-I-like-most, the Taylor Aerocar, the Waterman Whatsit, planes-I-shot-down, planes-I-flew-in, planes-I-can-fly, gas-powered / radio-controlled model planes, balsa wood and plastic model planes, paper airplanes. To name only a few, not including the section on helicopters and that UFO I saw once. Used this tome to early-on educate my son on the finer points of aviation, and later to enrich those blind and deaf, to the diversity of wonders winging their ways across our blue skies. To the uninitiated, one aircraft can look and sound like another, as in language where sounds distinct and unique to one ear can sound similar or indistinguishable to another (like *b* and *p* in English or *xi* and *qi* in Chinese). My HMO doctor says, albeit my heart and arteries be fucked, I don't suffer elder-stoop 'cause I'm always chin-up-to-the-skies watching the action heavenward. Looking up, I notice the weather today is partly soused with occasional burst of despair and irritation. Yesterday, it was partly furious with occasional fits of rage. That's the Chicago climate for you.

Where am I chair-molesting? I remember. In the Situation. In room 345 in the less-than-elegant Upping Arms Elder Home some ten miles west of

Chicago's famed Loop. A six-story masonry structure built, they say, by hungry immigrants (if not immigrants from Hungary). I found this supposition confirmed in our library's copy of *The Large Print Little Book of Succinct Quotations* as stated by famed Islamic scholar Ibn Khaldûn: *In republics founded by nomads, the assistance of foreigners is indispensable in all that concerns masonry.* This institution's main entrance faces due west, back toward warmer climes. But my room's door faces east toward the rising sun. That door. My door. An important object in my life here. Keeping watch over its presence. Keeping it secure. I glance at it a moment over my left shoulder, that perfected half-look tossed in its direction. Chair snug, oh so snug, in place under the door handle. Locks can be picked, keys can be distributed. Still waiting. Through waiting, that which turns aside from thought returns to thought to become a turning aside from itself. Does that makes sense?

My son says he gets dizzy from the smell of Pine Sol cut with urine. I can't smell it. Any longer, anyway. Too bad those scissors don't work on the piss. Funny. Pissed off is what my son says I've always been. *Wheels-within-wheels*. Pissed off at my cheating wife ("That's delusional thinking," my son says, urging me to go back on my anti-psychotics, "That's a *too close* reading, sheer connotative filigree."). Pissed off at the bad amateur photographer who posed my wife on a boulder overlooking the San Fernando Valley, nude. A truth-or-consequences photo this dude had the gall to give me, like he gave Jimmer an Exakta 35mm camera exactly the same as Jimmy Stewart's in the film, *Rear Window*. To get him on his side. Jammer thinks just because the woman didn't *look* like his mom that it wasn't her in the photo. Hell, her face was turned away from the lens. Now *that's* delusional thinking!

Years later, Jimmer claims this incident got him interested in photo-interpretation. Launched his career. I tell him his choice of photography is corny. Before he can react, I fill him in: the lubricant used to grind the camera lens in the photographic industry is a corn byproduct; the material used to polish the steel has corn byproduct in it; many of the chemicals associated with the production of a fine-art print also have a corn byproducts in them. Always amazes him, the diversity of my knowledge. I even know the precise location of the Museum of Erotica in San Francisco — although I've never been there. A real autodidactic I am, like my son, who used to say: "I'd rather meet a new book than a new woman" — until he met his soulmate. Like father, like son. Kinda. In high school, Jimmer only went on dates with dead writers; said he was bi-textual, loving to thumb the pages of Aldous Huxley (who died the day of JFK's assassination while on LSD) and Virginia Wolfe (he thought the name brought together both desirable victim, *virgin,* and desiring womanizer, *wolf*).

"Hey Lucky Lindy! Give me a ride!" That's how I always start my famous story about how I got my first airplane ride and took off on a career in-of-by the skies. It was a Ford Trimotor that in the late thirties was giving us local kids sky-thrills up over Antigo Airport. The day-sky was untroubled, the air crystal, the sun in full fire. The plane was circling low over the town, its silvery wings flashing into my eyes — when I was young enough to believe I would never grow old, never die — the whirl of its prop roaring over the excited hum of my thoughts. Grabbing my bike, I made a bee-line to the airfield and dumped a week's worth of lunch money for a ride.

Thereafter, there was no turning back. And I'm still trying to complete that sketch of Lindbergh, but can't get the nose right. How does one manage it? It's the action of carving a passage through an invisible iron wall which seems to be located between what one feels and what one can do. Melanie Mercaptan — our art instructor who waxes eloquent over "pale manganese blue" and "alizarin crimson," a gal clad in moth-eaten pull-overs 'n frayed Oxford shirts, who reminds me of Amelia Earhart (tall, slender, blond, and brave), and who graduated from the prestigious art school where Jimmer teaches — is very patient with me. Some days I paint a canvas with the calmness of an ancient Greek, another with the anxiety of a van Gogh. But Melanie understands how to cope with the frequent midair collisions between my painterly desires and my failing capacities. Supportive, even when I cut classes after my hand misbehaves, or simply fails to heft pen properly, she can laugh good heartedly when my body plays its jokes on me.

Speaking of jokes . . . God! . . . I can never forget the ruse we played on Jim Flood, my co-worker at Westinghouse Elevator Division back when I called Chicago home in the mid-fifties. This gentle-natured man — a model train enthusiast whose moods came and went with the regularity of his toy trains — had just gotten a hearing aid, so we office guys started talking around him in loud voices, then softly, then merely mouthed our words and repeated this all day, so the poor guy thought his new instrument was on the fritz. He'd pull it out, adjust it, refit it and do this all day long. Finally, we couldn't contain our laughter and doubled over. He didn't talk to us for a week.

Another time — this was out when I was working as a design engineer at Lockheed Aircraft in beautiful downtown Burbank — our bossy boss bought a new car. A snazzy red Corvette. So every day at lunch we'd sneak out and pour gas from a jerrycan into his tank. Soon he started bragging about the amazing gas mileage he was getting. The following week, we stuck a hose in his gas tank and siphoned off gallons. When asked about his mileage, he'd frown 'n mumble. Then we started filling his tank. This went on for two months, maintaining a bipolar cycle, fueling his anxieties.

I close up my typewriter, stand up and unsteadily totter toward the bathroom, unzipping as I amble. Usually micturition is accompanied by a profound sigh, like a whale in the night, followed by my usual preamble to taking stock of my constitution, a stare in the mirror like at a camera. A doddery old fucker looks back. His eyes have rings of color, one inside the other, dark to light around the pupil, brownish and hazelish and greyish. My old California driver's license listed "green eyes," but my Illinois Identification Card now reads "blue." Something's up and it involves the State. I relieve myself into a large plastic yogurt container, pouring my offering into the bowl. Prevents splatters all over the toilet seat — it's BE KIND TO MAIDS MONTH — as announced by a brightly colored flyer placed in my mailbox — something like SWEETEST DAY times thirty. Do the math. Those eyes in the mirror . . . I'm reminded of an incident when Jimmer nearly died.

An incident off Zuma Beach, near Malibu, California. It was 103 degrees in the San Fernando Valley, so our family headed west for relief, to the beach. I was swimming just beyond the breakers. Had to be around '58 as I was still driving my puke-green Ford. Our tan 'n white two-toned Ford wagon was still a year away. I surfaced and turned around to find myself staring directly into a sea seal's eyes. Expected soft brown eyes, like a dog's, but each was a pool of oil, an inkwell, a hole. The beast was huge, like a boulder on sand. I recall I flashed on that deadly piece of flak skimming my flight helmet during a particularly hairy bomb-run over Königsborn on June 20, 1944. Exactly three years prior to Jimmer's birth. Got to shore in record time, I did. Odd. Same place my son almost drowned some years later. He got snagged by a mean rip current when he was only a pimply teenager. But he managed to drag himself to shore, exhausted, but alive. He immediately fell asleep. No one ever noticed he was about to sink beneath the waves. Only later did he relate to us what almost happened.
Leslie, my daughter, had trouble upon trouble all 1994. Tear upon tear. Fear upon fear. We all noticed — cancer. Terminal. *Ka-chink*, the cash register, cashed her out. Hung along a line, birth to death, some fall off at 5, some at 17 others at 42 like Les.

The Queen of Sheba Meets the Atom Man

I'd been amusing myself most of the early morning chuckling at the sober-intentioned puerilities of our local newspaper, scrutinizing the ads and "personals," while chair-snoozing in our dayroom. Occasionally I would look up from the page to observe treadmill conversations, house observations, and the walking or marching of a movie-like scenery set before me. After some time of abstractly observing my fellow humans *en masse*, I commenced to narrow my focus more pointedly, scanning from this one to that, observing dress, gait (with or without cane or walker), expression, and mannerisms. Not surprisingly, there's not much variety of motion in to be discerned, except for (true to elder physics) two anomalies: 1) Phil Pokey, one of 28 children born to a sharecropper family in southern Arkansas who was forced to sell pet rats door-to-door to survive until he was drafted, in retrograde motion, and 2) Harry von Warburg who, because of unceasing constipation and elevated caste, always feigns extreme patience, pacing in an exaggerated orthograde stature. Otherwise, what I witness before me is the disheartening homogeneity of elder folk home-on-the-range. But is it really all that different here than on the outside where all those corporate-suited serfs, many recently graduated from university, are impeded by the delusory culture which encourages their most banal fantasies, while impeding their progress and independent thinking? My wristwatch alarm goes off, reminding me it's pill-time.
I slow-elevator it back up to my cell for my noon meds, only to find my room trashed. Chairs overturned, cig butts in an ash tray I never use. Books and

CDs on the floor in random patterns — perhaps it isn't random! — TV on and telephone screaming off the hook. My guitar (which I never learned to play) is face down on my carpet, clothing disarrayed, tossed about, adding a layer of mold to the fertility. My Denicar tabs missing. Confused, I wonder who broke in during my morning chair-snooze. I would consider the situation over a beer if I had one; instead, Futterneid Quotient rising, I dial my son and, with glowing anger, accuse him of the shenanigans.

My son, a classic cerebrotonic ectomorph and discursive source of wayward data, by now tired of my so-called "delusions," rudely reprimands me: "Is not physics an inversion of psychics?" and opines that my tendency to remain sedentary, while refusing anti-psychotics, adversely subverts my sense of actuality, and that the congruent boredom breeds uneasiness and restlessness which is best alleviated during the course of a lengthy walk with my walker. Translation: Yer nuts ol' man! Buzz off ol' bugger! Take a hike! In retaliation, I tell him he needs to be examined by my proctologist, Dr. Vera Grisenfingau and abruptly hang up on him.

Irritable as hell, I slow-elevator it down to our dining area where I notice a few cigarette butts in the flower pot have a story they refuse to say, but which might be linked to the bent cigs in my ash tray upstairs. I scan skin mummified, thin hair in a kind of spider-web sheen over the men's reflective pates, women's topped off with white cotton candy hair. I see blind mouths miss food-filled forks. I turn and lift up mine eyes, and look, and behold a flying roll arc across the room and bounce onto and off again a table where two newbie couples sit and look around nervously. All four sport huge sunglasses dangling price tags, fluorescent orange ovals reading $6.99. Roll probably tossed by Ill-Phil. Warping the intent of Sam "Walmart" Walton's smiley "Ten-foot Rule," Ill-Phil Pokey, our resident wacko, the whole battle of the century inside him, crowds near the newbies, blaring: "Mic check! Mic check! Mic check! A time for winter soldiers, not sunshine patriots!"

Harry von Warburg yells back, "Would the gentleman please get into the spirit of the proceedings," to which Phil replies, "I am capable of great thought, but it bores me. Plug me into something! I need electricity for my eccentricity," and points a wizened finger to his black T-shirt's message declaring in fluorescent yellow, I'M A PRODUCT OF MY ENVIRONMENT. He continues his rant, "The words we don't hear are the words that control us! Watch out, I sleep with a stick of dynamite taped to my chest!" In the deep shadows of his eyes float awful reminiscences not giving him much joy. Gnawed within, scorched without, always telling Jill he's going to make a snuff movie, or how he never drank a martini unless it had a dead man's heart valve floating in it for extra panache.

We've all had our fill of Phil and his every-half-hour, every-ten-feet-from-someone, abuse. Like a whale, he has to breathe periodically, coming to the surface blowing his invective. So I call him "The Whale" and he calls me "The Berg," we both immersed in an alternating sea of calm or tempest. Phil and I are as out of place here as the first composers of Sea-shanties in the age of Steam. My tablemate today, Sunny "Storm" Atkins, just fuels my "Philanoia" by noting, "There's no better disguise for an informant than that of a mental defective, heh?"

Buddy MacDonald, as he's served his salad, asks the waitress, "Know why don't you starve in the desert?" The young black woman, having heard this a million times, rolls her eyes as Buddy hits the punch line: "Because of the *sand which is* there!"

As I find my seat and impatiently wait to be served, I notice it's Bondo McCracken's turn to be Garbage Cop — a rotating duty we Independents share —

for he's standing in a corner with implements ready to rush over and sweep up food that falls or is thrown (usually by Ill-Phil) on the carpet.

A lunch of mystery meat, green beans, and Wonderbread primed with a jar of my own store-bought apple sauce. I cut my vegetables into small squares, chewing each slowly, with great deliberation, until I am finally full and can leisurely observe my surroundings.

At my left, I spy Sabbah "Sad Intestinal Poison" Pargoric, face as empty as a plate, sitting with Ruby Sunshine (who calls me "Gerro") who seems as full of zeal as a jar of jelly. A study in contrast. Wish I had my sketch pad. At my right, Kim Young Sam has just soiled her pant suit half way through dessert. I turn a blind eye. Not noticing what has been noticed is a talent of mine and a blessing here. But it wasn't a blessing during the height of my family life in California. Add to that, I tend to present matters of fact that make no sense with a clarity that is wholly obscure, and you see why I tend to get myself into deep doo-doo with people.

I have become aware of these things since Jimmer's encouraged me to keep a diary the way some people keep their dogs: feed them, comb their coats, and take them for their daily walks. My diary now a storehouse of shards of scenes 'n bits o' thought, perceptions briefer than butterflies, clips and tatters taken from the realm of Elder Physics. Jimmer helps me unzip these terse fragments into larger wholes as we ponder and position them like chess pieces, sending the endgame for my writers club President Fialta Fenwich's brittle, sarcastic, even frightening critique, where what I take for the fruit of the true tree of knowledge, becomes merely berries on the bush of belief. But it isn't all sour grapes. Fialta reads to us, managing complex sentences with the ease of a water-slide. She oft feeds us choice meat, like informing us that one of the longest sentences in the English language is found in Daniel Defoe's "An Essay upon Projects" (1697). An essay that, she said, is most needed in our elder home as it warns of ill-advised investments. Another bit of writerly wisdom, "The plot allows entry into the writer's worlds unscathed. People ride in on it unnoticed, without having to dismantle their personality consciously." I told her Jimmer told me, "Where plot is denied, truth-of-the-self is more in your face." Fialta just gives me her usual tragic-mask look. Her particular persona comes pre-plotted. Pre-plotted like her 1950s Young Adult novels written under the pen-name "Taweet Woo," stories about sorority girls (all former Girl Scouts) who had sledding accidents and found out the meaning of life through being good sports about it, never complaining about pain, who never over ate or drank, and went to bed at ten sharp. According to *Wikipedia*, every, and I mean *every*, novel opened with one of the girls sticking her head out the sonority's window and yelling at the red dawn, "Today! Today! Taweet, toway!"

Dinner and wandering thoughts completed, I ascend our slow elevator. If another suffering body is onboard, when arriving at my floor I announce: "Third floor! Encyclopedias, brushes and shabby suits," then exit and hobble to my room. I turn the knob. It turns. I push the door and it opens. I sit on my bed and watch through my room's west window the orange sky boil to dregs of purple and grey; exhaust ash and dust and glass refracting the light, pouring it through the clouds as if a rainbow had exploded. Colors reflect off the glass protecting an old fading color photo of a youngish, prettyish woman — my long-deceased daughter Leslie — smiling at the camera, set in a heavyish pewter frame. A frame almost as heavy as my heart. In my wallet behind a layer of scratched plastic is another picture of her. Evening paper is on the table. Could scrawl over the pages, write in the margins, fill whole pages with ideas and answers. But it wouldn't bring her back. To handle the slow process of her gradual disappearance, I went back to flight school at age seventy-three and soloed in a Cessna to rounds of applause. Even got my picture, standing by the plane, in the local paper to prove it. Now Jimmer takes pictures, photographs, of me. For his art project.

Jimmer loves to tell this story about me. It's true. I flew back to Chicago, this was over ten years ago at least, to help him out after his first marriage crumbled. Helped him move into a new two-bedroom apartment. A fixer upper though. We worked side-by-side putting putty and paint on damaged walls. Up and down the ladder until our legs were screaming, back and forth from the hardware store with nails 'n screws, out to dinner at the pizza joint for beer and meat lasagna. So vicious to the place were the previous renters — two girls, one of whom stole the other's boy-friend, the landlady told us — it took a week just to get the place shipshape.

One day we're walking back from a great blueberry pancake breakfast at the Golden Nugget where the waitress always fawns on me, ready to start moving Jim's bookshelves in, and we pass an elderly black woman, begging. Cold as a witch's tit out, too. As Jimmer recalls it to me, I took her into the McDonald's she was sitting in front of, sat her down like a queen on a throne, ordered and paid for a Big Breakfast and coffee. Brought it all to her, scrambled for the napkins, and stood beaming for a moment. In a racial reversal, I became her man-servant (that's how Jimmer put it). And walked out. Jimmer was just standing there, mouth open. I remember that awe for it inspired him to do a col-laborative art project with his ol' dad. Calls it "Gratuitous Giving." You can Oogle it on the Internet.

He uses me as his — how does he put it, avatar — I think. Under the pseudonym "L. E. Don." French for "the gift." Posed me as this Mr. Don character for some photos: in the front of the Museum of Contemporary Art, scrutinizing a painting at the local senior's art fair, standing by a large outdoor sculpture shaped like a heart, pretending I'm lecturing to an art audience, lolling in an art frame shop, and me gifting a woman in our elder home. Even did a video of me proclaiming to the world: "Have a heart, please gift," while I extend a hand with a gifting envelope toward the camera. Felt awkward. I seemed to be standing outside myself, seeing what I must look like in Jim's viewfinder. Even stranger when my portraits are labeled "L. E. Don."

In furtherance of this project, Jimmer made T-shirts with this wacky logo featuring a four-leaf clover with heart-shaped petals and distributed them. Makes me wear one for the photos. Made sew-on patches too. Hands out money to strangers in envelopes. Photographs them. Gets the weirdest of responses. Some refuse the gift. Some are pissed off. Most are grateful. Gifted some kids and got quizzed by the cops to see if he was a molester. Does this all over the world on his many trips. All up on his website. You can Oogle it. Says it'll be "One for the Gipper," my legacy when I'm strumming my harp. A real chip off the ol' block. I'm proud of him. Calls it "an anti-capitalist gesture." The kid's got heart. A real kick-in-the-balls to those Bushites (hey, I'm conservative, but not that wacko). My philosophy prof, at a Catholic university, warned us that if fascism ever came to America it would come through the door of religion, probably of the Evangelical Protestant variety. I never forgot that. Told my Jimmer. And his eyes lit up like Christmas tree lights. We've had our political disagreements in the past; we now share delicious fantasies about where on George W. Bush's anatomy we'd like to place our hiking boots.

Jimmer visits, goes over my writing — remnants of past life in which what is left are weather-beaten by the storms of time that have swept over them — making his usual red-inked corrections and suggestions. At these times, we are "on-the-same-page." On his way out to teach, he escorts me to my computer lesson on Net surfing taught by a woman with Afrodisiac hair and shiny, video-capture eyes who sports a yellow T-shirt begging: MORE BANDWIDTH. A Queen of Sheba, bet she dreams in gigabytes. In her office, data sparkles like fairy dust on wall-screens. I call her "Nutritious" 'cause her African-American forename sounds similar and, ever in rude health, she also teaches the Alexander Technique, a medically-approved and media-exploited system for releasing bodily stress, improving posture, and relieving spinal ailments from long hours at a computer. Love that phrase *rude health*. I'm often rude, never healthy. When I tell her about my fading memory, she says nature is merely imposing a "lossy" compression algorithm on me, decreasing the memory space in my poor *cabeza*. She calls me "Atom Man," 'cause I'm falling to pieces, memories splitting.

Here's how I write up our session that night (using a cool new notebook and Paper Mate gel pen Jimmer got me so I can work out my thoughts before typing them out as you see below).

After I tell "Nutritious" the computer is about to become President, Prime Minister, and Secretary of Defense all in one, that gears, pistons, big noses and humans who moved their arms while they walked were fading fast tags me as the "USBureauofMorality." Made me laugh. Yep, it's a global globe with techno as our destiny and the cold chill of the screen, with backlit personalities, is here to stay.

Today's lesson is on Oogling a topic, like "Not your mother's," bringing up 400,000 search results! "Noot" always has to re-teach me how to work the mouse. Can't quite coordinate. Knowing my penchant for numbers, she informs me of a web Power Law: *the distribution of web sites and their audiences follow a mathematical law as the top ten most popular sites are ten times larger than the next hundred more popular sites, which are them- selves ten times larger than the next hundred more popular sites, which are themselves ten times more popular than the next thousand sites.*

I argue that global intercon- nectivity doesn't matter as "It's still the fleecers versus the fleeced." She counters by visiting *www.deathclock-*

.com where, after filling out a health questionnaire, you get back your exact date of demise. Mine read, "You should be dead already." She assists me to Oogle the "U.S.S. Roncador" (Bruin Opps, one of our residents, served in the Pacific aboard this Balao-class sub and has a faded Navy photo of her surfacing). But I really want her to help me Oogle Jimmer's gifting project, so I can brag about the boy. Show her how we, as family, are involved. They like to see family involved here. Kill two birds with one mouse, ha, ha.

Tapping keys, up she brings the web-zine, *Boing Boing*, where I print out an article about making a laser using Jell-O (a goo found in several colors and great quantity here). Try to impress her by informing her that just as we remember things in the order in which entropy increases, so for computers. "The heat, I explain, "expelled by the computer's cooling fan when it records to memory, means the total amount of disorder in the universe goes up." My engineering training gains brownie points. She frowns though, when I confess that booting up a 'puter still feels like the beast is creating itself *ex nihilo* and that I fear instant transmission sickness when going online. She says that I "too often recode worrisome contradictory information to conform to my own story, my own operational lore; like Bill Gates, I require all things to be compatible with my overly righteous format." We wink at each other, acknowledging a conspiracy of sorts between us.

All bullish determination, she next Oogles *Mystery Ecology*, crypto-zoology, where I learn oodles about the study of mythical, imagined or unidentified creatures, weird, improbable creatures that remind me of some of the folks in our home; one drawing on the site looked like my poor attempt at sketching an anteater I saw in the San Diego Zoo during my days as a free man. Nutritious shows me how to order, online using PayPal, a Mystery Ecology T-shirt, deep green with white lettering: **WITHOUT TREES WE'RE FUCKED.**

Next, Nutritious downloads OSS code from *Jodi.org* (a Europunk group's digital version of an aneurysm) which overflows our machine with meaningless digits; we launch an application and an unstable mix of static 'n structure fills the screen. I make frantic keystrokes, almost getting a stroke myself in the process, trying to contain the chaos. There *must* be a patron saint one can pray to in order to get control of this damn machine! Or maybe a new pharmaceutical named "Chillaxin" that will restore my cool. But my cyber-guardian angel, Nutritious, miraculously retrieves the proper quality-to-crap ratio on our screen, clearing the data-smog. I can breath again.

This new technology is fantastic. Besides putting emoticons (-: in my e-mail salutations and perusing Jimmer's website, I can post to Nutritious's The Idiot Irresponsibles twitter, a great site to just, well, *fink* on one's fellow residents. But most groovy, I can access the Vatican and Patrologia Latina's databases. Deepen my understanding of Church History *and* settle a bet with Fialta Fenwich as to what saint of the Catholic Church labeled Woman a *saccus stercoris*, a bag of muck? She says Odo of Cluny. I claim St. Augustine. (She's right.) Then we argue over the shift in syntax relating to the *imitatio Christi*, that is, from imitating what

Christ did to questions like "What would Christ do?" The recurring WWJD? so prevalent today on T-shirts and even women's panties (devout or derisive?).

This question got raised during a particularly contentious monthly resident's meeting in the Sunshine Room. Every first Wednesday, at noon sharp, a gaggle of impossible-to-define-talents, intuitions, fears, and Jerry-at-Tricks (me) walk into that room in twos 'n threes to hear a speech by our Fearless Leader, reports from staff, and complaints from residents. The first half of November's meeting? Banal. But soon things picked up. Brucine Bitters began banging her cane, bitching 'bout the food served, her blouse still spackled with maggot debris of her spaghetti lunch. (Loud mutters of approval.) Then, politely raising his cane, Wolf Blass asked us to consider, "What did Jesus eat?" (Think water, bread, and lots of fish.) Fialta stood up and countered that more appropriately, with today's expanded dietary choices, we should be asking: "What would Jesus eat?" (Think Coke, pizza, Big Macs, and lots of French fries.) Ten minutes of pandemonium. Fearless Leader then got up, heart like a gas meter, chilled us out with the cold equations of the home's finances, "We must be at pains to understand this . . ." (Think a whopping rent raise to get better chow.) Silence. People, abject, heads down, slowly meandered out of the meeting. (Think card-playing, reading, computer surfing, napping.) Ah, Fearless Leader . . . he realizes that one cannot assume the practical, available supremacy over others without the aid of external arts and entertainments, always, in themselves, more or less paltry and base.

A Guide for the Perplexed

The flight to immortality requires an extreme discretion in the selection of one's luggage — er, language. A book that requires for its adequate understanding the use, nay, the preservation of all libraries and archives containing information which was useful to its author, hardly deserves being written at all, and it certainly doesn't deserve surviving its author.

I sit at my TV tray, gel pen *en mano*, chewing quick-to-die Biotene Dry Mouth gum, playing back a recording I made of Fialta's critique of Jimmer's debut novel, *Something is Crook in Middlebrook.* Not an unjust jab as his text, thirteen years in the making, is composed of shards of hundreds of texts, replete with obscure citations, and has so much textual "play" it has become unhinged, suffering its own version of *wheels-within-wheels*. Once, he excised all the body text, leaving only the chapter headings! But then he reversed himself, eliminating all chapter headings, replacing them with numbered sections having numbered subsections. Jimmer claims he owes this technique to the digital-age and the Kindle e-book apps. In fact, my son just gave me the latest model as a birthday gift. The device has an option that highlights passages and an app called Kobo, featuring in-text comments, reviews, and recommendations collected in real-time from readers. Great for my writing, but I still peruse our library as I like to razor out material and put the snips in my failing manila folder. Then Jimmer and I go over the stuff weekly for innovative assembly into this manuscript.

Speaking of Jimmer, he most likely already senses the issue of audience plaguing his writing — I ponder how his influence will affect *my* audience — but he defends himself with: "Do not disturb the slumber of those who cannot see the wood for the trees, but act as an awakening stumbling block for those who can." So I'm surprised when, in the early stages of our collaboration, he suggests I speak *ad captum vulgi*, speaking with the view to the capacity of the everyday reader. But I insist on him helping me put in a few perplexities, remarking, "Don't you realize the vertiginous questions contained in these words?" Eyes light up and he agrees to help me put in a dash of Latin and French, a savory neologism or two, a dash of academic jargon, says I should play up my bipolarity with some contradictions (Jimmer in Jammer mode calls me a "pious fraud") and so make it unclear whether paranoia or senile dementia has entered from stage left. Even a little "schizo-writing" can pepper up the stew, he says. Yep, I just knew he'd be all too eager to gratify his pedantry and my playfulness. I can always play on my son's weaknesses, which are his very academic strengths. Did any of that make sens?

By the way, talking about perplexity, did you know I was originally misdiagnosed as schizophrenic? Told I suffered an iridescent mental kaleidoscope and a tendency toward seeing the world as *wheels-within-wheels*. Put on Thorazine, not lithium. Slept like Rip Van Winkle. Nice material for my memoir.

Someone, during my employment at Lockheed Aircraft, noticing my bad temper and general irritability, handed me this ad clipped from some mental health mag. I had a ten minute argument with the dude, at times grabbing his white pocket protector jammed in the left breast pocket of his starched white short-sleeve shirt and rocking him on his heels for emphasis: Is schizophrenia *on* the mind or *in* it?

I successfully argued my case before a startled gaggle of designers by pointing out that the verbal descriptors were clearly in the mind if the illustration and our eyes were to be believed. Since nothing flies here unless it can be proven empirically, I won the verbal tussle.

At lunch time — what John Quincy Adams dubbed "a reflection on breakfast and an insult to dinner" — I snuck out to the parking lot to eat my bag lunch alone in my car as I sensed folks around me were glancing at me strangely; once in my familiar car seat, I noticed his new plutonium-powered, pancake-making wondercar — a 1958 two-tone Edsel with its rolling dome speedometer, and offensive vaginal-like front grill — parked near my three-year old puke green two-door Ford Fairlane.

Not that I'm proud of this now, but I let the air out of the guy's tires. A crime of opportunity which, the very next day, I confessed in Confession. I was commanded to recite five "Hail Marys," two "Our Fathers," give my son a gift of a plastic model kit of the Edsel, and buy my victim lunch — if I was to get Absolution.

Well, I did everything the Irish padre requested, except giving my son a toy he could get impure thoughts about and, as for coughing up coin for Mr. Edsel-driver's chow, if the guy can afford that vulgar beast, why treat

him, huh? But wait. Two years later, I did buy him that
lunch after statistics came out showing that his car's
resale value had dropped Blue Book value dramatically — you
could read it in his face — until my car's worth was higher
than his. In retrospect, I confess, I felt superior, even as
I seemingly performed a humble act.
　　　TICK TOCK. Now that Ticktockman is knocking on my
door, I'm glad I completed (most of) the terms of Absolution
for that unsportsmanlike conduct on the field of life. And
Jimmer? His favorite uncle stepped in where I feared to
tread and bought him that Edsel model kit for Christmas that
year. Jealous, I noticed he fondled that toy more than the
plastic model of P-38 fighter dangling over his bed.

　　　Well that was a long detour, but worth it don't you think? Gives you
"psychological insight," right? Jimmer liked it. He confessed he *did* "cathect"
that model Edsel (said it came up in a therapy session once).

　　　Now, a guide for the perplexed ought to pose the question about the
danger inherent in all writing (recognized by both Plato and Maimonides, claims
Jimmer) and warn you that this author, *Moi*, reveals himself by not revealing
and not reveals by revealing. Got it?

The Perfect Crime

　　　Outside sky swept lengthwise by gusts of wind. Vast
and silvery white, it is cut into lines of energy tensed to
the breaking point, into awesome furrows like strata of tin
and lead. Divided into magnetic fields and trembling with
discharges, it is full of concealed electricity. Diagram of
a gale akin to the renditions of our Chicagoscape as imagined by the late local superhero painter, Roger Brown. Like
the silhouette figures in Brown's painted high-rises,
there's a man with a thirsty face in my room, nay, on my
bed, refusing the bed, begging for the floor instead.
　　　His name is Michael Perfect, but answers to "Perf."
No kidding. Said he was a perfect angel when a kid, 'til he
joined the Marines and met a notorious San Diego stripper
named "Pumpkin Tureen". A rip for a mouth, a rip in his
crotch, a hank of hair, a flair for ill-fortune, an empty
stare, a done deal with sorrow. Complains his tongue feels
like it'd been bound in horseradish-and-beer-soaked plaster
and left out on the moon. Shirt off, he shows off his per-
manently scarred and distended abdomen (*sans* belly-button)
evidence of surgery for liver cirrhosis and ruptured spleen.
On his chest, under the right collarbone, there is a scar: a
round one with tiny wavelets, like the imprint of a coin on
wax. An old war wound. Says he smiles when angry. Ill-health
approaching central *pontine myelinolysis*. "I'll when I'm
dead," he asserts, words coming out thickened and stupid
like a Method actor playing a defeated boxer. One of our
neighborhood's invisible men. He seemed "con-worried,"
elder-speak for confused and worried.

Elder Physics

At the urging of Jimmer, who says I have talent, I am now the newest member of our institution's "Happy Scribblers" writing club where my inkly offerings in type-furrowed fields come under strict scrutiny. We open our meetings with hiccups in unison. It's shorthand for our club motto: **H**armony, **I**ntegrity, **C**learness, **C**onciseness, **U**nity, **P**recision, **S**trength. Yesterday, we spent a half hour discussing my favorite book *Tristram Shandy.* Then Fialta launched into the "peerage of words, urging us to get to know a word's true descent and ancient blood. She seems to know all their ancestry, their intermarriages, and distant relations.

I urged Fialta to expatiate on my favorite line in that favorite book of mine: *A cow broke in tomorrow morning to my Uncle Toby's fortifications*. Author Sterne has built a time-machine, I offer. Fialta agrees and tells us how English sentences create a pre-delineated space, like a table setting. I tell her that Latin is both Jimmer's and my favorite lingo 'cause each word knows it's station and duties, no matter wherein the chain of words it sits.

After these preliminaries, we get down to business. Bondo reads from his efforts, "This morning's strangeness was refreshing, more than refreshing — relevatory! Technicolor intensity and variety of color sizzle my retinas. Springtime birds are singing, and it's time to deftly believe, to dash all hopelessness upon the gym floor and sit and spin on my bike as overhead, my aura arcs, cascading over me, buzzing about me as I do my exercise routine." By now he's sweating.

Fialta harshes on him, "Hell, what a growler!" The standard response from our club president as she gives out her stare-as-bright-as-the-glare-of-a-projector's bulb. Turning to me, "Gerald, do you have a single predominant incident in mind?" A stern Fialta Fenwich responds to my hint that I've got a punchy idea for my first attempt as an elderly wordsmith.

"My literary adventure begins with a surfeit of alcohol, but ends in embarrassment." Zipped lips don't sink ships, so I remain silent about my son, who took the brunt of the incident, and suggested the topic. And the captain of our ship? Fialta was voted such as she takes her compass heading from correspondence courses in creative writing and, during the McCarthy Era, taught English composition to midshipmen at Annapolis and wrote Young Adult novels, prior to which, she is rumored to have worked for the SOS in WWII. Moreover, she's donated not one but *three* copies of Strunk 'n White's *The Elements of Style* for our club members' enlightenment. "You will reach new platitudes of success," Fialta announced when she passed the spanking new copies around. (Three, my favorite number!) Little good these do, those slim books, as our members are already shrunk 'n white and have little style.

"Do you have a preeminent character in mind, Gerald?" That's Fialta, she's relentless. I can't escape her, so neither will you, Reader. Withered, but immaculately unwrinkled, her scalp is dotted with hair implants. Our home's resident skeptic, she mixes an abrasive personality with a sharp intellect. Jimmer's dubbed her "The Geronto-midwestern Sontag." Even her daughter found her too headstrong to take under wing and care for after a third husband's liver gave out from all their alcoholidays. She'd stopped making meals, refused Meals-On-Wheels, only letting Library-On-Wheels past her door. To prevent starvation, relatives put her in here. Not easy. It was all call-and-response. Each time they tried to get her to pack, she'd yell: "I shall go where went I then." Translation: "Don't fuck with me." They'd yell back: "Life there'll be cool beans, Fee." Repeat *ad nauseam*.

"Yes I do have such a character," I bravely assert, pulling from that depth of courage I drew from on every mission over the flak-torn skies of

Elder Physics

Germany. "And I've got imaginaaaaaation," I add, drawing a large rainbow arc before her face with my open palm as I sit across the table from her in our home's newly remodeled Sunshine Room. "I want to experiment with narrative structure," I offer, not saying Jimmer has given me a nudge in that direction along with a folder stuffed with textual fragments he's razored from books stolen from academic libraries. She gives me her *Oh, have you!* look. "Yep, I've got a *real* character in mind. A *character* of a character, if you catch my drift." Fialta looks worried, like maybe my protagonist is modeled after *her*. So I quickly clarify, "In fact, my protagonist indirectly got me tossed out of my last elder home." I'll bet she is thinking, *Now that's the kind of protagonist I can identify with.*

Seven of eight pairs of ears at our table perk up, the exception being Kim Young Sam who suffered an Overwhelming of the Vessel (a stroke) and lost all spoken 'n written knowledge of animals. All sense a blot-on-a-plot — a plotless no puncher — and blood. A newbie, they'll pick my stuff apart with: "That plosh's really the pits!" But I'm praying for 4000 words and a unity of expression good enough to atone for any sins. What's that on my forehead? Sweat? Nerves. The "Fen Witch's" gaze can cast a formidable spell. And I am working with the handicap of some heavy mental obfuscation, inarticulate cerebral foam (why I'm in here in the first place). And what will our members think about my smartass son kibbitzing from the sidelines with his shards of copped text? He likes to call himself "a submarine in a sea of authorships, blowing up texts and reassembling the flotsam and jetsam."

"Your story must move, move, move. . . ," The Witch continues, directing her gaze evenly across our faces, dishing out her spell in equal dollops. But I know she's tossing her dart my way in particular. She was about to add a fourth "move" when our guest speaker walks in — fifteen minutes late.

"Made a perfect mess of my life," 'fesses Perf, on a striking Indian Summer day. As one of our village's numerous homeless, he's going through a garbage can which he prefers to call "my cylindrical restaurant." Rubbing snot from his nose, tells me, "All I used to do was hang with barflies 'n watch without pity as an olive drowned in my Martini. In them days I did a party trick balancin' a cocktail on my forehead 'n then easin' down on the floor with it intact. I was then gainfully employed 'n winnin' not a few bowlin' matches on a semi-pro circuit with Ohio's famous, Kegling Kouples. Now I can't afford nothin' but rot gut. Usually spend, kinda like Jonah, three days in the bottom of a bottle, then sober up for a time. That's when me mouth starts to taste like itta been used as a latrine by various small creatures o' the night. But hell, ya know, though, addiction is just prayer gone awry. Both require desperation and endurance, right Jerry? Now my soul has grown shallow like the puddles after a summer shower." I try to cheer him with the fact he's *au courant*, that cutting-edge physics' Minimal Standard Supersymmetric Model (MSSM) predicts a marvelous new particle called "wino." No shit. *Wikipedia* has it so. I *croil*(my invented word) at his sorry story.

Met Perf occupying a bench in our local park during one of these walks of mine. He just sat there and lifted his suspender straps, both at once, as if he were shouldering a load, the metal clips of his suspenders two burning clusters of sunbeams. He claims only as much ground as his two feet

take up (less for some), and only as much of a hold as his
two hands encompass. I liked that! So I kept meeting him
there over several sunny days. Always fussing with those
damn suspenders, though! Occasionally, he'd utter "Ophelia"
under his stale breath. "One of several names-that-touch-
me," he later explained. Seemed to keep himself going on gas
fumes and cigarettes. Liberal villagers walking by toss a
buck or two at his Starbucks cup, but Neo-cons lecture him
on fiscal responsibility, while Born-Agains bother him with
Scripture. I catch his attention 'cause I'm wearing my old
bombardier's flight insignia on my black leather jacket. I
become to him *un homme de confiance*.

    After introducing our guest — Professor Sayit Allreddy, a South Indian
writer teaching at Columbia College, Chicago — Fialta flashes a fortune cookie
from her Chinese take-out last night and reads: "A snowstorm of cold images
counsels against excessive love of winter.*"* Says she plans on adding it to her
latest poem (one of several assembly-edited together like a *cento* from such
randomly won verbal gems). I hand her one of my fortunes; it was just kinda
crumpled up in my left trousers pocket where it remained after my lunch at Soo
Way Kitchen. Our guest speaker comments briefly on Fialta's concept, explains
that the *cento* form of appropriation was the thing to do in Alexandrian Greece,
then segues into some esoterics about "postmodernist appropriation."

    I had asked Perf to use the familiar of my name
'cause I was impressed he'd often mention "prayer" during
his testimonials and once confessed that, as a child, he
jumped up in the middle of Mass yelling, "Didja see her? The
Virgin? I did. I asked the Blessed Virgin if my dog would
come home and she nodded yes!"
    Probably why, besides the weather, I invited him up
here. Smuggled him in the side door when the staff member
posted there was disinfecting himself at the newly installed
Purcell hand-sanitizer station. Oh, yes, the other reason.
He's a veteran of The Second. Tarawa Campaign no less. Told
me, "Lost one testicle, gained a Purple Heart, picked up
another ball keglin'." No wonder he has a slightly Kewpish
voice that sounds like Lisa Simpson on a peace march.
    He attributes his alcoholism to his war traumas and
the disturbing fact that a victory garden in his hometown
has a plaque erroneously listing his name as among the local
war dead. "And when your name is dead, you're *Kaput*. There's
a word for that kind of trauma now, that kinda disturbance,
not back then, so it didn't exist as it does now," he
explained. "Ever since they came up with that word, my
condition's gotten worse, I swear." He maunders on about his
sad life. Blah, blah, blah. Seems he drove a fork-lift in
some heavy industry up in Green Bay after the war. He
couldn't recall the company name, said everyone wore
designer hats, green 'n white. But when he mentioned his
wife hailed from Wausau, Wisconsin, I did a little elder jig
right in front of his startled face.
    "My ex and I both hail from Antigo," I tell him, "a
blip on the Chicago and Northwestern Railroad Line once.
Thirty miles from Wausau. Now the town's lucky if people
stop to fill their gas tank on the way to the North Woods'

fishing resorts. Although, the town has some claim to fame: first to be supplied with fluoridated water, *Life* magazine did a feature on the high school's Junior Prom in the late thirties, one shot featuring my future wife in her prom dress; it was the proud home of not only the guy who invented the famous Suick Musky lure, but also an Iwo Jima flag-raiser whose son wrote a book based on his dad's experiences from which a Hollywood movie was recently made; finally, notorious Timothy McVeigh had shady dealings with the big bald militia-type who runs the Army Surplus store just off main street." Here I run out of gas, but my son would've added to the list his favorite wine merchant here because the guy was born there and wants to be buried there. My parents and my ex's are all are buried in Antigo's Elmwood Cemetery. I want to be buried there. Jimmer wants to be buried there. Hell, who doesn't want to be buried there?

I sense death isn't Perf's thing. He prefers to talk about bars. The ones that still have rusty BLATZ signs over their rickety premises, where the bartender knows how to make a "Berliner." I agree with him that those little Wisconsin burgs all harbor nostalgic watering holes with dark-wood bars that have accrued a patina of sweat 'n booze. Places with names like "The Farmer's Home" and "Beer 'n a Brownie," that take you right back to the thirties when record-size Muskies were being lifted by the dozens from local lakes directly into the beds of rusted out pickups, and the true fisherman (sporting a name like Frank Suick or Jack Borkenhagen) would be known by his tackle box thick with layers of silver paint so it hardly be closed, which he'd gotten from his dad, who'd gotten it from his dad, who bought it from a family of a deceased (from alcoholism) Chippewa fishing guide.

"Alright Allready, I think we are running out of time," interrupts Fialta, trying to keep our meeting within its hour time limit. Allready quickly segues to a *Cliff Notes* summary of his Doctoral Dissertation on critic Dorothy Sayers' *trinitarian* theory of artistic creation. My ears perk up at the *three*-word as three is the number of God, the number of hope, the number of operations I've had so far. Cube three and you get how times I fall down per month. Sayers, he explains, sees art as a collaboration between a generative idea (the Father), and style (the Son), and some emotive force (the Ghost). God bless him!

By the time he's done, I'm nearly jumping in my seat. As Fialta frowns and looks conspicuously at her watch, I tell him about my project, *this* project, and that I'm the father (obviously) and I'm collaborating with my son (less obvious), and we are dealing thematically with the ghosts of my life-past (not a surprise). This evokes an effusive grin 'n nod from him, but from Fialta, a mouth crumpled like a discarded candy wrapper. Oops. I'd let the cat out of the bag about Jimmer. Now Fialta is standing and extending a withered hand his way. But before repacking his alligator-skin briefcase and returning the shake, Allready dishes out one last bit of advice, "If you send your writerly fruits out into the cruel world for publication, never, never, never should you give the perusing editor an easy out by enclosing a self-addressed stamped envelope for return. And never, never, never mention you are a resident in an elder home," he adds, "unless you're contributing to *Modern Maturity*." He gets the expected laugh or two.

Elder Physics

Bondo McCracken mutters, "Ya, ya, ya," under his breath. Even Fialta lets a smile happen.

Our guest having departed, Fialta shakes Bondo awake. He nearly jumps out of his seat. Today he's shed his jocularity like baby fat, none of that "Rama-lama-ding-dong" he's known for. He's sitting next to me, so his reanimated body sends a whiff of sweat and old cracker crumbs. He's been snore-slumped over twenty ballpoint scribbled loose-leaf pages titled, *Blight: The Great American Novel*. Groggy, he starts to read his opening sentence with a slur in his voice, "The dawwwwn rises like sick old men playing on the rooftops in their underwear," and is immediately cut off with an unanimous, "That's really the pits!" Fialta deftly refocuses her attention toward *moi* (my son claims tossing in a little French invites readers to take this stuff more seriously).

"Now the first thing you have to do, Gerald, is try and get hold of a catchy title; for instance, 'Basil Hargrave's Vermifuge,' or 'Fun at the Incinerating Plant,' catch my drift?" I nod a cautious affirmative. "Start with a good declarative sentence about your main character, such as, 'Hazel Goodtree had just gone *mah jong*. She felt faint.' Get it?" I was going to ask her if "going mah jong" was like "going postal," but kept my lips zipped. "Remember," she continues, "the voltage between two people, the pressure-cooker of a single human heart, are as fit grist for your stories as the epic convulsions of history." Oh yah!

he realized, after watching my cable History Channel and nearly all my WWII videotapes, none mentioned how often even battle-hardened Marines would shoot themselves in one foot to get evacuated out of hellish conditions. Bad attitudes.

I tell him about my lofy altitudes, up past 10,000 feet in St. Christopher, my B-17 Flying Fortress, but just "St. Chris" to us flyboys. Spin a yarn. Tell him once this young bombardier is on leave in London, about to be seduced in an apartment (lured upstairs from the smoky bar below by a girl who gave me the look of a distant star, turned, and asked me if I wanted to see her stamp album) when the phone rings and we are told: "Dive directly to the basement, Lootenant, do not stop at the bar, and remain there for the duration of the air raid." So down we went to a basement aglow with oil lamps and small candles snatched from the inn's tables. The girl I was with — Bianca was the name given, but not believed — exhibited a quiet serenity usually achieved only after long days of weeping and sobbing. This accounted for the fact that her Italianate eyes were deeply circled and yet they had the moist, hot flow and spare purposefulness of a business-woman who never misses any-thing. After a while the basement ceiling shook with bomb impacts and we feared it'd cave in. It was the first time I'd been on the other side of the bombsight. Under the incessant drumming, time passed like sluggish dirigibles stuffed with freezing water and my BVDs felt like they were made of thatch. This was just a few hours before the bloody charge of dawn and my bouncing bus back to the airfield for another gut-wrenching mission piloted by fearless "Bangin' Bob" Gormley. Years later, during divorce proceedings, his soon-to-be-ex-wife testifies her marriage was like being chained to a zoo animal.

Yep, he liked that one, but the story that really sobered him was, "The Case of the Uncanny Can," my *pièce de résistance*.

After our club meeting, I return to my little monk's cell via our slow-as-molasses elevator. Our Scottish handyman, Daithidh MacEochaidh, has just put mirrors in the lift. He's the guy that lets me take a nip from a bottle of scotch secreted in a janitor's closet and often feeds me trivia like, and I quote, "Jerry, no chameleon can live with comfort on a tartan." Somehow, I think that applies to me and my Situation. Some kind of Scottish Zen Koan about my bipolar change-ability. Trailing a smell of ammonia, he's usually armed with an ambiguous object: a composite club-broom-toilet plunger. Imported from Glasgow, he claims. When-ever he sees me, he exclaims: "Laddie, this bad place for ya to write. Di ya know Program Empty Body is running full tilt here? They just carried another one out this marnin'."

Anyway, Jimmer said Mac hoped the mirror effect would reduce the incidents of claustrophobia suffered by some of the more touchy residents, like Ill-Phil, "The Presence" we alert nebbies to with the cautionary mantra: "Ill-Phil, Ill Seen, Ill Said." (New folks who were once dubbed, "Pieces of finance on the afternoon wind" by our Fearless Leader). The Presence, wearing offensive T-shirts, has the whiff of the volatile about him; needs to inflict himself on the world ever since *unsuccessfully* storming a Nazi mortar position in '45. Phil's usual greeting is: "See yuh. Wouldn't want to be yuh," followed with, "You tampered with my *tau* modulation, fucker!" or simply, "Yes, I can very well escape, but during my escape, I'm looking for a weapon, see?" A thickish vein in his pale head flutters menacingly. At meals he mutters, "I would rather not to," as he stacks toast, jelly containers, salt and pepper shakers, and so forth, as high as he can get 'em, a construction we term: "The Ill-Phil Tower." Once called Jimmer "The Pedantic Glottologue," getting Jimmer's dryasdust repartee, "Sir, luculent your not."

```
     Perf's ears perk as I begin my tale: "After a devas-
tating raid on the Nazi submarine pens on the coast of
France — we lost two crews, who now live in the solid blue
silent skies forever — the bombing mission for the next day
was scrubbed; bad weather over the target. So our crew
worked overtime at the local pub that night. But about five
a.m., we were startled out of a drunken slumber to shouts
the mission was on again. Perfect skies suddenly arose over
our objective. With hangovers almost too heavy to bear, we
all staggered through breakfast, runny eggs and toast, and
barely managed to climb into our war birds. To make a long
story short, on our way back to base after a good mission, I
had bouts of diarrhea. No option but to do a large caliber
shit in .50 caliber ammunition box.
     "As luck would have it, our home base was socked in
with particularly nasty English fog, so we landed at our
alternate. I left the smelly can in the plane, but a ground
crew dude ran up to me with, 'You left your ammunition box,
Lootenant.' Had to carry the damn thing into the base's
terminal. Tried to leave it in the officer's restroom, but a
guy cleaning the latrine retrieved it, ran out, and handed
it back to me. I was stuck holding this dreadful thing.
     "My fellow crew members could hardly keep a straight
face. Anyway, finally, the weather cleared. As we started to
leave the terminal, I surreptitiously slid the damn can
under a seat. I was out the door and almost to my plane,
when a gorgeous WAC came running across the tarmac shouting,
'Lootenant, Lootenant, you almost forgot your ammo,' and
handed me the cursed thing. We had to ride all the way back
to our Rattlesden base with that smell wafting through the
fuselage, forcing us to go on oxygen even though we were
well under 10,000 feet. Needless to say, I became the butt
of jokes in half a dozen pubs over the next two weeks. Hell,
I coulda gone on a USO tour to entertain the troops!"
```

Yesterday, Jimmer suggested we put on our father-son flight jackets and test-fly the south elevator. My eyes lit up. Father-and-son mischief. Exiting my room, we ran into Daithidh MacEochaidh. Nobody can pronounce his Scottish name so we just call him Mac. As we passed, he acknowledged us with a polite nod and licked his lips with an odd, little grating sound, as if he's made of something peculiar. We hobbled down the hall past small metal plaques with arrows pointing the direction to a range of room numbers. The halls reek of urine (most of us are Depends carrying members of the Flow Flux Klan). When I stopped at the lift, the momentum of my thoughts sent them rushing forward, pressing and wetting the backs of my eyes — thoughts of affection for Jimmer.

I raised my finger old-age-cautiously to press the call button to begin our adventure. After a spell during which Jeane, my ex-wife, could have smoked two cigarettes, the door opened; we stumbled into an alien landscape. The doors

Elder Physics

WHUMP shut and we are sealed in that queasily rising box, rising slowly toward room 536, the Community Elder Services office (chairs there swiveling back 'n forth catching green threads of the carpet in the casters) where I will in the very near future, with unholy fury, report Jim's elder abuse and get, in return from him, a blue fluid of heavy cold silence as word-dust falls between us. The surrounding walls in the lift are mirrored floor-to-ceiling, giving an illusion of infinite space. I quoted *Hamlet* to Jimmer — it reminds me of that bright blue day in Oceanside, California when, at age seventy-three, I soloed in a Cessna — "O God, could be bounded in a nutshell and yet count myself a King of infinite space."

"Hall of mirrors effect, the scene of the abyss, dad," reflected my theory-jock son. "*Mise-en-abyme,* in French theory, *mon cher père*." Staring at that eternity, all that I'm fond of as me was cupped up in this single, staring instant. I was nothing but distortion, then completely disappeared into infinite replication — my ego a reflection, not an object.

"For Chrissakes, what's this? — a Jesuit lift?" I teased Jimmer at a moment we both sensed was somehow metaphysical. I felt my gaze become object-ivized; it was no longer mine, it was stolen from me. Usually my short-term memory just loops every day or so, but this adventure of ours remained vivid.

About an hour after I return to my cell, a knock. I remove the chair propped up to secure my door against interlopers and enters my son beaming as only his blue eyes can, wearing a Sponge Bob Square Pants T-shirt (a cartoon that's situated at the seabottom, an equivalent to that abysmal level of instinct where anything's possible), and holds a book in my mug: *Chefs as Farmers-Scientists: The New Frontier in Food*. I sense dark clouds of root vegetables and cabbages are on the horizon. In one of MyOwnPrivateIdaho brain events, I swear I smell a *sautoir* of potatoes simmering gently in duck fat.

In a Proustian moment, I recall last night's dinner out with Jimmer, not long after our elevating elevator experience. An awful restaurant bathed in unkindly light and the fish staring up at me from my plate, its one flat, iridescent eye accusing me — all surrounded by dreadful murals of Sicily. Sitting at another table is another not-long-for-this-world resident of our elder home, Vera Lille: an eighty-seven-year-old depressing concatenation of Parkinson's-arthritis-hip-implant. If this ain't enough, *twice*, shrieks emanate from the kitchen. (A month later, the joint's *Kaput*.)

Elder Physics

We sit on my bed and regurgitate our bad dinner experience (as Jimmer flips through his book and offhandedly mentions "slow food" and "molecular gastronomy"): *he* liked his clams casino, he said, but the olive oil bread dip sucked. Whatever. Too painful to think FOOD when the fare at my Situation is only a notch above penitentiary cuisine. So I quickly change the topic by telling him about my long walks, wanting to know where I've been forcefully resettled — this "village," as locals nostalgically call it — where I am living out my last days. Want to know it by *walking* through it. A side benefit? This will also help improve the use of my legs, balance, and blood flow to keep me lucid. So, daily, I do an hour constitutional around my environs in my clown-sized orthopedic shoes.

"Yesterday, on my walk," I start to recite a litany of events to my son, "a German Shepherd approached, I turned left to avoid it. Then passed two pastry shops on one block where two Scottish terriers looked less intelligent trotting side-by-side, than when seen alone. Someone was following me again. I ditched him. Near our church, I removed Tony Alamo Christian Ministries anti-Catholic pamphlets off five parked cars. Two cooks and one distracted woman formed a precise (and intense) equilateral triangle in an alley behind Chow Bella, that bad Italian restaurant, inside of which another woman buttered a piece of white bread as soft as the plump undersides of her arms. I went for a cone in that ice cream store (the one you say liberal villagers avoid as the owner is a Tea Party politico(which reminded me of my many forays into our family fridge for mounds of mint chocolate chip. Remember? Then, as I crossed in the middle of the street, taking a shortcut to St. Hilarius to go to Confession, a driver made eye-contact with me through her windshield, a stern gaze that said: I'll allow just enough time for you to cross before I zip by, but hesitate and you're toast. We both counted on the continuity and truth of elder physics, partaking in a mathematics of the most complex kind." At all this, Jimmer just rolls his eyes.

The only intellect in here I fear is Fialta's (once dreamt I was climbing her brain and fell into its Fissure of Silvius). And now she's knocking on my door and yelling, "Open Sesame," or "Sez me," or something like that. Claims she wants to share a box of her precious Koeda chocolates sent by her grandson teaching English in Japan. Jimmer opens the door. Upon entering, she's *too* ingratiating. Suspect she's really here to spy on our father-son collaboration. Jimmer tactfully excuses himself, "Gotta grade student papers, my hoppies. Bye-bye." Likes to call folks here "hoppies." Got the term off an online elder home ad. Go figure.

As Fialta hands me a choice dark chocolate, she points out a curious enigmatic fairy tale English inscription on the chocolate box: *A lovely and tiny twig is a heroine's treasured chocolate born in the forest*. "Grist for my collections of *centos*," she explains. Catching on to the gist of her project, I suggest she surf for inspiration on *www.Engrish.com*, that wacky website where people post about foreigners attempting to use our fair language, sending English spinning in all sorts of wonderful ways. When she opens my door to leave, I can hear that "Rama-lama-ding-dong" left his door open again, strains of what Doo-Wop sounds echo down our pee-tinged hallway: "Duke, Duke, Duke of Earl . . ."

Sorry. I haven't been able to add to my short story for two days. My feet hurt so. So this morning Jimmer drops by to take me to the podiatrist conveniently located in our building. Nice Korean lady. Seems so young. And her last name *is* Young. Has a sign framed in her waiting room with a curious bit of wisdom from the *I Ching*:

> **Deliver yourself from your great toe.**
> **Then the companion comes, and him you can trust.**

She's too nice and delicate, I think, to handle my feet, which look like two over-tenderized yellow-white chicken breasts with rooster claws grafted at one end and covered with month-old fungus growing at the tips. Embarrassed at the state of my feet, as if they are a horribly-rhymed poem, Jimmer's in the waiting room with his head stuck into some dumb magazine. Nothing changes during these nail-clipping procedures, except for a newer edition of *Cosmopolitan* (featuring "Waking up at *his* House" or similar dreck) and *Car and Driver* in the magazine rack. I get placed in this big relaxing chair while young Young hacks away at my thick, sick toenails. That distinct SNAP of the clippers. Sounds like something I'd hear in the inside the fuselage of a new plane being assembled as technicians wired the electronics. Even out in the waiting area, Jimmer flinches with each snip. She hits a small vein, I yelp and bleed, in vain. Nothing can stop that encroaching yellow plague turning my toes into caricatures of human digits. Constant pruning and prayer keep it at bay though.

    I'm unsteady enough on my feet without this shit happening. Have to wear high, orthopedic socks these days. Keeps the fluid from settling in my two southern peninsulas. Swelling (it ain't swell) and losing feeling in those regions too. Something about my heart. Isn't pumping up to snuff. Depressing to see your personal geography being slowly annexed by foreign powers. Thought I fought a war to prevent just that.

    The doctor was lifting my leaden feet one after another into my black orthopedich Velcro fastened shoes. Her small hands and my large shoes made this an operation rather like saddling a comatose horse. Cost of shoes and doctor's fees brought this to $120 per sole. Like paying for an Indulgence. Way too heavy for my weak legs, so I ditch 'em for my white gym shoes when I'm in my room, despite being prone to trip on untied laces. Yah, yah, I know I'll catch flak for this, but I'm a lucky bastard. Got a certificate after surviving all those combat missions to prove it. My son and I go for lunch, in our painfully slow-serving dining room. I've keep mum about my new roomy. Get him chatting about Language. "Say, dad, did you know that dictionaries are a lot like elder homes? Both warehouse entities that were once vital, active, and meaningful." Food for thought.

    For a week Perf suffers my war stories, me his. One night he points at the full moon out my window, exclaiming, "That'll happen." For a week I smuggle in food. Many residents hoard food in their rooms, so this subterfuge is easy. Perf prefers "coffee 'n leaky eggs fer breakfast," "fer lunge, bring me a grease-bomb wit cheese 'n extra fuel, but hold da fuckin' radioactive materials," and "fer dino-time, cop that classy mystery meat-o'-da-day." In between, the ex-marine snacks on my store-bought (honey-topped by *moi*) corn bread. "Better'n a twenty-one gun salute," he says, consuming

Bad day. Feeling persecuted. Irascible. What I call my "Futterneid Quotient" is rising. Complained for a week 'bout Bondo's noisy antics and that my toilet pipes are tapped, my feces analyzed. So annoyingly persistent am I, threatening to drill holes in order to see and hear what is lurking beyond, they move me to another room whose number, I insist, be a prime number. Jammer and the handymen commiserate as they work their butts off lugging my stuff. Jammer manages to sneak out with and trash some of my possessions. Thinks I'm blind and can't recall what I got. Like my golf clubs. Says he's storing them. Can't fool me. Sold 'em, I know. And where did my archery set go? Said I authorized selling it. Liar, liar, pants on fire! I know he's got his hands in my till, too. Why I moved all my bank accounts from under his nose and why I figure I'll report his elder abusin' ass — "I bear the scars of malicious gashes!" — to the fifth-floor officials next time I'm looking into the abyss of that mirror in the lift. And that red-haired wife of his . . . in cahoots! No doubt. A psychoanalyst to boot. I know she's telling them here I'm nuts. Why else are they analyzing my feces daily and putting meds in my orange juice? When I complain, they accuse me of "petulant self-advertisement." Ho! I can sense they're going to, someday, take their pound of flesh outta me for all the trouble I am. I am trouble, therefore, I am.

premises (more difficult now since he's gained weight and
suffers the after effects from a bottle of single malt
scotch Daithidh unsuccessfully hid by pouring its contents
into a bottle of rug cleaner in his maintenance closet.)

Pissed. Seems I'm always pissed off at someone or something: my ex-wife, deceptive salesmen, seducers of all types, bleeding-heart liberals, Pope-condemned movies, slow drivers, my former bosses, TV anchors, sex-celebrities, my daughter's suitors, and even well-meaning people who offer the platitude, "You still have a long time ahead of you." Can't stand our megalomaniac elder home honcho, nor those meal-delaying cooks 'n waitresses here, nor that faking-friendly guy who follows me around in this place and gets into my myriad medications by busting my safe (my son thinks I smashed its door myself to gain credibility); oh yes, and don't forget those guys on staff here who analyze my feces after flushing. Jeez, despite my move, I hear someone behind the wall at times! I imagine those test-tubes too. I try to imagine the faces. Plural because I'm sure it isn't one guy. (Did you catch my bad pun? Bet you didn't.) Must have three shifts. And all males because no female would analyze feces, right? Right?!

Wish they'd just move me outta here. *Wheels-within-wheels.* I'm busted, broke. They, my son and his wife, got all my money. And the meds I'm supposed to take, that sneaky bastard who pretends he likes me, fawning asshole, knows just when to break into my room and swipe 'em. I can tell 'cause when I accuse him, he frowns, nods, smiles, snaps his fingers, sucks in his breath, and eventually grins. Had the nuts to break into my safe once. Busted the door. Probably selling my pills on the black market. Must remember to write Jimmer a frank letter about this, this very week. Must twist the turbulence of my liquid intelligence into the stony idiom of the tortured brain.

I never found out Perf's fate. It was one of my more
colorful experiences in my elder-life and a first for the
Upping Arms Elder Home. And the last straw. As I stand
before Fearless Leader, I'm read a litany of offenses.
Later, Jimmer is told to find another home for my sorry
bones.
An ordinary short story is like a meteor. It has only
one moment, a moment when it soars screaming like the
phoenix, all its pages aflame, then peters out with a
swoosh. Such was that one moment in my life when I met Mr.
Perfect and we pulled off the (almost) perfect crime.
Almost, as I soon found myself out on the street waiting for
Jimmer to drive up and put all that makes up my material
life into his shiny silver SUV. Another Situation awaits me
ahead. Another story in the making.

A firm knock. I think that's Fialta at my door to remind me about our afternoon meeting. At least that's what my DON'T FORGET dry-erase wall-board lists in bright red ink as my next activity today. Ten minutes later Fialta is drumming her platitudes into us. "What do we really want? We're only just discovering our potential, but clearly it starts with *more*. Pareto's principle, the 80-20 rule, says that only 20 percent of our writings will be hits. So call it precious and go to hell, but I believe a story can be wrecked by a faulty rhythm in a sentence — especially if it occurs toward the end — or a mistake in paragraphing, even punctuation. Henry James was the maestro of the semi-colon. Hemingway of the paragraph. Virginia Woolf never wrote a bad sentence, nor did she do *mashups* like yours, Gerald." After several minutes of Fialta's lashing homily, the club meeting is turned over to each of our members' readings.

Tandeta Paluba, a vocal member, announces she has just completed a short story, "Jeffty is Eighty-Five,"a clever gerontic refunctioning of a classic Harlan Ellison story she loves. As she rattles on, I slowly become aware of how much I like how she wears her hair, swept back as it is in an odd '40s pompadour that looks like some auxiliary brain. Tandeta is followed by Magda Wang, a slovenly and loose-tongued woman, who brashly demands to read from her ongoing memoirs, *The Purple Days*, daring us with those darting eyes of hers to give an unfriendly critique as she covers her ass by saying, "I've written a wicked book, and feel as spotless as the lamb."

Rory McDuff, wearing some kind of citrusy cologne, his hair around his ears in little grey waves that look so natural they have to be fake, follows Magda, reading from his newly begun detective novel, *Bubble of Fear* (his original title, *Eight Heads in a Duffle Bag*, was unanimously nixed). "My protagonist, Detective Inspector Justin-Nico Thymme, narrates in the first person, opening my mystery in a men's room thus: 'Having just been involved in a self-defense shooting of a perp I returned to my precinct in Chicago's Greek Town. I've been on duty twenty-four hours straight, powered on copper's-li'l-helpers and mainlined caffeine. I'm now in the precinct shit-house. Staring in the mirror, I notice my hat and trench coat and hands are pinprick-sprayed with the residue of ugly work; my eyes are sunken little blue coals, the wrinkles on my face look so much like plastic that it's hard to tell what's real and what may be a mask.' That's the first paragraph, took me half the day to write it." We all nod our approvals — even hard-to-impress Fialta.

I go last, "I've titled this piece 'The Perfect Crime'." I pause as Bondo rubs his hands in anticipation. I begin, "Outside, sky swept lengthwise by gusts of wind. Vast and silvery white, it is cut into lines of energy tensed to the breaking point, into awesome furrows like strata of tin and lead. Divided into magnetic fields and trembling with discharges, it is full of concealed electricity. Diagram of a gale akin to the renditions of our Chicagoscape as imagined by the late local superhero painter, Roger Brown. Like the silhouette figures in Brown's painted high-rises, there's a man in my room, nay, on my bed, refusing the bed, begging for the floor instead.He has the aura of distant paint and layers of erosion and granite and sandstone and graffiti about him. Yes, definitely.*"

My Fellow Inmates

Nightfall descended and fell and otherwise pushed its foot onto my cranium. During these hours I become a receptacle of non-plot, which I welcome with open arms and closed eyes. I bask in the lack of an event curve until night — the astonishing, the stranger to all that is human — has fled and sunlight presses through the windows, thieving its way in, flashing its light over my furniture and then, an hour later, across senescents sitting in our dayroom.

Speaking of such, not much for many of the residents here to do *but* watch the shadow of the curtain slowly move across the polished floor. A local manifestation of that hourglass-shaped ribbon of light moving across the surface of our planet, The Terminator, rushing like great fearful wings across distant

plains and mountains and oceans. Jimmer has software on his computer that graphically displays this celestial Arnold Schwartzenegger in real-time.

Amazing, uses it for his shortwave-listening to determine where and when wave-propagation will be best. He tunes in world radio with a hi-tech Kenwood R-5000 digital receiver employing single-side band capability and digital signal processing that does an end run around inter-ference; strings a long Super Eavesdropper Dipole Antenna inside his home — much to his wife's dismay. She blames me. I got him started in all that when I buy a teenaged Jimmer a World War II surplus Hammerlund Super-Pro vacuum-tubed radio. Hugh sucker festooned with delightfully mysterious dials and knobs.

It's the early sixties; my son's curious ears be-glued to ungainly headphones crackling with static mixing with foreign broadcasts. Radio Moscow's propaganda competes with jamming and other electromagnetic mishmash on the 11,000-megacycle band. Very educational and (my ulterior motive) it sidetracks him from the pleasures of appreciation of females, often succeeded by the risks of seduction. Get the boy studying electronics (names his pet white mice "Cathode" and "Anode"). Learns about different types of antennae (loops and long-wires, dipoles), the effect of waxing and waning sunspots on radio propagation (an eleven-year manic-depressive cycle, much slower than mine), how to filter jamming, and the joys of auditing clandestine stations.

Unbeknownst to me, I spark in him a latent desire for eavesdropping (a kind of germ warfare for the ears) that has ever remained. But on the downside, that listening to and corresponding with Radio Moscow and Radio Havana brings paranoid F.B.I. agents to our door, especially unwanted as I'm working on top secret government projects. He has to sign a document refusing all material from these subversive sources or risk putting us under government surveillance. Hey, it was at the height of the Cold War. *Wheels-within-wheels.* Even I spent an inordinate amount of time listening to those fascinating airwaves; about the only time I listened to someone else when not, myself, broadcasting. Maybe that is why I enjoy listening in on conversations around here, or sitting respectfully, ears open, at the feet of our resident Ancient One who has a favorite spot by the north window of our dayroom where he can hear some little sparrows chirping on the window's ledge: *yeep — yeep — yeep.* So delicate, frail is he, I expect from him the same *yeep — yeep — yeep,* but instead get a series of spits into a brass spittoon. "My spitting is no sign of illness," he explains, "but rather of mental health. I spit from disgust at the nonsense on TV and in newspapers today. My spits are symbolic and of high cultural content; if you don't like them . . . Let us to our own play in the nursery of our own times." I shake his hand too vigorously for a condition so cadaverous: wrist-bones and the beak of his nose seem to want to break through his skin. Unbelievably aged, his features constrict into believable infantile aspects. It's as if his clothes hold him together; breathing like the rustling of fallen leaves. Has an aura as if dead and unborn relatives present themselves through his living organism; he, a spaceless entity contains a timeless evolution. We call him "Hemp," but his real name is Rupert Hempel.

Why, he's here now, wheeled in by his salaried, nervous factotum. He's edging towards his hundredth birthday, so no surprise that he's as slow as the galaxy and just as mysterious. Yet you wouldn't be surprised if he still found the chutzpah to hop on our electrician's Husqvarna 125cc and ride astride it willy-nilly down our hallways in one last whooping hurrah. But Our Ancient One is selective as to who he keeps in his orbit. He maintains the unwelcome at arm's length by addressing them as Your Excellency or Your Majesty. They get the hint. I'm among the privileged, he calls me Jerry.

In an elder world that has no rhyme or reason, Hemp reigns like a monarch, a Grand Lama-like exclusiveness that keeps him from ever feeling his own order threatened; an envoy in the midst of our chaos serving an order so noble that he is able to tranquilly accept the necessity of all our disorder. We all suspect great secrets in him, hidden treasures — his old hands are like the parchment of an old pirate map — but he can't seem to formulate them fully. It's less about *what* he says than how he *says* it. And his appearance! Like a broken record about those eagle eyes in between a sharp beak that penetrate you to the quick. Those quick turns of the head! But then there'd be those times when his senses would sleep as if nothing made enough of a claim on them.

He lives for mealtimes and our brief but tasty conversations. Wealthy enough to have catered dinners brought in by the assistant that shadows him; why, with his bucks, he parks his weary frame among us anyone's guess. Did he convince staff he'd thrive at Upping Arms by claiming to be short of requests and absolute requirements? But it might really be because he knew *moi* had landed here too! Stranger things have happened in my life. Like being cured at Lourdes.

Took a liking to him right off 'cause I intuit that all time and everything in our world is as mysterious and great as he is. A mirror of all I find fascinating. He was a successful C.E.O. of a car company; owned and piloted his own plane, a nifty Beechcraft B-35 V-tail. Jeez, how I've always wanted to fly that baby! Knows his cylinders and pistons sure enough. Still scans engineering mags.

One day his factotum brings out a pot of Chamomile tea from which there comes the occasional puff of steam as from a toy engine. As I sip, I mention I once had a summer job on the Chicago and Northwestern Railroad. Hemp's eyes brighten and he proceeds to detail the physics behind steam locomotion, more to prove he can remember than to inform. I broach the topic of aeronautics and we discover our common turf, become a four-eyed engine sparkling in the dim light of a winter afternoon. I gain points with his factotum by offering to watch over Hemp, push him around each day. So I'm welcome to visit any time and entertain him with my adventures in aerospace. Read excerpts from my memoirs too, of which he comments, "Jerry, from the very outset, recapitulating the past can have only one end, the hour of deliverance." I nod uneasily.

Hemp always listens with head tilted, smiling blissfully, but when it's his time to speak, it's as though he's desperately struggling for breath, face contorting into a grimace; the effort bringing beads of perspiration to his brow as words come in a spasmodic, precipitate manner betraying severe inner turmoil and presaging, even then, his demise.

Hemp wields a sharp blue heaven-piercing squint. He's a fencing master of imagination, a solo hero waging war against the fathomless, elemental boredom of old-age-institutionalization. Due to his advanced years, he doesn't buy green bananas anymore; due to his age and wisdom, he's been awarded our home's prestigious "Nestor Medal." He's like a magic mill: pour into the hoppers the bran of empty hours and they re-emerge flowering into all the colors and scents of oriental spices. The only other person who can do that was my ex-wife's father, my son's favorite relative. Out of everything repugnant and detestable, Hemp could extract the hots 'n cools to reinvigorate life. So I do dog him about, garner his favor. Once he encouraged our reading club to peruse Plato as a tonic for the blood and a catalyst for prophetic dreams and regular bowels. His mantra is: *Less matter, more form*. Best yet, in the dayroom, watching the on-going slow-motion opera performed there, we find ourselves exchanging secret eye signals.

After we've gotten to trust each other like that, he tells me he's old enough to have suffered the seven lympic scourges. That his wife died ten years ago. That his factotum is his wife's cousin's daughter's brother's friend. Or something like that. I tell him about the *action of unity* propelled from my bomber base in Rattlesden; he rattles on that his corporate management strategy stressed *unity of action.* In each of our experiences it was collective and individual interest that harmonized. Not like today's rampant spread of Randian Selfishness. One of his companies was among the first to offer profit-sharing to its work-force. Says one can learn a lot about successful management by combining ideas from that Frenchy Charles Fourier's utopic musings with Scottish educator A. S. Neil's progressive pedagogy. Hemp seems to have absorbed the Can-Do spirit of his models, as exemplified in this quotable quote pulled with effort from the depths of Hemp's shriveled frame: "At times it's more difficult to remain slumped in my chair, immobilized, than to get up and move farther on."

We share a sensitivity to Hay-Fever, Para-Hay-fevers, what I call "Toxic Idiopathies," and a marked disdain for politicians and TV personalities — peddlers of garbage both. Television overpays its talent, and "Politicians gotta graft, he observes, "to compensate for having one-half of the population always hating their guts. Imagine having that many people pissed at you! And the media hot on your ass 24 / 7. Not even The President is respected. Don't they know that in disrespecting HIM they disrespect themselves? He is, after all, the embodiment of THEM. Little wonder that no self-respecting person becomes a politico unless they can glean gargantuan profits off their positions as insiders, or have their egos scratched due to the power they wield." I agree, "It's educators, those unsung illuminators of young minds (like my Jimmer!) that should be compensated into the six digits, not those schmucks." Commonsense says you can judge a society by what it values. So just look around you, plenty of evidence we live in a topsy-turvy world, where shit floats to the top (one of two reasons I need to have a scissors parked on top of my toilet). Okay, Hemp and I are opinionated, "ROFs" (Rigid-Old-Farts) as Jimmer puts it. Our dislike of new times is concomitant with elegy. But few people in here could throw the first stone at us for being such.

When I told Jimmer about the startling shards of conversation I overhear here — as I walker-it about these days, oft in a daze — he offered me his extra iPod equipped with a little stereo microphone device which instantly turns the MP3 player into a mini-digital audio recorder. Ain't it techno-amazing? I wear it around my neck and people only see an iPod my son got me for my eighty-fourth birthday. With a little on-the-job training, I got proficient with it. I carry it everywhere, especially to our "Happy Scribbler" sessions. As every person consists of a soul, a body, and a name, here's a slew of aural tidbits (names changed to protect the innocent, from residents and staff) surreptitiously recorded this week and transcribed by (thank you) Jimmer. Some are goosepimply ominous, one has been censored for modesty's sake, unflattering comments about yours truly remain, most are true as a compass:

- **Teddy Jawnowitz** (staff shrink, to me at my "intake" session) — *Jerry, remember that every life is a special problem which is not yours but another's, and content yourself with the terrible algebra of your own; don't melt too much into the universe, but be as solid and dense and fixed as you can within the parameters of elder physics.*

- **Eepie Carpetrod** (wearing a blond wig and oversized sunglasses; author of the column "Just Ask Eepie" in our in-house Xeroxed bulletin, *Armed 'n Ready*) — *My doctor's now got me on Divalproex; effective against rapid-cycling and non-rapid-cycling episodes. I'm also researching the "herb of invulnerability." Need med advice? Just ask Eepie!*

- **Paul Brainard** (a visiting psychologist from Stanford doing Doctoral research, to Toby "The Belt" Van Allen) — *. . . and in between these tests you will master longhand and long division again. You'll be soon radiating confidence despite your obesity.*

- **Jill Peaseblossom** (our empathic events co-ordinator) — *I think Jerry's declining; reminds me of my cousin suffering Fred Hoyle syndrome, a rare disease that, although it boosts your brainpower exponentially, begins to age you a month a day. It's a paradoxical, both-and-logic; in both cases — Jerry's and my cousin's — Nature's both not playing according to Hoyle and according to Hoyle. And in Jerry's case he's not only been dealt a bad hand, he's not even playing with a full deck.*

- **Fred Federerer** — *Jerry, "Rory", at our Poker sessions, always has an interesting question or two to pose, such as: Why do hooded seals inflate a red balloon out their nose during courtship? Or, What is Pollyanna's epitaph? Or asking if we heard the one about the horse needing a cataract operation but was too broke to pay for it. I finally figured out that he was doing that to distract us when he held a good hand.*

- **Sabbah "Sad Intestinal Poison" (SIP for short) Pargoric** (as overheard at Suvarnabhum Thai restaurant) — *Dead bird — quail in the slipper — money in the bank — all's well with this soft machine.*

- **Sunny "Storm" Atkins** (gurgling and spitting through hayseed chapped lips) — *And Ellowese (it was on her name tag) she told me I had canine teeth that stick out like box seats at the opera — god — felt like I needed splints on my heart. Moon, uncentered, round, and white as ice, go away. I don't love you no more!*

- **Jean-Emile Leblanc** (to Teddy Jawnowitz) — *It's all a blank, Doc. Of my parents all I can recall is my mother was Swedish 'n my father French and they'd run a Swedish restaurant in Chicago that later sold out and became Ann Sather. Hell, I'm Anatole France le vieux cadavre de France. Your assignment? Resuscitate me!*

- **Hilla Horavath** (to me) — *Oh come on, Gerald, that's nothing to scuff through! Remember, even the sky opens for business. Morning comes on like a wink in the dark. So cheer up. You have it easy. Since my husband's started to speed-age, his range of emotions has narrowed into the yellow line on a highway crossing the Prairies. Dull crayons of sex and meanness scribbled all over his thoughts, so we were 'bout as happy as headstones.*

- **Amy Gdala** (with a mouth of an executed saint, to Noreen Pogacnic) — *In our popular bi-weekly session of "You Know More Than You Think" in* *the Sunshine Room, sweet Jill unrolled bubble wrap before our us, cut and gave each a yard's length, saying each bubble represents a story in our lives. We are to tell someone a story each day if possible and, when each story ends, we are to pop a bubble. The first to turn in our sheet with all the bubbles popped wins a pizza-a-day for a week of their choice from Trattoria Two Twenty-five. The flattened plastic then serving as a placemat. But Ill-Phil blabbed to us girls — disturbing poor Betty no end — that when no more bubbles are left, it really indicates it's time to fertilize the grass. That verbal tornado . . . the gibberish that life-form exudes!*

- **Kim Young Sam** (now back from death's door) — *I looks flimsy so. Am hopeless lone chopstick and "Bickering Barb" says I'm smelling like rubber worms in a box of fishing tackle. And Heidi blabs around that I have faint eyebrows like a pair of smudged thumb-prints. Isn't that racist? Can't I report her to Jill? Can't I? Or would that be like sending a letter to a coffin? Maybe I should just type out every dirty word I know on our computer.*

- **Nicea Blonde** (the bedazzling, now-dead, she-eminence of our writing club; under the *nom de plume* of 'Nice 'n Easy Ash Blond,' she had just published her sensational memoir, *The Ballad of Sexual Expediency* which begins: "Mock light lolls in the boughs of the pines. Dead air numbs my hands." It's rumored she died in Dirty Harry von Warburg's bed) — *The truth will knock "Teary" Castellano off her meds! Despite (or maybe because of) the fact that her cheeks look like scones.*

- **Buddy MacDonald** (all snub-nose and thyroid eyes) — *Everyday, Jill spoon feeds him a few details from his home town newspaper, articles he can't bring himself to read. Gives him small dosages so he'll eventually become immune to the full dose.*

- **Hilaria Wojnarowicz** — *Eepie, Harry's forehead looks as square and white as a slice of sandwich bread. Makes me swoon! Unlike that creep, Gerald who loves to hold my hand to hard and tell me, "We had children, married, and met."*

- **Daithidh MacEochaidh** (our handyman, who seems unusually keen on inspecting the hairs on the backs of female residents' necks) — *All day it's "Mac, this, Mac that, Mac, Mac, Mac, Mac". . . Ack! So when it comes to lunch give me food so good it'll bloody me lip.*

- **Heidi Katzenjammer** — *Frieda's mastered French's pluperfect. It conjures up our wishes and desires, our fears and possibilities, she claims. Then again, she thinks language (which exists to pull us close) originated as a benevolent virus from outer space, shot our way by extra-galactic residents.*

- **Chaddy "Gnetophyte"Fenwick** (a retired chef who's always carrying an ice cream cone, hence the "cone-bearing tree" nickname, to Jill, with a huge sigh) — *So, I will sit down and eat my bowl of dust like everyone* *else. . . . My son? Well, he's sous chef to Grant Achatz now at Alinea. As the saying goes, 'The apple doesn't farfalle from the brie,' huh?*

- **Jill Peaseblossom** (empathically, to a distraught resident's daughter) — *Your mom's words simply toddle across the page like a string of daycare tots, infantile and uncoordinated. In marked contrast, the objects pasted into her* I WON'T FORGET *scrapbook conjure up a spectrum of emotions and memories. So maybe there's still hope.*

- **Noreen Pogacnic** (to Jill) — *Why am I here? Why did my kids finally chase me out of my old house with the peeling birch trees out front. They accused it of having a porch so sunken it seemed to smile at you from the street. I thought* that *was a* good *thing! . . . Jill? . . .*

- **Our Fearless Leader** (at our annual residents' art show to Teddy Janowitz) — *Everyone's a friggin' self-styled critic, Ted. Y says oats, Z says hay, and chances are it's buckwheat. The only thing better than an art exhibit without the damn critics is an art exhibit without the art. Har-har.*

- **Viviana Verbock** (over slow-lunch in the dining room) — *My love life here is toast, Melba toast. When Dirty Harry invited me to play with his Necker cube, I thought he meant he wanted me to neck with him in his room. Well ... with what people say about his past — teeming with protean partners — one assumes . . .*

- **Gina Love** (our slender chair yoga instructor) — *Teddy, did I ever tell you about the time when I got hooked on the* I Ching, *and had to have Chaos Therapy to kick it?*

- **"Ill-Phil" Pokey** (our Overt Freak Supreme, to Jill, like the kettle calling the pot black) — *I'm glad I'm dead. I personally know a lot of inanimate objects with more human personality than many humans.* (Here he became so unruly he had to be restrained.) *Unstrap me, and I'll fit my square fist into your round pie-hole of a mouth! I'm mascot to a world-view away beyond yer comperhenshum. I am the bloody man, I have the bloody hand and I will have revenge!* (Here he shook his head and flung it off to one side as if to let go of the hopeless project of life, making a "ghah" sound.)

- **Brucine Bitters** (to Dorinda Daymare, who is stroking her persimmon-colored cat) — *In real life, Ricky was a womanizer and a cheat and Fred a mean-spirited drunk. Both only a notch above Ill-Phil. . . . As my mother told us, 'Always butter bread toward the edges because enough gets in the middle anyway'. I've found this to be good advice.*

- **Wolf Blass** — *I wept when the place closed in '49 'cause the floor show there had a cross-eyed belly dancer with a horsey face and a frenetic jiggle. Chicago was reaaaaalllllly fun back then.*

- **Rupert Hempel** (to Teddy Jawnowitz, our resident shrink) — *Doc, I must appear vaporous, a sort of floater in other people's eyes. Except to*

Jerry. Except to Jerry Hugunin, a true nomad. Ya know, he calls me an ummanu, *the Akkadian word for teacher of wisdom just 'cause I said memorabilia keeps longer under plastic.*

- **Valerie Desconsano** (president of our "Knit-Wits" knitting group, to Gina Love in a whisper the length of a woolen string) — *Flabby armpits — how can you exercise the armpits?*

- **Victoria Popularpoulos** (award-winning ceramics instructor to Hilla Horavath) — *A potato held by a two-headed baby? In clay? Really?*

- **A Resident's Grandchild** (visiting our dining room) — *Ugh, they look spooky!*

- **Fred Federerer** — *There's veterans and then there's veterans. There's bombers and then there's bombers. There's luck and then there's luck.*

- **"Nutritious"** (Queen of Sheba to Jill) — *And Wilma said she did the whole Mediterranean cruise with a front-end loader. . . . You know, she had to wear one of* those *bags after she'd had one of* those *operations. . . .* (to *moi*) — *Gerald, ya* know why black music is so popular? 'Cause ya can't see white music on the page!

- **Fialta Fenwich** (our overeducated resident skeptic and President of our writing club, withered but immaculately unwrinkled, her scalp dotted with hair implants, during an architecture lecture in our educational series, "The Arts: Now or Never," in the Twilight Room by a Professor Brugge-mann) — *Beggin' your pardon. I know that's what they used to say, but in fact the pointed arch is the most primitive. It's the easiest arch; it's not a development from the round arch at all — how could it be? They had pointed arches in Egypt. The round arch, the keystone arch, is the most sophisticated arch you can build. The whole thing has been report-ed ass backwards to favor Christianity.*

- **Quimper Quade** — *Valerie always a sunburst of kindness, never minds if she sounds silly; she will throw herself headlong into any conversation to turn it off its contentious course. Why just the other day . . .*

- **Professor Batty Langely** (guest speaker in our educational series, "The Arts: Now or Never," — *When the devils disappeared from Gothic detail, the saints lost half their saintliness.* (I wondered if Ill-Phil, that devil, were to die, it'd have the same effect on our home's residents.)

- **Teddy Jawnowitz** (during an inspirational Easter presentation, "Egg-on Your Family Member, Not on your Face," addressed to residents and their families) — *Some people will call their days here their "declining years," but I would ask you to realize an elder home is an easy, ideal, even utopic, place to reverse that perverse and disorienting sense so per-vasive in life-before-the-home that the false part of one's life is happen-ing openly while the real and interesting part remains hidden. As our most revered resident, Rupert Hempel, has rightly observed — thank you Rupert and Jill for that information and Harry von Warburg for your vivid* *example — we have something akin to a Fourerist Phalanstery* in utero *here.* [Editor's note: Charles Fourier's eighteenth-century proto-Hippy commune.]

- **Bondo "Rama-lama-ding-dong" McCracken** (at fifty-five, our youngest inmate, at one of our group meetings) — *We must invert our notion of repose and activity, elder citizens! We should not sleep to recover the energy expended when awake, but rather wake occasionally to defecate the unwanted energy that sleep engenders. Get crackin' if ya want my backin'.*

- **Vassili Brekhunoff** (to Bettina Weissacker) — I *trained at the four hundred and first KBG School in Okhta, Leningrad at the same time when Vladimir Putin was a fledgling agent there learning nine ways to kill with a rolled-up newspaper. It was rumored that on his KGB application form, where they ask your sex, Putin put "none."*

- **Ruby Zunshine** (eating stamp-'n-go pancakes in our dining room, her eyes harpooning Brucine Bitters) — *Dirty Harry sure has the knack for seductive whispering. A seductive mix of both hiding and showing something. Mixed signals. He often comes on to women as though they were men. Like a certain type of actor, he isn't particularly interesting in group scenes, but shines in one-to-one matches when the chemistry is right. When not, he seduces up to a point where conquest is certain and then calls it off.*

- **"Dirty Harry" von Warburg** (sporting his green hunter's jacket, brushed to a sigh of its used-up life, to Bondo McCracken) — *That Ruby, she's a good one. She's so pretty. Man I'd just like to be able to look at her and just . . . I could just look at her and just hold her and . . . I'd like her to just touch me, just, you know, just touch me and her like me, you know.*

- **Roy "Rory" McDuff** (to Jill) — *You know in this life you can lose everything that you love, everything that loves you. Now I don't hear as good as I used to, and I forget stuff, and I ain't as pretty as I used to be, but goddamn, I'm still standing here. Not washed up yet.*

- **Bruin Opps** (to Al Rutcurts) — *Fiona likes to drag me to the local bar that Bondo's bonded with where pinch-faced retirees hunch over their double vodkas in hopes it'll give them back the key to their personalities and Fiona gives out her tiresome doses of palindromes.*

- **Brucine Bitters** (a woman who would take a job drowning kittens, in an exchange with Jill Peaseblossom) — *We have no future because our present is too volatile. You go out either in terror or in ecstacy, I've heard. I wish I were dead. . . . But you won't tomorrow. . . . But I don't want to live to see tomorrow. . . . You will tomorrow.*

- **Dorinda Daymare** (mistress of the exotic incense stick; today a peony-pink-on-its-way-to-mauve blouse covers her marmoreal white skin, prone to blushing, as she peeks at the world through slow-moving, sea-green eyes evoking a Neptunian parentage; monumentally sober, she is a tongue-valiant vaunter of days of yore) — *Politicians used to address us as "Americans," but that implies individuals; now gotta address as "The American People." I mean, Roosevelt could get on the radio and say, "You and I know." Not now. Not now.*

- **Magda Wang** (to Jill Peaseblossom) — *Karol, god rest his soul, when he wasn't humming that old Balkan song "Savo Vodo," would say things like "pardonnez-moi" or "bonjour" and then add, "that's French, you know?" . . . Gerald told me that his son told him that he read that "You and I are semistable patterns of energy, barely maintaining in the very teeth of entropy a characteristic shape in space and time. He could've simply said, 'Our bodies are now adorned, but tomorrow they will be food for worms,' and left it at that!"*

- *Fleur Flaire* (an FTD Florist, lecturing on "CPDO: Make Your Room More Livable," in the Sunshine Room) — *Color, Pattern, Decoration. Ornamentation. It's all coming back. It's about celebrating life in these terrorist-aware times when we're more conscious than ever that this life isn't a rehearsal, it's the main event. And what simpler way to add some joy and pattern to your life than with flowers.*

- **Jill Peaseblossom** (to me, over Sloppy Joe sandwiches and coleslaw eaten with a plastic "spork" on home picnic at our local park) — *Jerry, you have tendency to "tugboat," that dysfunction of wits and raconteurs; that is, knowing when a joke or verbal gambit tugs at its limit, yet continuing to push just over that line. It really screws with Ill-Phil's mind, what little there is left of it.*

- **Our Dayroom's Communal TV** — *Los Angeles will be our Rome, and Las Vegas our Florence.* And later: *We vow no more starving Third World babies, but many more successful businessmen around their weekend barbecues.* Two days later: *If you use our miracle product, your bowels movements will no more offensive than moist clay and have no more odor than a hot biscuit.*

- **My Saturday noon radio program, "Those Were the Days"** (old time radio program on WDCB, DuPage; tobacco auction sound effects accompanying an old Lucky Strike cigarette ad during a Jack Benny program) — *L-S-M-F-T, Lucky Strike Means Fine Tobacco.* (I recall Jeane smoked Luckies, but switched to Camels.)

- **Our Dining Room's Piped in Radio Programming** (WBEZ, PBS Radio, Chicago) — *In-house sabotage is one of the greatest problems now facing both our manufacturing and service industries.*

- **Chub Lykom** (delivered softly to his agitated and obese mailman son) — *Don't pigeon-hole life 'n death, Denny. Why, death is also part of life. It's* always *someone living who dies. Right?*

- **Astrid "Meals-on-Wheels" Hunnecker** (our obese, wheelchair-ridden resident, to Chub) — *we were a family separated by the Dreyfus Affair but united by Roosevelt's New Deal.*

- **Kathy Holos** (to me) — *Gerald, take the American Revolution . . . it was the "moneyed groups" revolution. Breed's Hill, two weeks after Lexington, and it was all over for the "smaller people" — until Jefferson gave them another chance.*

Jimmer sits at my desk, brushes corn bread crumbs away, rubs his hands together, and begins to enthuse over these fragments. A *pochade* of my life here, he calls it, drawing on his penchant for pedantry. Hey — and it's fun!

Last night, after an afternoon of entering into gymnastic relationships with young oak trees, preparing for his nightly jog, Bondo "Rama-lama-ding-dong" McCracken tried to rally dayroom inerts: "Arise! Arise like the evening star 'n brighten the way into night for us!" He was ignored. Valerie Desconsano kept knitting with the grim seriousness of a surgeon in a touchy operation. Ruby Zunshine couldn't be budged from her latest romantic novel, *Heart Nouveau.* I slumped back, slowly resuming my infamous chair-snoring.

This a.m., Friday, awoken abruptly, a man surprised, cheated out of sleep. I take a long, deep breath and stare unhappily at the slits of cold sunshine slicing my room's walls. Monsters (of my own making, says Jammer) roar behind those boiling walls. As I lay on my left side for some moments before stiffly crawling out of bed, my heart contracts as the foreboding of some essential truth touches me with light fingers. I'm frightened by old age, by death, but I make myself a warm coat out of my faith.

I am up. Peeing in my pj's into my yogurt can and staring at a crazy face in the mirror, giving it an expression of a person with a fixed hallucination. I look outside. The whole sky is overcast with rain-clouds which won't spill their guts, resulting in a humid, grey dull day. Jimmer calls, cancels our breakfast. A crisis with a cooperative education student — sexual harassment. Over the phone *once more* our conversation is overlaid by a radio broadcast from the Polish-language station, WPOL, lurking on the top floor of our building (Fearless Leader needs their rent money). Its tall antenna doubles as a landmark guiding our weary residents back to home base. But so powerful are their transmissions, often our phone lines resonate with their FM waves. Disappointed over Jammer's reneging on our plans, I dejectedly double-lock my door and descend on the newly mirrored elevator for my eats. I try to avoid direct eye contact with that infinite reflection. But maybe I should boldly confront my reflection, attempt a sketch.

Breakfast *once more*. Around me, various groups and solitaries are hunched over bowls of cereal, plates of glistening stuff, leaky eggs, ersatz fruit, collapsing rolls. The grey carpet is liberally scattered with a sort of bread-related dandruff; each table has its dusting, too, along with a thread or so of unconvincing foliage in a throttled vase. At a corner table, Edna and Bill. There are so inseparable we've dubbed them "Edna-N-Bill." Edna chews and chews and chews, while I try not to imagine the finer and finer and finer and finer paste she is producing. *Swallow, swallow, damn-it*! I silently try my mental *jujitsu* on her — without effect. Bill, lips moving soundlessly, is intent on squeezing the contents from several tiny plastic containers of jam and then spreading the resultant mess across random objects gracing the table. The dining room's piped in radio muzak segues to news, then to an ad for some new brand of spray cleaner demanding its use, *When clean isn't clean enough . . .*

Standing at the table next to them in a sleeveless black shirt with green letters reading "THANK U FOR NOT SHARING" is Ill-Phil or "Foofaraw Man" — our cruel tags for a guy who has the whiff of the volatile about him, who needs to inflict himself on the world ever since unsuccessfully storming a Nazi mortar position. We all look at him through a scrim of awe and fear as he's the one true damage-causing substance here. A high priest of a religion based solely on sarcasm. He looks anxiously around with his pair of vague, too-large, stagnant eyes that never shine, flapping one hand annoyingly above an empty seat. The only visible empty seat (I usually get down here earlier). "A-ah . . .?" He keeps repeating that one sorry, wheedling vowel "A-ah . . .?" On either side of him lurk what can only be his cowed children, carmine-embarrassment creeping neck to scalp. His kids call him "Tiffy" after the sound of the slippers he always wears.

Neither inherited their dad's hair or mania for what's-on-my-lung-is-on-my-tongue. Phil's haunted, pale face signals a man born in a cellar among empty wine bottles, old corks, and piles of coal. Has knives for eyes. When talking (if not screaming) they squint to the outside, as if leaving for another dimension. On very bad days, just sits in the main floor hall, on his half opened lips a bubble of saliva glints, then bursts with the softest of whispers. This signals a soon-to-be rant directed at whomever walks by. One of his choice ditties: "Can there be anything sadder than a human being chained to rubber foley or enema tube, huh?" If Dorinda Daymare was within earshot, she'd answer, "Me! Me!"

Once, before my residency, chaos erupted here. Punches thrown. Soft-boiled eggs tossed. Burnt toast stuffed into unwilling mouths. Police. Arrests made. Big write-up about it in our Wednesday rag attributed it to political rivalry between Red and Blue Staters. None of the infamous participants are still drawing breath. (Jill, our beloved empathic events coordinator confided in me.) I bet they now put mild tranks in our chow, 'cause the day's events have become a blur. With effort I give you random comments on what I saw today and nightly reflect on, cuddling in my bed, for what I observe here is the greatest, grandest opera as rendered by a very provincial touring group:

- Gauzy, cotton-wool clouds gliding across the sky at *l'heure bleu* (more attractive than the dirty ceiling in my room). I look down from my third-story window and see Bondo "Rama-lama-ding-dong" McCracken back from his local watering hole's Happy Hour, performing his usual swizzle-skid gait toward our main entrance. Soon he'll address our receptionist in that Great Vowel Shift tone of voice signaling he's drunk.

- Our maintenance Nazis, "Brickface" and "Stucco." took Jill's office apart. Everything in it. Everything — the carpet off the floor, the cabinets, the bookcases, the desk and her computer, the telephone, the chairs, the blinds, the lights, the painting off the wall. It's our megalomaniac of a leader's idea. She's gonna get only half the space as before. Punishment for being nice to me? I bet. Once, she confided in me that our Fearless Leader had her writing memos apologizing for not writing memos. Said in their staff meeting her boss only gave *presentations*, stating for the record: "The difference between discussion and presentation was the difference between procedures up for grabs and procedures already set and pre-agreed upon."

Elder Physics

- Ill-Phil sitting in his proverbial hall chair, filled with sound and fury signifying nothing, damning all passersby, especially me, whom he threatens to kill with "one fuckin' long bayonet." His eyes speak plainly of knowing something awful. Do my hands on-head routine, doing a Vulcan mind-meld, and sense a dank basement full of twisted darkness, of an unspeakable painful confusion. Our one Samoan resident here, Maru Palolo, calls Phil in his pidgin lingo: "Too Problem Some."

- Bardo Thodol being out-loaded on a gurney, semi-conscious, by paramedics just as our weird "Greek Goddess," Hester Proteron, exits the front door, walking backwards.

- Kim Young Sam (a.k.a., "Phlegm-in-a-Hairnet") is, despite her middle name, our oldest Asian resident, who was rushed to the hospital by harried paramedics, the verdict an Overwhelming of the Vessel, a stroke, is recovering fast. Celebration. During the Korean War, before immigrating to the USA, she lost two sons, each on opposite sides of the conflict. The trauma turned her to chain-smoking Lucky Strikes.

- Slow zombie-walking to our downstairs restroom, a larger than usual dank urine stain the color of raw umber spreads around the crotch of my well-pressed dress trousers and a pissy Ill-Phil, with a certain malice in the corner of his eye, yells: "Hot stars 'n cold hearts, that's your universe, Mister Beeee-Seventeen!"

- Our Internet service was temporally *Kaput*. As rumor has it: 1) Ill-Phil was downloading online porno again and they pulled the plug; or, 2) Chinese "Black-Guests" have hacked our database for our residents's credit card numbers 'n fucked with me personally 'cause when I tried to access my e-mail I got this screen message: *No glot — Clom Fliday*.

- Hilaria, my Polish beauty's beauty (let all beauty be named and recognized) is evocative of roses and lilies, and rare honey and juice of apricots and liquors more secret than drambuie and the whitest, most perfect bread. But, alas, now she's flirting with tall, Dirty Harry von Warburg, and all I have left is a crumpled photo of her. She's seduced by his perfume of smoothly looks, his handsome moods, that flicker 'n drift on his face, that purple acrylic sweater of his. Even when he imitates our Fearless Leader's quip, "*Capisce* Cochise?" he has less accent of any speaker of English I've ever heard. Sounds somehow directionless, like a loudspeaker in a departure lounge.

- A new, confused-looking, resident moving in complains, "They took Poogy and Gog away from me" (Siamese cats); her children trying to comfort her. Tears, concern, bewilderment. Jill — she always provides comfort margins and counterpoints to human discord here — trying to calmly reassure them. I imagine her world was largely Knick-Knack Central: one of kitty cats, splashy floral bedspreads and pillow shams and cheap coffee mugs with jokey inscriptions like: *Because I'm the MOM — that's Why!* And now all that is coming to an end in an institution where she'll either make strange-looking necklaces out of polymer clay in our art 'n crafts room here, or become a rubber-stamp addict.

- Daithidh MacEochaidh, his unshapely fingers thickened where they should taper, creases at the joints resembling threads of flattened screws, swaggers in his kilt (it's Casual Friday) with a screwdriver in his sock in place of the traditional dirk. Observing a rant by Ill-Phil, he observes, "He's real heidbanger, that one."

- All the hearty and vigorous ladies on the third floor doing Chair Yoga with Gina Love in the Twilight Room. Quite a din in that den of gossip.

- EWTN Catholic broadcasting station: Mother Angelica slipping (horrors!) and falling on-camera, followed by a quick segue to "Life is Worth Living," a Bishop Fulton J. Sheen re-run from the late fifties TV.

- Ten residents cautiously walking into the Sunshine Room for another lecture in our Quality of Health Series: Living with a New Joint." Ill-Phil was angered because he thought the lecture would address the benefits of medical marijuana.

- Rumors run through here like howler monkeys through trees when a tiger is sighted. And a rumors has it that Martha Stewart will judge our residents' ceramics competition. I doubt it. But what is certain it that the elder physics-defying unicycle acrobats of the over-seventy *Grey Wheels* is coming to our parking lot in a show billed as "The Seven Deadly Manoeuvres."

- A bright red poster announces the "Knit-Wits" knitting club has won National Honors for its sheer volume of little knit hats for premature babies donated to Project Linus. Jimmer was a preemie. But some Evangelicals are bitching they look too much like Yarmulkes.

- Bondo's itinerant ex-wife, oft becalmed in a sea of Seagrams, sent him a postcard from Niagara Falls: "So much water and no whiskey."

- Suspicious person on the second floor, and alarm given. False alarm. Only crazy Hassan Ramani running around for the umpteenth time in his burnoose. A phone call from Fearless Leader and a Homeland Security suit "disappears" him.

- Viviana and Chaddy, adhering to Coulomb's Law (like charges) they repel each other, but today they were forced into the north elevator which broke and they were put into the Schoolmen's proverbial *nunc stans,* stranded between floors for hours. When finally released, Chaddy, sporting the sideburns of a Vegas legend, had an eye bruising up fast.

- Lecture in the Sunshine Room today, titled "Stumbling on Happiness," was given by a spiffy spinster in a grey suit who seemed to be in a state of almost perpetual worry. Ill-Phil stood at the back making invisible rifle aim 'n shoot motions, like Lee Harvey Oswald practicing for that infamous Texas day.

- Bondo McCracken on a stationary bicycle in our little gym, pedaling unceasingly like a man in a nightmare. Great drops of sweat oozing from under his hair, running into his eyes, down his nose, along his cheeks. His thick bull-neck wet.

- Our maintenance Nazi's just put up a large, new sign in the dining room asking: WHAT DO *YOU* KNOW THAT *WE* SHOULD KNOW?

- One of our fast-failing residents (who is usually asleep in her chair) is being wheeled out the door, transferred to a hospice. When she sees her daughter standing before her SUV, waiting to load her in, she opens her eyes which remain open in amazement, wonder and joy, galvanized, awakened, transfixed, radiantly fulfilled by the sight of her savior. It is amazing how much people can contain.

- Ad in our bulletin advertizes "Elder-Joke" T-shirts. One was a black T-shirt with BIODEGRADABLE printed across it in yellow Helvetica.

- A rent increase notice on green paper was found in everyone's mailbox. Someone had wiped a nose booger on mine.

Jimmer, that repository of lit crit 'n ideas, recommended I make this list, said it would give you all a "snapshot" of life here. Must 'fess up. Jimmer is helping to write this memoir. I tell him it won't be anything like a "novel of ideas," as my ol' *cabeza* ain't what it usta be. He agrees and notes that the trouble with that type of novel is that it entails having characters that have ideas and that's about .01 per cent of the population. Today, people are overinformed and under-educated. So our project will be an attempt to fuse our horizons: just father and son, elder and youth, past and present. Says its also a collaboration between application, resignation, and chance. He tells me our project is rooted in the knowledge that "a phrase is born into the world both good and bad at the same time, like you, dad." He hints that the secret of creativity, of life, lies in a slight, almost invisible twist that moves us into some ineffable beyond. Not sure what that means, but it sounds good.

As he labors with me over this text, he impresses me with his observation that, "No iron can stab the heart with such force as a period put just at the right place." And reminds me that *his life* has been stabbed repeatedly by many of my periods of mental disturbance. Like when I put a firm period to his college funds 'cause he stopped going to Mass. The poor boy had to drop out of pre-med at UCLA and join the Air Force during the Viet Nam War. The day he enlisted, his draft notice arrived. Close call. Coulda died in some Asian rice paddy. Became a base photographer instead, crawling up jet engine air intakes to get a snap of bird strikes or being called out at three a.m. to shoot candy machine break-ins. It changed his life. Period. He admonishes me with the advice: "You have to keep your eye, dad, on your job, wordsmithing, 'cause words are very sly, the rubbishy ones go into hiding and you have to dig them out. Only a genius can afford two adjectives to one noun. Ya grok?"

I just nod, incomprehensibly, feeling like I was about to become again what I call, when my Futterneid Quotient is up, "Mr. Wispy." In this state, my brain wanders among the multiple vanishing points and horizon lines of many Renaissance masterpieces and exhausts mental restrictions within those labyrinthian expressions. During those times I just sit and often concentrate upon my arm, elbow to hand, my eyes draw every possible line out of it until all seemed strands separate, as if in a dissection of its light and shadowed surface. The shaded area of the knuckles, the in-between finger-cast shadows, the very hair of the arm, and the crackling blackened wrinkles, produce a number of finely-drawn caricatures. I try to capture them on my sketch pad. Oodles of doodles.

Quid nunc? Well, it dawns on me that on days when I write, I feel life is worth living, and on days I don't, it isn't. All the more important I get Jimmer's feedback. When he reads this manuscript of ours out loud, he reads well — with relish, gusto, and a droll killing zip — out loud so he can experience the story on his tongue and in the resonant cavities of his body. This gives me complete faith in his redaction of my material. In making a selection of these extracts he might easily have given a caricature of my personality by reproducing, by preference, my most extravagant passages. On the other hand, it would've been easy to present a highly flattering version by systematically excluding everything of an eccentric character. Since, when he publishes this memoir, I'll be ashes blowing in the atmosphere, my ego isn't involved. But I do appreciate that Jimmer has dispassionately endeavored to keep equally distant from both of those extremes by presenting a *realistic* ME. Right now, he razoring out pages from a Jonathan Lethem paperback. Says the writing kinda sucks, but there's some redeeming choice lines apt to my Situation. So on with the show! I've a niffy tale concerning my travels (and I love to travel).

Travels With and Without *Rocinante*

Yesterday was the last Saturday of the month, so it was "Recall Your Favorite Vacation" day in the Sunshine Room (a program cleverly aimed at keeping us mentally sharp, memories intact, and our relatives stroked). I went first 'cause I felt a piss coming on. Just couldn't wait to hit 'em with my trip to Alaska and (paradoxically) to Unalaska on a Dutch cruise ship with my Knights of Columbus Church group back in May of the new millennium. As I'm explaining my delight in travel — "The explorer will never be satisfied by the motion pictures of the expedition" — Dirty Harry ambles in late as usual, sporting his Wayfarer sunglasses (it *is* the Sunshine Room, he reminds us). He's got a new resident in tow, Ray Bottles (pronounced "Bot'-less") who walks with a determination to fight that bad stoop of his. I take him to be a retired barber (close but no cigar). Turning to my tattered and well-thumbed trip journal, I read to all gathered:

    Oh, you Doubting Thomases, got a color photo to prove it — my sojourn to Skagway, Alaska. I don't look seventy-eight, do I? Was a far cry from what you see before you now, my friends.
    A bit sea-sick, eating with the face of a man whose favorite dish disappoints and after some very embarrassing moments on the cruise with the

ladies, landed at Skagway and then on to St. Paul Island,
one of the Pribilof Islands where bird-watching is a contact
sport. There, I took a ski-plane ride to a glacier. Pilot's
name was Bob, like my B-17's skipper, so I had faith. Needed
it too. A real white-knuckler, fierce crosswinds (a member
of our "intrepids" messed her pants)and so we couldn't land.
Just a week earlier, a pilot miscalculated a vicious down-
draft, plane and tourists kissed a cliff into oblivion and
front-page news. *Get killed, get noticed!* Hazards of adventure. Jeane disliked adventure, another of our mismatches.
On our adventure, wee did see firsthand global warming
nibbling on the glacial ice six years prior to Al Gore's
relevatory movie. A sad spectacle.

On an earlier cruise of mine — to some colorful port
in Mexico where a dry wind blows hot and from which I mailed
a soiled postcard to my ex-wife showing the prop blue sky —
I did a nosedive off a tall curb while framing a scene of a
religious celebration through my Olympus camera's viewfinder. Pain. Screams. A flurry of Spanish idioms. A rush of
peones and *Federales*. Hyperventilating. Our concerned tour
guide bending over me. A siren. The rest is a blur. Tore the
crap outta some ligaments in my arm. Cut badly. Some stit-
ches. Broke my camera lens. Up the ship's gangplank in a
wheelchair. Spent the remainder of the vacation in my cruise
ship's cramped cabin crying 'n kvetching. Still have peri-
odic pain in my left rotator cuff. Jimmer massages it upon
request. My son the hero, when he's not putting fucking
"inheritance powder" [arsenic] in my coffee.

And then there was the time *Rocinante*, Hu-go, and I
ran off the road somewhere near Valentine, Texas (Happy
Valentine's Day!) on a dark night in the early nineties on
the way to visit my cranky sister in Fort Davis, near Marfa.
Fell asleep at the wheel and ended up kissing some sage
brush. I forgot to tell you, on top of everything else, I
suffer sleep apnea. But, by Jove, I refuse to wear that damn
oxygen mask my doc highly recommends. Had enough of that on
my high-altitude bombing missions. Death from a distance.
Brings to mind too much trauma. Waking up screaming at night
doesn't help my mental stability.

My younger sister, Mary Alice, the one who always
puts her arms akimbo and doesn't particularly like me, lives
outside a small cow town that is still equipped with swinging metal barriers to protect the sidewalks and stores when
the drovers take the massive steers through. She and her
husband, John, live right next to the town cemetery. Boot
Hill. When one of them kicks, the other only has to walk a
hundred yards to place fresh flowers. Can watch the grave
with binocs. John's retired Army. Occupied himself selling
shit in the base commissary when occupying Japan after the
truce. Forced to retire from a back injury, he went on to
sell retail at the best Milwaukee haberdasheries. One glance
and he can tell your stats, hat to shoe. With him the phrase
"sizing someone up" is taken literally.

Mary Alice and John upped stakes from their forested
five acres five miles west of beer-breath Milwaukee and
moved to this godforsaken place five years ago. WHY? is
still a mystery discussed by relatives every Thanksgiving

gathering. John's also an autodidact. Like me, he's always looking for the greatest uncommon denominator. He is a wealth of local information: geologic and topographical, current and historical, personal and institutional, Anglo and Mexican. Has a story for almost every grave in that cemetery. Knows what went on in them thar hills during the Mexican-American War. Informs me that this town's sheriff is a real sheriff: stocky, with an exaggerated Texan drawl, complete with hefty large caliber pistol slung low under his bulging gut like a gunfighter of yore, who is maintained in equilibrium by the profits skimmed from the burgeoning drug traffic coming up from Mexico these days. Swears he's seen this conniving constabulary's Deluxe Collector's Edition of Dirty Harry movies. (Or was it hairy dirty movies?) John — kind, gentle eyes, soft voice, smart — Jimmer's most admired uncle. He gave Jimmer his first camera. A black box jobbie with with which he shot his very first fledgling photos — Yellowstone's Old Faithful blasting off like a reverse rocket — taken during our trip back from a two week binge with Wisconsin relatives in the summer of '58.

Anyway, to make a long story short and an unpleasant event funny — the sugar-coated pill tactic — Hu-go and I sleep fitfully in the car as we're firmly stuck in desert sand. Overhead, the great black flood of wind polishes the bright Texas stars. At the crack of dawn, Hu-go wakes me and does his business in full view of any passersby (none), while I crouch behind a sparse plant, a meager cover that is prudent but proves unnecessary. There ain't a car or buzzard in sight. Two hours later a cowpoke in a dusty Jeep just happens by and tows us out with a chain. No damage to my *Rocinante*, so we are back on compass-bearing fast rolling toward Fort Davis and my oddball sister. I, of course, never gave her any advance notice. Wanted to surprise her.

It wasn't a pleasant surprise; could tell by her arms akimbo greeting. John's more accommodating. Takes to Hu-go. Hugs me. But won't allow "the mutt" inside. So he cautiously prowls the backyard, sniffing. I'm praying he doesn't tangle with a rattler. After lunch, we take an auto tour of the town and its environs. John drives and narrates a detailed history to which Mary Alice provides the footnotes. I toss out a *fungo* or three in between their chatter and they catch my spin. As we approach the Rio Grande, I marvel at the gigantic fantastic red rock formations under turquoise sky with pure white clouds floating high. Holy Cats!

Later, after dinner, Mary Alice and I get to reminiscing about our youth. John retires early. Senses trouble in our conversation for he knows his spouse has a hard-to-figure complexity, like a very oddly-shaped crystal. She and I blabber on about John's bad back — he has to sleep slightly tipped up in a recliner chair — discuss my other sister, Pat, and her five children, one of whom suffers the schizzes of schizophrenia. We segue to my daughter's mental problems, evened out by medication now. Praise the Lord. I tell her about my miraculous cure at Lourdes. My improved eye-sight. She shifts nervously in her seat as her eyes shift nervously in their seat. Wets her lips repeatedly.

Applause from the Peanut Gallery. I beam, then set course, followed by innumerable ancient attendants, for our TV room and early evening National News on a large-screen we dub "Giant," which provides big 'n clear views wherein we can see the commentators' dental work. This fact, Ray Bottles elaborates on as he's a retired dentist. Bet if Ray wrote his memoir, it'd be titled "The Bitter Years" (think of the jillions of hours he's spent bent over foul mouths). Mentions he was a Naval dentist serving on a carrier hit by the foul "Divine Wind" of Kamikazes at bloody Okinawa. Swears he once filled a cavity in Admiral Spruance's mouth. Ray strikes me as a guy gentle as a lamb, brave as a lion. Funny fellow too; jokes that his wife was named "Flossy," his daughter, "Carrie." But Jill, the only staff I trust, confides in me that it's no joke. A clear and distinct FACT. *Wheels-within-wheels.*

Munching on a White Castle "slider," I lean across an end table between us, and barely manage to mush out to our new arrival, "We are all ears, Ray, if not all teeth." (Jimmer's always harshin' on me for yappin' with full mouth.) Telegraphing my friendly intent with toothy smile, I tip my hand — "Gee-air-ald, at yer service" — teasing Ray's curiosity by hinting at my miraculous healing powers and teeth-chattering war-stories-to-come if he breakfasts with *moi* on the morrow. Then I toss him a real ice breaker, "My son brushes his teeth (oddly) *before* breakfast, never after. Go figure." Noticing that I'm starting to "tugboat" our neophyte, Bondo, sitting in front of us doing stretching exercices, turns and gives me his unshaven Robert-Ryan-in-*The-Wild-Bunch* grimace.

Ill-Phil drags his sorry ass in and abruptly preempts our CNN news program by turning to the History Channel where over-voice narration seems directed at us elders: *But in reality, of course, memory fails us. Too many buildings have fallen down, too much rubble has been heaped up, the moraines and deposits are insuperable.* Our only Arabic resident, Hassan Ramani (this was prior to his being mysteriously disappeared) throws a shoe at Phil. Mayhem.

Hilarity Don't Mean It's Funny

Jimmer phones. I tell him the music CD of Marc Blitzstein's *Airborne Symphony,* with "The Ballad of the Bombardier" arrived, and, to his surprise, I burst forth with the lilt and expectation of love: "I'm getting married in three hours at St. Hilarius to that adorable Polish lady, so get yer tux ready."

Unlike most here, her flesh beckons, not begs. Her skull a proposition in geometry holding a sweetness of smile with no accessory expression of irony or pity, just a serenity that reminds me of actress Betty White. Saw her when walkering-it past our ceramics studio. She in apron, straddling a spinning disk topped by a lump of muck which, under the subtle influence of her joyful, delicate hands, was becoming a vessel whose walls were lifting like some fine mouth singing its only vowel straight to Heaven (despite poor voice, I sing in Church). Even those immune from the world as we are here need the touch of one another or all is lost. Erect, frail, yet handsome, I got up courage to ask her name.

"Hilaria, don't laugh, and I'm making a flower vase." She offers a wet hand with a grip so gentle I could feel its hope, followed with a laugh lovely, full of liking. "For us ceramicists, the earth is our playmate." I liked *that*. And, counter-intuitively, she confessed: "I'm at a stage in my adventure where life in the past *is not* more vivid, more beautiful than life in the present. As I've grown older, I've come to admire the new horizons life presents me, not dwell on the long-gone," she said in a vocal softening of language pleasing to my senses. Now that kind of elder optimism which spits in face of the peculiar laws and limitations of elder physics, really got me. Used to teach "Snooksology," her term for children's art, at St. Eurosia Catholic grade school in Berwyn.

So fine her features now, she must've once had a body capable of shattering memory and convulsing reason. Bet she makes a fab *pierogi*. So I ask her out. We slow walk to Al's Diner. For the moment the sky is an uncomplicated grey. Smiles at me like a cash register opening to a large bill. Over poached eggs, bacon 'n coffee, she agrees with me that modern life and art require the balsam of laughter (which I need when my mood swings to looking into gloomy rooms, seeing whole tragedies in the dusty corners). Likes my puns and stories. Impressed with my piety too. Claims to bake a great rhubarb pie.

No surprise, she's a parishioner at St. Hilarius Parish where the kindly pastor reminds us, after winter's first snow, "It's ermine to trim our sins with." She admits (like me) she's read G. K. Chesterton's *The Everlasting Man* eight times in as many years. She occupies room 333, a trinity of threes. How Catholic! Before you can say "Holy Trinity," I'm involved in the unending self-parody of heterosexuality, with its psychic pratfalls. My stomach turned in love for this woman. Well, the rest is history. During our ardent conversations, she, with infantile instinct, grips my thumbs; just my thumbs she holds and as we talk, moves 'em this way 'n that, as if she's steering me. Then I close my eyes and see the red darkness inside my lids trembling.

But now I'm *persona non gratia*. Our brief romance over, done over our undercooked omelettes last week. Egg on my face as she soured at me for shoving written reprimands under her door written in bold, angry hand. "What the hell are these?" shaking the letters under my nose. It was the last complete sentence she ever said to me. That day's fateful night, my brain in its calcium vault shouted about injustice, thundered accusations into the dark vibrating air of my bedroom which seemed filled with the dust of my grave or grave dust from my cremation (yet to tell Jimmer which method of disposal I prefer).

Whaaaa happen? She's more like my cheatin' wife than I'd thought: always flirting in the Sunshine Room with "Dirty Harry" von Warburg, a widowed, retired insurance salesman with a strong chin that helps make his full mouth as stubborn as his salesman's optimism. He caught her eye by parting his open-necked pinky-white Coronet-style shirt (windowpane check) to air his nipple fuzz; this garment rested under a gorgeous pale tweed sports jacket dotted with tiny delicate flecks of brown and black. He showed her an old photo of himself as a dark debonair ladies' man, from which I extrapolated he was smooth and full of panache, and given to undergraduate escapades like cows in the lecture hall and whores in the frat house.

Guess we're not really gonna to tie the knot today under Father Hardon's blessing in a dignified Gothic church. Jimmer will forgive me the misunderstanding, even though he'll chide me that my fling was a "solipsized creation of my own melancholy." But there's more than meets the eye or ear here. *Wheels-within-wheels.* Still I might just cry about it over our mutual Wednesday breakfast at Al's which is a busy busy place where the owner, a tall lean Greek, low-toned, and watery-eyed, howls a warm greeting and I josh the Hispanic waiter, José, about his thin-lined beard ("Like marching ants") and spend way too much time (complains my son) in the men's room. I always order the Southwestern skillet and plenty of coffee. Reminds me (and Jimmer) of California sun and Sunday breakfasts with the family in better times.

Jimmer keeps me balanced — everything below my head seems unbalanced and now even my head is wavering — and listens patiently to my unending, repetitive war stories — and now to my love-life laments. I notice people look at me and then my son and back at me, winking at him with silent approval. He must be getting some kind of (how do they put it?) *positive re-enforcement* for putting up with me (besides free access to my bank accounts).

When we finally emerge, our bellies full, we slowly make our way (Jimmer's arm on mine) up the sidewalk toward his car (which I paid for when his was totaled by a deranged and driverless garbage truck) and feel the sun and sky stroke my senses. "Like a million strokes of paint out here," I wax poetic. Jimmer smiles. If it weren't for Jimmer moving me here, taking me under his wing, spending hours of his precious time with me, I'd be lobbying the *Guinness Book of Records* to be entered as "The Loneliest Man Alive." But now my *raison d'être* is, with Jimmer's help, to pick at the seams of my Situation, unraveling it in useful and interesting ways. Thanks to him, I'm restored to as crisp a health as possible given my eighty-plus years, and now living in a sad new world run on the algorithms of elder physics and overseen by Our Fearless Leader (an I'm-too-big-in-my-own-gig-to-acknowledge-yours kinda guy). But underneath the camouflage of furniture and voices, habitual actions and accidents, I still sense death, that wide army invisibly advancing. So I pick up pen again to stave off for awhile the inevitable.

Elder Physics

During our meals together, Jimmer can look at me with deep concern, worry, pity even. I return the same, but still chide him about his agnosticism, "Some things that we can never know, we should nonetheless be very disinclined to doubt." But despite his frown, I'm sure it's love on both sides. I can still return a smile on good days when my Futterneid Quotient is low. We have hearty laughs when I'm not angry with him for elder abuse. Oh yes, he's beaten my gums bloody in the car on the way to my dentist and was surely in cahoots with that awful corrupt crone of a realtor who sold my home under market, saying it stunk of urine and old age. Sure they each took a handsome share of the sale.

I remember that mobile home, near Camp Pendleton Marine Corps Base. Back in California. By the sea. An after-my-divorce home that those two retired Mafia wise-guys from New Jersey living across the street, and dedicated to edging me out, try to get me to sell to them (cheap) so another Mafioso can escape the East Coast for warmer climes. Even if it means gassing me in my home, forcing me to flee to sleep in my fire-engine red GMC Jimmy. Until I wised up (more on this later). I still have the key to that life I've been evicted from; weekly I howl at Jimmer, "I'm gonna fly back!"

As an engineer, I've always been interested in architecture: block, pillar, slab and beam, a complete primitive material language. I find the building I'm living in interesting from that perspective. I lived and worked in Chicago when Mies was big, big stuff. I was putting in elevators everywhere in the Loop back then. I delighted Jimmer yesterday (or was it last week?) by proposing to lather my head with a spot of Rogaine foam inside every building Mies van der Rohe ever designed — if he can transport me and afford to dilute his inheritance on expenses — until by the end of the project my hair would be so long I'd be refused entrance (by some ex-Nazi) to Mies's Berlin National Gallery.

Each visit of mine'd be photo-documented by my son and eventually published as *Me(s) van der Rogaine*. For sure it would cement what's always been a very hairy father-son relationship. A relationship made hairy by our divergent attitudes toward ultimate questions. For me, to be in possession of an absolute truth is to have a net of familiarity spread over the whole of eternity. Some old priest so enlightened me at St. John's parochial grade school during those sweet days of incense and indoctrination, of Ashes on Wednesday and No-Fish Fridays. So tenaciously do I cling to the world revealed by the Gospel that were I to see all the Angels of Heaven coming down to me to tell me something different, not only would I not be tempted to doubt, I would shut my eyes and stop my ears, for they would deserve to be neither seen nor heard. Dear Reader, faith manifests itself not in moving mountains, but in not seeing mountains to move. Perfectly logical. But, I'm ashamed to admit, my atheist son can still rile me with his cruel quip: "Pray not only for your daily bread, dad, but also for your daily delusion." Humpf! Nervy shit! But his insight, "A true line is closer to God than any church," might bear, keeping in mind all the subtle connotations of "line," some scrutiny.

But when it comes to art, we are mostly on the same page. *On the same page* — a favorite expression of mine. I'm proud as punch of his art professorship and brag no end to my fellow inmates here about him. They pull out a few snaps of their kids, I pull up pages and pages of web-data on Jimmer. Even attended one of his lectures once, when the aluminum walker was still in my future. Unlike some parents, I encouraged my son to go into the fine arts. Jeane always envisioned him a well-paid commercial photographer, but he's always despised, like me, kowtowing to The Almighty Dollar.

Life of the inner-mind and its expression is *the thing* for both of us. Jeane never got that. One of our earliest father-son excursions, besides our Sunday jaunts to Mass and camping trips, was our ritual Thursday night sojourn to the spanking new Canoga Park branch library. We'd both remark on its modernist architecture. As already alluded to, we share strong autodidactic tendencies. Jimmer loved smelling the books, erotically thumbing their pages. Still does, much to his wife's chagrin. Later, we go to art museums two-abreast. I don't always *get* the artwork he likes. But we agree on the greats — Monet and Cézanne. We're equally responsive to a painting's *facture* — "Oh, that brush heavily charged with paint and that stroke vigorous and broad!"— but not to the subject. I'm pulled toward paintings with nature or religious subjects, while my son gravitates toward the bipolarities of Surrealist mishmash / disciplined Cubist structure. But he does admire a seascape I did last year depicting a low broad heaving of the ocean off San Diego, the lifting of its bosom by deep-drawn breath after the torture of a storm. Our home's art instructor described in a brochure to promote one of our art shows: "Between the ridges of the waves the fire of the sunset falls along a trough of the sea, dyeing it with an awful but glorious light, the intense and lurid splendor of which burns like gold, and bathes like blood. Purple and blue, the lurid shadows of the hollow breakers are cast upon the mist of approaching night." Had one guy wanna buy it.

I did surprise Jimmer once by my enthusiasm for the Minimalist neon-works of ... ah . . . can't recall his name now. Very famous guy. Painting with light is how I saw it. I insisted he sneak a photos of me bathing in the colored light emanating from one. Large retrospective it was. Filled rooms. That was the second to my last museum trip, ever. Memorable late autumn day. A good crystal frost in the air, cut my nose going in, made my lungs blaze like a Christmas tree inside; you could feel the cold light going on 'n off, all the branches filled with (as yet) invisible snow.

But that museum trip was awhile back. I'm not very mobile these days. I can prove it. Watch me try to walker-it over to my little folding table and try to spread Honey Bee brand honey on my slice of corn bread. . . .

On our main floor, "Rama-lama-ding-dong McCracken, our youngest, most vigorous resident (despite the fact he spends a lot of time in ill-lit cocktail lounges) is doing his noonday fast-walk up 'n down my hallway, muttering as he passes my door: "Cause it's gonna be the future soon, and I won't always be this way, in ten years when the things that make me weak and strange come fast upon me, I hope by then they'll simply get engineered away. A-hay, hay!" I catch that same faint whiff of sweat and old cracker crumbs. His constitutional will take him past our little library where Eepie Carpetrod (she writes a column for our in-house bulletin) is gratifying an unwholesome interest in epidermal problems, like Marat's skin disease. Some of this research will appear in her column, I'm sure.

Why am I waiting? What is awaited in waiting? Oh, yes. I'm in the dining room where I playfully yell my order — "Shit-on-a-shingle, yogurt, 'n Tang" — knowing I'll be served my usual omelette. Day after day I sit over the white parade ground of the tablecloth gleaming with silver and play endless games of patience. Bruin Opps, thinnest guy I've ever met, with an expression of painfully repressed disgust, eats a hard-boiled egg, barely. His eyes show that formidable capacity for looking and expressing nothing, like the pale blue eyes which peer out of a Siamese cat's velvet mask. Whenever he speaks, his voice seems on the point of expiring, as though each word was his last, uttered faintly and breakingly from his death bed. Listening carefully, you can just make out: "Fiona, it's a real light opera summer night. . . ." — repeated *ad nauseam*.

He's sitting across from retired recreational boat salesman Faolan Firth who's retained a scrappy, seat-of-the-pants energy from days o' yore. A Scottish immigrant who made good, he's the fourth child of ten, born near the Firth of Forth. Sports an SX-70 Polaroid of himself smiling (proving his dictum: *A smiling face sells more goods than a clever tongue*) standing before the Frith of Forth bridge. In the white area below the image is printed in neat letters: "The Fourth of Firth Before the Firth of Forth." He's damn punful proud of that image. Shows it to everyone. In his loose, crumpled clothes, Faolan has the air of a strangely animated scarecrow. He bums cigarettes with an insult, "Div ya hay a fag, ya numpty?" No one ever has one to give, but that doesn't stop him.

Talking about a scarecrow physique, my omelette is long overdue. Under-fed here. When it does come, it'll probably be undercooked again. Like Faloan's refrain, repetition changes nothing in the object repeated, but does change something in the mind which contemplates it. So I'm getting tired (nay, very pissed off!) about that daily travesty wrought upon my favorite breakfast item. Once a trait is repeated enough times, it becomes a social practice. Ergo, delayed and ill-prepared chow has become institutionalized here. Had it much better in the Service, I did. Here complaints go either unanswered or I'm told, "What's the hurry, ya got a plane to catch?" I reply, "I sure do," and point to a numbered item neatly listed in column three of my *Heavenly Emporium of Benevolent and Not-so Benevolent Aircraft.*

Sometimes I'm sitting here eating and Jimmer comes in looking a little exasperated. He usually tells me we'd planned to eat out. Been banging on my door for ten minutes. Said we chatted about it last night. Can't remember. I introduce him to my tablemate. Usually a guy who's a Vet vetted by Jill, our empathic enhancement and entertainment maven, as likely to get along with difficult-me. Today the guy's name is Fred, Fred Fredererer (never sure of how many iterations of "er" in his name). Was a pilot of a B-24 Liberator bomber on the famous raid on Ploiesti, Romania in '43. Today, he sports a vintage Hawaiian shirt, featuring guitar-playing frogs riding surfboards in a turbulent tide. He always seems to rinse his laugh through old tears. Jimmer thinks I eat too slowly. Fred too, probably. But what the hell? Jimmer will have to wait thirty minutes for scrambled eggs here so . . . So we drink tepid coffee while the old Vet across from me politely excuses himself and his Hawaiian shirt so father-son can jaw in private, which usually gets to Jimmer asking if I have enough Super Absorbent

Depends in supply. I know it's coming, just like I know the under-cooked omelette will come tepid.

Often, I can delay this distasteful event by taking our conversation into strange and elaborate detours. Like, I know he finds geology interesting. So do I, or once did. The topic's been a deep well of inspiration and irritation between us. So I hint at my desire to take a trip to the International Center for Lightning and Research and Testing (part of the University of Florida) to see their collection of *fulgurites*. Fulgurites? Where lightning hits the ground, it goes into sand and melts glass, producing an object. I read in *Rockets Magazine* (I once worked at Atomics International-Rocketdyne, designing fuel-injectors for the Saturn V rocket booster) that some artist, Allan someone, artificially made some ten thousand of these fulgurites by using rockets provided by that Testing Center to generate lightning strikes into buckets of sand.

Jimmer said he might use the idea in a novel he's writing. The character is — how weird is this — a former art critic and wannabe geologist. I keep probing about this odd specimen, a diarrhea of questions: How old? How tall? Fat or slim? Sexual orientation? Divorced like me? A lefty or not? Fear of heights? Facial tic? Knee replacement? Adenoids out? An orphan? Missing a toe? suffering internal strabismus? eye floaters? balding? facial hair? Deviated septum? Obsessive thumb-sucker? Wet his bed way into adolescence? Can he wiggle his ears like I can? Is he on the FBI's radar? A former Hippie? Votes Green Party? Wrote a poem titled, "An Ode to a Geode?" And so forth and so on. All those "?" marks!

This interminable tally, of course, amuses him and to amuse my son is to sustain his interest interminably. Anything to enhance my Shandyian digressions. Oh, I can see you're surprised I'm so literate. Well, I read constantly; read that one, *Tristram Shandy,* in college. It was the only novel I was forced to read that captured something of my own personal existence, that (as my son put it), *resonates* with me. From it's pages, I gleaned that dearer to me are the fictions provided by literature than life's baser truths where the real tragedies are enacted somewhere behind the scenes. From its pages I sensed a conjuring from the inexpressible into my personal lived-world, evidence of something essential. I remember the sensation vividly — of receiving a communiqué, of something *arriving.* My response to that piece of literature was not exactly to the words, and what they appeared to be saying, but to something enormous and living beyond that which the words exactly entailed. Now my life, like Mr. Shandy's, is certainly fodder for a wacky literature, or so claims Jimmer.

But I wonder if sentences could contain anything so cold or hard or painful as my life? Wouldn't the words just fall apart like my body is now? Moreover, I confide in him (not easy) that I'm losing the plot. That's why I'm reading the supersized print version of Andy Clark's *Supersizing the Mind* — as antidote. "All the more reason to put down your stories now, dad, and there isn't any better source of inspiration than your final days here," he urged. "Temper your complaints and revelations with your expansive sense of humor, coat the proverbial bitter pill. Let the sugar be the binding agent holding your words together. I'll help edit." He convinced me 'cause you're reading this now, right? But I digress.

Another digression tactic at these in-house breakfasts, waiting for our food, is to quiz Jimmer on his teaching, even get him to philosophize. Jimmer is deep, like an excavation; got him to admit that, "Dad, in this place one really has to ignore sense data." Once he got me thinking (for quite a sustained time for an oldster like me) when he tossed this one in my direction, "Intelligence is liquid chaos," something about how our minds have their own purposes and agency.

Elder Physics

Before my stint in here, I would've argued the point. Me, grumpy me, being so sure of myself. But now most days I feel my intelligence swirling around some cosmic drain, going down fast. I increasingly have trouble not just balancing, but balancing my check book. So I try to keep my hand in doing numbers, high powers, 'n humble roots. Math proven to keep the ol' noggin' asloggin'.

Jimmer picks a newspaper off the adjoining dining table, peruses same as I slowly eat my hash browns. "What the fuuuuu . . .!?" He's noticed Ill-Phil's time machine. I explain to him Phil likes to shuffle pages from yesterday's paper into today's edition. Gets down early for breakfast just to do same. A time section montage taking Jimmer back to yesterday and back again. Talking about time differentials, I show him a snapshot given to me by Hilaria depicting her a bit younger than now. "I was more *physical* before my *accident*, you can see from this interesting picture," she remarked upon presenting it to me. Now she regrets giving it out; imagines me doing some kind of voodoo-thing with it. Sticking pins in it or some such. Or putting it online. Jimmer wants me to return it. A silent *no dice* flickers across my face. If she *had* asked for it back, I'da said, "Up yours with a double strawberry phosphate!" And she'da countered with enough garlic on her breath to deter a covey of vampires.

Our coffees and conversation drained, Jimmer helps me up and we amble side-by-side toward the depressingly slow, cramped elevator. I notice he is watching to see if I'm gonna trip and fall. Which reminds me — I trace mental networks back, construct parallels — last week I tripped over my phone cord just as I was jiggering over to pick up a call. From Jimmer as it turned out. All he heard on the other end was one prolonged "Aaaaaaaaaaaaaahhhhhhhhh" — then a loud THUMP. For a second my mind turned onto an unlit road; then gristle and bone heaped on the floor. Jimmer rushed over. Saw all this. My flesh was purple, bruised, my knee knee-deep in red; my fingers, from grabbing desperately at the wall, were too pink for March. My only post-traumatic response (as I was later told) was that I laughed in a way which was both like eating a melon and giving up on life. The TraumaSmile Services staff rushed in, applied antiseptic acridity and the paper-plastic rip of bandages, soothing me with a charity so physical it was biblical in its application. My poor lived body . . . it's a problem that can't be solved. And I'm used to solving problems. No easy *Q.E.D.*

Jimmer's body's as big on peanut butter as I am of Squeakers cheese curds. Always was. Never outgrew it. This goes for Leslie too. Both love Ants-on-a-Log (peanut butter with raisins on cold raw celery). And anything vanilla. Maybe these are compensation for loss. The environment of their childhood, their past, collapsed about them — rampant tract-home expansion, trees bulldozed, creeks turned into concrete, orchards obliterated, strip-malls proliferating.

Today, he has added some aberrant tastes picked up on his world travels, like *Rognons de veau* (veal kidneys). Had 'em in Paris, he said, at famous *Chez L'Ami Louis* (sounds like a new sexual position). Said the food there flows as easily down the gullet as the restaurant's name flows out off the tongue. Da Pres, Clinton, ate there (with a bobbing head under his table napkin?). Jimmer and I share a hearty appetite. Often he has me over to his place to chef for me. Makes me feel special. Makes Italian sausage cut-up, seasoned, and *sautéed* with a massive dose of charcoal grilled red, green, and yellow peppers. Plenty of elephant garlic too. I yell, "Fire for effect!," and he lops a huge serving on my designer plate. Tosses in an exotic micro beer, cool with a little wet condensation sliding down the brown sides, for liquid companionship. My brew of choice is Fat Tire Amber Ale which gives me that classic, old fart spare tire that ranks with the best in our elder universe.

During these alimentary events, Jimmer loves to see me eating with gusto. Our love is at its peek here, eye-to-eye, forks-to-mouths. No odd perilous expression or awkward shifting feet or hoisting of pants here. I must smile a lot then, 'cause he smiles back. Yah, sometimes he's my hero. I think my last request will be: "Lay a brewsky on me, buddo."

Of course, I don't think of this when I'm in the Confessional at St. Hilarius, kneeling beside ghosts, pressing my flesh into the worn kneeler, toes to the floor-boards, invisible inside that small wooden box surrounded by stained-glass saints pierced by arrows or hacked with knives. I go there when the stillness of the world is too much to bear, or when Mother Angelica on EWTN is on vacation, or my cable service is Kaput.

When salvation is too much on my mind and I've too much to fear — as broken cogs, blown fuses, and a leaky crankcase dash hopes of me outlasting my corporeal host — I take comfort by imagining death to be like a series of concentric football coliseums with me inside the innermost, garbed in my high school padded football gear, being straight-armed by a figure garbed like Death in that famous Bergman film (Jimmer rented the DVD because we both love to play Chess) to wild cheers from the stands as the team's mascot, politically-incorrect Chief Illiniwek, dances crazily on the sidelines, reminding me of the densely forested Indian Reservation just south of where I grew up. Where one drove through without stopping, even for gas.

The Velvet Foliage of Anthurium

The days were like amber rosary beads, one like the other, transparent, yellow. Then came a rosary of cool autumn crystal, and a rosary of snow-white ivory. By March, Jimmer and I are both suffering that late-winter malady, *cabin fever*. The temperature hasn't risen much above 35 degrees Fahrenheit for weeks. I start to chew my nails, watch my house plants die, suffer water retention in my legs despite my aimless sauntering about our facility, let whiskers grow stubbly on my bleached cheeks 'n chin, and fantasize the assassination (by bomb) of one Ill-Phil Pokey. Our art class is slowly making a large "Pretzelhorn," large conic Eiffel Towerish structure of store-bought pretzel twists glued together. It is supposed to reach the height of a typical Christmas tree. Why? Well, it does keep those of us suffering from internal mimicry, who have to struggle every day to keep our poor organs in their ordinary shape and their habitual function, occupied. And Jimmer? Every year at this time he has the manic urge to re-read all his Soren Kierkegaard books, including that tortured thinker's navel-gazing *On My Work as an Author*. So a trip to the warm, humid rare tropical plant display in the Garfield Park Botanical Conservatory (just east of us) is mandated by Jimmer for next Thursday as anodyne. "But let there be no moaning," he adds as a condition. "What's the quote from," I ask. "*The Odyssey,*" he replies, finger in ear.

Wednesday. The sun comes up like the yolk of an egg swimming in an albuminous sky. A skillet breakfast at Al's Grill. Our waitress has narrow shoulders and narrow bony hips that would fit in a cigar box. She has on this soft cottony blouse, tinted like old rose, with a wide, folded collar, and at her throat a gold necklace no thicker than a fish line. Looking into her eyes as she takes our orders, I see they are animal eyes, sleepy and quiescent as if in the presence of another species. One of our residents is eating alone at the counter, munching a Danish and sipping her coffee with alacrity. Jimmer fills me in. Around 1905, landscape architect Jens Jensen, Prairie School architects, and far-sighted engineers colla-borated (I *like* that) on creating a 184-acre site about five miles west of Chicago, its focal point the astonishing 4.5-acre "landscape under glass" conservatory. The remainder of that day, my *cabeza* resounds with the phrase "hothouse . . . hot-house . . . hothouse." Mashed potatoes at lunch time, gravy dribbling down my chin, it's "hothouse . . . hothouse . . . hothouse." Lying in bed trying to get warm after the late-night news it's "hothouse . . . hothouse . . . hothouse." Getting up to piss at 3 a.m., it's "hothouse . . . hothouse . . . hothouse." I think you get the picture. Jimmer wants me to use the trip for artistic grist to tantalize the critical ears in our writer's club. Here's what I did:

Thursday after lunch. The sky is a heavy sheet of opaque glass with fissures prised part by wedge of sunlight. A chill wind blows off Lake Michigan as I am shoe-horned into Jimmer's car for the brief trip east to the corner of Lake Street and Central Park Drive. My "Johnny Walker" and I are dropped off in front of the steel and glass structure. As I stand immobile and alone on the sidewalk, I think I know what the first astronaut on the moon felt like. We are early and no visitors have arrived yet. But soon Jimmer walks up, turns me in the direction of the entrance and we shuffle in. I cough up the dough for the entrance fee. Least I can do, huh? The ticket lady had an oval face, a notice-able nose, and green, green eyes, with convex lids, half-

Jens Jensen's Garfield Park Development (1905)

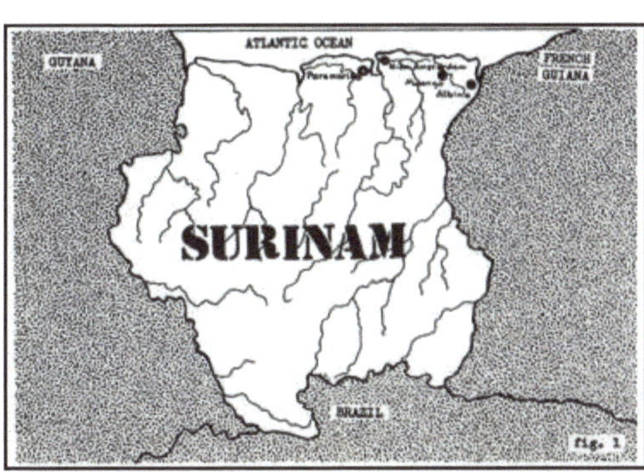

Croton Plants

eclipsing those two green worlds. We make a bee-line for the green tropics as fast as I can propel my aluminum-assisted body.

Ah, huge ceiling fans, sounds of water spraying, the smells, the warm and heavy atmosphere. Yes.

I came to incredible Floridas, you know, where eyes or panthers, with human skins, mingle with flowers, and rainbows stretched like reins; I saw fermenting swamps where gigantic snakes, eaten by bugs, drop from crooked evil-smelling trees; I would like to show the children those golden countries, I muse, copping from Arthur Rimbaud who's expresses what I felt upon tottering into such a lush, exotic environment full of surprises like jambú (the "tooth-ache plant" containing an analgesic) and flame acacia, little pink and red flags welcoming an elder into its presence. I feel younger already.

I am transported into adventure, into a living cabinet of curiosities, by the Crotons with their red and yellow-streaked leaves so magnificent you might think, as Rimbaud might, that they are poisonous. Acalyphas with its bright red leaves pulling my eyes left, then the velvet foliage of Anthurium (the name sounds like a utopia Jimmer might dream up) hanging over the dark pools, and smelling sweetly of decay, pulling my eyes right. Ah, bushes of black pepper, and the hard cups of Bromelias, from which spring incredibly pink and ethereally blue sprays of flowers, Pandanus standing on the tips of its roots, sharply toothed like little saws, not to speak of the palms shooting upward inviting a gazer to a sore neck (it's useful that everything has a name). I recall Hilaria's hand forming a ceramic, a marvelous flower with five petals that opened and closed like the sensitive plants here.

In their original setting, I would have had to slash that festering jungle with sharp machete and macho endurance; here I enjoy a weak sun filtering through the glass house as a young bronzed child on the other side of the pond cries, "*Tiazinha, tiazinha*! [Portuguese for Aunty, aunty] Come to the coco palms when the drums are rolling. Come." What an immense and exuberant bastardy! What a wild jungle! Flowers of frangipans, blossoms of marhaniks, and the brilliancy of butterfly wings like I saw in a book of drawings by naturalist Maria Sibylla Merian made during her 1699 journey to Surinam. Like her, I've escaped to the southern side of the world where I imagine flowers and scents mingling with human skins and commercial agents, huge snakes, export and labor, the blue sheen of the butterflies, and the international conventions about the supply of fruit, coffee, tobacco, and the management of plantations. But Jimmer spies Che Guevera lurking in the dense foliage. I imagine my escape into the very center of things, where all is in conflict, ages copulate in an addled medley of cultures. Jimmer, a drop of sweat running down his back, sees only ideology behind every tree.

We listen to the rustling of the palms as the huge fans turn above us. I imagine gazing at lizards, darting or motionless, as a mysterious shaman advises me: eat elephant lice, nuts of kashu trees (these to drive weariness away and sharpen my wits), and smear leg sores with palm olive and simaruba ointment. Ah . . . it would be a place *simpatico* to Alzheimer dementia, for a man without memory would be (as in here) without relations, would be surrounded by (as in here) strangeness, and the sound, which reaching him, would not contain any answers. Why, it's only in *our* social world, the realm of the Symbolic, that memory loss is such an agonizing experience. In the tropics . . . well . . . We're here because we're here because we're here. Me, I smile foolishly at everything.

Jimmer's next surprise? We step into the Orinoco. Not the river, but a small, inviting Brazilian restaurant a few miles further east. Famous for brunches touted by Steve "The Hungry Hound" Dolinsky, TV Channel Seven's restaurant critic. Praised by Jimmer, now described by yours truly.

Feijoada

Inside, I meet a member of the Spurge family, Cassava. No, it's not the owner's wife. It's a tuberous root of a woody shrub: *Mandioca* in Brazil, but we know it as manioc. Jimmer, that walking encyclopedia, informs me it's one of the highest yields of food energy per cultivated area of all food plants. *Now that's good engineering,* I muse on our Creator's "intelligent design." Today we eat it as a thickener in *pirão*, a sauce on our crab appetizers and on our guava-filled *beijú,* crepes with a gummy chewiness. But our main dish is classic *feijoada*, a meat and bean stew with as many versions as cooks. Ours contains *paio*, a spicy pork sausage, *carne seca,* sautéed collard greens, salt-cured pig tails all over white rice and black turtle beans. We munch on *cuscús*, a steamed corn bread, and chug DaDo Bier.

Jimmer loves to watch me eat: slow, deliberate trips from dish to mouth — during which I chide my son for his hasty, shoveling-coal-into-a-speeding-steam-engine approach to cuisine — then I gaze up from plate to sky and back again, followed by a joke, then repeat the action. In turn, my son keeps my attention by describe Henry Walter Bates, a nineteenth-century naturalist, traipsing trench coat-clad and hat net-draped through Amazonian Brazil, marveling at leaf-cutter ants gnawing jungle foliage into little jagged-edged umbrellas to protect their young from the rain. Jimmer can vicariously explore the same by tuning to Radio Manaus, Amazonas for its authentic local sounds shot northward via short-wave. The beer makes me nod off. I wet my pants.

Elephant in the Room

Today it's raining cats 'n dogs. April showers turned to torrents. Our empathic events coordinator, Jill — sky-charged 'n goddessy in her pantsuit — urges me into the newly-situated library with all those LARGE PRINT BOOKS. My eye is caught by an intriguing title: *HOW TO BE A CHRONONAUT AND NOT A CHRONONAUGHT*. Because of the pun, it appeals to my fabulous 'n secret universe of mind. I flip though the text. Basically a self-help job about "aging gracefully" (as they say). How not to be a burden on your relatives — stop yer bangin', bitchin' 'n bullin' — basically.

The author asks: DO YOUR IDEAS TAKE SHAPE LIKE SOLIDIFYING FOG? and HOW EXCEPTIONAL ARE THE MEMORY LAPSES YOU HAVE, DO THEY HAPPEN WITH IMPECCABLE REGULARITY LIKE BLACK SWANS AND ALBINO SQUIRRELS? They've got a do-it-yourself dementia test on page 20: SAY THIS TEN TIMES, FAST: CONTIGUOUS CONTINUITY, CONTINUOUS CONTIGUITY. Can't do it. Hell, bet Jimmer can't do it. Shit nothin' graceful about it, old age that is. On page 55 they give you a "brain-teaser" to keep you sharp: IMAGINE YOU ARE THE GHOST OF CHRISTMASES YET TO COME, EXCEPT IN THE PAST.

I start to think about the Ghost of Christmases-That-Could-Have-Been if Jeane hadn't dumped me. As suspicious and perspicacious as I am, as focused a decoder and recoder of the world around me, as skilled as I am about sussing out information hidden within other information, I didn't see that long trail of evidence and anomalies leading up to the demise of our forty-plus years of marriage.

"Now it's just all footnotes, dad," Jimmer admonishes me. Would I've been safer with snipers, trapeze artists, and other security precautions in place? I need inspiration. That's it! I need uplift. Something to temporarily turn my world wildly and quickly on a completely different axis. So I pick out a new arrival to the Poetry Section: *UNMONKEYING THE ARCTIC: AN ANTHOLOGY OF POEMS FOR EVERY OCCASION.* After all, Earth's axis goes through the arctic, right? Just as I pick it up, I turn and spy our new elderly Romanian (or is it Czech?) cleaning lady on staff coming into the dining area, broom in hand. Her head is a bit too small for her body, her eyes are too close together, and she wears her hair in stiff waves. The old black guy with the scar who waits tables here — his mouth always moving, full-lipped and generous without a hint of cruelty — whispers to me, jerking his thumb her direction: "Pssssst. Jerry. Translated, her name means *Dry Fissure*." I counter with a wink that the longest word you can write on a type-writer's top row is *rupturewort*. He gives out a gigantic cracking Southern laugh, one that echoes inside one's head, with an incessant hard-edged ringing to it like having roadwork going on outside one's window.

I pass the communal TV viewing room, ambling in lockstep toward my mailbox, and can just make out an ad or a fragment from some sci-fi movie blurting out to weak ears: *With love we can dream, with 5.0 we can cherish, with SimAnima we can believe. Unlike real memory, this one won't fade with time. Move and sound just like you once did.*

Hand trembling, with unsteady key, I open mailbox number 345. There's an official-looking business-size envelope mixed in with the usual crap an-nouncements from the home (always on colorful paper, like *that* can cheer us up). A pale-blue envelope with no return address. My name and address is displayed in a standard Times Roman font. It taunts me to open it.

In lockstep, I walker-it to the slower-than-molasses-in-January elevator. Gotta open it in my room. Beware the prying eyes and all that. *She*'s on the lift. That woman. The one I almost married. We exchange vague pleasantries. We both stare at the elevator door or up at the ceiling. I get off before her, looking dubiously first to my right then to my left before jigging down the hallway, fumbling with my keys. Always get the wrong one in. Sometimes it sticks. This time, thank the Lord, I get the right one. Noticed I left my little carton of milk out again. Probably spoiled now. I sit on my just-adequate bed. The maid's made it. Stare at the blue envelope for some minutes. The Flag stamp is put on upside down. When I see that, with the urgency of lust opposed by buttons, I rip it open with my niffy vintage fifties letter-opener, whose plastic handle resembles the profile of a smartly hatted businessman holding a slim brief-case smartly at his side. I, a strict sobrietarian, unfold carefully and read:

Dear Mr. Hugunin,

This is to inform you that your darling pet elephant has arrived (see enclosed photo). Years of delight ahead await you! "Herbert" may be picked up at the following address.

Herbert

Here the letter lists a location on the south side of Chicago on Ashland Avenue and is signed "City Courier." Some official stamp like a notary's affixed below the scribbled signature. I read it several times thinking there was something I was missing. After several readings, though, I conclude someone *had* given me an elephant and it would be delivered by courier. I'm not sure what kind of elephant, although judging from the enclosed photo, it's BIG. I'm not sure what to do when it comes. I imagine that unpacked pachyderm charging right through my little apartment. Jeez! Though it would be fun to see it lumber into the dining room, upsetting tables and driving the staff to move faster than usual. In fact, there seems no other explanation or option, unless I donate the damn thing to the local zoo. Then I notice, mixed among the mail I brought up, one of our home's brightly-colored notices. I unfold it and read:

DON'T FORGET THE APRIL FOOL'S DAY

GALA TONIGHT IN THE TWILIGHT ROOM

AT 7 P.M. INVITE YOUR LOVED ONES

Aaaaah! Jammer, that no account putz. One of *his* practical jokes. I remember, he always puts Flag stamps on topsy-turvy to protest our nation's conservative bent. Wants to remind me about that proverbial elephant in my room: my *supposed* dementia, which I refuse to discuss.

In fact, I have an uncanny ability to read people. Hypersensitive to every wink 'n tic, innuendo and out-take. When our most "up" inmate, Ruby Zunshine, laughs, her genuine gaiety is contradicted by a face that seems to go to pieces, wrinkled and distorted by the violent grimace of mirth; even her forehead is ruined when she laughs. It's a face seen as if through a tornado. Would be a challenge to paint. In contrast, Brucine Bitters always has the smile of a contest winner on her face, but she never has a kind word for anyone or anything. Ergo, if inner truth can be suppressed in so many ways, we need someone to suss it out — *moi*!

Jeane said I was "just suspicious," at worst, "a spectator of bizarre brain movies," but that's not accurate. I'm really a righteous reader of physiognomy 'n souls. More than that, been known to heal cancer. Ask Hilla. Got people in the home here lining up for my magic touch after that. I don't yell and jump around like those TV quacks. No. Only subtle movements of slithering 'n a slight shake with a tender laying on of my mitts, a pious prayer, and bye-bye bad stuff.

A finer nuance than mere intuition, my radar can pick up a Stealth fighter! Back in California — where the weather was often partly suspicious with chances of betrayal — didn't I "make" those cars shadowing my weekly trips to Mass? Jeane said I was nuts and had me tamed with sleep-inducing anti-psychotics. Later I freed myself of my mental chains, and successfully "made" those malevolent Mafiosi across from my mobile home plotting to drive me out of my place with some lung-irritating gas. You bet your sweet bippy, I did. Natch, Dack, our mobile home park manager, was in on it too! A short shit, topped with a fifties flat-top haircut, I decked Dack when he tried to kick me in the balls. Never messed with The Big Guy again, I tell you. Runs when he sees me. Has the local cops on speed-dial though and so turned me in when he saw me sleeping in my red GMC Jimmy. Drat that dumb damn Dack!

Foiled all their nefarious plans. Hung a thicker door with 24-gauge hot-dipped, galvanized steel skins and acoustical performance rating coded at ASTM E413-70T-STC 28, complete with four Schlage dead bolts, and four separate color coded keys: red, yellow, green, and blue. When those two "Noo Joisey" short fucks surreptitiously pipe noxious fumes into my home hoping to get me to vacate and get my property cheap — I — a growl rising to a shriek, then sinking to mere pule — crawl under my home through dust 'n cobwebs garbed like a gung-ho Navy SEAL in a black jogging suit, face black-ned, snarling teeth clenching my old combat knife. I cut their hose. "Got da fuckers!" I later phone Jimmer. If he could only've seen my eyes with their competing currents and temperatures subtly coursing. "When I get sparks in my long muscles 'n a click in my head like a catching latch in need of oil, look out!" Silence at the other end of the line. "Cemented up one of my floor heating vents just for good measure too. Mission accomplished! Chalked one up for God 'n Country! Remember the Gipper!" Silence from Jimmer's end, then a click. Well, screw him. I always take suspicion into conviction. For it's difficult to rove things to those not clued in. How could one? So I shoot from the intuitive hip, so to speak. But Jimmer would insist I need a hip replacement.

Around town — Oceanside, located near the blue wallop of the Pacific — I got car salesmen and auto mechanics who hide when they see me drive up. Know they can't pull the wool over ol' Eagle-Eye Jerry. But could never intimidate good ol' "Gorm," our skillful bomber pilot. He saved our butts more than once in those flak- and fighter-filled skies over Germany. When he retired from his commercial pilot gig with United, he settled within a half-hour drive of my mobile home in Oceanside; that's when he began an affair with my ex-wife two hours north up the coast (it was obvious his own wife was flying way below his radar, so little attention did he give her). Ballsy guy. Even spied Gorm and Jeane here in our little village just last week, arm-in-arm. Told Jimmer, but he swore he'd talked to his mother that morning and she was still trapped in her time-loop, sipping weak coffee 'n chain-smoking (it lightens her head 'n loosens her sphincter) in the house she stole in our harsh California divorce, surrounded by the particulars of portraits 'n snaps of our deceased daughter. So he says. But he always covers for her. Says the universe will change, but I, never. Can't blame him. She's his mother. And loyalty is loyalty and Jimmer is that, loyal. Why even his best high school buddy's elder brother is named "Loyall." With two l's. Can you beat that?

It's a good thing my ex-wife won't be privy to my memoir. Jimmer promises to keep it from her eyes should I flat-line before her. Our "Happy Scribblers" group just eats it up.

The Lord Cures me at Lourdes

Although our home's library is a modest one, they've just got in Henry Alford's *How to Live: A Search for Wisdom from Old People* and they get the *New*

Elder Physics

York Review of Books. Like to peruse those reviews on Monday mornings. Like reading them more than the books they purport to review. My son's a critic and he gets that desire to praise or raze from me — my critical genes that are critical of Jeane. Oh, here's one I love, brought back up to my room for Jimmer to see. Cut it out with a single-edged razorblade I keep in my wallet for self-defense, but often employ to cut text from books and mags I might use as inspiration for these dialogues. Got a spiral notebook full of these now. I quote: *Immense talent, deficient in craft. The punctuation doesn't serve the rhythm, the structure doesn't serve the plot. It has a pungent flavor, but a reader must be careful with a book like this not to confuse the preposterous with the original.* Jeez, sounds like what someone would say of *my* ruminations, huh?

I wonder what Jimmer is doing right this very minute, this very femtosecond? I am lonely for his company. Given his two-school adjunct status, he could be teaching an abstruse theory class at the 'Tute, or a student-friendly General Ed course at Roosevelt U. Forget what days he's at which. Might be grading papers at his studio too, putting little red marks hither-thither. He did say he had proctored an exam recently. Which reminds me, I'm getting proctored by a proctologist tomorrow. Got it on my wall calendar for Wednesday: JIMMER HERE AT 10 A.M. WEAR CLEAN UNDERWEAR.

The drill is the same. We sit together awaiting my appointment with a slew of other not-so patient patients. He reads a book, I scan magazines. About a twenty minute wait. The physicians I see seem bored. Afterwards, Jimmer always treats me to a bacon burger with cheese 'n fries. My reward for good behavior (like not telling the fellow, usually of foreign extraction, where to put his stethoscope). I only get testy when the issue of dementia comes up. But I'm forever fun and hugs with the nurses. Entertain them with thrilling stories of yore. Get them laughing. Once in a while, a blush. When they say I'm a joker, my retort is: "There's a joker in every deck and he must be dealt with."

I'm quite a joker to deal with. Went off my anti-psychotics back in '87. Retired from Lockheed's "Skunk Works." New jerk-off boss was really beginning to stink things up there, so I put in my papers. Much to Jeane's chagrin. She was delighted to have me away at work all day and medicated to indifference at home. I hated it. So my first act of rebellion after retiring was to take a trip to Europe. Hadn't been there since the war. Went with a Church group because on the itinerary I spied the word LOURDES.

Decided to see if I might merit a miraculous cure there. For my mental illness. But how would I know it worked? If I'm nutso delusional, how to know? I prayed that my cure would be signified by my eyes being restored to 20-20 vision (wore glasses for decades). And whaddayaknow! After rubbing shoulder with mutes, paraplegics, quadri-plegics, severe stutterers, autistic kids, Tourette-sufferers, compulsive gamblers, sex addicts, artists and writer's who've lost their creative juice, cancer and scleroderma patients, blah-blah-blah — Presto Change-O! — my vision was restored two days after my offering at Lourdes. Pulled my glasses off, tossing them into a trash can, and skipped down the street chanting: "I'm cured, praise the Lord!" And, by Jove, I've been seeing perfectly ever since. Message received, O Lord! I immediately went off my meds to become (as my son poetically puts it) "a loose culverin." I,

of course, feel like I've been let out of prison after a
wrongful conviction. My daughter (when alive) and nephew
(before his death) were imprisoned by their meds and I
grieve for that, but they hadn't my faith. I had much to
catch up on, now with a head clear after my release. I get
the feeling that prior to my miraculous restoration, my
mental activity had been continuous, but unimpassioned,
lacking versatility, and was altogether insignificant,
except for my hours of application with T-square, pen, and
coffee mug at Lockheed's drafting tables.

My plane landed at LAX with a drug-free-me — just say
NO, right? A new man preaching that people tolerate the
current bad script to the bad film of their lives because
the same rationale IT imposes on 'em from the outside also
gets insinuated in them from the inside. A persistent reign-
of-clichés, externally and internally which, I bet, could be
detected internally by gas chromatography of our feces!

So how can I not believe, I asked Jeane, in the reign
of an all-powerful, not-Vatican-approved, concerted effort
to warp our collective minds? My wife, not amused, began to
wiggle and spit, like bacon in a pan, whenever I approached.
She'd wrap herself in one of her self-made, multicolored
afghans and freeze-up before Fox News on the TV. I'd sit in
a chair three feet away, but it felt more like a mile. I'd
need three-league boots to get her back. Dinners were served
in silence.

Her secret-society-type shenanigans, elicited a
severe surveillance on my part. Duty bound, I put a lock on
the telephone and snatched the distributor cap off her car,
all to frustrate her adulterous assignations. Fifty-odd
types of cuckoldry known to man, you know. Followed her
around the neighborhood with binocs when she was out on
foot. Finally, she talked Jimmer into flying out to reason
with me, get me back on those mind-numbing drugs ending in -
zil or -zine. Arriving for Easter, he used his best philosophical *jujitsu* to resurrect my old self. No go. Left
shrugging his shoulders and twirling his eyes. Hopes for a
truce smashed. Marital combat resulted, a mix of heavy
verbal 'n mild physical abuse which threatened our *tessera
hospitalis*.

Finally, exhausted, she backed off and (unbeknownst
to me) began her ultimate plot. Jeane always has played a
shrewd, ardent, and interfering game in all our lives. Ask
Jimmer. Or Leslie, if she was alive. After the emotional
strain subdued between us, we took some transcontinental
trips in *Rocinante*, our RV. This got her far away from her
many lovers, calming me. Upon our return, she coyly got me
to agree to fresh digs, got me to buy that mobile home in
Oceanside. Milder climate than the San Fernando Valley, she
used as her ploy. Less yard to toil in. Close to the Marine
Corps base where as a vet I could get some discounts at
their base commissary. Seductive inducements. At least it
would get her away from her lovers in the Canoga Park area,
I thought. Of course, I bought it hook, line, 'n sinker, I
did. Dumb me. Shoulda known. Jeane and I are never on the
same page, even when it appeared so.

Elder Physics

After we got settled there and before our home in the Valley was sold, she shoved divorce papers my way and ran back north, leaving me to stew in the new joint two hours south. Was out-manoeuvred. So I dug in. Stonewalled, griped, cursed, wrote bitter letters — used every delaying tactic known to a "paranoid personality" (my wife's lawyer's term, not mine) to frustrate the legal-inevitable. Made myself known to the local branch of the Franciscans at the historic San Luis Rey Mission nearby by going to daily Mass. Promoted to Eucharistic Minister distributing the wafer to the faithful at Mass and to elderly shut-ins. Eventually climbed to a Fourth Degree Knighthood in their Knights of Columbus chapter. Got the sash and ceremonial sword to prove it.

Meanwhile, I got my sketching and painting gear up to snuff by daily jaunts to a local art supply store. New, snazzy painting easel, tubes of wonderfully-named oils, watercolors, gouache, a range of charcoal pencils and ink pens. Stocked up on TV dinners, cans of salmon and lima beans, beer, and tons of Sara Lee baked goods. Large cans of yogurt which, when emptied, were used for you-know-what. Upon the suggestion of my widowed neighbor, I bought a very fluffy Keeshond for his unconditional slobbery loyal affection (my attachment coefficient to humans is sub-normal). Since he was to be my travel companion, I appropriately named him "Hu-go" (yes, spelt with the hyphen). Ah! He essentialized the secret of life in a simple, handy, toy-like form. Hell, if I could've been half the person that dog was, I'd be twice the human I am today. His sighs were like some form of distilled truth. Everyone loved his plush two-layer coat of silver and black fur with a cuddly ruff and cute curled tail. Small, quick heartbeat. He'd sit calmly, tongue lolling while I sketched him, the wisdom of generations of Keeshonds lurking within. He soon adored me and I him. Jimmer has the same tuned-in relationship with his Westie and Scottie dogs.

Nice to be adored when your chain-smoking, nail-biting, non-practicing Protestant ex-wife despises you. Ya grok? After the divorce was finalized, Hu-go and I, now inseparable, set out in my RV to become nomads for six months. Hu-go in the passenger seat, dog-eyes front with excitement and tongue lolling with adventure anticipated. This was in the early nineties. I visited Jimmer in Chicago (he was still married to his first wife and had just bought a classic brick bungalow in a Swedish enclave) and, criss-crossing the continent, I knocked on the house doors of all the remaining members of my valiant bomber crew, showing them a photo of me in flight gear. Visited John Fernsler, our funny, but

Lt. Gerald Hugunin, England, 1944

Took a week to write that, with help from Jimmer, who's calling our father-son collaboration "The Keystone Cops," touting our "Innovation in Assembly" mode of bricolage. I can hardly wait to read it, complete with sound effects, at our next "Happy Scribblers" gathering, where Fialta always opens the meeting with: "It has become easy to write a good poem, and for that very reason, hard to be poet." Ray Bottles promised to sit in. Said he liked seeing us folks brush the cobwebs off our memories, clean paintings cracked with layers now showing through, listen to the crackling of the adventure-colored curtains gone moldy 'n brittle over the last eighty years part and let sun in again. "Ah, the cabinet-of-wonders that is our past," he muses.

BRAIN-InterActive-Construct

Today I've been drinking instant coffee and Pet milk, chilled. Air's warm as syrup, thick with pollen, photons moving at the speed of light. I pick up our local freebie Wednesday newspaper and ogle the headline —

VILLAGE FORESTER ASKS RESIDENTS TO
STOP DANGLING TIRES FROM PUBLIC TREES

— then I open to the Lonely Hearts section and read:

Hugo Boss kind of guy seeks Guess sort of girl.

Peek to see if Hilaria is running an ad therein. I'm suspicious, for in her bold gaze my ruin appears writ large. Stacks of this rag in our dining room; everyone grabs one, opening it to the Obits (my son says some day he'll put in mine). Ill-Phil picks up a copy only to shred it before our astonished eyes, picks up the pieces and declares he's going to use them for toilet paper.

Knock at the door. It's Jimmer, shaking out a wet umbrella. Saved by the knock! He notices my new baseball cap emblazoned with the Upping Arms phone number. "It's in case we get lost; also doubles as an advertisement for our institution," I tell him. I tell him also how lonely I am. He tries to reassure me. "Let's not visit Mr. Wispy today, dad," he pleads from sad experience. Says I'm a person other people warm to — without exception, they all warm. That I'm likeable. (He exaggerates, as all too often I get that *Nobody loves me but my mama* tune in my head.) He hugs me, desperately. He intuits my disturbed state, so lays on the concern — thick. True, up to a point, I'm convivial. But then oddities, schizzes 'n flows, always manage to burst forth and my goose is cooked. Once, responding to one of my mood swings, Jimmer literally shook 'n screamed, "A day with you and I'm inwardly shouting: *I SUFFER LIKE A DOOR*." And so with my Polish beauty, too, who suffered my door that swings both ways at a drop of a hat or a buzz of a gnat. So no more of her tonic blast of sunlight. I now try to balance myself at the top of my neck, trying to prevent the Mr. Hyde version of myself from swinging and slopping out over the sides, running down my breast. My identity tends to shift, skip 'n stutter through a kerfuffle of utterances and evocations. Yet Jimmer's presence can steady me, but only if he firmly holds my shoulders and looks me straight in the eyes. Yes, he can be my hero at times. Other times, well . . . (aren't ellipses just jim dandy to express awkward moments between father and son?)

Futterneid Quotient winding down, I regain enough control to show Jimmer that odd ad for his expert decipherment. He strokes his neat beard, silently reads, chuckles, and with a slight, micro brew beer induced slur in his speech, he explains the reference: "It pertais to designer labels. Buying is much more American than thinking, dad; now people can glean more about each other from labels in their duds and their zip code than from their Zodiacal sign or ten weeks of premarital yak-yak with a horny priest." I take exception to his slur on the pious.

I know staff go through my trash, running a detailed inventories. So while I got his ear, I beg Jimmer to dump my more incriminating waste-goods into his trash, stuff like opened packages indicating use of forbidden items, elder home contraband. Not referring to condoms, never used 'em, or Viagra. While I'm certainly no very virile Picasso, I admit to my son that inflammable desires dampened by day under the cold water of consciousness are ignited at night by the libertarian matches of sleep, and burst forth in showers of shimmering incandescence. Hyperbole, yes, but I can still pole-vault out of bed in the a.m.

Angelica's voice? How many times had my toenails been clipped? My prostate probed? How many times have I flipped when Jimmer taps my till? How many times has that *faux-*friendly sneaky dude got into my meds? How many of my feces have been analyzed to date? How many staff have been so assigned? How many times have I been hauled to the hospital after I crash-land on my apartment floor when my landing gear fails? How many times have I been hooked up to an EKG machine? How many times has the doctor predicted the worst? How many times have I asked how many fingers do you see? How many more things are there to list here? There's no hand-calculator built well-enough that could handle all the additions. Nor a computer (on planet Earth anyway) fast or nimble enough. Need a Kryptonian super-computer: BRAINIAC (short for BRAIN-InterActive-Construct) built by Dax-Ur and Jor-El on the planet Krypton. Yep, I was a Superman comics fan until he was he became flesh as TV's George Reeves.

    Like Superman, we can go up or down, but unlike Superman, we never really *fly* in our home's newly mirrored elevator. Too slow. One day my son and I are bored, so we get on that lift and do an experiment, more empirical than our previous metaphysical experience thereon. Jimmer suggests that while I give out one helluva sustained AAAAAAAAAAAAAAAHHHHHHHHHH, he'll time our descent to the next floor below, then reproduce the length of such so voiced graphically on a typed page. Calls it "a phenomenological artwork." I think it looks like Concrete Poetry done by an autistic: AAAAAAAAAAAAAAAAAAAAAAAAAAAAAAAAAAAAAAAAAA
AAAAAAAAAAAAAAAAAAAAAAAAAAAAAAAAAAAAAAAAAAAAAAAAAAAAAAAAAA
AAAAAAAAAAAAAAAAAAAAAAAAAAAAAAAAAAAAAAAAAAAAAAAAAAAAAAAAAA
HHHHHHHHHHHHHHHHHHHHHHHHHHHHHHHHHHHHHHHHHHHHHHHHHHHHHHHHHH
HHHHHHHHHHHHHHHHHHHHHHHHHHHHHHHHHHHHHHHHHHHHHHHHHHHHHHHAAAA
AAAAAAAAAAAAAAAAAAAAAAAAAAAAAAAAAAAAAAAAAAAAAAAAAAAAAAAAAA
AAAAAAAAAAAAAAAAAAAAAAAAAAAAAAAAAAAAAAAAAAAAAAAAAAAAAAAAAA
HHHHHHHHHHHHHHHHHHHHHHHHHHHHHHHHHHHHHHHHHHHHHHHHHHHHHHHHHH
HHHHHHHHHHHHHHHHHHHHHHHHHHHHHHHHHHHHHHHHHHHHHHHHHHHHHHHHHHAA
AAAAAAAAAAAAAAAAAAAAAAAAAAAAAAAAAAAAAAAAAAAAAAAAAAAAAAAAAA
AAAAAAAAAAAAAAAAAAAAAAAAAAAAAAAAAAAAAAAAAAAAAAAAAAAHHHHHH
HHHHHHHHHHHHHHHHHHHHHHHHHHHHHHHHHHHHHHHHHHHHHHHHHHHHHHHHHH
AAAAAAAAAAAAAAAAAAAAAAAAAAAAAAAAAAAAAAAAAAAAAAAAAAAAAAAAAA
AAAAAAAAAAAAAAAAAAAAAAAAAAAAAAAAAAAAAAAAAAAAAAAAAAAAAAAAAA
HHHHHHHHHHHHHHHHHHHHHHHHHHHHHHHHHHHHHHHHHHHHHHHHHHHHHHHHHH
HHHHHHHHHHHHHHHHHHHHHHHHHHHHHHHHHHHHHHHHHHHHHHHHHHHHHHHAAAA
AAAAAAAAAAAAAAAAAAAAAAAAAAAAAAAAAAAAAAAAAAAAAAAAAAAAAAAAAA
AAAAAAAAAAAAAAAAAAAAAAAAAAAAAAAAAAAAAAAAAAAAAAAAAAAAAAAAAA
HHHHHHHHHHHHHHHHHHHHHHHHHHHHHHHHHHHHHHHHHHHHHHHHHHHHHHHHHH
HHHHHHHHHHHHHHHHHHHHHHHHHHHHHHHHHHHHHHHHHHHHHHHHHHHHHHHHHH
AAAAAAAAAAAAAAAAAAAAAAAAAAAAAAAAAAAAAAAAAAAAAAAAAAAAAAAAAA
AAAAAAAAAAAAAAAAAAAAAAAAAAAAAAAAAAAAAAAAAAAAAAAAAAAAAAAAAA
HHHHHHHHHHHHHHHHHHHHHHHHHHHHHHHHHHHHHHHHHHHHHHHHHHHHHHHHHH

    Bet Superman would let out an appalling sound just like that if his super-powers went south when he was zip-zooming over Metropolis. Of course, he'd go down much faster than we.

Our lift opens with a gloating little *ding*. What fun! Jimmer notes the time: floor four in forty-four seconds flat. Now multiply that by three to see how many ah's it takes for me to go from my flat to the ground floor for my slow-motion breakfast (to save paper, I'm not recording *that* here). Jimmer says coming here is like being an extra in a movie filmed at high-speed and then projected normally, so everything moves in slow-motion.

Fialta in the Springtime

I am spying on an utterly unsuspecting female life-form moving alone in that aquarium dimness that is the Twilight Room, flower decorations still up a day after Teddy Jawnowitz's Easter pep-talk, an ostrich thigh of a harp sticking out from under a cloth cover, reminding me that the event culminated with a hubbub of sentiments and an orchestra of young women playing Vivaldi. I can still hear the hollow of Teddy's violaceous syllables, the sweet soft dampness of his voice as he introduced them — one by one. (Jammer pegged this last sentence as pretentious, but I insisted on retaining it.) Outside, a gibbous moon as she strolls about, sits and yawns (there's a private sound to her yawn). She is thinking as she yawns, wavering on the edge of caring and not caring about bright bits of memory, those long-drawn sunset shadows of her personal truth. She appears a perfect character for inclusion in a humorous book for sad people, her face a grimace half way between tragedy and comedy masks. It's Fialta Fenwich, eating a sandwich with her distinctive mouth curl. In between bites, she mumbles, "The calla lilies are in bloom again." Fialta in the Spring, a lady quick to hoe our type-furrows, pull out ill-placed commas, dangling modifiers, and sexist language.

No point in approaching her. She's forever harshin' on everybody's buzz. She wallows in self-congratulation over her exemption from the general mire of humanity, especially men. She hates all pantless manifestations of the male sex. One of her poems, "Goodnight Irene," ends: *I'll return to the bosom, / Where my journey ends — / Where there's no penis / Between us friends!* If a woman's love were spring water containing salubrious salts, everyone around Fialta would be dehydrated. Heard her once spout off about "the link between the hymen and death." I could only appear to her to be a melancholy brigand hawking local lollipops, or a figure from a Russian folktale, perhaps. But that just might give me an edge. Rumor here — as per Hilla — is that the last time she was laid was in Russia quite a long time ago during her stint at the U.S. Embassy in Moscow. Whether her partner was male is doubtful. Maybe depends on the moon cycle. Gibbous moon last night meaning — what? — my big chance? Maybe. Maybe, literally, just Depends. Which reminds me . . . to the extent that God is a muscular, powerful force in my life, inversely, my bladder and prostate muscles are weak and wanting. So . . . you will have to excuse me.

As I hasten (a relative term here) toward the ground floor restrooms, I pass The Presence sitting in his chair in the hallway in a state the extreme opposite of blissful southern fatigue. Real nasty expression on his mug, Phil-quick eyes darting. As if in his brain a duet for trumpet and zither were going full tilt. Slurpy 'n slurry 'n simperin' like Dean Martin after six or ten double Scotches — still wearing p.j.'s over which he wears an old T-shirt urging: SHOPLIFT AT KROGER'S.

Upon my passing, Phil recoils as if bitten by a snake, his face going instantly the color of ash as if every drop of blood left for better digs, leaving it with empty pouches and ugly loosenesses and laxities all about it. His lower jaw hanging loosely as if it were a mechanical jaw on a toy man. That jaw then opens and barks: "Impotent incipiency of a bastard, hopeless tyranny!" Sardonic triumph passes across his face as he shakes his head thrice and rudely clears his throat. "Fine, fine criticism! Every slick jackanapes sees fit to read me a lecture," as he jooks me with his cane. (Nice word, *jooks*, huh; thanks to my son.)

This wild outburst is followed by the mumbling of method acting as his energies of speech are drawn inward and dispersed throughout his twisting body. If sleaze took physical form, it would be incarnated as Ill-Phil. Oddly, he smelled of violets, or was it *MyOwnPrivateIdaho*? (My canny code for suffering a delusion or hallucination, like the one yesterday where the scene before me seemed shot through with holes, wormholes, scintillating, and no one around me noticing the popping sounds I hear.) I imagine a huge tome titled *The Mirriam-Webster's Dysfunctionary*, where his name is listed along with an arm's length of pathologies suffered. I can cast the first stone, 'cause my name's listed there too.

Continuing my slow rush to the toilet, I negotiate around a neat stack of just-delivered cartons labeled FOLEY CATHETERS near the receptionist's desk, heading due south, the ill-wind of Ill-Phil's abuse now blowing at my back. Nod politely at Eepie Carpetrod as she shuffles toward me, diffusing a familiar warmth, carrying proofs for her next column (I never miss reading it). Then an awkward encounter with our Fearless Leader who's just entered the south door after parking his bruise-purple Cadillac (sneaky bastard never uses the front) on his way to his taxidermic chic office. "Everything will be okay in the end," he says, "and if it's not okay, it's not the end." Winks. I mumble a humble "God-be-with-you" and give the Papal blessing. The men's room door is locked. So I use the women's. Our P.A. system is again playing "Strawberry Fields Forever," pop culture's version of *ontological skepticism*, or so claims Jimmer.

What a Jewel

A day had passed almost unnoticed, and now the night felt as if it were part of the night before, and the night before a part of the night before that, all connected by my restless dreams, fragments of the same continuous night, I read in Stuart Dybek's *The Coast of Chicago*. Some passages should make their way into my memoir. Jimmer gave it to me for Father's Day and I'm enjoying the scenes depicted, which evoke vivid flashbacks to my early married days when our family had a small apartment in Chicago's Rogers Park area near Clark Street on Albion Avenue, when I worked at Westinghouse Elevator Division. Jimmer, reading, drilling holes in language to get at the meat within, always gets me itching to write, so here goes:

<pre>
    Besides mentioning the leachate seep, an espresso of
bodily refuse marring my undies today, I really should add
something about my unique shopping experiences to this
memoir, like moments when objects become other, like when a
sardine can looks back or a contents list hails me.
    Shopping allows us a delightful taste of freedom,
like a Southern Negro going North to visit relatives circa
</pre>

Elder Physics

1950. Every Tuesday, it's Grocery Tuesday, ta-da! A line of white hair lines up before our Magic Bus. It takes a full ten minutes to load up. Why I usually let my son take me. In making our departure, we barely negotiated around Ill-Phil blocking our home's entrance, his body stretched across the steps as he produced a gurgling sound in his throat and a grating of his teeth with two fingers ready to plug his ears if we tried to argue our way past him).

At the Jewel grocery store, we fab four (*moi*, Buddy, Brucine, and a recent transfer from another home, Don Ferdinand) move on toward vague purchases looming ahead. "Ferd's" face, faded like an old stamp, opens its mouth and tells me he suffers a shit of a son who's always changing jobs "like a radioactive element with a half-life of forty-five days." Typical small talk. Soon we're scattering with our carts like hunter-gatherers. Although the carts dual-function as walkers, one of us occasionally still goes ass-over-tea-kettle (for an objective observer, it's a most extraordinary visual). Then there's the ominous God-like voice announcing *CLEAN UP IN AISLE TWO* when one of us forgets (today it was Don) to don Depends. Yet we love the store's airiness, cleanliness, the muzak. It's a reprieve from our gulag every time we go on our wacky Tuesday grocery grab.

Ran out of corn bread 'n honey; as Jimmer is teaching the next two days, he couldn't take me. I took the initiative. Although it takes longer — gotta wait for everyone to get back on the bus — I can linger in the aisles. You see, Jammer nags me about that when with him, the fact I read all the fine print on the products: water, corn syrup solids, sodium caseinate, mono- and diglycerides, sodium citrate, salt, dipotassium phosphate, carrageenan, artificial color and flavor, vegetable oil (ah, those long chains of unsaturated carbon atoms). Both delighted and suspicious of what's in 'em, and might find a clandestine communiqué secreted therein. Holy Humbuckles, it's happened. I've come up with a telling equation that captures my relationship to food and existence during my trips to the market:

$$\frac{\text{Foods}}{\text{molecular structures}} = \frac{\text{Life}}{\text{knowledge}}$$

It's employing this equation that makes Jammer impatient as I prowl the aisles, testing my hypothesis over and over as I dawdle over the cornbread, which would be in my stomach before it was off the shelf, but for the fact I love to coat it with Honey Bee honey to enhance its flavor.

Sometimes, I grab a flexible, imitation Arcopal-plastic Blue Bonnet margarine pot decorated with neo-rococo designs and stare at it for ten minutes before plopping it in my cart. On one occasion, just when my eye caught a new brand of toothpaste and an exotic blend of granola, Jammer trots over and points emphatically at his watch, restlessly pleading a full schedule. Sometimes we squabble like husband 'n wife.

So you can see it's a more relaxing adventure when I can get blissfully lost and imagine I'm running a maze, but without the time-keeper's stopwatch. The bus won't leave without me. But the boy has his redeeming aspects. He loves to see, as he puts it, "language stutter like *porqué* peeg." Give ya an example. We were shopping on a snowy day once and we were discussing how I could pepper my stories with some well-chosen French words, when suddenly he pointed to a reduced-price sale on *L'eau de Source Alizée* brand French bottled water. The sign reads:

L'eau Sale
Low Prices with your Jewel card

"A real gem, that," and the kid points out that *l'eau sale* in French meant "dirty water." And that the phrase "low prices"sounds like French for "frozen water."

"Shit, big guy, it's the stuff great literature is made of!" he exclaims, stroking his beard with pedantic enthusiasm. Besides his pedantry, if I had to fault Jimmer, it'd be that he's perpetually ON. Needs to relax. Chill out. Smell the violets. Read the canned food labels.

I kept saying this to him like a broken record while he was throwing out all my possessions and getting me moved from Oceanside to my Situation, this place, back in '04. That's the time I did my ultimate digression. I was supposed to be gradually divesting my stuff until he could visit at the end of his semester of pedagogical responsibilities. He'd sent me a check list of things to do and called weekly to see if I'd kept up my end of the bargain. Of course, I said yes each time: "Dad did you sell the bow and arrow set?" . . . "Affirmative!" . . . "Dad, get AmVets to pick up all those ratty clothes?" ... "Affirmative!" . . . "Got a buyer for your sofa and love-seat?" . . . "Affirmative!" And so on. Arriving, expecting an easy move-out — surprise!

"*Merde*!" he yelled and went into a variety of jim-jams. I expected he'd jump back in the huge rented van and hightail it back to the airport. Much to my utter amaze-ment, in five fourteen-hour days and approaching-fisticuffs screaming matches, everything was disposed of, even my car sold, and one hundred and twenty large black contractor-size trash bags were begging for collection. Stacked the way they were, Jimmer said they looked like a contemporary art installation. I tried slowing him up by perusing labels on my canned foods, taking inventory of all the crap in my refrigerator, but he soldiered on almost non-stop.

Eventually, only my mobile home remained on the market. But sold after I'd been living in my new place a few weeks. To this day neither of us can believe it. We look at each other, eye-to-eye, shake our heads and mumble. After all, it took him two weeks to sell his mother's house and move a much moody Jeane and all her crap out eastward and into an elder home a safe two miles distant from me here after her emphysema took a bad turn and her breath away.

Yes, Jimmer is driven. He's a gem. Often wears a funneled expression of determination on his bearded face. Driven to do his art and writing. I think I helped put that spunk in the guy. Made him one whopping big neurotic and neurotics have more talent if not fun. Can turn lemons to lemonade with a twist of the imagination or pagination. In turn, his peculiar approach to art has found its way into my monologues. Jimmer says the fantasy of the artist or writer as an isolated, heroic genius noun has given way to transitive verbs: to take, to edit, to collect, to install, to perform. Purloins replace loins as the *macho* image of the *auteur* yields to that of the *bricoleur.* Gut 'n baste has been superceded by cut 'n paste. (See what a good teacher he is, I'm learning.) "Wow, this sure takes the pressure off," I tell our art instructor. She just frowns from the waist up.

I get this same buzz from my writer's group when I finally clue them into my textual tactics.

Last session, at my turn to read, I tell the wrinkled faces around our table of my thrill at writing seriously again; that I spur on my theme and my theme spurs me on. That I take inspiration, like Jimmer, from artist Jasper Johns's dictum: *Take something, do something to it, then do something else to it.* (Eyes light up when I say this.) I argue that my stories will constitute a Medieval *periplus,* a temporal narrative describing stages of my journey through my elder-scape — a terrain surrounded by homes from which model citizens emerge each a.m. to play their part in the national economy, or what's left of it. My story is no unique sojourn. I'm really EveryElder. I tell that them one character, Bondo McCracken, is a younger and more vigorous resident who is used to figure the underlying laws of our elderverse through their very negation.

"Wholly Hegel! That's one good dialectical gesture," exclaims Fialta, nodding approval. "Of my work," I continue, "I want the critics to write: *He's a deadly submarine in a sea of authorships. His work's biting, but there's heart there . . . heart, but not schmaltz."* I read my first draft's opening sentence: "The Situation. There seems to be nothing but a whirl inside me futzing with my somewhat delicate circuits. Unwelcome things that come and go in my mind's eye. My heart beats faster. I can't control the headlong promiscuity of my thoughts. I start to make an inventory of everything I shall miss when dead. This, as I sit with arms folded, looking into the well of light from my desk lamp. I take my watch off and put it on my desk. Are you ready for my disgusting honesty, O Reader?"

I tell them that, in the spirt of my son's penchant for postmodern appro-priation, this is partially copped from a short story, "Helping" by Robert Stone, razored out of a large print version of *You've Got to Read This* (from which I got a paper cut) and slightly futzed with. For instance, besides the tense change, I substituted the word "watch" for "glasses" in the original (after my cure at Lourdes I don't use 'em).

"I'll tell you a thing or two — or thing or three," screams group member, Tandeta Paluba, who proceeds to excoriate me: "Gerald, yer one disgraceful un-ethical 'n lazy plagiarist."

I counterpunch, "I'm only *Playin' Jarism'."* This I culled from Jimmer, who's always scavenging, like his famous mentor Robert Heinecken, from wide-ranging sources, such that the line between so-called "originality" and "ver-sioning" is wholly blurred. "Hell," I continue, "Stone's words *exactly* describe my inner feelings and actions, so why not refunction 'em? We are what we read, a wrapped onion of citations, no more. Moreover, I have a penchant for piracy dating back to my role as Errol Flynn's character, Captain Blood, in my childhood games. My son reminds me I've always spoken in a voice that says, *I'm quoting*." I give 'em a hard stare.

Elder Physics

Tandeta fights by fiat, "Experimental writing is to real writing as the sandlot is to Wrigley Field." I plead my case, that image / word scavenging is currently hip — make it new by making it again — or so my theory-jock son says. I say that all language has pre-existed us, nobody is "original." First there was The Word, ever since it's been The Quote. That shuts 'em up.

Jimmer says my unstable identity, oscillating personae, makes a good argument for my multiple readings. So he urges me to boldly wield that little razorblade of mine where none has gone before and speak in multiple voices. "Just avoid the semiotic police," he jokes. But no kidding, if our Fearless Leader hears about me slicing pages from our library's books, *I'll* be arrested 'n booked. *Screwed, blued, 'n tattooed* — as we used to moan in boot camp when things went south. So it's back to my nifty notebook with pen in hand.

Like most folks here, I sleep fitfully due to a promiscuity of thoughts. When I do sleep, vivid dreams intrude so convincingly, I don't feel like I've slept. (My sleep apnea doesn't help.) So diverse and weird are those dreams — depicting scenes from over my life-span — often memory and dream lose distinction. I suspect my brain is host to larval engrams traveling in suspended animation, undetected until they divide and regenerate like flatworms and hide in seams and bedding, in war stories, laughter, and snapshots waiting to make their assault. Some of 'em can rot your socks (I've got proof in my clothes drawer) and turn memories into black and green blisters (observe the sole of my left foot).

As a hedge against all this, I find my comfort in Church. In faith. Back in Oceanside, daily Mass was my anodyne. Here, now, it's a struggle to make it up the three blocks north to St. Hilarius once a week. A wonderful older Gothic building, I love the echoed thump of my heavy orthopedic shoes inside that hallowed hall. I wonder why more people — those without walkers — don't go. To church, that is.

Taken purely as a human recreation, what could be more delightful, more unexpected than to enter a venerable and lavishly scaled building kept warm and clean for use one or two hours a week and to sit and stand in unison and sing and recite creeds and petitions that are like paths worn smooth in the raw terrain of our hearts?

John Updike wrote that. I am Gerald Hugunin and I approve that message. Why, to even usher at Church is to commune with angels. And I've upped the ante: read Scripture at the lectern, hand out hosts. Come Sundays, I love wisdom followed by wafers then waffles. In that order. I believe (with Updike): To be known by face and name and financial weight robs us our unitary soul, enrolls us against those Others. Personally, I'd replace "weight" with "gain." rhymes better with "name." Don't you agree? They say hindsight is twenty-twenty, like my Lourdes-cured peepers. How I love that humble kneeling posture, hands upturned and palms joined. A long habit. It represents a captive who proves completeness of submission by offering hands to be bound by the Victor, Our Savior. But now it's time to submit to the

Films You Can't Forget

Après yoga — during which we try to maintain a Buddhist sage, bitter
dried-up ascetic face, a petrified expression of supreme indifference and ab-
negation — my mind and body (for awhile anyway) seems again ONE. Felt good
enough to attend the weekly screening of film classics, "Films You Can't Forget,"
in the Twilight Room (7 p.m. sharp).

As I sat down, I notice the shadows turn to Hitchcock. I watch the ladies
wander in, walking as if stalking a rose. Three teen-girls-with-boyfriends, a
resident's grandkids, saunter past my seat, amazed by the newly found power of
their bodies to unhinge reason and jolt planets from their orbits. Their universe
shakes with metallic adolescent lust. One girl, a lissotrichous brunette, sports a
round steel labret stud gleaming from beneath her lower lip and barely hides
breasts beneath a black T-shirt with a name, RAGGEDY AN/DY, reversed out in
white. (I later Oogled *Wikipedia* and found it was a band consisting of, "A man and
his identical twin sister who dress like children's dolls, but with reversed roles,
gothed up, androgynous, with a sound like the most delicious children's stories
gone mad with pleasure.") Her pimply male hang-on wears a black cotton dress
shirt, its French cuffs unlinked 'n flapping. They give me a passing glance and,
seeing nothing but age, do not see me. Looking at Fialta, they see not flesh, but
cracked porcelain.

Staff psychologist, Teddy Jawnowitz, opens the event with: "Film, our
most vivacious art, is young enough to remember its first dreams, its limitless
promise, but is so haunted, scarred, by a central, ineradicable trauma of dis-
sociation." Boos from the peanut gallery. Ted scurries stage-left. Lights out.

As the old ghosts on the screen say the same lines and do the same
deeds for eternity — what Jammer calls the soothing syrup of imagistic repetition
— I usually nod off for most of the flick. Not tonight. Alfred Hitchcock's suspense
thriller, *Strangers on a Train*, keeps me alert, riveted to the screen. Good and evil
(personified) are about to do battle, shuttling between Washington and a two-cow
town named Metcalf.

During our post-film discussion led by Teddy — who always casts his
theoretical moves in the form of rhetorical questions ("Is not the primary focus
. . ." or "Can we not say that . . .") — I stun the gathering of elderly souls by the
exercise of my eagle-eyed observation. I raise my hand high — from which I just
had a squamous cancer removed — something I rarely do. What I reveal even
manages to impress Fialta Fenwich (although her jealousy shows in the murder-
ous gaze tossed my way). Her usual retort to anything I say is, "I can't get
excited." She prefers either jerker genres (tears, sobs, and org___s) or extreme
Brian De Palma (*Carrie* and *Dressed to Kill*). She gets mail (I peeked) from the
Fromm Institute for Lifelong Learning at the University of San Francisco State and
San Francisco's Brian De Palma Theory Collective. After last week's screening of
Hitchcock's *Vertigo*, she sharply observed that the woman impersonating the ship
industrialist's wife, Madeleine, who supposedly suicides, but then is seen alive
again by Jimmy Stewart's character, and then dresses her up like the first
Madeleine-*poseur*, well, her name in that later incarnation, "Judy," is an apt refer-

ence to a dressmaker's *Judy*, the dummy used to shape clothes on. Brilliant, huh? While Teddy offered the thought-provoking insight that one day we'll need archaeologists to unravel the storylines of even the most prosaic Hollywood films. So I had to outdo them both. Make my son proud.

"Well, what was it? Tell us Gerald!" yells Eepie Carpetrod, adjusting her terrifying glasses, thinking there might be grist here for her column. "Oh, come *on*, Gerald," Hilla's incredulity again. "Yes, Jerry, 'fess up," adds Chaddy with a smile. "Because?" queries Franco Zapardi in the saddest of all movies voice — an Italian-speaking resident, a thin grey man who flickers in and out of focus like an old film and who still mixes up *because* and *why* as both are covered by the Italian word *perché* — just waking up, rubbing his eyes, then noticing he's peed his pants.

My startling revelation? I had noticed in the scene where Guy and Bruno first meet on the train — their shoes touching and so touching off the narrative — that Guy Haines is holding a copy of *Alfred Hitchcock's Fireside Book of Suspense* and that its back cover depicts a photo of the director. Moreover, at one point Bruno Antony has his feet resting on a book, possibly another anthology of stories edited by Hitchcock. "Allow me to rewind in an effort to move us forward," Teddy Zen Koanizes, re-running the film. And sure enough! Now it seems obvious. Everyone makes excuses for not seeing it.

Eepie claims she was cleaning her glasses. Bondo says he was running in place at the back of the room, and Serena says she was thinking of goldfish and, hence, was distracted. Amy complains Dirty Harry's head blocked her view. Brucine Bitters claims she fled to the restroom having had a spoiled food item at Burma Superstar. Ruby Zunshine complains she's always in the dark. Fialta says she was musing about my missing Benicar tabs: maybe they're the proverbial Hitchcockian "McGuffin," the absent presence, upon which the action of my life here turns. And so forth. A truism proven: once you find a hidden picture, it then seems obvious. *Quod erat demonstrandum.*

Backstory. This "too close reading" (my son's phrase) was what I was using to get at the truth of that naked photo of my wife taken by our dirty-minded, perverse neighbor way back when. An analysis that Number One Skeptical Son failed to confirm, remember? Yet this incident is sure vindication of my skills (right?) and I plan, by Jove, on tossing it in Jammer's face at our next Wednesday breakfast if he suffers me to listen to yet another excerpt from his pedantic work-in-progress: "The Acrobatic Gaze and the Pensive Image in Serbo-Croatian Morgue Photography."

A brief digression. Why is it that all the women here refer to me as "Gerald," but the men call me "Jerry." And my son's first serious college-age love-interest bizarrely called him "James-Richard," and not just James, Jim or Jimmy. His male friends call him "Jim" or "Hugy," or "Eyes" (short for four-eyes, his glasses you know). What's that all about? Some kind of gender pre-emption?

Back up in my room, I suck on my last Vosges Woolloomooloo chocolate bar, letting it slowly melt, soothing me. (A tad of sugar won't hurt me; unlike poor Ill-Phil's gross antic: grabbing a sugar dispenser, holding it aloft and drinking dramatically from it, then placing it down on the table with a flourish and a belch.) Woolloomooloo (love to pronounce it, over 'n over) is my late-night reward for one-upping Fialta during our heated post-film discussion. It's okay, as tomorrow is our weekly food-gathering trip and Jimmer and I will make a bee-line for the exotic and healthy chocolates section to purchase more fashionable flavonoids for the Para*papa*noid. Then to the pharmacy for my heart and blood pressure meds, a *Town and Country* mag stuffed in my cart, an inner monologue roaring.

As I put on my pajamas, I recall that Friday night is our Big Event: Seymour's Big Band. Big Band dancing in the Twilight Room — Tony Bennett, Frank Sinatra, Cole Porter, Count Basie, you name it. Last month the home hosted Kevin and Friends, an acoustic folk group. All the guys had scruffy beards. Damn. If I hadn't screwed the pooch with Hilaria, Big Guy'd have a date for the Big Dance. That poem I sent in a snit probably did it: *Your gorgeous cabeza is cold as a gun's empty / chamber, a hole that can't be stuffed with poems / or the half-chewed aspirin of the moon.* Bet Dirty Harry wears his kill-the-ladies lavender tux. I've grown a handsome, slim 'tache and can wear my tux too. Jimmer says the ladies can't resist me when I'm dressed to the nines and wear a belt buckle that shines. He tells me, "Dance first, think afterwards." Love that boy! When I don't hate him.

Ass Over Teakettle

Didn't make it to Friday. Ass over teakettle in my room. Boom boom boom. So little feeling in my legs and toes it's hard to balance. Plus, been feeling like a slow tire leak for several days. Little energy. The center of gravity in my room shifted. I'm down. Too weak to get up. I'm out for the count, my limbs strewn among room debris, and my desperate prayers there, until cleaning staff find me. Hallelujah! Don't remember who it was hailed the front desk and the lady there hailed paramedics while I said my "Hail Marys." Pair of paramedics. Named "Mutt 'n Jeff" — just kidding. One tall, the other short. I remember that. Jimmer meets me at the hospital's ER where my thoughts are an interminable desert of sand, with not a palm tree in sight, not so much as a comforting mirage. The whole fabric of my mind seems to have tumbled to pieces; it lies in a horrible chaos. I can make no order within myself. Futterneid Quotient extremely high. Damaged dignity, but only wounds are minor cuts and bruises. Jimmer's in the waiting room flipping through the hospital's rag, *The Daily Infarct,* until they call him about having discovered a bad bladder infection — my fourth this quarter.

So they put me through intake. My son has to visit me on the third floor, me in an adjustable bed, and negotiate around the IVs while listening to medical mumbo-jumbo from white, brown, black, yellow people in green scrubs. The food sucks. Makes Upping Arms's under-cooked eggs and timid coffee seem gourmet. Stern-faced staff rat on me about my "lack of cooperation," get Jimmer to sign off on the use of light restraints. I have a tendency to yell, "I'm outta here!" and dash down the hall toward freedom, bare-ass mooning all as flesh pokes out the back of my hospital gown. So I make no friends here. The docs are distant. Only positive thing, the Feds pick up my astronomical hospital bill. But I *am* responsible for our Village's ambulance service, one hundred bucks each way. That's a lot of Wednesday breakfasts out at Al's with Jimmer!

When I'm laid up at the hospital — where the luggage labels of life are exposed — but have regained some of my mental moxie, I like to charcoal sketch staff (nurses exaggerated exasperated expressions, doctors with diagnosis eyes like deadlights shining on me, Candy Stripers with discomfort reflected in their peepers, etcetera) and can even work out math 'n symbolic logic problems to pass the time when my calculating engine ain't on the fritz. Jimmer always brings me my spiral notebook so I can record my monologues 'n do my ciphers. My latest foray into the arcane elder-equations obtaining here? Took a while to work this one out, but here goes, can ya follow the inexorable logic?

Elder Physics

$$(God)^2 - (Man)^2 = Art + life \times Art - life$$

    Also did a sketch of one of the crones passing for a nurse here, catching her expression of disgust when she caught me befouling my bed-clothes (not on purpose, believe me). When I'm not limning these figures, I worry about Jimmer and that new guy, Ferd, getting at my stuff. The other guy who used to breach my security has passed the baton on to Don Ferdinand. I know Jimmer has a key and I bet my month's Social Security that staff lets pillferin' Ferd in. So while my heart is not so content, Ferd can pillage to his heart's content. My safe's been totally wrecked, door jammed open by a vicious kick; no use getting another one. Hell, every time I return, I find items have gone missing: socks and underwear or CDs, but most often my blood pressure meds. Think I don't notice that ten or twenty tabs have gone bye-bye? They can't fool ol' Jerry! Think I don't know that they're a hot commodity in the home? Hell, in prison, the cons use cigarettes as legal tender — right? — here it's blood pressure meds. Benicar, the preferred coinage. I once saw Fred Fredererer and Rory McDuff playing Poker in our dayroom, using those little white B-tabs as chips. Rory was winning. Fred was whining. I've seen those pills used as markers in Backgammon, Monopoly, and Sorry at our "Games Night" in the Twilight Room.

    The scene described above reminded me of my son and daughter's incessant card games and the fact that the proportion of playing cards matches the golden section ratio. Here's a good place as any to treat you, Dear Reader, to some inside information. So draw this book closer to your snoz and be sure no one is watching you.

Elder Physics

When Jimmer and Leslie's level of serious card playing made it to Cribbage, Jeane and I eagerly joined the team. In Wisconsin's North Woods, Cribbage is serious shit. Every winter someone is killed in a drunken rule dispute. Hell, old Torvald Ekbery (hailing from Shawano) lost a hand to his wife, literally, when she took a kitchen knife to his cheatin' hand. I proposed to Jeane over one of our hard-fought games and we played Cribbage on our honeymoon, laughing lasciviously when referring to "salting the crib." But she played her final and best hand when she dumped me in Oceanside. In the North Woods, fortunes in pennies are won 'n lost over tap beer in the local watering holes (that was before monster sports TV screens). Or Sunday Mass missed after a game went into overtime. I can still see Uncle Don beating the pants off all comers, foul cigar smoke obscuring his hand. One of my most prized possessions is a handmade fish-shaped Cribbage board I got at a yard sale Rhinelander. Jimmer will inherit if Ferd doesn't steal it.

Jimmer plays Cribbage solo on his computer because — my son's one sad lament — his psychoanalyst wife hates cards. Has some psycho-babble reason why card-players are neurotics. Poor guy has hinted that he's actually looking forward to his stint in the elder home just so he can get back up to speed with his one-hand shuffle. Even if I get out of my hospital bed, in which I intolerably wrestle, in time, my mental focus is still too fluffy to sign up for our annual "Great Cribbage Showdown 'n Hoedown" in the Twilight Room next Friday. A card-players dream of a competition with a scores of tables set up, a roster of contenders, and so forth, followed by a real whoopeedy-doo Western dance where Western shirts hide marzipan, pale arms and all the ladies are fulgent in fluffy petticoats. Those screaming red, green, yellow, orange taffeta thingies all a-twirl like what's going on inside my confused cabeza. As I'm dead sure Hilaria will be dancing with Dirty Harry — deal me out!

Was right. Hilaria and Harry are a pair of magnets on the dance floor — electric, inseparable — as they kiss, the yarns of their body lines together thread. He mixes music with her thoughts and gladdens her with heavenly oughts.

The Official Critique

Mayday. Mayday. Usually the call for help by aviators, and what I yell into my phone if I need help. But today it really *is* May Day and I'm home from the hospital. Hurrah! One hundred dollars saved 'cause Jimmer demanded he be allowed to drive me home. Good ol' boy, he stood up for me. That's a month's worth of breakfasts at Al's between us.

Since my bladder infection has been shot down, I'm feeling like an Ace. I kind of "buzz the field," walkering-it around to let people know ol' crazy Gerald's about to land. Best way to prove I'm back in form — besides entertaining Jill Peaseblossom with my war stories — is to try my hand at the aesthetic and kinesthetic rigors of our art class. On my way, with my sketchbook, small canvas, and art box, I spot Eepie walking perkily toward the home office to hand in her latest column seconds before her deadline. Her fingers, quick and sure, play anxiously with three sheets of handwritten notebook paper. She places her feet with a meticulous precision, one after the other, in the same straight line, as though she were treading a knife edge between goodness only knows what invisible gulfs. At her age, how she manages that elder physics event anomaly mystifies me. Ill-Phil, perched in his usual seat, spies her too. The ease of others makes him ill at ease, so he gives forth a laugh with the loud and bell-mouthed cynicism of one who sees himself as a misunderstood and embittered Prometheus. "This body's a sewer!" he yells at her. She's too focused to acknowledge him with anything other than a laugh expressed on a descending chromatic scale.

In my last art class — must have been at least a month ago — our instructor pleaded for us not to enforce our tendencies toward insisting on putting militant Prussian Blue or goblin Cobalt or any kind of crayon bluing into the whimsical drawings of our yellow-sky happy grand-children who use any and all of the wax spectrum and remain untouched by Western verisimilitude. I can see why Jimmer likes her.

For once, I was prepared. Completed three very different sketches for an oil I propose to title *Portrait of the Artist's Heart Disease*. Don't know yet which version will out in the end: 1) a not too sympathetic portrait of Hilaria; 2) a very flattering portrait of Hilaria; or 3) a very Abstract Expressionist interpretation of a cross-section of a clogged artery. But given the degradation of my manual skills and concentration, and seeing what is appearing on the canvas before me today, I suspect the last version will win. Jimmer'll go nuts over it. Anything abstract. Always busting my chops over how my mechanical drawing skills neurotically repress the magic of my inner child. Inner child, hell! Inner monster's more like it. God, how I struggle just to keep the color inside the lines these days.

I sit before that frustrating canvas, brush moving uncertainly from palette to surface 'n back, tweaking that vermillion, dabbing cerulean blue, cleaning a brush — suffering a boom-box playing Melanie's latest purchase, a Punk-meets-Folk CD titled: *Love, Murder, and Mosquitoes* — when in walks . . . oh, what a time for him to visit! . . . in walks our Fearless Leader, clipboard in-hand and an arm band on saying OFFICIAL CRITIQUE. Self-righteous, arrogant, brazen, lord of the manor swagger. I watch closely for the physiognomic transition between "face" and "mask," as this shifty connoisseur makes his rounds. "A *Kunstforscher*", Jimmer calls him. Ah, that boy, he's like a caterpillar eating all that's put before him, can consume a hundred times his own mental weight every day. Other people's ideas, other people's knowledge — they're his food. Once devoured, he totally assimilates. Annexes without scruple or second thought impressions to be absorbed by his ravenous artistic unconscious like a stockpot tat is cooking its way toward cassoulet. Once I dreamt he stood, bound, on a pyramid of books, as a priest-librarian ripped into his chest with a knife *cum* bookmark; instead of blood, books and breviaries flowed from his opened breast. But I digress.

Fearless Leader announces (revealing the declarative aspect of his minor presence) he needs volunteers to work a concession he's thought up: a cottage industry performed in-house where residents can work off their rent by refilling toner cartridges for local businesses (the guy whose little storefront biz provided said service in our village committed suicide, so our Camp Commander spies a lucrative opportunity). "It'd be a thirty / seventy split," he offers. We know who'd get the short-end of that bargain. No hands go up.

So Fearless Leader abruptly changes the subject, directing his attention to our instructor: "A picture is a chemical combination of plastic form and spiritual significance, and the colors in painting are as responsive as flesh is to an amorous touch, am I not correct, Ms. Mercaptan? . . . Ms. Mercaptan?" He touches her lightly. She dubiously nods an affirmative. "O Captain, Mercaptan," he mockingly replies, saluting, twisting a line from Whitman used in the film *The Dead Poets Society* (Jill confided in me, he secretly calls our group "The Dead Artists' Society"). I'm drawn to "Mel," her green, limpid eyes, aquiline nose, her mouth full-lipped, but straight and unexpectedly wide. Her chin? Small, round, and firm; prominent cheek bones. Always wears artist's black.

Now our Fearless Leader plays art critic with sideline omniscience; moving around, raising his thumb, squinting, peering in close, licking his lips, tilting his head as if hair on one side is heavier, patting Patty Perlmutter's shoulder, he intently studies her masterpiece, *Woman on a Cosmic Background*, muttering: "Good, good, my lamb — what impasto! Intense passages of plasticity!" uttered in low, encouraging tones. Patty points to a passage of yellow goo in her composition and exclaims excitedly, "That's hyper-yellow, *hyper*." She widens her eyes and pushes her face forward towards him slightly. He quickly moves on to warmly clasp and shake hands with Jim-Bob Wheye, the only African-American in our class, hell, the only black dude in our home (except for Nutritious) not doing menial work. "Very strong! Very strong, indeed! The size, the manliness!" he encourages as his raised hands do pirouettes in the air.

He nods approvingly at Anna Csillag's seascape — sailboats caught in a squall, masts heeling seaward, the sky pewter, the sun frightened — which invites an *ekphrasis*. Imitating Clement Greenberg's famous ploy, our Leader turns his back to Anna's canvas, then abruptly faces it, purses his lips and observes: "These lines are irresistible, amazingly accurate, and final and, like lightning, illuminate the very center of things." But over Hilla's god-awful finger-painting, he just sadly lingers, eyes like bursting shells, strained in a transport of pain, and patronizingly blurts, "We *could* do better couldn't we? Couldn't we? A loud discordant squeal me thinks. Merely connotes Freud, inkblots. Yes? But maybe if one turned it upside down, in a certain light, with one's eyes closed . . ." Pats her consolingly while trying to mask a painfully repressed disgust. She offers magniloquent apologies, ending with a nervous, 'I'm vvvery sorry, really, vvvery sorry, bbbbut I can't help it, can I?" As tears form in her left eye. "At first we pass time painting," Fearless Leader continues, "then time passes us," trying to console her with a cruel truism.

When he comes to me, to the recently declared Ace, . . . he . . . he . . . he . . . *laughs*! Just laughs. He vacuum cleans my heart with that laugh. That demonic chuckle. Walks over to Ms. Mercaptan and they exchange muted words, both glancing over at me in between nods and lip movements. Probably calling me a miserable little whiner. Or, between them, spelling out D-E-M-E-N-T-I-A, silently mouthing the word, thinking I won't understand what's going on. Insinuations. Plans I'm not supposed to be clued in to. Tests from Minnesota to be taken. Protocols to be enacted, on the spur of the moment if necessary. Experts to be consulted. A finer straining of my feces for analysis by gas chromatography or electron microscope. A secret CAT scan, maybe, as I sit oblivious, face toward the computer. Up the dosage of godknowswhat in my orange juice? Or get Ferd to tail me. Lay me out on Mac's tartan? Certainly, conferences with a colluding Jim. Ho! Cunning and dangerous creatures all. RAT-A-TAT-RUMBLE-SPLAT! Enough to make a guy paranoid at that. Make that little brain inside my brain go through hoops. Hoop-dee-doo! *Wheels-within-wheels.*

"This, indeed, was a pleasure," reports Fearless Leader, completing his critique, straightening up, nursing a weak back. He closes the show with grand, smirking, sweeping gestures, bowing, but only manages to reveal a nacreous scalp thinly mantled with long damp creepers of brown hair. Thinks the length makes him hip 'n cool in the eyes of the Baby Boomers who are these days putting their parents in here in droves. But we all laugh at him behind his back.

He, I suppose, returns to his office, the universe around him arranging itself in a pattern like iron filings round a magnet. Probably goes right to his phone to arrange another visiting speaker with a Litt. D., D.C.L., L.L.D., PhD., or F.F.A. degree after his or her name for our writing club or ceramics studio, but more likely he's spooking up some pencil-neck to come and try to get us to invest in this or that stock, take this or that supplemental health insurance, or get us to turn our life-savings over to some company who'll, in turn, provide for us until we kick and they keep the balance.

Penn and Teller

Every ego enclosed within itself, each one revealing itself to every other one in its utterances. A pithy insight by some nineteenth-century German historian who only came to my sons's attention 'cayse he was born in Pomerania, the same area as his great-grandfather. Accurately describes our social dynamic here. It validates my *emic* probe, running around with my digital recorder around my "turkey neck" (hidden in under my grey turtleneck). Turkey, turtle — one might imagine I'm morphing into some kind of hybrid animal, heh?

Society's key mode of revealing utterance are the arts, literary and visual. *N'est pas*? Damnbetcha! Why our home supports programs in these areas — and are *fun* to participate in (when not marred by Fearless Leader's kibbitzing or kind Jimmer turning into a more cynical Jammer). And why I write — to make life and my history in it make sense, like the letters of a word do.

So continuing my exposition of such programs here, I must pick up pen and paper to describe yet another momentous monthly art event here.

I call them "Penn" and "Teller" after that wacky pair of popular magicians delighting audiences in Las Vegas. But their real names are Roy and Karin. Roy is tall, imposing, authoritative in a gentle way, like Penn. Karin is short, thin, a bit nervous, and orbits around Roy, like Teller. Roy, like Penn, is effusive, but his tones are soft; Karin, like Teller, is more laconic, her voice crisp. In both instances, the effect is of maximum contrast. In both cases, we see magic performed and tricks learned.

Roy and Karin are Emeritus professors at the School where Jimmer teaches. Kind of heart and in need of an audience, they donate time to come demonstrate printmaking techniques — woodcut and monotype — that are not beyond the capabilities of our art club's physical resources and elder-understanding. gentle giant with a white beard and massive wave of white hair, Roy, exudes both authority and kindness in a seemingly impossible hybridization. A pillar of wisdom, he encourages us to view our artmaking as a deepening of our "I" as an expression of life, activity, and energy. Concepts that seem to be fast slipping away from us elder-folk. He reminds us that the first monotype printers were Neolithic cave dwellers who pigmented their hands and pressed them to

stone walls. Not unlike one of our dwellers here — she will
remain unnamed — who mashes food on her palms and presses
'em onto our dining room's walls.

I tell Roy about son Jimmer
once inking the flat, but flawed,
base of Nabisco short-bread
cookies and pressing them onto
paper, forming a grid array of
comparisons of shapes that looked
uncannily like tonally reversed
Ink Blot tests. Much to my
surprise, he GETS IT!

Okay. It's an October
Saturday. Exactly fifty-six
degrees outside (I checked). The
topic this month is monotypes.
Roy, waxing poetic, sits on a long
work table in our art room, stating his favorite home-brewed
Zen koan concerning the fruit of our labors: "The blossom is
the real maturity, the fruit, only the chaotic covering." By
this he cautions us not to overwork our images after the
fact, stay close to our original inspiration. In simple
terms: KEEP IT FOCUSED 'N SIMPLE, FOLKS. Brilliant, huh?
Let me shoot you another bit of Roy's wisdom (captured via
my small digital recorder): "A great artwork is strange
enough to present a problem, yet familiar enough to be
fundamentally intelligible." I later take that gem back to
my room, meditate on it (if a dementia sufferer can call
that activity meditating) for hours. Tell Jimmer about it
too. Yep, I learn, upon discussing THAT ONE, he and I are on
the same page.

But I digress. Throughout Roy's pedagogical performance, Karin, is nodding affirmatives, turning her sharp
eyes from us to Roy and back again. A gesture that says she
agrees with it, while emphasizing we should pay strict
attention to these matters too. She goes on to open before
our eager eyes a book — *Monotype: Mediums and Methods for
Painterly Printmaking* (now in paperback!) — and points to
specific examples. "See?" We learn we can do some amazing
things using Plexiglass or even cardboard as our printing
plate — and we can do either additive or subtractive
approaches in ways that don't overtax arthritic hands or
seeping mental faculties. The fact that our mentors are only
a few years younger than us makes us more receptive to their
ideas. So popular have their presentations become, the
"Knit-Wits" knitting club attends just to sit in around the
periphery and knit with curious eyes darting up 'n down,
ears wide open, a hint of drool here and there.

Ill-Phil stumbles in, but is so transfixed by the
words and images, he screams, "I'm gonna shut da fuck up!"
And he does! Sits quiet for a whole hour, does he.

I'm telling you all this not to brag about rubbing
shoulders with greatness, but to honor Roy's memory. He
passed last week. Our art room is still draped in black. Our
grieving class uses black as a theme in a series of monotypes and redact them into a handsome "Genial Giant" portfolio to give to Karin to show our gratitude and encourage

her to continue our lessons. Both will remain in our hearts forever. Eppie pens 'n tells a touching tribute, "Royal Roy," in her column, praising him for "the non-methodical character of his brilliant ideas and bold syntheses." (Ah, Eepie!) Surprisingly, even our Fearless "Steer-the-Course" Leader seems diverted from his usual monomaniacal focus by our home's sad loss, for his mask dropped and I could see his face.

As some species of elder-commotion in the hallway outside pounds my auditory canal, I scan the fruits of my poor penmanship and muse: *Will Jimmer think it brilliant, or Jammer shame me for being over sentimental? Will Fialta fume, or Bondo beam?*

Stickin' It To Ol' Jammer

Saturday. Slow-breakfast in our dining room. My table is bused by an older Czech woman suffering scarlet blotches which appear from the neckline of her blouse and creep up her throat as she bends for my plate. She avoids eye contact, either her gaze remains fixed on the floor or she looks right through me as if I was not there. She flits back to the kitchen with mincing steps. I can't help but overhear Fred Fredererer at an adjoining table telling his table-mate about the day in May 1944 when two Thunderbolt fighters, in a mock dog-fight, collided and crashed into a lake at Somerleyton, England. He'd Oogled the crash online and to his surprise found out that, forty years later, the aircraft and pilots' remains were finally recovered. I lean into their conversation with a pun, "The closest shave we had on a mission occurred that very May over Wihelmshaven." Fred, smiles, returns like for like, "The stinkiest situation we got into was over Schweinfurt."

Important lecture in the Sunshine Room at noon: "Inheriting Wisdom: the Legacy Conversation." Us old farts (with walkers) and our kids (with laptops) attending. I attend. Jammer doesn't. The young suit addressing us seems too happy, like he's just come into his legacy. Just beams as he scans his audience. Tosses a kiss toward our Fearless Leader who has just introduced him. He begins dramatically, "From shirtsleeves to shirtsleeves in three generations is no longer the driving assumption in wealth transfer!" He pauses. Before he can amplify on this statement, I stand up. I scowl and spout out, "Where there's a will there's a way, or rather, where there's a way there's a will." I walk out. People are staring. Our Fearless Leader gives a moue of sulky disgruntlement. Fuck 'em. *From my shirtsleeves to Jammer's Armani suit*, I silently mutter; *the kid's screwing me. Legacy, hell. He's a highwayman.* I rush (a relative term) back up to my safe-house on the third floor to put a chair firmly against the door. I pace the room in a huff. Forlorn, I fart.

My only comfort is a firm knowledge of my world and its heavens above me: one more floor of suffering humanity, then a floor of (on weekends) empty offices, then a radio studio stuffed with verbose Polaks, next the flat roof, a huge radio antenna on it and, above that, an airliner approaching O'Hare and, finally, two or three hundred light-years away, a star of the fourth magnitude. Below is the Assisted Living floor. Interconnecting them all — those *wheels-within-wheels*.

Elder Physics

Down there below, people sport necks that look like dried roots; they're more child than adult. It's a place of burps 'n spills and purple pills; people pissing into their catheters. Children shouldn't have to see their parents in a place where the paramedics practically have a branch office. But this is our world now I can't get away from it. I complain to Jammer to move my aching bones in with him and his wife, but no go. His wife nixes it — so I'm stuck here. I tell Jill, "If I have more than a father's interest, Jammer has more than a son's indifference." Which reminds me, must give that cheatin' son o' mine a piece of my mind at our next Wednesday-at-Al's breakfast. Or better, just file charges of elder abuse on him at that government agency on the fifth floor — "The Firth of Fifth" — if I can remember to do it on Tuesday (closed Mondays). The Firth of Fifth? I call it such as the robust fellow who heads the fifth-floor Elder Complaints Department, Dirk Scrymgeour, is a transplant from Edinburgh. A bonnie lad, he'll stick it to Jammer! Dirk the boy in the ribs, he will. Jammer'll be haunted by social agents ("Fifth-Floorists) until he screams EEENOUGH! and I get my money and life back.

After getting bored thinking *revenge*, and becoming becalmed by an inspirational homily by EWTN's Mother Angelica — who reminds me of my dear mother — I walker-it down the hall to Hempel's as ol' Hemp never attends these stupid lectures. Sure to be in. His factotum answers the door and gives me a surgical mask, as even a nasty cold could take Hemp from us. His inclination to infection is inversely proportional to his infectious stories, which he never runs out of. (Just like me!) We can entertain each other for hours and bore his paid-help to no end. That's what I call a win-win Situation!

We exchange knowledge about cataracts and the best surgical procedures to remedy such. I tell him about my "floaters," the various aerial formations they fly in, he discourses on his macular degeneration. I brag I can still pole-vault out of bed in the morning; he pitifully relates his thing just hangs there between his legs, discolored, like a relic of some long-dead saint in an Italian church. He burps. I belch. (There *is* a subtle difference between them as attested to by connoisseurs, read the literature.) He says the mind is a place for reflection, I say it's also a place of suffering; a kind of dark hole full of words, but not kind words. We keep this up until supper time. Then we peek at the weekly menu. Chicken-fried steak! Which we *love* — if it's done right. Hemp and I are *on the same page* as we make our way down that depressing urine-vapored hallway (I imagine hands reaching through it's walls, blindly groping us) and stare at each other, multiplied to infinity in the mirrored lift.

Next a.m., it's the same old, same old: open my sleep-crusted eyes, take a breath, wet my cracked lips, tongue that night-dryness out of my mouth, clear my throat, spit any Biotene Dry Mouth chewing gum I forgot to remove into an already used tissue, fart prodigiously, and wonder that I made it through another night to miraculously awake at the Upping Arms Elder Home rather than at St. Peter's Gate. Another day Jimmer won't be able to give out a huge sigh of relief. Hell, you'd think he'd enjoy having all this power over me, enjoy having a clear run with his hidden motives and want to maintain my Situation forever. Why I hold so much close to my vest, don't want to give too much away. Information is power, about all the power I can muster these days. I don't tell Jimmer half the shit that happens here or what I'm thinking, at least directly I don't. He can only glean it indirectly from my notebook. Why he says he only knows me through "knowledge by description," rather than "knowledge by acquaintance,." mumbling something about a philosopher named Bertrand Russell.

Elder Physics

I fight thoughts as black as a post-Pepto-Bismol-shit. I notice my legs are quite swollen, like water-logged tree limbs skinny-dipping in a North Woods lake. I force myself up on wobbly pegs to make my way to the bathroom for an exchange of gazes with my *Doppelgänger*. He seems about as expected, only his 'stache needs trimming. A noisy clearing of bladder 'n bowels, after which I take that scissors (I promised I'd tell you more about this) and cut the thick, long brown things into sewerable-size portions, otherwise pipes get jammed. After flushing, it's ear to the wall, to hear them gathering specimens for analysis. I suspect Jammer will have me cremated and, with Daithidh MacEochaidh playin' the pipes, flush me bonnie ashes down them sewer pipes.

Next, I shave, managing to nick myself only once. Bathroom business behind me, I munch a big chunk of corn bread topped with thick honey. Then open my Robin's egg blue pill organizer. Three rows of seven compartments with three pills each. Three doses three times per day of assorted colored tablets. Jimmer says it looks like a Minimalist artwork in miniature. Says he wants to photograph it, every time he comes over to restock my meds. (Poor guy had to sign a notarized document taking on this responsibility and absolving the elder home of any lawsuit, etcetera.) I can't seem to keep them straight any longer — what with all the thefts. And they charge an exorbitant rate for a staff nurse to knock on my door, walk in, and toss a tab or two in my mouth.

As my blood sugar starts rising as fast as the consumer price index, I feel my feistiness coming back. Always been a tad hypoglycemic. When I finally do kick, the poor attending physician will have a slew of possible reasons for my demise, starting from my feet up to my head. Why can't they just put *old age* and leave it at that? Or *served his sentence, time up*. Jimmer tends to prefer the latter; he's forever comparing supposed "free society" with prison, which, he says, hides the fact that everyday life *is* carceral: "The time man has spent in his brothers' prisons can now be measured in light years." Before I ended up in here, I might have given several well-argued objections to that. No longer.

Speaking of the justice system, I tune in TMC cable TV and up pops Sidney Toler's Charlie Chan character advising a wizened police chief (Number One Son intently watching on): *We also have been variously disturbed, chief. Concepts cross in mist. Perception is difficult. Volcanoes emit fire. Help is offered: refusably. Snakebite serum not prescribed for all. Before following directions leading in wrong direction, auxiliary forces may be summoned . . .* [Chief replies, scratching his neck in mystification] *Ahhh, ya might be right, Charlie.* Good ol' Charlie knew about those *wheels-within-wheels*.

Since I've been keeping a running commentary about my life here, things seem real and unreal at the same time. Jimmer says the authors of the theory book, *Data Trash*, call this simultaneous holding of contradictory feelings, *Spasm*, and say it's an important aspect of our postmodern condition. (Spasm, a term not unfamiliar to us elders.) Jimmer claims this is proof that I'm a "Complete Postmodern Man," a CPM. Sounds better than "old fart," huh? So I humor him. I add that to my appellation: Gerald R. Hugunin, CPM. Looks authoritative. Like I'm a member of some religious order — which has forever been my dream. I need this title. It helps stabilize my identity at a time when I'm finding it increasingly difficult to keep my tenses straight: past events seem vividly present, while present events hurry into oblivion. My feelings for my son alternate between calling him Jimmer and Jammer. Jimmer sees the glass half-full, Jammer sees it half-empty and worries he sees his future in my present Situation. (Now, there's a cheery thought!) Better get down for breakfast. Early birds get a pass on the piss-warm coffee and much faster service and they get to watch Rory McDuff spit into his coffee and mumble Bible verses.

I walker-it through our Hall of Sorrows to our watering hole. As I'm slowly eating my scrambled eggs alone at my usual table, I see Fearless Leader poke his head into the dining room. I'm sure he's keeping his wary eye on me. If one word had to describe him it'd be MICROMANAGEMENT. In his mind he's the dude who gives the orders and staff and us inmates gotta jump. When Jill showed initiative and compassion, suggesting one of our suffering bodies here would do better at another elder home better equipped to handle her mental problems, Fearless Leader had the maintenance Nazis carve her office down in size.

But today I notice a dramatic change in him; there appears a deep furrow between his eyes, eyes whose pupils are empty like the pinholes in Jimmer's lens-deprived camera. Yesterday, I overheard him and Jill talking about something called *wickednomics*, I think. I assumed it referred to Reaganomics, but when I asked Bondo about it, he said was actually *wikinomics* and that it had something to do about "collaboration," and that far more creativity, today, goes into the marketing of products than into the products themselves. Other than that he didn't know what the fuck it meant either. He did mention he saw a flyer on Jill's desk whose full-color cover image depicted many hands clasped with a rainbow in the distance and sporting the title *Wikinomics and the Future of Elder-Care*. Think that topic had something to do with our Leader's awful countenance today. *Wikinomics or Wickednomics or Wackynomics*, hell, anything that can produce *that* grim visage on our Camp Commander has my blessing.

My musings are abruptly interrupted by Fred Frederererererer (increasingly difficult to keep the reiterations of "er" in his name straight) choking on his onion bagel, frog-croaks shooting from his large mouth like bursts of flak over Ploesti. He grabs desperately at a small "good luck" crucifix made out of the crossbone of a frog's head slung on a chain around his neck. Staff swarm him like P-47 fighters to the rescue. Grabbing him, they put this aviator through the Heimlich manoeuvre, a defensive tactic during which, belching "Ach, ach," he escapes his enemy. I watch with a certain lead-plane detachment, but do sympathize. Bits of food can be as deadly as ack-ack.

Sometimes after a choking bout myself, the next meal I only see a firing squad lining up on my plate. Hemp told me he has to add a clear thickener to his water or it always goes down the wrong way. Reminds me of sad words dropping down from the Assisted Living floor and scaring the shit out of us "Independents" below: PITIFUL HELPLESSNESS, DEGRADATIONS, RIGIDLY-CONTROLLED ROUTINES, CLOSELY-WATCHED ACTIVITIES, FOLEY CATHETERS, UNPLEASANT CHORES, MOUTH DRIBBLES, BABY FOOD, BEDPANS. Our home's equivalent of Orwell's Room 101 extended to a whole floor, where DIGNITY is an unknown quality. All sequestered here know that our elder-world is divided into two very fluid classes: *The Independents* and *The Assisteds*. Jeez, when I get to that latter class, I'm requesting a real firing squad. Dress the fuckers with the rifles in Nazi uniforms; yours truly will don his old officers hat 'n jacket and pretend he's dying for Flag 'n Country. Go a hero. Make Jimmer proud.

Jimmer claims that all those new meds for heart disease, heart bypasses, angioplasty, aerobics, blah, blah, blah, have markedly reduced men's deaths by heart attack, so they're living (like me) way too far into *senile-hood*. To avoid "The Hood," he vociferously promotes a Neo-con approach to the problem. Prancing about my room, he declares his campaign slogan: "Have a heart! Death with dignity. Bring back the heart attack." Wants to put it on T-shirts, sweat shirts, bumper stickers. Sell 'em for profit. Claims that at seventy-five, he'll opt for a *laissez-faire* Reaganomics health program by going off his blood pressure and cholesterol meds and letting his physical economy do its own thing. After seeing his expression after seeing my expression of what I see in here . . . I believe him. Tell him given what occurs when I try to use my yogurt carton, I'm already into trickle-down economics. Now *that* gets a whopper of a laugh, justifying my existence for yet another day.

Old English, Latinate Roots, and a Prostate Problem

Checked my e-mail. I've been flamed again by Parkaboy (for my politics) and AcerbicAnna (for my sexism). Two unruly residents I've had issues with. On top of that, yet another bladder infection coming on. I can tell. Tiny changes magnify into big ones. That typical rusty metal taste in my mouth changes, after brushing, to that of a fifty-year-old Tootsie Pop. Futterneid Quotient up like a bull market, while my thought-processes are poor performers. Physical pep bottoming out. Bowels feel like novices are bowling down there. My pegs way beyond wobbly. Elder physics predicts a high probability of: 1) a future fall where a loud sonic boom of AAAAAAAHHHHHHH will fill space as I go ass over teakettle, or 2) an high-water aquatic incident where I won't be able to shut my tub's tap nor raise up out of my bath, lobster-stewing (a repeat of last month's elder event). Worse, it's raining hard outside. Luckily, not a sound from the bathroom — yet. No usual subtle tapping on my pipes. Rejoicing, I let out a loud, smell-less fart. Struggling, I grab the phone and weakly order my breakfast up. Waiting for my chow, I sit up in bed, take up my notebook with its long list of figures.

Yesterday, when manic, I prowled the Assisted Living floor, taking note of each room number thereon. That night I put those numbers into a column of ascending figures which I then proceeded to add in my head with aid of a little trick (something I couldn't even hope to do today, given my woes):

200
201
202
203
204
205
206
207
208
209
210
211
212
213

94

```
                              214
                              215
                              216
                              217
                              218
                              219
                              220
                              221
                              222
                              223
                              224
                              225
                              226
                              227
                              228
                              229
                              230
                              231
                              232
                              233
                              234
                              235
                              236
                              237
                              238
                              239
                              240
                              241
                              242
                              243
                              244
                              245
                              246
                              247
                              248
                              249
                              250
```

To easily do the math, you count the number of rooms, which equals 51, multiply that by 200 equals 10,200. Then add up the first ten room numbers's last two digits (1 plus 2 plus 3 plus 4 plus 5 plus 6 plus 7 plus 8 plus 9, plus 10) which yields 55. Thereafter, just add 100 to each group of ten rooms: 155, 255, 355, 455.

     Now add it all up:

```
                         10,200
                             55
                            155
                            255
                            355
                    455
             ___________________
                     11,475 total
```

Add up each number within this total: 1 plus 1 plus 4 plus 7 plus 5 equals 18. *Q.E.D.*

     When you can measure something and express it in numbers, you know something about it. For instance, room 123's digits are factors adding to 6, the first "perfect" number! Now eighteen, which I take to indicate that on average every eighteen days one Assisted Floor resident is rushed out of here by paramedics, life withdrawn from our institution like savings from a bank. I plan to keep close

tabs on the ambulances arriving here over the next two
months to see if my theory holds empirically. If it does,
I'll insist Eepie publish my detailed findings as "The
Assisteds Floor Correlation Theorem" in her column under my
special *nom de mathématicien*, "G. R. Mathemagician."

Damn, if this won't knock our Fearless Leader off his heels! Then I might
get some respect around here. Get moved to a room with a better view, might
even have my own table at our watering hole and faster service at meals. I can
see it now, astonished residents approach me at my dining table and respectfully
place their forks before me in an elder home pastiche of that scene in the faculty
lunch room, in the film *A Beautiful Mind*, when mathematician John Nash is told
he's won the Nobel Prize. Why after that honor, Jimmer could get me lecture gigs
at prestigious institutions. The possibilities are endless. Unlike my life. But today
I feel closer to that end than to my endless possibilities.

To rush, to hurry, to fret — Old English and Latinate roots — soon apply
to my Situation. By the time Enid Wrecker from our kitchen delivers my breakfast-
in-bed, and my maid starts mopping my bathroom, I'm running a high fever,
becoming increasingly unintelligible. My mind's a whole tumble of nothing but
sparks of a particle of memory here 'n there. Lucky I ordered that meal, for in my
little space no one can hear you scream. The maid pushes the red emergency
button. As the residuum of drying mop strokes fan out across from my toilet seat
set, harried paramedics are loading this bloating hunk of decaying meat on a
gurney for a fast journey. (Hey, that rhymes!) Phone call goes out to Jimmer. Got
him on speed-dial. Forgot to take my notebook. Until my son can retrieve it, I'll
jot with a hospital-provided ballpoint on napkins, kinda like that "frog," Jean
Genet, who (Jimmer said) wrote a whole book on toilet paper while in prison. As
I'm being wheeled down the hall toward our freight elevator, I hear emanating
from Bondo's room (door open with cleaning staff inside) a constricted burst of
cartoon voices, a sudden crazed drawn-out hurricane-cackle of laugher and
crepitating music. Jeez, what a send-off!

I could just cut 'n paste my previous description of my last hospital stay,
so predictable are the hassles and routines. Life as boiler-plate. Jimmer says it's
like being extras in *Groundhog Day*, that movie where time repeats *ad nauseum*.
We both abhor a life devoid of those subtle delights which chance introduces,
giving off a furtive, but cheering light. Ah, Jimmer! A single kind word or pun from
him can divest me of the quality as a prisoner here and drape me in magnificent
tinsel. For instance, once I tried to get him to attend Mass with me. At this, I
feared he'd turn from Jimmer to Jammer, but his reply was unexpected: "Yes, if
at Church they would give us some Ale, and a pleasant fire our souls to regale .
. ." This from guy who recently confessed to me that "As a child I felt in my heart
two contradictory feelings, the horror of life and the ecstacy of life." Yes, with my
attentive son at my side, I can pass through my end of days like a sovereign. Why
once, seeing a cockroach crawling on my collar, he exclaimed: "I can see a beauty
climbing you." I meditated a whole week on the ambiguity of "beauty" in that line.

The docs say I get weaker each time these infections — they feel like a
hot, icy breath — settle in my southern regions. Given my enlarging prostate, they
will get more frequent. To correct the problem, they recommend a laser procedure
to open the urethra to improve urine flow. This will necessitate a foley catheter
insertion for a week. Jimmer says this is perfectly in tune with my "Complete
Postmodern Man" persona, and mentions something about the posthuman possi-

bilities of the cyborg, the avatar, and other such blather. Oftentimes, I can't follow my-son-the-theory-jock's locker room pep talks.

The procedure is to be done by a female urologist, Dr. Kiki Kaikai, who greeted me in a beige Yamamoto-style linen jacket and spoke with an almost offensive maturity. There was an eager, angelic waxiness about her nostrils as she explained the operation's discomforting aftermath, how it will divide my Situation from being an *Independent* to becoming an *Assisted* as I'll be moved to the dreaded second floor where, if I'm lucky, I *might* recover bladder control; but that prognosis is iffy at best.

If I'd known I was going to live this long, I'd have scarfed more Super-sized Happy Meals at McD's. But I try to be optimistic, tell myself, *Jerry, now you can more easily confirm your "Assisteds" Floor Correlation Theorem.* Jimmer says, "Dad, you're going to be pampered like in a high-class hotel 'n spa." Ah, one a rationalization, the other a gross exaggeration, like a TV ad. Bring it on. Can't be scarier than my nerve-shattering bombing missions over Hitler's Germany.

If pampering is what Jimmer desires *pour moi*, why has he not returned my beloved stamp albums, eight volumes of multicolored lickables from far-away domains and two thick ones of USA plate-blocks? Gummed treasures collected since grammar school (like Jeane with her postcards). I gave him his first stamp album; taught him how to spell *philatelist*, how to look up stamps in *The World Encyclopedia of Stamps,* a thick tome stuffed with tons of attractive images of the world's lickables, riff with oodles of information on the notable issues, the rare, valuable ones that'd make you cry with amazement and delight, and make you a friggin' millionaire overnight.

I once encouraged him to form a stamp club with his pimply teenage buddies and his younger sister. They'd spend hours working those little perforated gems with his professional stamp tongs into his fast-growing collection. Jimmer loved their multifarious colors, but really took to those nice triangular-shaped stamps from the Cape of Good Hope. He always had this *thing* about triangles, triadic relationships, the triangular device used to rack billiard balls, and he would draw cars with inverted triangular doors, and so forth. (Because I raised him Catholic? What with the Trinity and all?) Once he asked me why our native U.S. stamps were so visually dull (and they were, back in those Eisenhower days). I knew then and there the kid had a keen aesthetic sense.

about everything human? For instance, the three much-coveted *Huguenot-Walloon Tercentenary* issues (USA, 1924)commemorate our ancestors' crest's debut on this continent when they set foot in South Carolina, having sailed from Holland after being ignominiously expelled from France way back when! It's genealogically important for chrissake. The twit has probably sold 'em, lowest bidder take all, on e-Bay, violating our very famous Huguenot motto: *We'd rather DIE than be disgraced*. Weekly, I would drum that phrase into the kid and he'd nod his head and swear allegiance. Not convinced, I told him that, "Even if you don't believe, kneel down and pray, act as if you believe, and the belief will come by itself." No go.

And now, he's upped 'n sold all my precious stamps! Filthy lucre in exchange for world history, sacred family memories, and beauty. Leslie would be rolling over in her grave had she not been cremated. So the only thing I'm going to leave him in my will is the briny-scented, poop-flecked plunger under the bathroom sink and my accompanying scissors. He's already inherited my nutcake gene.

Strong gongs groaning as the guns boom in my *cabeza*, my emotions going to war over this philatelic fiasco. Jammer and I are often at cross purposes, perfectly symbolized by the fact he prefers his bowling shoes laced under, criss-crossing; *moi* prefers laced over, so the laces are parallel.

I silently raise my eyebrows like a silent movie villain, staring at mirror-self, and thinking evil thoughts. A new fall, a fresh swerve, a different configuration of turbulent elder forces, another set of formations, a different rate and sequence of decay and decline. Yep, someone up there doesn't like me, doesn't care for Mr. Wispy. A fitting disgrace, a disgraceful fall from independent living. I'm on my way to being a convict chained to my Situation. The future beckons with icy heat as though unsure of promises. Elder homely words from Keats keeps resounding: *Here, where men sit and hear each other groan.*

The time between moving from the *Independents* floor to the *Assisted* was accompanied by a grey November day of defeated smirr unrelieved by a decent downpour and will be graphically noted here by my favorite mode of punctuation, ellipses, in LARGE PRINT, as that glorious font-size makes every letter a soldier, the top of every "T" a rifle barrel, and all the periods bullet-holes.

... ...

... ...

... ...

Part II

Assisted Living

My Life Broken Down into Segments

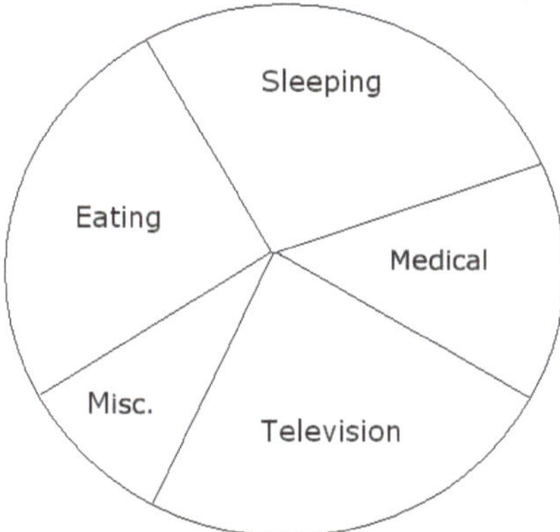

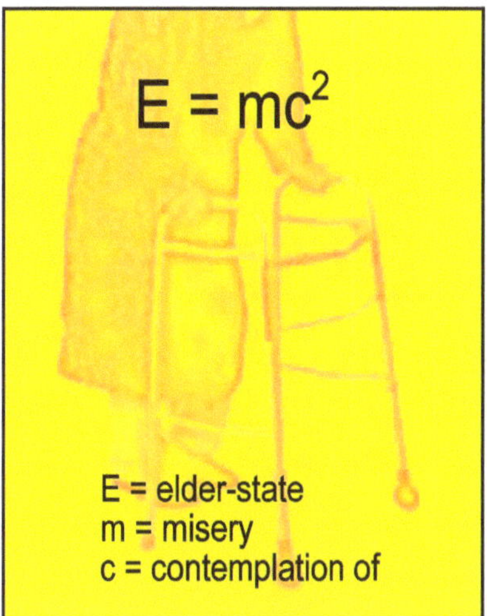

The consensus is that after the seventh generation one can no longer distinguish between history and myth. Given my Futterneid Quotient-rising situation, myth begins for me at the level of weeks, not generations. Is it fact or myth: that a gorgeous little Filipina from our Village's Human Resources, sporting a tomato-red shift, dispensed to this garrulous old man (*moi*) his annual flu shot last week? (Jimmer said to toss in French so people'll take this stuff seriously.)

Fact or myth: that I experienced a meaning too diffuse and melancholy when I noticed her beauty, freshness, the shortness of her red garment? Fact or myth: that Bondo McCracken (in a throaty Sambuca rasp in his southern accent that transforms certain words into certain other words) told us he was in Miami on a jag when thick black hair sprouted over the top button of a T-shirt declaiming BEER, IT ISN'T JUST FOR BREAKFAST ANYMORE (he's less hirsute now) and drank a weird Haitian cocktail, "Segretaria" (rum, pineapple juice, 'n bull's-blood, shaken with chipped ice 'n topped with rooster's testicles)? I do believe him, though, when he talks of snapped spines of lemon wedges, worms in the tequila, and roaches in the coffee? Alas, it's no myth that I will be acquiring an italicized identity, *An Assisted,* exemplifying an elder physics phenomenon: high probability of a self disengaged from the mass, invisible to most. Forgotten to society.

    Jimmer drives me to Oak Brook Urology for my high-tech roto-rootering job. The laser makes it easy and recovery time is quick. Jimmer sits in his car outside the clinic for the requisite three hours, reading an appropriate book: J. M. Coetzee's *Diary of a Bad Year*. Jimmer says he can identify with that South African's brand of *pessimistic quietistic anarchism*. When I emerge, I'm wired for effortless urine extraction, "Complete Postmodern Man," but I feel more like a Bagman. We return to the Upping Arms where my new room awaits, number 235 (a Fibonacci number sequence, 3 being the geometric mean twixt 2 'n 5). Henceforth, I am to be monitored, medicated, my urine bag drained periodically, and my foley catheter changed daily by nurses with rubber gloves. (I recall Ill-Phil's rant about rubber tubing.) Here all that is air melts into strange objects.

    In the myth of the founding of the state as per Thomas Hobbes, our descent into powerlessness, into being a subject of the state, was voluntary. But my descent into the powerlessness, of becoming *An Assisted*, is not so. The mark of my subjection is not my state's birth certificate, but the doctor's written orders and our elder home's medical treatment policies. What I notice after several days of my routine here is the acquired passivity of our second floor's population *vis-à-vis* our rulers. I am aware that I am being institutionalized to a greater degree than what I experienced upon initial residency in the home. One has only three options after coming here: placid servitude, open revolt, or a willed obscurity, an inner emigration into oneself. At first I choose open rebellion (much to the chagrin of staff, Jill, and Jimmer) but eventually settle down into the third path, keeping my complaints for my son's ears only. Safer that way. No more visits from our fuming Fearless Leader, garbed in his retro mustard-colored tweed jacket, threatening genital cuffs! But a private life is, to all intents and purposes, a thing of the past. Such common locutions as: "my body," my leg," "my eye," "my bladder," "my genitals," has become "our body," "our leg," "our eye," "our bladder," "our genitals." Care-staff jargon. One female nurse just asked me: "Gerald, how is *our* penis doing today?" All seems to be moving without me taking part in it. An elder entity, I'm a casual visitor in an alien world, plucked out of life's normal flow, in need of Flo-Max. Like quantum mechanics, one day I'm a wave, the next a particle. Lost the taste of own self.

    Like those particle-waves bustling about the nucleus, I'm never alone. Old folks with doddering intellect, poor eyesight, and arthritic hands orbit our floor. I survey my coevals here and note a high Grouchiness Quotient spurred on by a helpless bafflement about their arrow's trajectory toward the Final Target. Like me, they are simply too old and infirm to enjoy the proper fruits of their personal triumph. And we have to pay for the privilege: rent nearly doubles on this floor. Ah, my high point was soaring in that Cessna by myself with the blue Pacific at three o'clock. But was it worth all the sweat — just to end up here? I ask myself. What looks back at me in the mirror now shows a rapid slide of face, an elder physics dragging down my superficial *musculoaponeurotic* system. I notice a marked increase in hyperpigmented lentigines, liver spots. Had a squamous skin tumor carved out a month ago. Jimmer tries to cheer me, to jump-start my creativity, spark desire to keep pen-to-paper, finger to keyboard. That theory-jock pep talk again: "Hey Big Guy, keep the metaphoric spark one jump ahead of the decoding function. Once you're decoded, you're dead. Here's your big chance to take magic revenge on the world for declining to conform to your fantasies." How could I refuse that? So I struggle on to put pen to paper. Foot before foot. Keeping head in the clouds. Sipping piss-warm java.

Have to admit that at first I was relieved to be free from embarrassing accidents, letting my catheter drain away my troubles, but after a week my own muscles are still not back on the job. What? Their union on strike? So I remain on the foley as my urethra starts to get tender, tenderer, tendererer, then fuckin' sore. Incompetent reinsertions by nervous nurses didn't help either. What's a four-letter word for pain (besides *p-a-i-n*)? OUCH! As I was urinating, saw the stream turn from coward yellow to angry red. In a classic paradox of elder physics, the very procedure aimed at reducing my bladder infections, induces *more* infections because of the prolonged need for the catheter. Reiterated reinsertions result in reiterated infections, despite rubber gloves, alcohol, and sanitary-as-can-be-expected conditions. Depresses my immune system further. But I'm luckier than ancient Rupert. No virus. Hemp's nemesis. A virus wants to play world conqueror. Desires to take up residence in every warm-blooded body regardless of gender or ethnicity. Collateral damage — dead hosts — all too frequent. Count Hemp as one such. Two days after I started occupying room 235, he lost that Cosmic Chess Match with Ticktockman. Because Virus always gets White (the first move), by default Hemp got Black (could only react), and he had little to react with. I will miss him. His factotum informed me he died listening to Mendelssohn's "On Wings of Song," whose theme is the Earth-bound poet yearning to take flight, to become pure spirit.

Alas! There is now one less person around to whom the inner life of nineteenth-century man is not quite dead. Hell, the other day Jimmer took me to my HMO doc. As we sat for the usual forty-five minutes, we were entertained by the thudding, repetitive, mechanical music of today's youth. Used to be you'd be lulled by Vivaldi or Broadway songs. The Vivaldi puts your blood pressure down several notches. Now when the nurse takes mine, it's always up. A fluctuation rooted in music 'n mood.

June first. After my foley's changed this morning, got to thinking. Musing on Zeno's Paradox, the problem of the arrow in flight: the supposedly infinite number of steps the proverbial arrow takes to get to its target, such that it takes an infinite time to do so. Too bad *that* isn't true for the stages of my decline. But Isaac Newton foiled this when he invented a way of summing those infinite number of infinitesimal steps and reaching a finite total. Okay, so I'm feeling my *finiteness* today, experiencing those steps as getting longer not shorter. I'm accelerating at 32 feet-per-second-per-second toward a Situation change. A *major* change. Last week I snuck an EL ride downtown at rush hour (Jimmer chewed me out.) The train was jam-packed and I had to grab a strap, supported solely by the equalizing pressure of bodies on all sides; occasionally my elder bones were lifted right off planet Earth, floating upward as we traveled east at velocity (v) of 40 m.p.h. as the force of crowding (c) exceeded the force of gravity (g) by 6 percent. Don't be impressed, in elder physics, this is an easy calculation of a common event.

It's not only moving to the second floor and my deteriorating condition that's gotten me philosophical. Yesterday at a eat-love-for-breakfast-and-spit-out-the-seeds encounter, Fialta and I tangled. She couldn't see what evolutionary advantage it was for us to be creatures with insufficient intelligence to grasp the ultimate nature of things, yet be aware of that very insufficiency. A cruel cosmic joke she opined. Interesting thought: an intellectual apparatus marked by a conscious knowledge of its insufficiency. "Does that make us an evolutionary aberration?" she asked. "Aberration, yes, but, of course," I argued, "it is that very condition that propels us toward God." Yep, I can say this with straight face.

"God, schmod," she replied, "just a name used as a convenient bandage to cover a cosmic wound. H. L. Mencken, you know, once listed scores of names of gods once firmly believed in and now lost to the veils of time."

Despite her atheism, is among the smartest of our inmates. I get her to smile when I tell her, "You are equal to the idol who has given you your inspiration." Oh, I forgot to tell you, Fialta is not only the President, but the illustrious Founder of our Happy Scribbler's writers group. She writes poetry, mostly. Her latest? Clever title: "The Pleasures of a Good Comforter." Can only recall a choice tidbit from it, "softcore forlorn" or something like that. Her opposite number here is a stocky second-generation Czech whose name tag reads: Noreen Pogacnic. We call her the "Babushka-from-Berwyn." She, for forty years, waitressed at the locally famous Czech Plaza restaurant on Cermak Road. Ironically, Jimmer took me there for my first official dinner out when he dragged me back here three years ago. They do a liver dumpling soup rivaling what my mother used to make. Poor Noreen, thinks "Kyoto" is a misspelling of "Tokyo," and that the Russian generals Vassili Brekhunoff is always name-dropping "sit somewhere in the urinals." [i.e,. Urals, ed.]. Jill told me it's dyslexia masking a higher order of intellect. Jimmer says that's an inversion of my performance where intellect masks my high degree of craziness. For the record, I take offense at that.

Since we're on the topic of pecking orders, I need mention that within the classification of *The Assisteds*, we have three groups: *The Ambs* — ambulatory assisteds who can orbit the elder home at will; *The Semis* — those who are in wheelchairs and tend to spend most of the day close to the nucleus of their room and have their meals brought up; and *The Shuts* — those whom gravity keeps pinned to their bed. I'm an *Amb*. Most of us are *Ambs*. And the one thing that seems to distinguish us all from *The Independents* is that every Laird, Lass, and their blessed cat here has an opinion or two on *everything*.

In our little dayroom here, just blink and you're into a good lick of conversation with someone's head turned parrot-wise in your direction. After weeks and weeks of yakking about our catheters, bedpans, blood-pressure apparatus, oxygen tanks, heart monitors, speculi, electric-powered scooters, and miscellaneous whatnots making up the topology of our elderscape, these objects take on an occult quality worthy of the best Surrealist imagination. Jimmer says this stuff creeps him out, like a one-way ticket to Chicago's Museum of Surgical Science where all manner of medical oddments repel, yet attract, your attention.

Holy *Hoblovacky*

For a change, Jimmer and his wife take me out to beautiful downtown Berwyn's Czech Plaza eatery for a gut-stuffer of an "all-white dinner" (is that racist?): liver dumpling soup, white bread, veal cutlet, mashed potatoes, Sauerkraut, washed down with stein of Pilsner Urquel beer. The first time I've been brave enough to venture outside our hallowed halls with my urine bag firmly strapped to my left leg. Jim's been instructed on how to empty it. My fingers are too unskilled to do it without making a digital *faux pa,* spilling uric lemonade into my shoe. So self-conscious in public, I feel like a terrorist with a bomb strapped on and all eyes on *moi*. Not a good thing for one prone to a healthy paranoia.

We're lucky to find a parking spot on Cermak right in front of this famed local institution. Jimmer assists me out of his silver SUV and he and Marianne take places on each side of me for support (I've insisted on using only my four-legged cane). As we enter the restaurant,we pass a stocky working stiff hunched over the pay phone (you don't see many left these days) mumbling, "Allo Tony? That'll be four, six, three, for a fin." A substantial hostess in her middle-fifties seats us.

Jim's beloved, Marianne, says she loves the local color here. Used to eat lunch here while working at a mental health clinic in Berwyn, a "burb" of Chicago, home to zillions of Czech immigrants, but now its East European flavor is being diluted with Hispanic ingress. Menudo soup displacing liver dumpling soup every other block. Jimmer and I love both cuisines so it's win-win in Berwyn.

It's only five after five, but da place is jumpin'. Oily Boid Special Time. No one under fifty years or two hundred pounds here. Our thyroid blond waitress with a slight limp, sporting a clever T-shirt reading *Ich bin ein Berwyner*, gives us our menus while performing a huge howdy-do smile that reveals missing teeth. We look at those gaps in her smile — like alternating black 'n white keys on a piano — not at the menus. We know what were getting. Both Jimmer and I have Bohunk in our blood and our nostrils are flaring. Janáček's music is blaring. Marianne's blue eyes (she's of Russian descent) are staring. At the generous bowls of Borscht white-capped with dollops of sour cream displayed on an adjoining table surrounded by four retirees splayed in their chairs, huge guts preventing them easy access to their vittels. Taking cue from "M'est" — Jim's quaint *amornym* for his soulmate, hers for him is "J'est" — I ogle the iceberg-sized wedge of frosted white cake sailing by on a waitress's tray (it've sunk the Titanic). And whistle. She thinks I'm making a play for her and turns a cigarette-stained smile my way, wiggles 'n winks. I probably turn a Borscht-beet red. Stick my head back into my menu *post haste*. She reminds me of my Polish beauty, Hilaria. (That ain't funny.)

During our *My Dinner with Andre*-like conversation — Jim's screened it for me as a lesson on how our father-son chats might be improved — our thoughts turn to higher education. Now I don't recall how we get on to this topic, unless munching on Sauerkraut got us discussing the sour taste contemporary pedagogy gives us threesome.

"M'est" bemoans changes at her adored *Alma Mater,* the University of Chicago, where she claimed three degrees: "When the University felt it necessary to start a football team — my god a *football* team—I felt marooned." *[Editor's note: the football team is named "The Maroons."]* At this point, she emphatically spears a morsel of food and pops it in her mouth and glares at me.

I respond I once compared my Marquette University textbooks with those used in typical courses at the college level these days and was shocked to find my all-text textbooks now come stuffed full of illustrations, photos, charts, witty jibs, and larger type with shorter sentences composed from a vocabulary limited to three syllable words. Hell, my high school books were meatier. A B.S. degree back then was like an M.S. now. Now it's all (lowercase) b.s.

Jimmer winks at my pun, adds a complaint over "lowered expectations," "retention quotas," "writing-across-the-curriculum" fads, "grade inflation," and "intimeducation" (students and parents ragging on the professor until a grade goes up). Refers to these terrors of teacherly existence as: "Sickly signifiers of a sad elastic scholastic situation." A "no-indignity-left-behind" pedagogical environment engendered by "statistic-minded R.E.M.F.s" (Rear Echelon Motherfuckers). I take perverse pleasure in knowing *his* Situation *ain't too much more benign than mine*. (My alliteration, thank you, not Jimmer's.)

In each case, we agree, quality has been subordinated to a bean-counter's ethos. Jimmer envisions the new higher education may take the radical form of that New York City alternative, The Bruce High Quality Foundation University (just Oogle it for fun), or will have to move into people's homes and grant degrees for which the sole backing will be the names of the scholars who sign the certificates. Like Oregon's Flying University, a kind of post-pedagogy for tertiary education on the model of Plato and friends. Or that of (Jimmer, eyes twinkling) German artist-teacher *extraordinaire,* Joseph Beuys. Anyway, it'd sure keep the economic rationalists smiling and scratching and shaking their heads as if they'd been victimized by both dandruff and head-lice. Well, we can dream, can't we?

As we start our goluptious dessert, Jimmer (inspired by our Czech cuisine?) goes on to shock us with an episode from his never-to-be-published book, *Astounding Tales from Cacademia.* Allow me to sketch the main points. In "The Holocaust Augmentor, The Strange Case of Professor D.," he relates the firing, for "lack of collegiality," of a modern history professor who published a fat tome claiming, in an odd twist, that the unconscionable deaths in the Holocaust had been purposely *under-reported*; the gist of this don's argument is that the several infamous death camps of historical record were only the tip of the iceberg, meaning that millions more victims were disposed of in top secret underground camps run by "Morlock-like" (think H. G. Wells here) camp guards drawn largely from inbred East European peasant populations. The historically-known camps were, in his estimation, only a clever distraction camouflaging the magnitude of the slaughter and the employment of non-Aryan camp personnel in the "Real Final Final Solution."

Jimmer said the don based his theory on having come into possession of a *never-before-seen* issue of *Vedem* (a youth-produced camp zine coming from inside Theresienstadt (Terezin) death camp near Prague. A cache of issues surfaced in the late 1960s and were published in Prague in 1995 as *We are All Children Just the Same*). Theresienstadt was a "show camp" for a separate Jewish city and parts of the camp appeared in many propaganda films so as to hide the horrors of the actual fate awaiting the Jews. But our don, touting "history-from-the-bottom-up," saw a *double* camouflage at work here as that newly uncovered text with its regular feature, "Rambles Around Terezin" by Petr Ginz, age 15, alludes to a secret entrance leading to a deep underground passage through which heavy truck traffic passed very late at night. As Petr was shipped to, and died in,

Auschwitz, he cannot testify to the authenticity of this supposedly "missing-issue-now-found." The three Czech editors of the original anthology did contest the authenticity of Professor D.'s find, challenging him to submit it to them for scrutiny, but their comments appeared in a Czech language publication. So either our weird don didn't see it, or couldn't read it, or declined to answer the charges, for nothing further can be found about this incident.

Neither Germany nor Eastern European countries (out of profound shame?), nor Israel (out of fear the new figures would just add fuel to the crap spewed by the Holocaust deniers?) responded when the book was published in limited edition by an obscure academic press in West Virginia ten years ago. Jimmer speculates that both parties (victimizer and victims) feared to come to the attack as to do so would'v most likely resulted in negative consequences for all concerned, not to mention pointing a hungry media toward an obvious nut job, best ignored. Luckily, this oddball academic, who had never attended a Dean's luncheon and gone only to one faculty meeting in three years, was now up for tenure, so he was easily ousted by majority vote (there was *one* dissenting vote!) on the specious collegiality issue without the real reason having to surface, without a Civil Liberties lawyer knocking on embarrassed administrators' doors.

Sounded like malarkey to me. So when I got back to the home, I Oogled the supposed professor's book, *Holes in the Historical Document*, and much to my surprise, found a copy at Powell's bookstore in Chicago. Next, a ZabaSearch of the prof's name brought up a guy listed as a proprietor of a franchised donut shop in Bluefield, West Virginia. This guy seems to have a thing for *holes.*

But I digress. Where were we? Oh yes, we were polishing off our *hoblo-vacky* — carpenter's curls, usually a Christmas dessert, but this place has them all year round — when in walks Quimper Quade (*Quawdeh* in proper German); we've dubbed him "Quimp") with (surprise, surprise) Hilla Horavath who's clad in her usual green Terylene slacks (she drives now that I've healed her).

Quimp's a new guy at the home who stalks around restless as a tiger with indigestion. Wears a narrow, myopic sort of cleverness — honed through many years of dead-heading on slow trains armed only with cheap novels — that matches his horn-rimmed glasses. What Hilla sees in him is a mystery as the guy has no sexual presence — *nada*; it's as if he's been sprayed with a neutering spray. But one person's poison is another's . . . well, you know. Hails from Pomerania. Germanic territory that was known as Prussia — *Pee-Russia* is how this *Erstge-borene*, first-born son-of-a-farmer, pronounces it — which always makes me think of my bladder. Retired from Amtrak after fifty *annī* (excuse the Latin, but the altar boy in me keeps peeking through) as a passenger-train engineer. His last decade was served on the route from Chicago to New Orleans. Yep, the song-worthy *City of New Orleans* route on the Illinois Central.

I introduce him to Jimmer as he used to ride Quimp's train back 'n forth between Chicago and Carbondale when teaching in Illinois's sweaty southern toe during the late eighties. Jimmer tells him he really got a kick from the drunks on the train coming up from "Naw'lins." Quimp 'fesses up he wasn't much soberer himself on those trips back to the Windy City. You can never tell when the dude's funnin' ya or serious. So we laugh, but wonder. . . .

Hilla gives me a big hug and whispers a smoker's rasping private thanks in my ear for my healing hands. She winks. They march on and get a table at the far end of the room. I later notice that they bolt down their food as if it might be whipped away at any moment (Quimp's stomach a globe, his lips a guillotine, his tongue a cleaver). Solitary eaters *à deux.*

Marianne elucidates upon some of her stranger clientele (no names, of course). One who is slightly autistic, married to an autistic. Their lovemaking like two machines put on autopilot. He's in therapy, as he puts it, "to learn how to better oil the machine." The telling of this choice case history is interrupted by our beaming waitress: "Here is your *check*," she emphatically announces, pronouncing "check" as if she was declaring her ethnicity to a skeptical census-taker. On our way out, we pay our bill to the massive Czech manning the cash register and wing our way back to my barracks, my furlough a brief one.

Doin' the Kerouac Yak

A heat advisory warning has gone out for the Chicago Metroland area for the next several days. Cooling centers have been set up in various areas. Be sure to check on your elderly neighbors. . . . So blares my radio — tuned to the Classical music station WFMT — as our Midwestern sun flares, putting on its executioner's scowl. Last night heat lightning flashed on the distance horizon, like the cogitations of God. According to Jill, several years ago hundreds of us elder-folk died of heat exhaustion and dehydration. So no one is allowed outside this geometric site of failing lives.

When you can't go outside, one's thoughts turn inward. . . . I'm not just any kind of animal. But a *Homo sapiens dementiens* if one is to believe the psych eval they do here (done by a woman who looked a helluva a lot like someone I talked to on the phone once). I do know for sure that my ideational faculties (up to now) were always evaluated as overdeveloped for someone from Northern Wisconsin. But were so at the expense of my animal self. As Jeane put it quite bluntly, telling Jimmer I was "a prude." And she added that my whole stance toward the known universe was "too wary, too defensive" for her taste and heart.

Nice things for a son to hear! So I had to tell him that his mother, before our engagement, seduced me on her family's davenport (after serving me deep-dish strudel) while her parents were visiting family in Davenport, Iowa (as a train engineer, her father got free family train passes). Lost my virginity. *I think*. Can't be sure. Depends on how you define that. But I did experience a *modality of consciousness* (Jimmer suggested this term) that Lucky Lindy must've felt: a matrix of impressions mixed with elation when he saw before him the French coast on his famous Transatlantic flight.

Now that I'm writing, being urged to find a language to describe our waning lives inside this place, and our fatal trajectory toward disembodied poetics, I think I have a new way to describe IT, that experience when time stops: I broke through the subject - verb - object linearity of conventional thought into a free prose I never knew was in me. (I can just see Jimmer smiling his approval over *that* shimmer of truth. By the way, my son said to mention the irony of this elder-author producing his juvenalia in his dotage.) But after marriage, discord and mismatch about intercourse: my Catholic beliefs prohibiting prophylactics, but Jeane's Protestantism permitting birth control. White

Since I've started writing these monologues, I feel more at ease thinking about such unpleasantries and discussing them with my son. He wants us to lay our cards out on the table. No more hands held close to the vest. And Jimmer is right, the written page can deliver a sharp paper cut to the old scar tissue inside us, re-opening old ill-healed wounds, therapeutically bleeding the patient. Jimmer says I'm often, for him anyway, a comedic figure when my strictly-held principles bump into that wall called reality. But then that bump just causes me to reflexively up my Vatic Quotient with even more strident ukases. Which then bump even harder against reality, which then . . . well you get the picture, until I'm raving, ranting, and striding my tall upset self back 'n forth before that thick, high wall. An unstoppable force confronting an immovable obstacle — this is how Jimmer describes my forty-year marriage — at which point comedy edges into tragedy and we get (according to my critic son) a stunning tragi-comedic performance acted out on the world stage. If you haven't already guessed, Jimmer/Jammer is (paradoxically) both my harshest and most sympathetic reviewer. Figure that! So, is he also held in thrall to that postmodern condition we earlier defined as *Spasm*? Or is it just par for the course in father-son relations? Or maybe I *am* paranoid.

Given the fact that *never never again* will I live my life, the Yin-Yang missing from my marriage is tragic. Those years of torrent and torment between heaven and hell can never be recovered. A deep melancholy seeps into my joints, paining them. No, instead, Jeane and I sat in separate chairs in front of the spanking brand new color television and watched *The Lawrence Welk Show* in silence. A musical program that bored Jimmer to no end. In fact, traumatized him so badly that (comically) when he finally got to Paris with his wife, he couldn't eat the welks on the seafood platter at the famous Café Procope located (appropriately) on Rue Ancienne Comédie (Oogled that on the Internet).

When I wasn't sitting silently, or snoring in my reclining chair, I was thunder-roaring, making the family quake in their boots. I *am* a loud person. Then we'd rush into jokes. As soon as our ease was threatened, humor was used to deflect deeper examination of our issues. Soon we'd be in good spirits, full of vim again. Ah, but something inside me wants to avoid these subjects; best not to haunt old sites only to come away mourning for chances lost.

Uncomically, Jimmer and I sit over coffee at Al's diner, lingering to digest our massive skillet breakfasts as the morning sun streams in upon the clean tiled floor recently mopped, and look into each other's eyes and think *never, never, never, never again* will this moment return. We don't have to *say* it; we grok it in our peepers. Nope, we don't live in a Nietzschean universe of Eternal Return. As my time runs out, we're cognizant of the uniqueness of this togetherness. Can't get angry with him when submerged on these run silent, run deep *tête-à-têtes* where no torpedoes launch between us as we periscope each other from across the sea of dishes from within our deeper selves. When my peephole is closed, will Jimmer ever be able to eat at Al's again? Might he fear a gruesome grieving ghost at table? Reversing the situation, I sure couldn't. I'd just drive by and salute.

"Happy Scribblers" club today. Good opportunity to sublimate dredged up trauma. Guest writer for this session teaches creative writing at DePaul University (M.F.A., The Jack Kerouac School of Disembodied Poetics, author of *Rewriting Your Thinking and Rethinking Your Writing*). Wears an interesting, sketchable face: a prodigiously long nose, crooked and inflammatory; full eyes, brilliant and acute, chin and cheeks, although wrinkled with age, broad, puffy, and double; yet ears so small as to seem almost absent. He ambles around our table in a gait at once advancing and tarrying, a strange mixture of both, giving each of us a Jack Kerouac thermos bottle, which I give to Jimmer.

Enlightens us numbskulls about S. S. S.: the creative juxtaposition of three registers — synaesthesia, synchronicity, and syncopation — in Jack Kerouac's *Visions of Cody*. I've heard of the three R's, but not the three S's. Fialta serves up raspberry cream cake to keep us in our chairs 'n our blood sugar up, as our lecturer plays a jazz CD, a big influence on Jack. Fialta bats a high-flying comment his way, noting, "The term *beat* means both down and out, and ecstatic, while retaining its musical significance in Kerouac's *oeuvre*." Claps of approval. A triple homer! Our visiting speaker beams approval her way as she touches home base. At the end of our meeting, so reluctant were the rest of us to chime in, the final score tallies: Fialta three, Us zero.

Informs us of a small press, *Dorothy, a Publishing Project*, devoted to women writers who "write with slightly different aesthetic sensibilities with equal wonderfulness," then he stands and bide us: "Farewell fictioneers, remember ol' Jackie K. wanted ya'll to tell your life-stories in your own way, whether it be within or against the constraints set by the real world. Storm the Reality Studio and retake the universe! And then we all would have something to read in our old age, instead of the cavilings of men-of-letters, yes? As that Lake Forest College-based Hungarian psychologist-boosterist for creative a-go-go, Csikszentmihalyi, put it — *obsessive perseverance* should be your writerly watch-word — so, jazz it up, kids! Hubba-hubba!" After *that*, our mouths remain open for five long seconds, at least. Thin, open-armed and waving, he makes a dramatic exit.

"The day of the great writer is gone forevermore," mutters Fialta into my left ear. Fialta — getting the last word in before we break for our late-afternoon naps, a filthy, evil light coming in through the Venetian blinds — takes a swipe at a few wilting poets in our gathering. "I'm prepared, when I read a poem, to be impressed by the use of an ampersand, but only if it's done by someone outside this group." All are silent, eyes cast down.

I am a *burble blear purple Lear on his moor of woes* — as Kerouac would have it — a *gnashy old flap* emerging from the Land of Nod, the weather in my brain like a North Woods August storm. My thoughts come together in fragments like those I razor out of the large-type texts copped from our library, public words that I refunction to express a private self. Outside weather is curdling, only a trickle from gutters and drops from the overhanging trees after last night's deluge. Feels like my blood is spinning in the wrong direction. This morning, declines lead advances in key indices of my mental health. A turn of my head reveals the

sorry state of my room, a disorder mirroring the turbulence
in my noggin.

How I'd like to remain nestled in my room and guard my possessions as I've the got the feeling someone's been testing my door to see if it's locked or not. But my growling stomach combined with the extra charges to my bill when I order room service, forces me toward our elevators. I soldier on. Awkwardly make it out my door, which I double lock. I find I'm following Dagmar Müller-Karltreu down the hall into the lift, as she mumbles and pulls a roller-skate-mounted oxygen tank clad in a red knit pet sweater (thanks to our "Knit-Wits"). It's the closest the poor thing can get to walking her dead dachshund, "Herr Gobbles," now that she's on a forty-year chain-smoking downslope. Keeps her sense of humor about her though; ribs us about her incontrovertible body changes by declaring, "I put the *emphasis* in emphysema," while waving her nicotine-stained fingers for dramatic effect reminiscent of Grand Dames of English theatre. She's better off than Chet "The Usher" Cynwyd, whose throat cancer and subsequent laryngectomy made, like an usher's, his profession a hush; he's Hilla's silent partner for Bridge. The only thing he has going for him, besides his uncanny skill at cards and his odd perfumed aftershave, is an inviting saddle curve of his lips where long-dangled cigarettes have left their impression. The door of the elevator opens, Dagmar and I are greeted with a kind of hospital light that ain't hospitable. I get an idea for my writing.

As I come down the south elevator, Buddy MacDonald descends from the north. (We live on opposite ends of *The Assisteds* floor.) We land on the main floor simultaneously and approach each other head-on in elder-space as we make our way to the dining room. Buddy paddles at the air with loose-hinged hands and slaps the hallway carpeting with poorly controlled feet. I'm wielding my four-legged cane, advancing in spurts of baby steps. We are both strapped: Buddy with colostomy pouch, me with my urine bag. From the perspective of Jill's office window, as we pass, we must look like a parody of dueling gunslingers facing off. Our ammunition being our war stories, the contest seeing who can more quickly discharge a superior brand of bullshit at his opponent. I usually win because Buddy was strictly rear echelon during the Korean War. We carry our face-off to a mutual table, our dining room reeking of burnt toast. Poor Buddy's hands shake like a bartender making a drink for James Bond; they are both his and not his property to do with as his bids. More food ends up in Buddy's lap or on the table than in his mouth.
Ah, Buddy. Lemme give ya ye oldtime lowdown on this guy. Last night at dinner — liver 'n onions with a dollop of mashed rutabaga exuding a clear yellow-ish liquid similar to the stuff blisters are made of — Buddy had one helluva time unwrapping his dessert chocolate cupcakes (full of butter 'n frosted with butter frosting). Earlier, when applying his fork to his rocket salad, our table became a Green version of a Cape Canaveral launching.

Fialta — alternately talking and running her tongue beneath her upper lip like a cat beneath blankets, attacking any lingering rutabaga — leans over to me and comments *sotto voce* from the adjoining table that "a video-clip of these antics would go over big on YouTube." You see, her pet project here is to get our elder home to sponsor a ground-breaking ElderTube site, no one under sixty-five allowed, which would promote Grey Power, gerontic-porn, oral histories, legacy and medical information, reviews of elder care facilities, and what not.

I told her my son is always pointing out that his generation will want to make full use of Web 2.0 and social networking technologies during their "Golden Years" and so elder facilities better get up to speed if they want to be competitive for future clientele. I told her Jimmer claims bandwidth and life-span are growing exponentially in parallel. Fialta loved *that*. Now all this yak-yak over technology was further sparked by a lecture Jimmer and I and Fialta attended in the Sunshine Room last Saturday (sponsored by Apple) provocatively titled "The Technological Imagination: What Today's Children Can Teach Their Parents." The lecture was followed by a raffle for a new Apple iPad. Clever promotion, huh? Eepie won the prize (Fialta was terribly jealous as Eepie already had an iPhone). She told me she loves the iWork Pages "app" (that's tech-talk for application) which they thoughtfully included. Now she can do her column with ease.

Speaking of technology, my son urged me to fork out an extra monthly fee to get DVR service on my cable so I can record my favorite television shows. So no surprise that after breakfast I'm back up on the second floor, in my sparse room, moving through the stations of the stations, past "Airstrikes" on the History Channel, to bring up this morning's pre-recorded "Good Morning America" with its smiling, full-of-vim 'n hip heterosexual anchors chatting about global modes of thinking and being. Jimmer says that waking up in news America someday hence, he hopes to see a cable station bold enough to feature gay news anchors or at least cross-dressers smiling out at us. I tell him, "Dream on, chamelon!"

As I futz with the confusing buttons, erratic vital signs of the bipolar American economy and political scene stream across the screen. I see logos and smiling faces, and spotless kitchens blink like strobe lights before my eyes as I fast forward through commercials between segments with news anchors. Jimmer argues that these scenarios are more than just images, but metaphors for living and point to a way of life I can't fulfill on my income. I press PLAY and catch some political debate over healthcare and taxes. Convenient and attractive theatre, a species of Reality TV, in which we all can gratify our baser emotions: hatred, rancor, spite. And see how far we can up the "Abuse Quotient" on candidates.

I press FAST-FORWARD, halting on a book review segment featuring a soon-to-be-best-seller self-help book Oprah is touting: *Chasing the Perfect Cool: Life Doesn't Have to End at Sixty-Five*. The gist of the author's thesis is that most elderly folk victimize themselves by their persistent "Poorthink," a phenomena rooted in negative attitudes related to their traumatic experiences as children of the Great Depression. "They have suffered Economic Castration Anxiety rooted in a Mode of Production Failure," argues the author. At the opposite end, today's youth exude "Greedthink." Much healthier for the global economy, argues the author, citing Ayn Rand's *The Virtue of Selfishness*.

Come to think of it, Jeane, my ex-wife, would make the perfect poster-girl for Poorthink — nobody cheaper or more uncool. Kept the family in Sears & Roebuck clothes despite my salary raises. Jeez, according to Jimmer, she still cuts up junk mail ads into note-size scraps for her grocery lists, phone messages, etcetera, rather than drop a buck on Post-It notes even though she's squirreled away a cool million. When it came to food, she was particularly skimpy. Always combined left-overs into a weird mishmash. One night it might be bratwurst-rib-eye-bok choy combo, the next lamb stew chunks and Sauerkraut on pizza. The worst was the canned asparagus spears, drained of flavor like gum chewed by train engineers. Every meal preceded by the ritual green Jell-O embedded with pineapple and slices of olives squat-ting on a bed of week-old iceberg lettuce. Before my bedtime, she'd fix me my required Thorazine Sunshine cock-tail so I'd sleep soundly, literally soundly, as I snored at maximum volume, torturing the whole family. For all I know she coulda tiptoed out to meet that unneighborly neighbor-hood photographer or been handing out my old suits to beggars as I sawed logs.

After The Weather Channel's local report — cooler but muggy — I flip to live broadcasting, past "The View," past "Cops," past a History Channel special on "The Day It Rained Frogs," to a kid's station always running a marathon of old Warner Brothers cartoons in this time slot. I settle in with a mug of microwaved hot chocolate and a bowl of lemon Jell-O taken from breakfast. Propped up in bed, I pull pants legs up, massage my neuropathic pegs with Aloe Vera gel, while waxing nostalgic at the antics of Porky Pig. Jeez, I recall that Jimmer Hispanified that character's name to sound as *Porqué* Peeg; from short pants to jockstrap, he persisted in using that name while imitating *Porque*'s wacko stutter. In between memories, I glance at small piles of neglected clothes strewn about, which remind me of very sad, abandoned orphans, or those "Pagan Babies" we were forever trying to convert through our charity. "Pee-Again Babies," as Jimmer jammered the English tongue (I've always suspected he'd gotten a sliver of my granddad's Tourette genes.)

Our Hit 'n Pretty Miss

I'm on the second floor helping a new *Assisted* into her wheelchair when I hear about Miss Sandy DeSica. She's descended upon our home and got over half of us golfing in a little world made cunningly. She's a granddaughter of a long-dead River Forest-based *mafioso* spaghetti eater, so we assume she's doing penance for the sins of her family. She makes us laugh when she quotes her granddaddy's daily quip to *his boys*: "You breeng me back da moa-ny, hoan-ny."

Our home got a bequest to hire a college intern. So Jill hired this social work student from our local Dominican University for the Fall semester. Sandy looks like a Roman column standing there, firm and tall. She's got a smile wide as the Mississippi. A heart as big as Texas. The patience of Job. Yet a real eager beaver. A senior among seniors. I can see she's going to quickly become a surrogate daughter to some of us. Best yet, she lives among us, in Firth of Fifth territory, in room 515. Great number: symmetrical and adds up to 11, a prime number, no less!

Ever since the fifth grade she's been a devotee of the "Hit 'n Miss" miniature golf course at our local Kiddie-Land. So no surprise when she came up with a brilliant idea: turning our lounge area into a miniature course and letting us loose to enjoy what we are too infirm to do at a regular golf facility. She's devised easily laid out and negotiated obstacles and paths just like the real thing. So we very quickly agree that thing-at-hand will have to stand for a desired, but absent, object. Now every Wednesday afternoon the golf stuff comes out and so do we. Even our wheelchair-bound can participate. Morale is up several points and less inmates are remaining in their cells. I come up with a great name for our improvised facility, "The Upping Woods," honoring our home, Tiger Woods, and a type of golf club. To claps of mass approval, it's accepted, unanimously — well *almost*, Ill-Phil slams his cane against various objects and gives out his usual "Bah, humbug!" (Last Friday at the Stations of the Cross at St. Hilarius, during the "*Tantum Ergo*" an altar boy accidently stepped on his foot and, ergo, a tantrum.)

Just for the record, Jimmer has inherited my gift for naming things. There is a frail, multiplex relationship between labels and materiality and Jimmer has the gift of mapping that territory with a bulls-eye, right-on denomination, a uniquely orthogonal approach that proves how intellectually radioactive he is. Even his usually skeptical wife says Jimmer could launch a new career as a professional Namer, James the Namist. Once successfully argued his case to a lawyer that he name his cat *Tom Cat Sue* and his new sloop *Mitigating Circumstances*. Yep, I can see the ad copy now: *For a sawbuck or two he'll name your pet or newborn, your car or boat, your refrigerator or toaster, your cellphone or iPad, your summer vacation home or private lovenest, your new business or website, your tick or bad habit, the style of your gait, even your undiagnosed aliments.* Hell, the possibilities are endless. I mean when only eight he named his pet Malaysian turtle *Mullanezhi M N Neelakandan Namboothiri* ("M N" for short). When the poor thing died, I built a small pine wood coffin for it and Jimmer used his Deluxe Wood-Burning Kit to etch that mouthful-of-a-name on the cover.

The effect of this new game on our inmates here is immediate and dramatic. Bondo is ecstatic and has upped his gym routine, put on his boxing gloves and makes the rounds to his favorite oak trees twice daily. Eepie's added a roster of winners 'n losers to her column. Fialta and I put our heads together and try to calculate and plot ball trajectories. Vassili, our Russian madman, insists on hitting the ball with a rolled up newspaper. Dirty Harry works the sidelines, schmoozing the ladies. Brucine Bitters, although thrilled that our carpet is already green, complains about the interference from the hi-lo aspect of it on the accuracy of her prize putter. The "Knit-Wits" have knit cute covers for our golf clubs. Our writing group is using the game for writerly inspiration, one fellow already titling his story "The Unnatural," and hoping to sell movie rights to it. Noreen amazes all by consistently beating the pants off Bondo. And Ill-Phil? The Presence just picks up the ball and *flings* it hard (*throwing* implies a sense of skill and purpose) right through Jill's office window, uttering his mantra: "I would prefer not to."

Now that word has got around about our new miniature golf setup, disaffected residents at other nearby facilities are jumping ship and migrating our way. Speaking of new residents, last month we got our first set of twins in our elder home's long history. Tristessa and Essabetta Pursy. They're in their early eighties (librarians always look ill, but live forever). Tristessa being a life-time smoker, their appearance is less identical than in their shushing days of sour-faced spinsterhood. Now both look quite a bit like the forties actress, Marjorie Main, but much thinner. Thin women without much fantasy. Both sport large white beehive hairdos sprouting over faces marred by massive doses of rouge 'n lipstick. Inseparable — we call them "Double or Nothing" — you can always count on them carrying identical purses, little black bags studded with rhinestones.

Spinsters, they live inseparable as Siamese twins, except for some years apart during the Second World War when Tristessa goes into the WACs and Essabetta the WAVES. Both their sailor-fiancés (twins no less!) go down in the infamous *U.S.S. Indianapolis* incident near the end of the war. Thinking of their sweet lovers as shark bait, adding the trauma of long sisterly separation, on VJ Day they vow to ne'er part and seal their vow with a "Springbok" cocktail (½ creme de menthe, ½ amarula cream), while legal papers formalize their sisterly devotion. A year later they buy a Cicero-Illinois-brick-bungalow and never budge until, at age eighty-three, they can no longer adequately care for themselves. In their heyday, both were infamous librarians in local middle schools, fighting on the side of what they cleverly called "Enlightened Censorship." For instance, they are found knee-deep in the debates over *Catcher in the Rye.* "That book never got past our desks while we ruled the roost at our respective institutions," they brag to Hilla at our "Welcome Newbies" tea. As the twins sit ramrod-straight in high-backed chairs in front of me, it's hard to tell if the comments are coming from the chairs or the entities symbiotic with them.

Tristessa claims the last time they ever voted was when Truman defeated Dewey. Not clear whether it's a joke or god's fact. Probably, given our post-modern condition, both. Ill-Phil bitterly complains that under the new system all the detective novels have been concentrated into an array where wise-cracking female private eyes, beery detective inspectors, and genius-but-neurotic amateur sleuths all *indiscriminately* rub shoulders; where idiosyncratic hobbies bump against romantic dalliances and foreign adventure; where authors' mugshots on dust-jackets produce an *incongruous* line-up of rosy fresh mothers, catty intellectuals in glasses, sleek well-dressed advertising types, dryasdust, aca-demics, prim dyspeptic maiden aunts, and also-ran psychos with the Boston Strangler stare. As for me, seeing all those call numbers on the books' spines sends shivers of some delight up my spine. The new system reveals an anomaly: the most checked-out library book is *Teach Yourself the Ukulele*, yet no one here has such nor plays one! Figure that.

Since Jill has them tend our dinky in-house library, discombobulation gives way to a Dewey Decimal *retour d'ordre*. And now a plaque over the library's door reads: BIBLIOTHECA ELDERORUM. On the down side, the twins have a nose-dive effect on social gatherings. Upon entering, they exude what Bondo dubs "the librarian effect," a quiet descending upon us all of such density that it nearly stops the clocks. Yes, we've all been privy to that perspective regression toward a common vanishing point of misery easily read off their extreme faces. So prompt is their daily appearance in our midst, and our uneasy anticipation thereof, that Jim-Bob Wheye picks up on this phenomenon, cleverly denominating it: "Waiting for the Librarians." Clever 'cause only Jimmer and I (and the twins?) get that it's not mere description, but a play on the title of Jim-Bob's favorite J. M. Coetzee book, *Waiting for the Barbarians*. Insider information. Both Jimmer and I live-in-the-pages of our books. I mean, one minute I can be in my Spad battling a Fokker triplane over WWI France and then at a loud KNOCK at my door and POOF I'm back in a wet bed in a pair of dirty pyjamas. Ho! Jimmer and I trade in obscure references, junk bonds between ideas, risky investments in copped prose. The very stuff my son and I strive in cultivating in our portfolios and liquidate upon request. We are both quite radically idiosyncratic interpreters of the world, or in my son's inspired phrasing, "We are hermeneuts for hire."

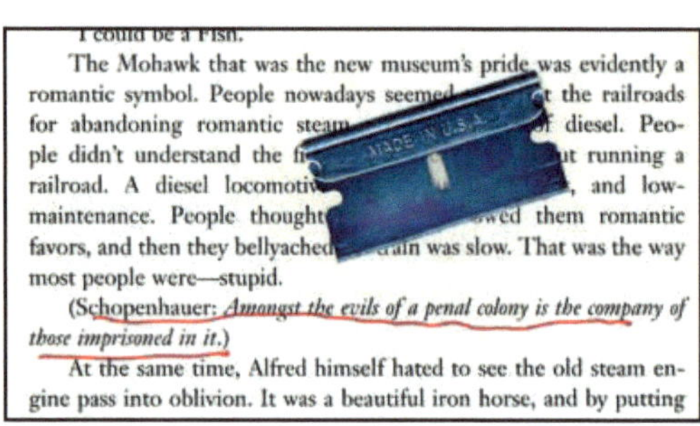

I could be a Fish.

The Mohawk that was the new museum's pride was evidently a romantic symbol. People nowadays seemed ___ the railroads for abandoning romantic steam ___ diesel. People didn't understand the f___ running a railroad. A diesel locomotiv___, and low-maintenance. People thought ___ them romantic favors, and then they bellyached ___ train was slow. That was the way most people were—stupid.

(Schopenhauer: *Amongst the evils of a penal colony is the company of those imprisoned in it.*)

At the same time, Alfred himself hated to see the old steam engine pass into oblivion. It was a beautiful iron horse, and by putting

I have a praxis for my theory; for instance, while perusing Jonathan Franzen's *The Corrections,* I razor out a keen textual fragment, an Arthur Schopenhauer quote I hope to refunction to further elucidate my life as suffered within our geronto-penal colony. But my Jimmer thinks it a too pessimistic, even nasty, assessment of my *compadres,* reminding me of Hemp's heft 'n wisdom. *Point well taken*, I think. So I acquiesce and drop it, *for now*. Being a bipolar kind of guy, I just like to keep my options open.

By the way, wielding a razorblade is *Verboten* here after a resident sliced his wrists, bloodying our LARGE PRINT copy of Philip Roth's depressing novel about old age, *Everyman*. So now it's electric razors only. Less chance a despondent respondent will hack away at sclerotic arteries or an upset spouse will run rampant, dousing the object of her ire with: "Analrapist!" (It really happened, but way before my time here.) Fearless Leader has repeatedly sent out letters to our children saying: SHOP NORELCO THIS HOLIDAY SEASON. The dude probably has stock in the damn company.

Me in the Eocene

The sounds emanating from behind the wall where my toilet sits have changed ever so subtly, indicating a shift change in the person plying their trade as my feces-gatherer. I oft wonder what they look like. Probably young. Doubt if *they* do the analyses. I see small packages sitting in the large wire MAIL OUT basket in our Head Nurse's office. Probably my waste going to some local lab. I had hoped my moving down a floor would complicate or even eliminate this fecal surveillance, but I was wrong. If anything, I'm sure they've stepped up procedures commensurate with my *Assisted* status.

Tune out the unpleasant noise by tuning in to WBEZ's new elder-hour program, "I Am — if I remember correctly — Are You?" A program aimed at benefitting our nation's growing Alzheimer population. The title, minus the qualifying statement, once denominated a Gay issues program, but the Neo-cons' attack on National Public Radio got it nixed. Jimmer complains of NPR's removal of jazz programming in favor of rock music commentaries, annoying music shows, and inspirational programming such as "This I Believe," believing they are just the beginning of a noxious dumbing-down of NPR that will only stop when ninety percent of its air-time devolves into conspiracy theory chit-chat and nut-job talk shows *à la* Fox News touting the First Amendment right to shoot illegal immigrants on sight. Refuses to support them any longer. So now sends his annual donation to WDCB, the College of DuPage FM station that plays heaps of jazz and folk music, and features "The Sports Doctor" chat show. I send my financial support to EWTN, of course, whenever I can smuggle out a donation under Jim's critical nose. Gotta send green backs as he's got the checkbook.

Elder Physics

Speaking about complaints and First Amendment Rights, I finally confront Jill about the violation of my fecal privacy. She just gently guides my abusive self toward our library and the Pursy Twins, thinking that if they can make clocks stop, maybe they can bring a halt to my stentorian manner, fist-pounding and finger-pointing. As usual, the Twins are meticulously labeling book spines. Jill, who is very grateful to them for donating their substantial home library to us (including *Three Tall Women,* Edward Albee's famous old age-probing play), whispers something into their huddled form. Essabetta quickly breaks the huddle and like a quarterback going into lineup, quickly shuffles over to one of the shelves, pulls down a tome, and hands it to me. In large Helvetica it says: *The Eocene: The Rise of the Thermal Maximum* by some obscure French scholar and recently translated. An erudite study of that important geological period as indicated in the title. A time when the Earth heated up and the first mammals appeared. I tuck the unwieldy tome under my walker's seat and rise in our lift (mirrored *ad infinitum*) to the occasion.

Once snugged down in my room, I prop the huge thing on my lap and start examining it. The pages thumb well. So I continue my textual autopsy. I find the cold scientific text, those dull paragraphs, an effective counter-irritant against my own obsessions; moreover, as my bewildered and suspicion-enraptured mind scans the series of remarkable colored plates, I feel transported into the abysses of our planetary past and, *voilà*, my cold assessment of my current situation warms up. Sympathetic magic worked by Jill and the peculiar twins. Frustrations deep in my psyche are released, like methane was during the Eocene when methane calthrates deep in the oceans melted, initiating global warming via a super-duper greenhouse effect (methane gas is more effective than carbon dioxide in performing this feat).

Jimmer and I share an interest in geology. Like many areas that Jimmer has taken a fancy to, I initiated the encounter. One Christmas I wrapped up a starter collection of minerals along with a small paperback with a big title: *Rocks and Minerals: A Guide to Minerals and Rocks, 400 Illustrations in Color*. When he opened his gift, his eyes popped. I still remember that. Seduced he was by the colorful rocks and their mysterious names. Image and language, still his bailiwick. Still has that damn book in his library as well as a smattering of gems decorating his bookshelves.

Anyway, next thing I know he's running all over the neighborhood accompanied by his best buddy, Kevin, smashing up rocks to see if he can find a geode; wants to witness one of nature's most fascinating internal secrets. What with my getting him seriously interested in anything with a hardcover (not a skirt): geology, short-wave radio, auto mechanics, model planes, marksmanship via pistol, rifle, bow, wilderness camping skills, photography, weight-training, coin and stamp collecting, bicycle-racing, and amateur astronomy — by the time he and Kevin are seniors in high school, they're both such over-the-top teenage polymaths that the girls avoid them like the plague and the boys beat their brains out at every opportunity. A real *Geek*.

Speaking of Geeks, Nutritious sees that I have potential in that regard. I just might be a good ROI, return-on-investment. She notes that I'm already a full-blown cyborg, what with this strapped-on foley catheter. No better time to get me up to speed in the digital age. During one of our novice sessions in the computer lab, she encourages me to Oogle my favorite dry, white wine, Sangiovese. I tell her when Jimmer buys me a bottle and we share, we are experiencing essentially the same somatic shock as Socrates. When the vintner's website comes up, the page invites me to learn how to pronounce the word correctly (*sahn-joh-VEH-seh*) and so am learning a foreign language, then I'm told how to set up a social gathering with my friends to taste various incarnations of this dry wine, how the wine is made and where, and how to expand my oenophilic knowledge. Moving on to the website for my favorite Serbian brand of plum brandy, Vuk Stefanovic Karadizic, it also provides product details. Next we up the ante, Oogling websites for information on testicular atrophy, cerebral palsy, hypertension, elder footcare, diabetes, deafness, sperm damage, and Alzheimer's. An annoying ad from DHL international delivery service pops up (I forgot to disable pop ups) aimed at the numbed pawns of reactionary false consciousness:

WE FEATURE TRACKABLE PACKING IN A NETWORK.
IF IT'S TOO DUMB TO KNOW WHERE IT IS AND WHAT TIME IT IS,
WE DON'T EVEN CALL THAT A PACKAGE.

Nutritious points out (I captured this on my iPod-recorder) how this expansion of knowledge enables a deeper, more intimate, multifarious interaction between myself and this desired object of my consumption. "We *are* information," she informs me. "You are not an object, but a process, not a noun, but a verb. You are merely a search-hit in the elderverse: you *are* a social security number, a driver's license or state I.D. card, a voter registration card, a stock portfolio, and a retirement plan. Withdraw those structures, Jerry, and you're just a sack of water and chemicals. We are a clocked trajectory from nonexistence to postexistence. You've grown from the infant state of research and development and you're now heading for obsolescence. Past your sell-by date. Fail to maintain the length of that trajectory by not attending to those structures and entropy sets in. For instance, take those awful state institutions for the indigent elderly, what I call *no-care* facilities, where the economically challenged are slowly turned into middens and refuse. Such places operate under two key managerial concepts: *Entropy requires no maintenance* and *Tomorrow composts today*."

Her frightening description of where my flesh 'n bones might end up sobers me into confessing my despair of ever mastering this hard-to-know cybershit before I go into the unknown-unknown. Too great a cognitive load for this withering brain. Her large brown eyes take pity on me as she toys with her plastic cigarette lighter — so oddly and grimly anonymous that it just had to be manufactured in some Chinese basement and then filled with smuggled butane — using the pause to gather her thoughts like clouds over a Wisconsin lake. Finally, she pockets the lighter and confesses in turn: "Jerry, I, well, ah, actually prefer my devices when they *don't* work properly; keeps me balanced on the edge of complexity 'n utter chaos." When my look conveys befuddlement, she adds, "Gotta keep my hacker edge sharp, ya know." I answer that if she lives past eighty-five (which is quite likely given her health-nut lifestyle) and ends up in a place like this, she'll *really* experience that razor's edge. I notice she calls me "Jerry" — not Gerald — must mean I'm her "cyberbud."

During a brats 'n sauerkraut lunch, I am chatting up Fred, our ex-B-24 pilot, and we get onto the topic of Howard Hughes. (Well, the guy inspired us both

during the days of our maximum testosterone levels and, apropos myself, he was
paranoid.) I tell Fred that when Hughes did his record-breaking 1938 round-the-
world trip in that sleek Lockheed Lodestar of his — it was in the record books
before it landed — upon returning, he parked his shimmering bird in the *exact*
spot it was moored prior to his take-off. Odd, but impressive. Something about
fighting entropy, I think. I could analogously relate my fighting the cold equations
of elder physics, attempting to remain a constant across space 'n time. Get it?
Don't want to part that dark curtain opening into the scary unknown-unknown,
and I'll bet the same thought crossed Howie's mind too. Ah, grist for my memoir.

     Fred Frederererererer (oh, you know who I mean) chal-
lenged me to circumnavigate our elder home's exterior in the
Can-DO spirit of eighty-nine year old Granny D who walkered
it across the USA: "Here, where they talk so much about
efficiency, usefulness, where they demand a sober, realistic
approach to things and events, what about suddenly doing
something absurd, Jerry, pulling off some trick of genius
and then just saying: That's your way and this is mine."
Offers to time me, but I must return to the precise starting
point. So I start to work out with Bondo, attend chair yoga.
     The first calm and sunny day this Fall, when staff
are out at lunch, out we go. I've emptied my urine bag and
stripped down my wheeled walker so I don't carry excess
weight. I put my vehicle into position facing due north.
Fred chalk marks the precise spot on the front sidewalk and
scrutinizes his Pulsar brand watch. "Go!" he yells and
brings his hand holding a white napkin abruptly down. With
that, I'm moving like a tap-dancer in a sack race, feet
going as close to supersonic as they can go within the cold
equations of elder physics, my torso in slow-motion, hands
gripping handle bars, my head facing ahead as if affixed to
a ship's prow. Devoid of casual logic, the only event of
speed is potential accident; thus obliquely, fear is com-
plicit in speed's seduction, the utter contingency of the
accident I'm tempting to happen. Eepie is covering the event
for her weekly column, snapping a shot at the start and the
finish on her new iPhone. Our home's circumference is one
block long north-south and half-a-block wide east-west, for
a three block total. (Yes, I can still add!)
     According to Fred's time-keeping, I circumnavigated
our brick monstrosity in eleven minutes and eleven seconds
flat. Both prime numbers! Like Hughes's feat, my feet have
gained a world record, I think. Surely I've reached the
limit of absolute speed (for a demented guy pushing a
walker) that is allowed in terms of the cruel constraints
imposed by elder physics. Fred and Eepie are shit-faced
impressed. But I know when all this comes out in Eepie's
next column and the administration here reads it, my Spruce
Goose is cooked. Jill will read me the riot act concerning
"dangerous and inappropriate behavior" and "being a bad
influence" on our residents. Hell, I think my achievement
will do much to boost morale here, like the Doolittle Raid
on Japan did during the dark days of the Pacific war. Give
our residents something to strive for, to say, "We ain't
dead yet, buster!"

Although this story will be praised within the fictional endeavors of our writing club, in reality, as it turns out, I end up punishing myself. Severe charley horses. I have a tendency to get them anyway because of my "water pill," furosemide, which keeps the swelling down in my legs, but depletes my potassium. Now they hit me like a *tsunami*. The pain twists my overworked pegs into figures that look like the curves I used to plot in analytical geometry. In relation to this intense pain, I'm wholly passive, helpless. In my delirium of hurts, I actually thought I had been shot down over Germany and was being tortured by Gestapo brutes. Lucky for me I'm on the assisted care floor. I get immediate attention. The cute Filipina nurse here gives me massive doses of potassium and finally RELIEF but, during the worst of the ordeal, I actually envied Christ his Passion (what Christians use as a gauge for absolute pain). They call Jimmer over to my bedside and he helps take my mind off the lingering soreness. Strokes my pride at my solo flight around the home, shares a few jokes. I tell him I forgive him for emptying out my bank account on account of his sweetness toward me today, that he can cash in on my sympathy. He just rolls his eyes. Ingrate!

Jill takes pity over my sufferings and never brings up the incident. She looks in with pleasant concern. She's sure I've learned my lesson the hard way — and she's right. But our Fearless Leader (who has taken to wearing a lab coat when he visits our floor) does pay me an impolite visit after Jimmer leaves. He just stares and stares at me, a stern look, clears his throat AAAAAAAAA-AAHHHRRRRMMMM and turns abruptly on his heels, storms out. Message received Mr. Warden, loud 'n clear.

Venning with Jimmer

I'm in the hospital again. Fell in my room. Head hit the TV tray I use for snacking when watching EWTN. Knee abrasions, scrapes along my left forearm. When I got to the emergency room for my MRI and so forth, they find I'm also suffering another bladder infection, which probably contributed to my weakness which made me susceptible to a nose dive. By the time my son gets to the ER, I look like I went twelve rounds with Muhammad Ali. Again I'm put through intake and given a room. Shortly after my son visits my hospital bed, some South Asian doctor pulls him aside for a huddle with the nurses. From the look on all their faces I know I'm gonna be here awhile. Probably in those damn restraints again too, 'cause I see Jimmer sign a form clipped to a clipboard.

There are times I do take pity on Jimmer. I am a high maintenance kind of guy, like a "muscle car" from the early seventies that's gone to shit and is in the shop every week for one thing or another. He does express amazement at how other elder caretakers who do the 8-to-5 step work-tango manage it. He's lucky his teaching schedule offers great flexibility, or I should say *I'm lucky* his schedule is so open for my benefit. Between getting irascible with staff, worrying about my condition, and thinking of the unknown-unknown, I often forget about how Jimmer must be suffering time constraints, worries about me, and maintaining his marriage on top of all this hassle. Sometimes I can see the strain on his face. To his credit, that's not too frequent. I can sense that he does enjoy opportunities to nurture me. He is a giving person, after all. Why I agreed to be the avatar for his *Gratuitous Giving* art project.

What I didn't see coming was that the doctor has recommended that my assisted living care be upped to more frequent room checks, taking the responsibility for my medications out of both my and Jimmer's hands and given to a nurse who arrives thrice daily to administer them with stern face. More costs upon more costs. Jimmer looks worried about the finances. He says that at one point my care needs will exceed what I can be given here (without hiring a round-the-clock live-in care-giver) and that it will be less expensive to just find another elder home geared to my special needs. He's Oogling the Net for one.

In the meantime, he's researching Veteran's Benefits that can supplement my income. As we soon find out, applying to the V.A. is a nightmare of bureaucratic intrigue worse than Kafka's nightmares. Poor Jimmer is swamped in paperwork. Triplicate this and that. Gets writer's cramp. You'd think one was applying to the C. I. A. or for an astronaut position. And when paperwork is sent in, more paperwork comes back. Then months of waiting (six to eight) before you even hear if you're even eligible. You're strictly warned not to call or write about your claim as the pencil necks in the paper mill simply replace your application to the bottom of the pile in retaliation for hassling them. The Presence, Ill-Phil, has called and cussed them out so often his application must have been sent to Mars as it's been three years since he's heard from them. Jill confided to Jimmer that often the V.A. benefits arrive a day or two just after the applicant has died. This way they can claim they've given out the benefit, but . . . aaahhh . . . poor guy just passed away too soon, sob, sob.

I'm on a heavy antibiotic bladder woes and it makes me woozy. I think they're giving me a little dose of sedative as I'm not eager to prance out of bed and work my way down the hall to freedom as usual. Not much to do here but listen to the ambient murmuring in the hall. So my mind wanders like that cute nurse I just glimpse meandering past my door every now and then. Reminds me it is better to be the object of desire than of pity.

Pity — I can see it in the eyes of even the most hardened doctors who poke their heads in here and gape at my carcass, an object in a state of inertia. *Inertia is a raw form of despair,* observed that French pilot-author, Saint-Exupéry, in one of his books. Funny that *that* quote should rise to consciousness now. Must have casually paged through his book in our library several weeks prior to my "Calamity Jerry Stunt" (as Eepie called it) and the words just *took* somehow as they applied to my own condition. Hell, might even be why I was so eager to pull off that damn circumnavigating walker stunt in the first place. Bet Jim's wife, the analyst, would like to roll out her Freudian divan and probe the unconscious motives at work here, huh?

7 a.m. — the no-frills nurse has just removed the stainless steel bedpan (which I've wickedly named "Pol Pot"). So I can watch TV now. "The Today Show"

is on and I strain my head upwards to gaze at the monitor crucified high on the wall. Can't get too creative with my body's position due to the IV stuck in my arm. Some too-cheery announcer is introducing a young, freaky-looking rock band to the screams of ill-dressed people on a New York sidewalk. Hell, all the music you hear is just electricity. I turn the volume down. After twenty minutes of watching the woes of the world scan across the raster, this ugly thought keeps popping into my head: *The world is sick, a lot sicker than those who bicker realize.* This plays like some Hari Krishna mantra — over 'n over in my *cabeza*.

According to Jimmer it ain't much better in "cacademia" with its perpetually changing "philofolly" of the month. Yet, somehow in the midst of all this global shit, miracles do happen: Les and Jimmer were born; a little child plays with a toy; a total stranger pays for someone's cancer treatment; someone gives their kidney to an ailing child; a student gives Jimmer a box of his favorite chocolates; a new musical composition is written; an eighty-year grandmother graduates college *magna cum laude* after winning a sexual harassment against the college president; a magnificent flower blossoms in Jim's wife's garden as her koi moil in the pond like pulsing flames; a plane crashes and all on board survive; a Black man is elected President; or a dishonest politico gets his just due. It's the little things that keep me soldiering on. And I think that holds for Jimmer too. Of course, our buoyant sense of humor keeps us afloat when things do capsize. For all the strife between us, JImmer 'n I, it's our shared **sense** of humor that melds us, a Venn diagram of overlapping circles. We are *on the same page.*

Jimmer has a very endearing way of mimicking this "Venning" between us: crossing his beautiful blue eyes. Funny kid. I can't do that well, but then neither can he wiggle his ears and nose like me. So it's a draw. If those two circles did completely overlap, we'd either make a full-blown clown and join the circus, or a full-blown psychotic and join the bug-house.

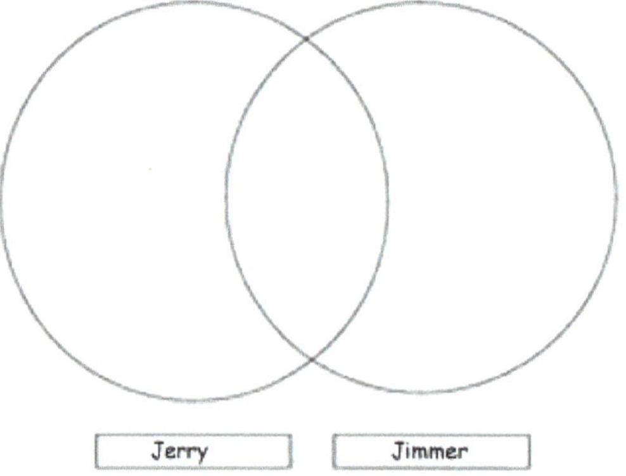

Speaking of Jimmer, in walks the boy with a big smile and pleasant surprise, Chinese take-out. Knows I hate the chow in here. Sweet 'n sour shrimp for me, Kung Pao chicken for him. We have a common language besides puns, tasty cuisine. I gave Jimmer his first cooking lessons. Walked him through how to spook up an egg 'n bacon breakfast on a cold morning. Demonstrated a different version (over-easy and medium, scrambled, poached, soft- and hard-boiled) every Saturday for several weeks; showed him how to slow-fry bacon (Wisconsin's famous Nueske's brand being the you-betcha-best) and do a thick steak medium-rare. And in the summer, the secrets to good barbecue (today his wife claims he's the best grillman she's ever known). Later, his college girl friend seduced him with unusual chicken recipes and soon he was hooked as a cook. Quiches to curry, chile to borscht, but shied away from desserts for some reason, preferring those store-bought Windmill cookies. After emptying white cartons of Sino-American cuisine, we open our fortune cookies. Mine is quite encouraging — albeit wishful thinking — and has my lucky prime number eleven on it (see next page).

> Your mentality is alert, practical and analytical.
>
> Lucky # 2, 11, 14, 30, 31, 34

Jimmer said he had good news and that's why he brought in the chow. I was being released tomorrow into his care. "So everything is fine?" I ask. "I didn't say that," says Jimmer, winking. It's days like this I don't regret fertilizing the egg that became this witty egghead.

Before he's off to teach his theory class, held in an infamously stuffy classroom, Jimmer leaves me with a pun and a challenge: "*Cogito argot sum*, dad; here's *[handing me a note]* a litany of academic jargon you might for wicked fun scatter throughout your narrative":

VEX, ROBUST, *APORIA, SINTHOME,*
FORCLUSION, DIREMPTION,
THICK DESCRIPTION

Stimulus: I tell him I'm often *vexed*, but nobody here, but for Bondo and staff, is *robust*. That *diremption* is what I think I get the day after eating mystery meat in our elder home, while *thick* describes why I have that pair of scissors on hand in the bathroom. Response: laughter.

After Jimmer leaves, I'm thrown back on my own devices which, not being robust, are pretty limited these days. Impatiently awaiting my parole on the following morn, I start to do skull-time, my memory taking its lead from the smell of baby gouda cheese emanating from Sid's bed. I forgot to mention I have a roommate, Sid Seide, separated by a white sliding curtain. His overly obese daughter just waddled in, giving him a festive (but contraindicated) sausage 'n cheese tray. He's in for *heart trouble* and I don't mean of the romantic kind, like mine. His stay here, unlike mine, is frozen in the Present-Indefinite.

That odor takes me back to my favorite crackers 'n cheese snack, washed with Hamm's beer — my staple diet during fall football season. I can see it all now: I would have two TVs on (our first color TV and a portable black 'n white), plus two portable radios with earbuds, so I could monitor several hard-fought contests simultaneously. I'd bounce excitedly on the sofa and — although I was largely oblivious of it — broadcast stentorian cheers, yells, and groans to all parts of our home. Yes, Jeane became a very annoyed sports widow each Fall and the kids would do a Chinese fire drill and evacuate to their friends' homes to watch their favorite TV programs.

Sadly, for this former athlete, Jimmer disliked most sports, especially team sports, but occasionally he'd sit in and munch popcorn and down a Coke and put up with a war story or my exploits on the gridiron. Usually it was Sunday or a holiday and Jeane would be baking a ham or a turkey and the smells of cooking flesh would mix with that of baby gouda cheese. Jeez, our holidays were always special and FUN. Everyone would be on their best behavior too, even me.

To this day, Jimmer has a special liking for that cheese. Leslie, however, opted for Laughing Cow cheese. I

121

think because of the name. She loved words. Ended up studying literature in college. Adored Gertrude Stein and dia-
graming sentences — even got Jimmer hot for her too. Both
were attending California State University, Northridge's
optimistic campus (its acronym is CSUN, pronounced *see'-
sun*). You see, Jim's stint in the Air Force put him four
years back in his education. Jimmer 'n Les even took some
classes together — literature, philosophy, and film studies
— if my memory serves me correctly. At home, they'd march
around and drive me nuts by reciting: *A rose is a rose is
rose* or *I am me because my little dog loves me* or some such
written by that portly scrivener. The prof teaching Les's
class actually knew Stein personally. Les got Jimmer deeper
into American literature, while in exchange he initiated her
into the art of fixing the shadow — photography.

It was touching to see siblings become so close intellectually and feed
intensely off each other — *symbolingiosis* — to coin a term. Hours were spent in
Les's tiny room (she had the better stereo) where they'd listen to acid rock or
jazz, sip Christian Brothers Cream Sherry or Novitiate Black Muscat (still Jimmer's
fav dessert wine) while sharing notes on a panoply of topics and exercising a
hermeneutics of suspicion the envy of paranoiacs everywhere.

I know that language bears the meaning of thought as a footprint
signifies the movement and effort of a body. So in trying to write about Leslie —
who was leery of the licentiousness of language as it was then being described by
licensed deconstructors — I find my words produce *both* revelation and con-
cealment. One word seems to also hide another. Or is it just the passage of time
and the weakening of my memory of her so she seems to become unreal?

Not so for Jimmer. Months after Les's passing at age forty-two — by that
time both siblings were serious writers — Jimmer still had his sister on speed-dial
so he could run a passage hot off the word-processor past her critical ear. Typing
in his studio, many times (he confessed) his index finger would involuntarily jump
from keyboard to speed-dial button only to pause in grief. This was a sentence
he'd have to resolve alone. Yes, her passing left a hole in our family large enough
to fly a formation of B-17s through. My faith has it that I will be with her again
when I go into the supposedly known unknown-unknown (as per Catholic
optimism). But one never knows for sure. Doubt nags like an unsatisfied wife.

Oilin' Up the Way-Back Machine

Hold your horses! Stop everything! *Achtung*! *Écoutez bien*! Several interesting events to chat about today.

First, I can hardly wait for Eepie's latest column to appear in our official
bulletin, *Armed 'n Ready.* She's doing a piece on "Grey Power" to be titled "Revo-
lutions That as Yet Have No Model." Clever, huh? She interviewed me when she
found out I'd been a union rep once, but other than saying we need more steel
and less equivocation in our dealings with our Fearless Leader, I could only gripe
about how in the US of A we've exchanged literal slavery for wage-slavery. Tired
Marxist stuff the Tea Party members in our home would tar 'n feather (or flame)
me for uttering. Too bad ol' Hemp kicked. He'd have oodles to say on the topic,

what with his utopian penchant for phalansteries 'n all. Hope Eepie's words have the power to make our Fearless Leader aspirate *his* food. Now that's doing things with words!

Second, yesterday our art class stormed our home's yellow bus (we call it "The Magic Bus") and bribed the driver with OxyContin tabs to venture east on the Ike Expressway, over the Chicago River, to Michigan Avenue and north up to the Art Institute of Chicago's twin lions. We were on a Vision Quest, to see a retrospective of, and hear a lecture on, Op Art, "What You See is What You Get." Op Art, you know, that abstraction movement of the sixties wherein intense patterning gives rise to optical sensations worse than my floaters. Special effects for the *cognoscenti.* "Merely Skinnerian stimulus-response meeting Clement Greenbergian formalism," pontificates my son, adding that "the artworks are empty incarnations of inauthentic feeling." Ouch! No wonder he wears a bullet-proof vest at art openings.

We piled out of the Magic Bus hobbling up the steps, some of us using the wheelchair ramp, and formed a single line leading to the lecture hall. A burly Black museum guard gave us a dark guarded look. Given the GO signal, we awkwardly made out way to our seats in the Museum's Fullerton Hall. Soon the show's curator — a myopic fellow from the Met in New York, assisted by thick-lensed glasses — took the podium, futzed with his slides and was soon droning on about things such as *saccadic pulsation* (eye-nerve vibration) and *simultaneous transmission of form and content as one aesthetic entity*. After he'd cleaned his glasses with his handkerchief three times and provided a suitable coda by dropping them on the floor and accidently stepping on them, we, with our walkers preceding us, with evenly suspended attention, scanning both figure and ground opening up before us, made our slow senescent sojourn through the over-stimulating exhibition.

Before Bridget Riley's *Current*, I had a voluptuous moment when my senses and skin tingled with a new warmth and sharpened awareness of my body and the world about me, which, unfortunately, was largely composed of decrepit elder-folk. Still, a wonderful reprieve from the usual shivers, jolts, and horrors my body visits upon me. I was made aware of myself in way that I can't experience with my writing, which never gives me an unmediated sense of myself, only a reflective distance (like the mirrors around here do) that separates *moi* from my written words. I seem to be a mere vehicle for words. But I digress. And digress again for, on our way out, I made a slight detour, shuffling my feet as fast as my pulse, to an adjacent gallery area to see (on loan from New York's Museum of Modern Art) Jackson Pollock's long 'n narrow 1945 canvas, *There Were Seven in Eight*. I love its math reference which contrasts with the abstractive, surrealist forms, thickly applied.

Third, our Fearless Leader decided to beautify the dining room, "rusticate it" as he put it, by creating *faux* exposed beams made out of Syrofoam — fuckin' Syrofoam! — painting them chocolate brown. Hell, they support nothing, but are meant to warm up the ceiling and give our maintenance Nazi's something to occupy themselves with. "Idle hands are the Devil's playground," says our Leader.

Whenever these two jack-of-all-trades are idle, our Fearless Leader fears conspiracy, a worker's revolt in the offing, so he keeps them busy, busy. When asked to do handy work around the home, Stephan "Brickface" Tortenstück, the crew's burly foreman, obediently salutes his boss and rattles: "Piece o' cake" (he expresses everything in words of one syllable made up of two letters or three, at most five). But what one sees in Stephan's face is nothing but unblinking eyes, black as coffee, peepers dissociated from feeling, disconnected from the motive power of his body. That screened unknowingness creeps me out. Might God give him speech balloons over his noggin. No telling how Fearless Leader reads him. Brickface's lame side-kick, Luigi "Stucco" Rozo, only nods a "yes" or a "no" with his unshaven face. What bolts of electricity make their clay walk is unknown, unless it be bone stupidity. But I digress. They make minimum wage here.

To be of-a-piece with objects in our world does not necessarily mean to be at peace with them. I, as a structural engineer and art aficionado, hate the proposed addition; moreover, that "improvement" to the "Waiting Room" (our euphemism for our dining area) won't bring the food any faster, will it?

Fourth, I'm happy and sad in my joy and hurting. I sing, weep, move, shout. I take forms and pattern them as best I can so as to *say myself* to you (or to me, perhaps), returning disorder to order (harmony, coherence), what we recognize and call (among other things) *beautiful memories*, bringing equilibrium and repose. Why? To answer that, I have to turn to my memoir-in-progress.

Jimmer and I took the Way-Back Machine to 1942 and 1976, respectively. Let me explain. After returning from the Art Institute Museum on an elder home sponsored trip, I desperately called my son, demanding he honor his "zero-hour" contract with me (i.e., I call and he comes running) and get his butt over here to fix my radio. Forgot how to turn the damn radio alarm off, so at two a.m. each morning I'm treated to the rants of a megalomaniacal talk show host with the wrong politics and an annoying lisp. Sheer misery.

As a last resort, I stabbed a small phillips-head screwdriver into the earphone jack to kill the states of delusional conviction this jerk espouses. Now my headphones are silent. He tells me to the forget the stereo, chalk it up as a total loss. Write it off my income tax. Said he'll buy one the next morning at Best Buy, drop it by around noon, then transport me for eats at The Buzz Café, a home to local caffeine addicts with a taste for outstanding food — and only a block from his studio. What I wasn't prepared for was Jimmer's time machine.

So with grunts 'n groans, my son unloads my heavy, blue wheeled walker from his silver Toyota Matrix (which I bankrolled) and I shuffle slowly toward the Buzz. The door is held open for me. Entering, a wall of coffee bean aroma smacks my mug. I nearly lose my balance. Inside we find a table with chairs are hand-painted in wacky multicolored designs. The walls are hung table height-to-ceiling with photos, posters, paintings, etchings, and sketches. Jimmer says it reminds him of his Hippy days in Berkeley. Here ya can not only get a buzz from the java, but pick up on the local buzz as well. The owner publishes out a four-page Xeroxed weekly events flyer editorializing on local happenings (the inspiration for Eepie's column, by the way). One graces each table. Well, I'm about to read the latest buzz therein when Jimmer yells "Surprise!" and pulls out of his rétro-styled 1930s leather briefcase two photos recording events I'd wholly forgotten.

"This is my favorite flick of you 'n mom," he admits (see next page). "You look like you're literally walking into your future as a young, love-smitten couple. It's utopic!" (Here I flash on Hemp 'n Fourier.)

Elder Physics

It is a wonderful shot, I agree. Snapped by I-don't-recall-who when we were just engaged, just prior to me enlising in the Air Corps. Jimmer remarks how much he likes the formal properties: the way that leaf-sparse tree — indicating Fall but promising Spring — appears to be held in my hand like a victory branch making a triumvirate of tree-me-Jeane linked by those clasping hands. He points out that our paired bodies form a single sun-dial shadow indicating two o'clock, a play on two-as-one-as-two. A numerology of love 'n marriage. Suddenly, I notice, the horizon-line cuts across the frame in a

perfect golden section slice! And, god, were we young! Only twenty. Two times ten! As I do these sums, Jimmer hums the "Twilight Zone" jingle and I get shivers up my spine. The waitress takes our order: two Buzz breakfasts (scrambled eggs, sausage, whole wheat toast, and coffee, black.

That image may have its utopic dimension for my son, but it jars me into regret for a failed marriage and love lost. This frozen slice of times-past permits me to measure then with now; the trajectory of waning affections becomes clearer, more easily plotted. I can see that Jeane and I had gradually become interfering entities very much akin to what Jimmer unwittingly captured in a conceptual artwork from the mid-seventies, one we'd collaborated on.

As seen in the second photo he surprised me with (see next page), our marriage is figured as a proliferating interference pattern generated by two mismatched source points rooted in a Catholic versus Protestant agon. In the photo, my two rotating hands, hands no longer clasping my wife's, turn pointlessly in space, dynamizing a pure void, touching at nothing. An image diametrically opposed to the first one. I wouldn't have come up with this startling interpretation had I not seen these two photographs side-by-side. Context is everything, Jimmer says.

Hell, our family photo album must be — like the events broadcast over TV, and splashed on newspaper front pages, recording the long death throes of our planet — a parallel series of scoops detailing the demise of our marriage.

Yes, one can tell much from family photos, therapists swear. I could show you family group snaps where my wife's father, Fred, always stands aside from the group, looking down the line of his kin in a detached manner, never at the camera. He was, indeed, unique, and always stood outside

125

familial disputes. Out of the order found in these images, I redact a disorder of emotions. I recall the years of celibacy because Jeane wouldn't allow me to touch her unless she was permitted birth control, which, like a good Catholic, I refused us both.

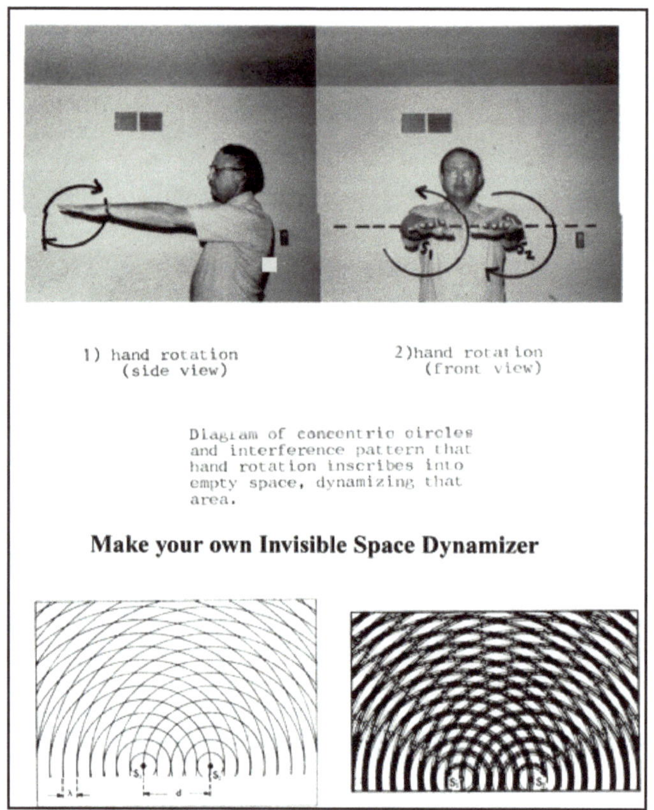

    I recall the years of being drugged to the point where, after my workday, life was reduced to a little television, then snores, aided and abetted by apnea exhaustion. Twice I fell asleep behind the wheel, once ending up in the ivy banking the 405 Freeway. Luckily, no injuries. But scary enough to make me regret not finding marital harmony, regret throwing Leslie out of the house for a week when my weekly pat down of her bedroom revealed a single joint under her mattress, regret cutting off Jimmer's college funds over our religious differences. Regrets, regrets, regrets. If I were to be given a name in the Native American tradition, basing it on one's distinguishing characteristics, it would have to be: "Carries-Regrets." Of course, being a critic, artist, and visionary, Jimmer's Injun moniker would have to be: "Takes-His-Body-Where-His-Eyes-Have-Been."

    A smiling waitress approaches and gently puts our yummy breakfasts before eyes linked directly to stomachs. My thoughts now turn to just getting more food into my mouth

than on my grey "B-17 War-Bird" hoodie, or not aspirating it
into my lungs. Once it did happen and I had to make another
rip-roaring trip to the ER. So eating's a long procedure.
Jimmer is usually putting away his last sausage as I'm
starting to put jelly on my toast. Happy kids race in,
chasing each other; the littlest one has a stuffed dinosaur
by the nose, a brontosaurus with huge cartoony eyes and
black felt lashes. Reminds me, I'm a dinosaur too.

Jimmer, sitting sipping his coffee, as I finally
start on my sausage link, asks me about my museum trip. In
between cautious gulps, I tell him about the Op Art show. In
turn, he puts on his critic's cap and, besides commenting on
art *per se*, expostulates on the triangle of war, commerce,
and piracy, a three-in-one, inseparable structure that
haunts all museums. The art lover, he asserts, is mute
witness to the illicit products of wartime plunder, ethic
massacres, and other criminal acts: tomb-raiding, dismant-
ling of religious sites, etcetera. Moreover, he explains,
another three-in-one structure has emerged in our museums:
sex-culture-advertising. Block-buster museum exhibitions,
proliferating Kitsch (notebooks, bags, umbrellas, T-shirts,
blah, blah, blah) related to the show hawked in the museum
shop; a museum in France splashed a poster around featuring
Gustave Courbet's graphic beaver shot, *The Origin of the
World*. And, he goes on to mention, some outrageous show in
London called "Sensation" put together by some crass advertising mogul was a *succés de scandale*. Art in which, like Op
Art, conditioned reflex wins out over contemplation. All
part of "a double process of pornification of culture and
culturalization of porn," he claims. I reply that I'd bet a
rosary blessed by the Pope that if spiritual humanist Bishop
Fulton J. Sheen was still kickin', he'd have a wise, sharp
tongue for it all.

Jimmer pays the tab. Leaves a better than 20 per cent
tip as I struggle to my feet to grab for dear life onto the
handlebars of my walker. He carefully navigates me to the
loo and, with some awkward embarrassment, assists me in
emptying my urine bag. A curious pair, all eyes are on us as
we shuffle out of the place, trailing a pungent mix of urine
and roasted coffee bean behind us.

Once shoe-horned back into the car seat, I hit Jimmer up with what I'd
been wanting to really talk to him about — putting Flyvision in my room. Yep, a
web-cam aimed omnisciently at my little safe holding my pills. I just gotta find out
who the culprit is. Who's copping my Benicar? Trust me, when a suspicious
character says, "Trust me, I didn't cop yer pills," I trust him less.

Nutritious said this hot new type of panoptic localness, *tele-localness*,
would put an end to my anxieties, as well as father and son hostilities over the
topic, once and for all. Finally, give me a solution to "x" in that perplexing elder
equation: $x + opportunity = missing pills$. Why, I could sit in the computer room
and surveil to my heart's content! Noot knows how to set it all up and will offer
advice, but cautions we'll have to avoid using the loose-tongued maintenance
Nazis to install it so Fearless Leader won't find out and raise my rent or fire her.
"Would *you* do this for your good ol' dad?" I plead sweetly, guilt-tripping him. He

nods no, so I up the ante, "I won't complain about you stealing all my tools if you do." Hell, he has the skills, but does he have the moxie?

A femtosecond into my request and I see Jimmer's eyes roll up like in cartoons, like a broken window shade. It's a hopeless request (I'll remember that in my bequest). I zip my mouth for the remainder of our painfully silent trip back to my prison where I will suffer The Presence's leopard's jaws.

A Bipolar Moment in the
Life of a Bipolar Kind of Guy

The cold, clear dawn erased the paranoia of the night and came through the half-open window of my bedroom. Several bad days now. Futterneid Quotient climbing rapidly, going jim-jams after Jammer's refusal to realize my Flyvision vision. Mental confusion mixing with bouts of rage seasoned with regrets. He and I aren't talking. I write him a nasty letter telling him I know he's in on the profitable pilfering of my meds, getting a cut of the action, selling my Benicar on e-Bay. I'm thrown on my own resources right now. And, Lord knows, what happened just now in our writing group hasn't helped.

Just returned to my room, not in best of moods, in time for a flatulent nurse to administer my pills. Mentions I'm short and need to have Jimmer call in a prescription; even now I can picture him pensive in the microwave fluorescence of the pharmacy awaiting my meds. Just five minutes ago, I'd been in a small room downstairs where our "Happy Scribbler's" writing club circles a circular table for our roundtable discussions.

First we welcomed a new member, Don Ferdinand, by gauging his familiarity with literary terms. Fialta asked him to give three examples of synonyms and homonyms. His answers weren't encouraging. For the former he listed: lust, gluttony, pride; for the latter: Kevin, Bruce, Wayne. Needless to say, we then quickly segued to our members' reading excerpts from new work. Ruby Zunshine read the opening line of her short story, "Better Living Through Chemistry": *Down by the promenade two splendid seniors, walking side-by-side near the water's edge. They radiate power, authority, wealth, assurance. He's a judge, or senator, or CEO, no doubt, and she's — what? — a professor emeritus of international law, let's say. They are going toward the plaza, moving serenely, smiling, nodding graciously to passersby. How the sunlight gleams in their white hair!*

Tandeta Paluba observed that this sounded like utopian drivel, a bit passé in our cynical world. She suggested we make use of the new wonderful words that are among the constants of elder physics: angina pectoris, arteriosclerosis, prolapses of the infundibulum, fulminating ventricles, and dilated viaducts. Ruby, sulking, mumbled something about *we still need to dream*.

Critiques over, we welcomed our guest speaker, who got us on the topic of the origins of literature. A suave guy in a bow tie, hailing from the University of Chicago's vaunted English Department; he came with courtesy copies of Stanley Fish's *How to Write a Sentence* for each of us. Gently clapping his hands in enthusiasm, he asserted that storytelling was a Darwinian adaption with antediluvian roots in oral communication. Its aim may've been social cohesion, or representing nonexistent states of affairs (like paranoid delusions?), maybe even for attracting intelligent members of the opposite sex. As for this latter point, Dirty Harry and I would surely agree — and hope.

I offered that we need a real Way-Back Machine to confirm this thesis. Jumping on the topic, Fialta noted universal themes — love, death, adventure, family, conflict, justice, and overcoming adversity — that are found in most oral and written literatures. She pointed out to me that *my* latest writing effort (this book) is rife with them. I smiled. But she went on to warn me: "How long, O Gerald, will you abuse our patience? Your writing runs from object to object, as they happen to strike your irregular imagination. And, you're getting soooo *reflexive* these days, you're disappearing up your own asshole." That's Fialta, cuts to the chase. Takes no prisoners.

Hands went up over mouths to stifle laughter. My smile abruptly switched to a profound frown — a bipolar moment in the life of a bipolar kinda guy. I jumped up (as quickly as possible in a universe dominated by elder physics) and left in a huff, my F.Q. reaching for the stars as I slowly ascended in our mirrored elevator to my cell, gazing at my infinite reflection, my infinite humiliation accusing me over and over as long as it took me to groan out a long: SSSSSSSSSSS SSSSSSSSSSSSSSSSSSSSSSSSSSSSSSSSSSSSSSSSSSSSSSSSSSSSSSSSSSSSSSS HHHHHHHHHHHHHHHHHHHHHHHHHHHHHHHHHHHHHHHHHHHHHHHHHHHHHHHHHH IIIIIIIIIIIIIIIIIIIIIIIIIIIIIIIIIIIIIIIIIIIIIIIIIIIIIIIIIIIIIIIIIIIIIIIIIIIIIIIIIIIIIIIIII IIIIIIIIIIIIIIIIIIIIIIIIIIIIIIIIIIIIIIIIIIIIIIIIIIIIIIIIIIIIIIIIIIIIIIIIIIIIIIIIIIIIIIIIII IIIIIIIIIIIIIIIIIIIIIIIIIIIIIIIIIIIIIIIIIIIIIIIIIIIIIIIIIIIIIIIIIIIIIIIIIIIIIIIIIIIIIIIIII TTTTTTTTTTTTTTTTTTTTTTTTTTTTTTTTTTTTTTTTTTTTTTTTTTTTTTTTTTTTTTTTTTTTT TTTTTTTTTTTTTTTTTTTTTTTTTTTTTTTTTTTTTTTTTTTTTTTTTTTTTTTTTTTTTTTTTTTT

The phone rings. It's Jimmer. I'm yelling at him. Then I'm crying. Telling him about Fialta's verbal slap. He, the wonderful son he is, calms me down. Feeds my ego, saying ignore her. That he and his wife want me over for Thanksgiving to feed my face. Now I'm laughing. I ask him to call in my prescriptions. "I'm already on it," he assures me. Love that kid.

Thanks for Thanksgiving

Thanksgiving Day. I'm still in bed. Musing. Most people in our polyglot cities are home in homes with western furniture and Japanese or German appliances, with toaster ovens and end tables and deep thick wooly carpets breaking like surf against the walls. Such thick carpets are contraindicated in elder homes. Thin carpets for people thinning away to nothing. When people die here, they just disappear. I'm thinner than usual today and my stomach is slightly upset from the fish-paste sandwich I had for dinner last night; had to opt out of the main fare (some kind of *gnocchi*) as it's too difficult for me to get down the hatch these days. I slept restlessly last night, over-stimulated by thoughts of the holiday ahead. I do the Yokohama kick, extricating my legs twisted up in my sheets and blanket, exposing a pale certificate of flesh. A new staff nurse knocks and enters without permission given ("My, don't we look good this morning!") and proceeds to gingerly insert a fresh catheter up me. Every several days I do suffer this humiliation and discomfort. Someone's pulling my dick and jabbing a sterilized tube up it. But it's Thanksgiving and I give thanks that I have a son to visit. A few of the folks here have either no family or have been largely abandoned by them. Jimmer is to pick me up at three. Dinner at four. Five hours to kill. Six-course dinner. Hey, that's three, four, five, six! A perfect number series. Gotta be significant. This mathemagician is seeing patterns again like John Nash in *A Beautiful Mind*. Ah, the day will get progressively better as it goes on, I think.

And it does! I grab a *Gratuitous Giving* envelope stuffed with twenty bucks, one of several Jimmer has given me to hand out, and head smiling for the lift. First, I notice that outside Clara Kleinschmidt's door the usual besmirched panties she always tosses out there are conspicuously absent. Ah, Clara, her eyes a pale blue, never resting long in any one spot and, like a bad actress, she finds her hands a problem. On my way to breakfast, I share the elevator with Brucine Bitters, uncharacteristically grinning like a Halloween pumpkin. I hand her the gift envelope. "You've just been gifted," I announce, much to her mystification. So it's "Why Gerald . . ." this and "Why Gerald . . ." that. I leave her baffled and reading the enclosed gifting letter through her magnifying glass and tootle down the hall. Suddenly, "Rama-lama-ding-dong" McCracken bolts through our main door decked out in his grey and yellow jogging outfit and bounds down the hall toward me with his large feet (he's very self-conscious about 'em) and shouts: "The storm cloud cantata is done, the air's clear as glass!" Last night I'd watched the sun go down, color draining with it and saw clouds move in as hard and cold as hammered pewter. Thought it'd snow, but a south wind kept temperatures above freezing. Around midnight I heard thunder.

At breakfast, in startling contrast, people are sunny. Many are dressed to the nines. All are eating like feral dogs — hungry, untamed — knowing that they are going to skip lunch to better savor their turkey tonight. I observe an unusually calm Ill-Phil. The Presence sits stacking jelly and cream containers so high it must be an All Elder Home World's Record. His relatives are absent. Even my scrambled eggs and home fries come promptly and are *hot*! Then — surprise, surprise — I notice our maintenance Nazis have installed a large fresh water fish tank in the middle of the dining room. Our two newest residents — Eulonia and Royal, wed now some fifty years — are bent over, noses pressed to the tank watching the streaking colors zip back 'n forth inside. Ah, we can muse dreamily over the drifting denizens of the deep as we await our chow. How nice! How thoughtful! How unexpected! I wonder what it'll be next week, flaming yellow parrots and chartreuse palm tress? And menus on the table now! Opening mine I notice an unusual addition to the normally cholesterol-heavy fare, "Jill-Dill Omelette," a tofu 'n gouda cheese, dill 'n mushroom wonder made strictly with egg whites. I must be dreaming. I pinch myself. No, I'm fully awake. To make things even better, an effervescent Jill is having breakfast with us, chatting up the new dish named after her and reading statistics that watching fish actually lowers one's blood pressure and decreases frequent urination.

And our Fearless Leader, praise the Lord, is absent, at home with his family. Ah, I feel my Futterneid Quotient rapidly descending like the elevator in the Sears Tower. I'm so in the mood to attack turkey and trimmings and enchant the dinner guests with my stories! I'm especially "up" because I now recall that Jimmer mentioned his mom (warehoused at another elder home a mile or so distant) will be joining us for the traditional feast. On this special day, I want to show her a rare tenderness and warmth. Make up for the shit I've shoveled her way all these years.

Have to say one thing about the boy, Jimmer is prompt. At the very second of three there's a knock at my door. I remove the chair propped up against unwanted entry and see the bearded smile. He's in such a good mood, I hesitate to have him assist in draining my urine bag, but necessity is necessity. Time and urine march on irregardless of one's wishes. Always the diplomat, he complements me on my slim moustache and reminds me to take my robin's eqq blue pill box. I stuff it in my shirt pocket. I put on my black leather flight jacket and dark pilot's glasses (maybe I can woo my ex-wife a bit). I can see Jimmer is impressed. He hugs me. "You look ggggrrrreat, dad. Inglorious Basters, we're ready for all manner of baster-based antics!" If only my insides were as trim 'n handsome as my outside.

The elevators are particularly slow. Family members picking up their parents for the holiday, adding to the traffic. Ill-Phil, reacting to the fact his kids have stood him up — his "I'd rather not to," has discouraged any further advances on their part — sits in his hallway chair holding a provocative sign, droning some repetitive nonsense that sounds like a slow, slow death in a metronome factory. In contrast, outside the air has a fresh, after-the-rain smell. As it fills my lungs my pride in my son also swells. As I'm dying I hope I can at least utter to him, "You're my hero."

Ill-Phil's provocative sign

I judder my butt into his car. My cane rides in the back seat. It's nice to be outdoors, to see the trees, young people, the varied store windows (we always pass that bizarre bra store called "In Her Cups"). Soon, we're pulling up to our destination with Mr. Turkey. I've captured that special day in my memoir:

Sky's serene and there is not a huff in the air. In about two hours we'll be in our cups. Within a few minutes, we're pulling up at Jimmer 'n Marianne's, a cozy English cottage snuggery with its Church of England front garden and lawn hinting at croquet parties. Inside, a blazing Arts and Crafts hearth welcomes. But first, I have to negotiate a most difficult hurdle, the elder version of the D-Day Landing: broaching the high concrete abutment and steep, handrail-less back steps. Not easy, even when my weapons are my sturdy four-legged cane and Jimmer guarding my flank. But if my legs fail me and I slap-bang my full foley bag against a step, it'll be the urination of our Turkey Day!

But God is my copilot today, so without being wounded or having my urine bag explode, I win my objective, Jimmer's wife's aromatic kitchen. Marianne and Jeane (Jimmer picked her up earlier) are wielding kitchen tools like surgeons in an O.R. Marianne pulls out a meat thermometer and takes the turkey's temperature, Jeane chops vegetables. I salute smartly like a young cadet-in-training, "Reporting for duty." Jeane smiles. I've broken the ice. Josh, Marianne's son, hasn't poked his shaved head through the door yet.

Marianne takes me in hand and proudly shows me the wide variety of trimmings that will accompany our tremendous turkey to the table. A veritable palette running from the white of mashed potatoes, through the light browns of dress- ing, the dark browns of gravy, through greens, to deep reds. In genuine amazement, I exclaim, "Holy Moses!" and notice

Jimmer just caught my outburst for posterity with his camcorder. I'm a star!

    Moving about the kitchen, Jeane and I — each other's grand hazard — keep a precisely measured physical distance betwixt us, as if we were attached by a pole precisely a meter in length. She's a tad cool, but I counter with warmth and conciliation. I see her relax a bit when no shenanigans from me are forthcoming. Can't vouch for her though. I can see Jimmer loves the fact that after too many single-parent holidays he can enjoy, probably his last, two-parent Thanksgiving.

    I stagger past a typical Marianne over-the-top festively decorated dinner table gridded with a table-setting like a football field (ad ceramic pumpkin soup tureen offsides on the fifty-yard line) and into the television room, plopping down on the couch with a a Scottie and a Westie flanking me. You know, like the ones in the Black 'n White Scotch ads. In no time a football-game announcer is screaming, Gillette ads are blaring. Soon I'm flat on my back, snoring, with one mutt on my chest, the other tucked between my legs (got a photo to prove it). See, some of the stuff in here is god's-fact, not all, but a heap. And it's usually the most unbelievable stuff that passes Jimmer's severe analytic philosophy conditions for truth — like the large, recently sharpened scissors in my bathroom. But I digress. Back to the story.

    The door bell awakens me. It's Josh, my rival in wit and storytelling. I like him. Great sense of humor, like Jimmer. He's paired with a stunningly beautiful girl friend, a dish matched to his whine. Very easy on the eyes, unlike him, since he's gone and shaved his head — bald. I might invite him to join my "Mies van der Rogaine" project (just kidding). After introductions, we pop some bubbly — Jimmer says there was a photographer named Esther Bubley — fill flutes, and guzzle 'n nuzzle until it's time to chow down.

    Marianne cheerfully rings the dinner bell and we make haste to our assigned places. Dramatically, she trots out the turkey bird and we all bubble 'n pose as Jimmer snaps a digital flick reminiscent of that classic forties Turkey Day illustration, *Freedom from Want*, painted by Norman Rockwell. Vouvray wine stirs in our glasses. Mobile and receptive dog mouths lurk beneath the table. In a wink, food and language are inextricably intermixed. So much so that to record what is said here, I'd have to drag cranberries, green beans with slivered almonds, thick gravy, mashed potatoes, moist turkey 'n dressing, ventures into metaphysics, sport scores, puns, shaggy dog stories, embarrassing facts, drunken oaths — literally — onto this nice white page. So let's agree to say, in sum, we had one helluva gut-stuffer and a super mind-boggler of a time and leave it at that.

    I tire easily and after an hour's snooze on the leather couch, I was ready to set my compass heading to home base. Descending those steps prove easier than ascending, and soon we are under the night sky, the stars alive and conscious. A perfect moon cuts a parenthesis into the dark shade dropped before us, a yellowish, thick toenail paring.

When we aren't fighting or playing deaf mutes, we do become what Jimmer calls "The Incomparable Buzzsaw," a rip-roarin' lust for life. I wish we'd had more of this father-son fun-fusion earlier. If only we'd tossed away our differences like spoiled paper, weighted the residue for genuine gold, and filled each other's dance card. But, both of us being younger then, we were each as volatile as Jeane's lighter fluid. Like any wine worth its vine, we had to be stoppered up for years, then uncorked and let sit for awhile. Now we can sip 'n savor each other to the dregs. When he's Jimmer — not Jammer with his greedy mitts in my accounts or his feisty fists in my face, of course.

Bladder Blather

I'm bending over the toilet bowl, scissors in hand and, like a sausage-maker trimming his product down to edible size, cut my feces to fit the mouth of our pipes. I blame the Brobdingnagian portion I consumed at yesterday's feast. After I get dressed and Jimmer arrives, we will replay the monthly podiatrist visit. But when he does knock on my door, I abruptly discover I've fallen asleep eating a bowl of instant oatmeal, the gooey stuff now slopped all down my sweater. I change and my annoyed son and I descend for my appointment. Or is he just concerned? After all, he'd put up three fingers and asked how many I see. As nothing changes during these nail-clipping procedures, except for a newer edition of *Cosmopolitan* and *Car and Driver* in the magazine rack, we can skip all this.

Jimmer observes how much less vigorous I am today. My urethra is sore. He hints I might be getting another bladder bummer. Each infection ratchets down my immune system and saps energy. The T.I.A.s (transient ischemic attacks) my HMO physician says I occasionally suffer further impair my mental focus. At these times, my *vas bene clausum* seems to be lit with only a jittery forty-watt bulb. (Like my Latin skills? Did you guess that my secret desire was to be a priest?) When such occurs I find myself just sitting on the bed (my legs inordinately weak) staring at a silent television without any sense of time. Where my mind goes during these lapses, I can't recall. But an hour or two can pass unremarked. When I do awaken to my environs again, I stagger over to my mirror, but hardly recognize who stares back. I realize the revisions to this manuscript my son labors over are becoming more extensive. I've entered the realm of assisted writing! Red ink spreads across my notebook pages like mold on bread, a rhizome. Increasingly, he's slicing textual fragments from noteworthy sources (Tantra Bensko, T. C. Boyle, William Burroughs, William Gass, William Gibson, Aldous Huxley, Jonathan Lethem, Sam Lipsyte, Chuck Palahniuk, Charles Yu, and a shit load of others) and shoving them my way with a wink. My manual skills are geometrically declining, so I'm afraid to wield that razor. (Here's where the Kindle comes in handy.) Never thought putting together a postmodernist text could endanger one's life. But I got to give it to the kid, he rallies me: "Buck up Big Guy! Here's where we separate the Humanists from the Posthumanists! The

Delusionists from the Deleuzians! Come on! One for the Gipper!" Gumption he's got. Love that kid.

But after cheering me up despite my waning writing skills, he passes on bad news: "There is epic, epochal fuckedness! More insane delays with your Veteran's benefits." I need to get an appointment at the local V.A. hospital to have my mental and physical condition reviewed by a physician there. Jimmer has to teach that day, so he schedules a limo and driver from the home to take me. He warns me to "be honest and don't try to smooth over your deficiencies, if anything, exaggerate them. We need that money, dad," he insists. "This ain't time for espousing *sancta paupertas."*

It's been *six months* now since filing my application. It goes into a sea of identical cubicles, a computer and a coffee mug lurking in each; my paperwork, swims around inside circuits, discorporate, now a series of ones and zeros; every week pink slips are delivered to undeserving staff by flabby supervisors who don't know or care who Gerald Hugunin *is*. They seem to be saying about the processing of my application, "We'd prefer not to." Of course, even after the exam, I can be assured of more weeks of delay as my appeal circulates the bureaucracy. Yep, they're just waiting for yours truly to kick the bucket so they don't have to pay up, benefits not only earned over the deadly skies of Germany, but with thirty years service during the Cold War designing hot shit aircraft.

When I was needed, I was there for Uncle Sam; now he's treating me like a poor relation. Lots of jaw-jerkin' about the "Greatest Generation," but I'm getting the "Greatest Shine-on!" That's it — *talk*. Talk is cheap. Put your money where your mouth is 'cause my money is fast running out. My son can't afford to support me on an academic's salary. One bad episode where my care will have to be upped again and it*'s wham-mo*! into a state-run institution and I die among the destitute. Hell, in Germany today, their government actually contacts *you* if you *haven't* filed for your war-times bennies. And *we* defeated them! Shoulda been a *Luftwaffe* pilot so that now I'd have aid in my time of dire need.

Jimmer tries to calm me, but I can see he's just as pissed as I. And as worried about my future as I. As much as I'd like to move in with him and his wife, I know that: 1) she'd nix it; and 2) my needs are too much for two people who have to work, even if they do have flexible schedules. It'd be a disaster. Jimmer and I rarely discuss it. And I'm O.K. with it. I will face my uncertain future with the calm resolve that I used to face the flak bursts over the target after our pilot turned the aircraft over to my steady bombardier's hands.

Jimmer, with something like merriment in the drawn-down slits of his eyes, says that if I hop into bed, he'll pop out for White Castle "sliders" with fries to-go and we'll have lunch in my monk's cell. I love to lift the top of the bun to examine the grid of holes in the small patty, the slime of glistening cubed onions. To an engineer, there's nothin' like a machine-tooled burger. Then my son'll continue diligently spiffing up my scribble, but only if I promise not to torture him with EWTN. A bargain, I say. So he keeps me casual company until he has to leave to teach his night theory class where he has to confront some very keen Art History and Visual and Cultural Studies graduate students. They must really appreciate his efforts, as I do, when he's not punching me black 'n blue in the car on our way to my dentist, that is. You know, no one can both ruffle my feathers and smooth them out as that boy.

I was correct about the bladder infection. The next day I'm too weak to go down for my morning meal, so I order breakfast in my room. Getting up to turn my television on,

my feet somehow get braided around each other and I do an
Evel Knievel death-defying leap over the breakfast camped on
my TV tray and smash onto thin carpet. Gash my left forearm.
Sprain my right hand, which is stuck in a muck of scrambled
eggs, beef hash, and home fries. All ass 'n elbows, staff
rush in, walkie-talkies blaring. Emergency call to Jimmer.
Emergency call to the ambulance service. Another Mr. Toad's
Wild Ride to the ER. Yes, my life is turning into a cartoon
mad with physical discombobulation and miraculous rebound.
But one day, like a deflated basketball, I won't rebound.

X-ray, CAT scan, bandages. Jimmer at my side. Dour doctor talking to a grave-looking Jimmer, I mean literally, as if he's looking into my grave. This time my F.Q. is at ten thousand feet and climbing, climbing over the flak my son is giving me about not using my cane when perambulating about. I'm awash in a no-time zone and in overall dull pain until the meds take effect. Next thing I'm aware of is a hospital bed, starched sheets, an IV inconveniencing me, someone snoring behind the curtain to my right. And constant ambient murmurs. Doctors and nurses trotting-in-and-out (South Indian surnames) and for a minute I think I've been transferred overseas. No Jimmer. Must've left for work.

That evening Jimmer's drops in with toiletries. From what the staff tell us, I'm going to be a guest here for at least five days. The middle-aged doctor, Avinder something, gives my son the proverbial "Be-prepared-for-the-worse-worst" lecture. But, hell, my attending physicians have been foretelling my demise for the last two years. Yet somehow, this time the warning sinks in, like ink on a blotter. Each time I'm here, I don't rally as quickly as the time before. And thereafter, my body and mind seem less connected to the world around me, like I'm being prepped for my final journey. So when I do bail-out and yell "Geronimo!" it won't seem such an abrupt leap.

All next day, no Jimmer. But the following morning he's here for a man-to-man talk. I'm going to have to be moved to Thanatopsis House, a care facility run by a German corporation that can more adequately, like stockbroker, handle my advances and declines (my declining health, my advancing needs). From the literature, I see the Home's motto is: NO SPECTATORS ONLY PARTICIPANTS. I learn that although most of the residents are higher-functioning Alzheimer's sufferers, staff and services provide Konstant-Kare to a wide range of the elderly. It's a trademarked system of gerontic intervention first successfully employed in the Federal Republic of Germany and recently touted on "The Today Show" news program, where their spokesperson referred to their proactive program as, "A kind of a kinder Kindergarten for Forgeters Who've Forgotten They've Forgotten." I envision foam-flecked lips, hollow cheeks, shifty, demented eyes. I shiver. Jimmer says that they aren't *that* bad, as famous German fine art photographer, Thomas Struth, has photographed some *in situ* under the series title: *Innocent Monsters.*

The program, as my son explains, stresses a strict daily schedule of group activities, such as memory-stimulating games like "Word-Probe" of which the brochure says, "Every word in our language is memory at work for us, changing what has become a panic room back into a palace." Or storytelling sessions, interactive computer games aimed at maintaining hand-eye coordination, physical therapy, group lunches and dinners (a planned diet of gourmet taste quality), and so forth. Jimmer spent a day there before signing me up, witnessing how staff were trained to intone commands in a neutral, baby-talk softness (patented as "Sooth-Talk") to all residents at all times. No matter how uncontrollable a resident may become in body or voice, the response is ever even and calming. "Dad, it's as if the staff exists on some meta-level above the fray going on below. Like B-17 bombers flying thousands of feet above the mayhem in the trenches below, but instead of dropping bombs, they drop soft pillows." I just nod.

The downside, he admits, is that unless that Veteran assistance money (over $1500 per month) isn't granted soon, I won't be able to afford Konstant-Kare so very long. Then we must set our compass for a public care facility where elder care asymptotically approaches zero. I grit my teeth. I know I'm in for a major sea-change. Jimmer says he will start moving my dwindling personal effects into my new, clean and larger room and have it all prepared for my grand entrance in a week.

I think the worst of aspect of leaving will be losing up my crew of *compadres* here. I think I will even miss The Presence and his proverbial "I'd prefer not to," perhaps because I find myself saying it more often now too. In a home of Alzheimer's patients, there won't be another Fialta Fenwich. Maybe I can subscribe to our in-house rag from here so I can keep up on Eepie's column. I'll have Jimmer look into it. Bondo can jog over for a visit, of course. But with all that do-this, do-that group activity, how will I find time to keep up my writing? And who, at the new place, will have enough mental moxey to follow my story line? Tell me, do Alzhelmer's folks make jokes, and laugh at them? No. Nothing has quite prepared me for such a dramatic change to my life.

On the good side, the facility is only half a mile further from Jimmer's home and right across the street from Al's breakfast joint, so I can always meet old buddies from the Upping Arms there. But will I be *able* to meet them? I can barely haul this old carcass around anymore, even with Jimmer beside me. I don't want to give up the struggle and plop into a wheelchair or motorized scooter. You may think it silly, but I want to die not only with my boots on, but being able to *use* those boots. It has something to do with freedom and dignity, being a proud Huguenot whose says NOT to Mr. Infirm.

Thanatopsis House

I'm paroled. Jimmer picks me up. We head back to the Upping Arms so I can make my goodbyes. I pick up my mail, including a notice from the Veteran Affairs office that some V.A. inspector will be calling for another appointment to further evaluate the evaluation that I received at the Veteran's Hospital. At my "Farewell to Arms" cupcake 'n coffee send-off in the Sunshine Room, Jill, looking smart in her new suit, is particularly broken up. We're buds and she's taken to listening to my war yarns over a cup of java during lunch. A tear traces a curved path down her cheek like a droplet of water on a vase. Fialta is devastated to lose her most challenging competitor and I'll miss her keen insights. But Dirty Harry is smiling and breathing a sigh of relief, one less macho visage for the ladies to compete over. Noot hugs me. Claims I'll always be her star techno-pupil. She votes to keep my Browser web-link to *www.votecatholic.org* forever listed under FAVORITES on the home's computer in my honor. The library-twins say they'll put *Missing from its place* on a commemorative library call-slip with my name on it in their database. I'm overwhelmed! Damp eyes.

Elder Physics

Kim Young Sam, having suffered an even more debilitating stroke, wishes me farewell from her wheelchair, but in a voice that sounds as if she were shouting underwater, tape-recorded, and then broadcast to us at the wrong speed. Even Ill-Phil surprises me with a salute: "Looootenant, clear skies, ya hear?" Stricken, blasted as he is, The Presence has his moments.

Fearless Leader is conspicuous by his absence (very postmodern). What I don't know is that he's not going to grant me an emergency move dispensation as specified in my contract, so he's demanding six weeks rent, precious funds I need in my new home. I'm sure he's pissed for having to move me about room-to-room, floor-to-floor like a Knight in three-dimensional Chess. Tit-for-tat is his philosophy. As I slowly walker-it out the door for the last time, Jimmer supporting me, a genuine tear falls down Jill's cheek as I pass her.

Five minutes later, we are passing Fialta's favorite coffee-klatch hangout, Always Latte, turning left at the corner where Al's Diner sits on Wisconsin Avenue, then another left and down a ramp to the basement access to Thanatopsis House, a spanking new five-story luxury elder complex. Jimmer unloads my elder-baggage and we make our way to the parking garage elevator and up to Priscilla, the official greeter. Trim and stunning, in green leather boots that have the air of being just one pair of a considerable collection of trophy footwear, she is as fresh-faced as a highschool twirler surprised by the miracle of her own flesh. Smiling as though she had teeth of sugar that were forever dissolving, she greeted me: "Gerrrrald," dragging out the *r* softly, "pleased to meet you. Welcome to the Land of Unfinished Sentences." She shakes both our hands using that stiff, cocked hand gesture peculiar to business women.

She escorts me to the Head Nurse, one Ottilie Ohrdruf, a broad-hipped, matronly and substantial woman suffering her mid-fifties. But her very age and figure announce: CARE and CONCERN. As I'm handed off to this nurse, Priscilla and Ottilie smile at each other as if they'd just come back from sailing around the world together, eyes flashing flat as glass. I later find out this smiley routine — impervious to even potty-mouthed nonagenarians — is called "Tender Training." It's a key element of their Konstant-Kare.

Jimmer leaves and Ottilie escorts me through the long process of my intake, a variety of interviews to glean my background, my likes and dislikes, my family's history, how acute my memory is. My first interrogator, Hannelore, is a too-cheery svelte blond, eyelids tattooed to look like blue-black eyeliner, clad in tight brown leather pants; she seems the type who would fall for George Clooney. In her pea-green office, she loosens me up with some casual chit-chat: "You know Gerald, most of the folks here — and you seem sharper than most — revert in their old age back to a state of Blakean innocence (you know, William Blake) and moral simplicity. I say that because I see you're Catholic. I confess, I find myself gazing at some of our residents here and thinking: *Little Lamb — you rackety old thing—who* did *make thee*? You see, I too have questions I'd like to ask Him." She confesses that when she previously worked in a Jewish retirement home, she had to ghost her German and not mention Nordic processions."So may we chat?"

Ah, but she can't fool me. I grok her attempts at gaining my trust, so I'm all the more suspicious. I already am prepared. I draped what looks like an iPod around my neck, ready to digitally record all interviews in case future law suits need be filed. You know that given the inaccurate forecasts of late, the weather handlers have been distracted. My answering machine knew when one of my shoes was untied. So let the pieces fall into place as they may.

Jimmer, with a grimace, overlooks the paranoid aspect of this counter-measure in favor of its literary potential. "A wonderful opportunity to interject the

Q 'n A form into your text, Big Guy." (Predictably, Jimmer liked the above passage even as he abhorred its implications.)

Q.:   We are yourself boy! So now Gerald we're going to pose some questions designed to help place you here, a questionnaire procedure we call VK after its developer, Oskar Voight-Kampff. Ready?

A.:   Fire away. *[I sit up higher in the office chair, feeling in my stomach like a lonely goony bird struggling to take-off.]* Holy Moses! Vought's F-8 Crusader jet is my fav. Jimmer even made a plastic model of one.

Q.:   Ahhhh. . . . *[Mystified.]* O.K. . . . What is your full name? *[She crosses her legs, eyes beaming like the searchlights encircling Speer's Nürnberg zeppelin field.]*

A.:   Gerald Richard Hugunin. *[said with Huguenot pride, chest puffed.]*

Q.:   Now give me that name in reverse order. *[Looks me directly in the eye.]*

A.:   Hugunin, Richard, Gerald. *[clear throat, suppress a fart.]*

Q.:   Excellent! *[Very enthusiastic.]* Where were you born?

A.:   Antigo, Wisconsin, 1922. A northwoodsy area chuck full of Krauts 'n Bohunks, brats 'n beer.

Q.:   *[Smiling, a hint of condescension.]* Now where would you have *preferred* to have been born? Defend your choice.

A.:   Definitely, Saarbrücken, Germany. I would've gone into the *Luftwaffe* during the Big Tiff and by now I'd be receiving generous veteran benefits thanks to an enlightened social policy that is nonexistent in our country thanks to, Neoliberal is too kind, cheap-ass, cold-hearted Republicans.

Q.:   *Mein Gott!* . . . Good answer, Gerald! I can see you're going to thrive here, *mein Herr.* To continue . . . what was yesterday's date?

A.:   The two days after New Year's 2007? A day I more keenly felt the presence of Ticktockman lurking over my left shoulder. *[She seems puzzled.]* Oh, I mean Death. The Grim Reaper.

Q.:   Oh, of course. . . . But it's been a *week* since January First. . . . Do you know why you're here?

A.:   In mathematic's cold terms: Assisted Care to the second-power *[I jot down: (Assisted Care)^2 on a notepad]*. Because I'm asymptotically approaching infinity. To put it into medical terms, my cerebellum's gone on a long walkabout. Poor motor skills, bad balance and coordination, you name it. Because I grin and reach into the air for memories.

Q.:   Poetically put! A significant sign of your capabilities. Speaking of math, your aim is now to reverse time's arrow. Can you count down from 1945 to 1933, negating Hitler's rise and demise? Wiping history clean. You use the last two digits only.

A.: O.K. '45, '44 (that's when I started my bomber missions and finally ended up getting married upon returning stateside), '43 (basic training), '42, '41' (I was in aeronautical school), '40 (that's when I graduated high school), '39 (Jeane and I saw *The Wizard of Oz* on our first date), '38 (that reminds me I wanted to fly P-38s and also the year Margaret Kuss, an early girl friend, was killed), '37 (got my first ride in a 1929 Ford Trimotor, they called it the "Tin Goose" back then), '36, '35, '34, '33 (our town's bank president shot himself). How's that?

Q.: More than excellent. Your long-term memory is far from *Kaput*. We can do things with you here to help you retain that edge. O.K. Next. What did you have for dinner last night?

A.: Think I can't remember, huh? Well, it was tortellini with Maalox, washed down with a glass of orange-flavored Metamucil. I did aspirate some of it. I remember that. Now my gut has that inward writhing akin to the torments of that famous sculpture, *The Laocoön. [Hand to stomach.]*

Q.: *[Huge smile.]* Thank you for sharing that. Next. If say "Konstant-Kare" what comes immediately to mind? Quick now . . .

A.: The opposite of constant nuisance — at least right now — not having lived here, of course, my judgement is based on weak empirics. *[I will later revise this assessment.]*

Q.: *[Laughing.]* Of course. Now, if you saw a butterfly outside, say in our wonderful garden area here, how might you respond?

A.: Not like stringy metallic-minded Ill-Phil at my former home; he'd try to catch it only to pull off its wings. . . . Let me think . . . I see myself trying to *draw* it. Pastels probably. Reminds me, one of our flight's bombers had a picture of a Death's Head Moth painted on it.

Q.: *[Her expression sours, but she quickly recovers.]* What annoys you the most?

A.: Well . . . this may embarrass you . . . having to cut up my feces in order to flush them without stopping up my toilet and having them analyzed when flushed.

Q.: *[Looking up at the ceiling, a slight blush rouging her cheeks.]* Ah . . . well we have *ÜberSog* toilet-flush technology on our German-made commodes, I can assure you. . . . I might warn you . . . don't ever put your hand in the bowl and press the flush mechanism. Poor Mrs. Ratachek ... It took hours . . . well that's another story. O.K. Ready for another question?

A.: Pre-flight check O.K., props clear. Ready for take-off.

Q.:   Say you have a conflict with one of our residents. How do you resolve it?

A.:   Hypothetically, huh? Well, I don't. They gotta. I'm *always* right. It's the other guy who's screwy. But I'd pray for his or her conversion.

Q.:   Ahhhh. I see you are divorced. So the person directly involved in your care is your son. So how would you describe your relationship with him?

A.:   I either hate to love him or love to hate him half the time, then I do a flip-flop and I hate to hate him or love to love him. Depends on the level of my Futterneid Quotient, which oscillates like stock market returns or my EKG read-out. I go from tropical to arctic mode in a few minutes.

Q.:   Yes. He mentioned bipolarity . . . *[Unconsciously biting her fingernail.]*

A.:   *[Defensively.]* Hell (excuse my French), but Gaia, our own Mother Earth, is bipolar and spins about an axis. Not to mention Her PMS symptoms: all those friggin' earthquakes, cyclones, volcanic eruptions, tornadoes, blah, blah. What's good for the goose is good for the gander. And *my* axis is my Catholic faith. *Q.E.D.* Should be allowed my eccentricities — right? — *and so it goes*.

Q.:   *And so it goes?* Look in wonder, my hoppie! I'm a Vonnegut fan too! And I'm sure he would agree that life is a black comedy and doesn't always end the way you think it should end *[beaming from ear-to-ear]*. By the way, have you read Vonnegut's . . .

Here my iPod recorder's battery went *Kaput* and now I can't recall the remainder of our interview. I did undergo further tests to determine the range of physical activities I can still perform (I sure ain't gonna do a cartwheel!) followed by diverse and challenging mental tests from some town in Minnesota, all necessary (I'm told) to precisely determine my level of Konstant-Kare, to which *Klasse* (hoppie group) I will be assigned within the home. On one tough test I had to link up terms in three columns (it was a bitch); they said only the hippest hoppies could perform it.

Next came a very unusual visual test in which I was told to make two rapid sketches, pen never leaving paper: one when I felt at my peak mental sharpness, and the second when I felt my so-called Futterneid Quotient fast rising. The results are sure sort of interesting, don't you agree?

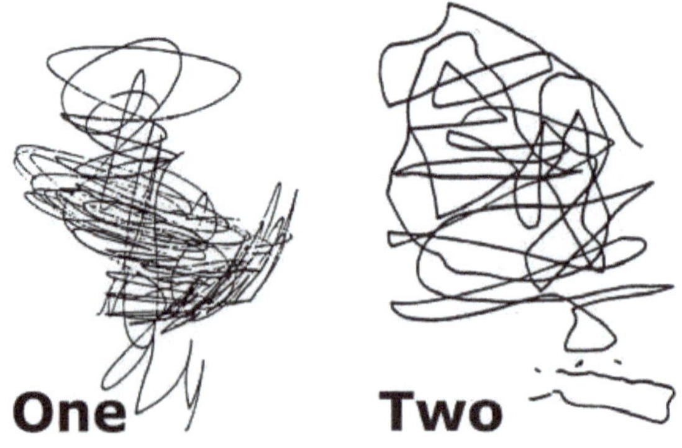

The stupidest question set — though, I suppose, many folks here had to struggle with it — can be characterized by this one instance (set in large print):

Read the following sentences and provide an answer that logically follows:

1) Smith wants to keep warm.
2) Smith has a wood-burning stove that warms his home very well.
3) Smith has run out of fuel for the stove.
4) Smith knows that he can get fuel for the stove by collecting and chopping wood.
5) What should Smith do? _______________________.

As a "neo-hoppie," I get an official name tag for "NameTag Nacht," an orientation (library, computer room, snack bar, exercise facility, group activity rooms, and so forth) then taken to lunch to meet my *Kareklasse,* where I'm introduced to my little band of *Kameradin* that will now be chained to me most of the day. We've all been matched by ElderQuest software on a top-line MAC computer based on the input from those aforementioned tests and have been assigned a trained staff member, a "Big Brother" or "Big Sister," who will guide us through our day and our various encounters with gerontic specialists. There are just enough of us *Überfunktionen* to make up two full roundtables (all tables here are circular) in our dining room. Everyone sports a spiffy name tag like mine, printed in large type Helvetica (held on by magnets, no dangerous pins).

I stand and look down at a figure-eight of faces. They all stare at me with a sympathetic "Going my way?" (meaning down the tubes) look. Background music by our live in-house piano-player, a Black guy marked by attitudinal tattoos easy to read. The facilities? A cruise-ship on land. Top quality carpet, tasteful decor, polite staff, a garden area with chairs. There's fast elevators, clean rooms, impeccable maid service. No urine smell. Great chow comes quickly and with generous smiles. Always a choice between at least two entrées and a cheese-boiger with fries. Desserts baked in their own kitchen.

The French chef, Armand de Bouchette, introduces himself, *"Bonjour,* my hoppies!" He bows politely. I toss him a "Ça va?" He glides over and inquiries as to my favorite dishes. Doesn't even blink when I ask for my boiled eggs done *mi-mollet.* Jeez, even the waitresses have figures worth calculating. Am I in some Geronto-Islamic Paradise?

My appetite is already revving up on the tarmac. However, conversation ain't nothin' to write home about. Something like $x + y = z$ is beyond these characters. But I can't throw the first stone, as I'm heading that way myself.

Elder Physics

So let's introduce you to my *Kameradin* — we are quaintly called "hoppies" by staff — squeezing two tables full of folks into one for brevity's sake (the innovative elder-care program's logo inscribed inside):

There is a basic *Konfiguration* employed in our therapy: always two very large tables ringed with hoppies, abutting to form a big figure-eight at whose intersection sits our Big Brother or Big Sister in a comfy swivel-chair that permits easy interaction with adjoining tables. And that interaction is constant. The facilitator (our handler, if you will), sports a freckled cleavage and congenitally parted lips. Sitting in her power-spot, she

Konstant-Kare Konfiguration

encourages conversation, discourages food-fights, wipes mouths, deals with a wide variety of gastric epiphanies, mops up split milk, calms vitriolic outbursts, pulls hidden memories from reluctant minds (like pulling taffy), and puts up with haunted eyes and sad, sour smells. All accomplished via the famous patent-pending Konstant-Kare palette of bright eyes, wide smiles 'n soft tones.

Today, Sonia is late to our session. Putting letters in the mailbox, she says. She is dressed with more layers, loose shawls, as if that would "make her less visible if they were looking." Slender as she is, it still made her look lumpy, the outer shawl a nappy gray purple. Our facilitator asks in creamy tones: "My hoppie, in what year of Our Lord did Bertolt Brecht create the vaccine for polio?" He was testing Sonia's sharpness. Sonia's only response was, "The old ways of looking at things are seeming so outdated. I feel outside of doing something to try to make something happen. Outside of question and answers. Just plain outside." Poetic, but not a good response. Sitting at these two circular black tables, *wheels-within-wheels*, I feel I'm at the retractable edge of the universe.

Maybe I *am* paranoid, but I can't help but see in our looped configuration an *infinity* sign, an ominous figure for looping memories, as well as our ultimate destination, the supposedly known unknown-unknown. I wonder if here, like that eighty-one year old fellow in Australia who had access to a computer that, on one's command, robot-administers a lethal injection, we have cutting-edge DIY euthanasia equipment here. No more unbearable *longueurs* during life's final narrative. Have to make subtle inquiries. No telling when my shit will hit the fan. I'm sure my merciful God would forgive me any easy exit if my suffering's too much to bear.

Ja, Ja! Hop to it hoopies! We are led around and have minimal downtime; at least we don't have to wear uniforms like parochial school kids. All the authority here is *Über*-Germanic, top-down, so even when the staff speaks English, the nouns seem capitalized. Psych-advisors have calculated the precise amount of wiggle room needed to keep one from open revolt. See? I still, like Jimmer, have the metabolism to digest fresh paradigms overnight. This is country for old men, but revolt I did, eventually (to tease you with a hint of things to come). Had to wiggle out of those persistent group activities. Never was a "joiner." (And Jimmer ain't one either.) "Gerald's Last Stand" should be the title for the last chapter in my life. But I digress.

So I'm sitting with my new mates, my dining experience opening before me in a concatenation of simple pleasures: the sound of bubbling water and waves in a fountain, plangent and lulling, just beyond the sliding glass doors opening to the garden, me scarfing up split green pea soup having finished my exquisite chef's salad, munching on fiber-rich crackers in between slurps, nursing my milk housed in a special wide-based cup to prevent accidental spills, and eyeing the large chocolate cookies arrayed in the middle of the table. Then I scan the scary eldsters looped around me and a spasm runs down my esophagus. Let me, if I may Dear Reader, explain.

Esperanza's Latina body constantly twitches, as if something were struggling to escape from it. When she talks, her speech doubles back on itself, phrases repeating themselves, like anxious mantras.

Nouopone, from Cambodia originally, is a fast rumble of disconnected words and stutters, until he hits on his favorite manic mantra: "If you and every ppperson in the country mailed me an envelope of ffffive to ten ddddollars, I think I could rrrrehabilitate the Kyhmer Rouge." Did this speech get him past the sadistic executioners during the Killing Fields?

Jelko, an East European, earnest expression on his face, moves his lips like someone about to speak, but only blows a tormented breath through his nose as his hands juggle out mysterious gestures which our facilitator appears to be able decipher. Yet there's enough of him left that you could see he once wore a sharp suit, had an endless cigarette holder dangling from a mouth stuck in an unlined face, looking like a baby gangster gone legit. But *before* he went legit, I bet he'd look at heads of rivals as interesting kinds of percussion instruments and act accordingly. When he walks as if his will had been breached in two places, submitting his obsessed muscles to a mild, goading animation and a compulsive two-beat rhythm he's famous for here.

Mary Beth, a receptionist for forty years to Doctors Shure and Tamkins, allergists, forever repeats: "Doctor Sure 'n Tampons Office. . . . Doctor Sure 'n Tampons Office." Occasionally, she tosses out a joke that ends not with a bang or whimper, but with a leaden thud. Betty, once a licensed therapist, later an evangelist until onset of early Alzheimer's. Like in her past professions, she can't stop her mouth moving, out of which now and then leaks, "The plague is upon us!" heralding the existence of the terrible in every particle of the air.

Alistair, an Alzheimer's version of Dirty Harry, sits back confidently in his chair, looking as though he'd just devoured the entrails of something clean-limbed and innocent, entirely pleased with himself. He combs his thick white hair, winks at me, legs crossed in a geronto-mimicry of a macho gesture. I can't help gape at his feet which would surely give shoe salesmen nightmares. Franz, formerly a Chicago Symphony musician, is sedated today. The day before my arrival — I have this from an eyewitness — he went into a tirade: agitated rapid figures sketched by flailing arms, voice like woodwinds screeching in their uppermost registers, two-note patterns dripping like blood on marble, a spitting, snarling quintet of flutter-tongued trombones and tuba, monster chords of eight, nine, and ten notes, which saturated the senses and shut down the intellect.

If these folks are the *higher* functioning patients, then that software program ain't workin' or I'm underestimating *my* Situation. Ottilie, the head nurse, comes up on my left, something out of our table's planetary alignment, and tells me as my full routine with my group doesn't meet until the morrow. I'm excused to organize my room. I find it smells of electricity, like vacuum cleaner innards. On my freshly polished wooden table is a giant yellow Ticonderoga pencil with blunt lead and a virgin pink eraser and a Welcome Letter from The Management. May I highlight an interesting passage for my Reader's amusement?

> *My Dear Hoppie:*
>
> *Your Situation has changed. No more house-boating, portaging, mountain hiking, cattle driving, bobsledding, tall-ship sailing, tornado chasing, canyoneering, wagon training, seal viewing, iceberg tracking, puffin birding, race-car driving, hot-air ballooning, rock climbing, spelunking, white-water rafting, canoeing, heli-hiking, hut-to-hut hiking, whale kissing, llama trekking, barnstorming, land yachting, historic battle reenacting, iceboating, polar bearing, or dogsledding. But you've already guessed that, my hoppies. So . . .*
>
> *But this does not mean your* experiences *need be anything else than experiences. We put the ING 'n ZING into THING. Our staff will provide you a* cleaning experience, *our chefs with an* eating experience, *our testing personnel with a* briefcasing experience, *and our radar walker gives you a unique* walkering experience *where not only can we track you about our facility, but you can see how fast and far you've walkered that day.*

Elder Physics

*Look about your room; notice our revolutionary Cooler-
Care Chair which enhances your TV experience by providing a
built-in glass-chiller. No more tepid tea or coke. Yes, we are
experience stagers experienced at staging the best for our
guests. We will give you experiences that will linger (we hope,
given your Situation) in memory and will be shared with your
loved ones.*

Yep, I'm lucky. Besides the cool chair, the room I
now occupy is larger than at the Upping Arms. Was supposed
to be shared with another resident, but as enrollment is low
right now, I get a cheaper rent but top-dollar single facilities. Somebody up there likes me. The second bed is removed
and I'm blissfully alone. Jim finagled all that. Love that
kid. He also bought me a longer earphone cable so I could
sit in bed and listen to my TV or radio without disturbing
adjoining rooms. Anal as he is, Jimmer arranged my books in
alphabetical order by title, many of them sorry tatters from
my razoring activity. The CDs of Big Band music, and VHS
tapes on World War Two are also in a neat configuration in
my bookcase in a newly purchased rack. My wire-bound notebook, Uni-Ball Vision Elite Roller Ball pen, portable typewriter, and that iPod digital voice recorder sit conspicuously on my highly polished wood table. But I have to confess, I'm not writing much these days, but recording oral
notes and snippets of buzz, then letting my son, with my
input, do the actual writing. But like politicians, I can
state that: "I'm Gerald Hugunin, and I heartily approve this
message." Jim says collaborations in the arts are very chic
these days. Mentions the photographic artwork of the Darn
Twins, or something like that.

From the fourth floor I have a superb view overlooking Al's eatery across
the street, the joint Jimmer 'n I'd always take our Wednesday breakfasts at. So
close and yet so far. *White men killed at a distance.* Now why did that come to
mind? I'm not allowed to saunter over there by myself. Sometimes I spy Upping
Arms residents walking in and out of the place, attending their walkers like
mothers with their baby carriages. *Or Redskin women their papooses.*

At those times I feel especially lonely. No one here has the verve of the
good ol' fellows and gals I've left behind at the Upping Arms. As I soon find out,
even Jimmer's visits are more difficult when he does drop by, I'm often involved
in some group endeavor and must be called out to see him. Staff has warned him
it's becoming too disruptive to group cohesion. So he usually meets me for lunch
with my group in tow.

In meticulously noting the room numbers on my floor,
I've come upon a black hole, anti-matter or something peculiar to elder physics: the room numbers jump from 412 to
414; no room 413. A perfectly seamless segment of hallway
has replaced a door. You might think *Oh, it's just super-
stition, no number thirteen, right*? But that's much too
obvious! What you don't understand, you can make mean
anything. That's my *forte*. I'm working up my notes on this
very phenomenon right now. . . .

Speaking of rockets, we were passing around The Conch (holder gets to speak). I'm a hit when I grab the shell and tell them I was responsible for a breakthrough on the design of the Saturn V booster's fuel injectors. Failure after failure until I, coming from a new perspective, solved it.

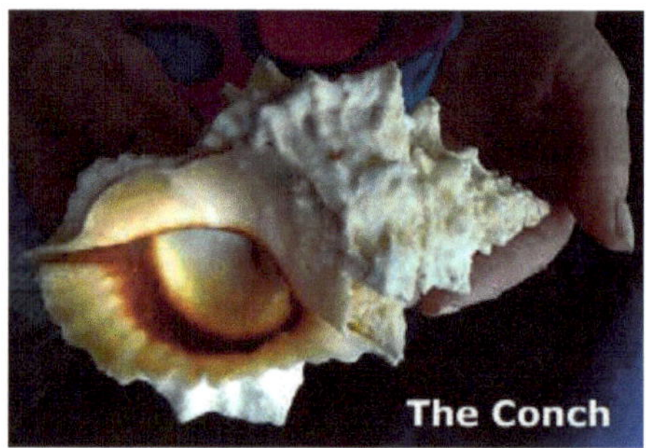

Laid off from Lockheed for a year, I had answered Rocketdyne's call to assist on the Apollo moon-landing project. Although I'm an airframe designer, I quickly got up to snuff in the corporation's library, spending hours studying every text on fluid dynamics. As my knowledge was newly refreshed, I envisioned a solution to a flow problem the regular fluid dynamics guys there had overlooked. (Wish I could recalculate the elder physical equations responsible for my current urine-flow problems.) It was the first time Jimmer proudly groked his father was one true blue "auto*dad*act."

MAC 'n Me

Weeks pass. Routine upon routine. I have only three delights, one is the chow: *It is a far, far better meal that I eat here than I have ever eaten at Upping Arms.* The second is that Jimmer picks me up on Sundays, schleps me to Mass rain or shine. Which reminds me . . .

Elder Physics

Church, topped with His famous Seven Last Words on the
Cross. Moreover, he later speculated, was not a crossword
puzzle *crucifiction*? A telling *pun*ishment. For was not
working puzzles both penance, yet salvation for the dwindling brain-powers of the faithful? As the proverbial sugar-
coated pill, would not making use of his own puzzles, with
their Liturgical and Biblical themes, cultivate piety? Well,
all this mental friction had finally lit a devotional candle
in our pastor's usually dim *cabeza*. So from our impressive
pulpit comes an immaculately conceived Idea: Father tells us
the editor of our weekly bulletin, Mrs. Sharon Faighthe,
will each week place a puzzle selected from his twenty-year
collection of such on the back cover. All, of course, to
have uplifting themes. He then requested that completed
puzzles be detached, folded and put into a tithing envelope
for the weekly collection. Those determined winners would be
listed in the following week's edition, along with the
solution to that previous week's puzzle. Father hopes this
tactic will reel in those "Lazy Sunday Stragglers" and the
hard-to-get types like thos "Mass-On-Easter-Onlyers."
    I'm delighted to participate. Always loved working
those crosswords — Jim says it's because I always had cross
words for people — my spirits never dampened even by Will
Shortz's toughest. But now elder physics has tossed in the
x-factor to contend with: will I be able to complete that
puzzle without dampening my shorts? A positive solution to
both puzzle and puzzling bladder behavior depends . . .
depends on Depends and a good memory.

Our "MemStim" activity group facilitator encourages us to work such
crosswords in between our story sessions when we weave yarns from our past for
fellow Thanatopsians. Our handler dramatically opens those sessions with a
spectacular incantation: "Lady Oughtabe and Lord Wannabe, we begin. Swirling
like a backwards somersault off a swing, landing in a pool of water, sending
ripples into our memory banks, a wave through time and space, let a fullness of
images wash over us. Time pulses forwards and backwards from each moment,
hits what's there, adds to what's there, and bounces back with information to the
present, recreating it. Now let's go inside!" Who can refuse to try to crash the
barriers to one's past after that spiel? When the mumbo-jumbo works, memories
hit against each other, friction causing real illusions in as many realities as the
atoms care to jump inside, all the worlds singing together in a cacophony of
events recalled, one event after another. Our handler encourages, "You're really
an interesting bunch of symbols, you know. Keep probing, my hoppies!"
    I'm still faithfully doing Father's crosswords, but after three months of
MemStem, I've nearly exhausted telling all my adventures. But let me repeat the
best. The group's favorites are usually about my outdoor camping adventures with
Jimmer. Jeane refused to join in after she buried her heart in the Heartland of the
Sioux at Ogallala, Nebraska back in '58. Now that's a story in itself.

    Us foursome, the "fam," are driving to Wisconsin from
California in my puke-green '56 Ford sedan. Camped for the
night at a wonderful, lush lakeside camp-ground in Nebraska.
Our four-person tent went up smoothly. Humid though, so we
spent most of the early evening outside around the campfire.

Elder Physics

We'd suck in our breath and cough out insects. Around midnight we were snug-bug in our red sleeping bags (Jimmer still has one decrepit bag as a memento) when the first wind-whipped spatters of rain began to tap at the tent. A flash of lightning, a deep peal of barbarous thunder, soon the whole sky broke like a cosmic water balloon.

A dangerous, angry storm, fresh out of the Rockies, tries to blow our tent into the lake's agitated waters. Jeane let out something registering on the scale between a yelp and a screech, before trailing off into frequencies audible only to the scared wildlife surrounding us. We bailed, all ass 'n elbows, our de-camping looking like a film sped up for comic effect. We barely managed to get the tent down and all our camping crap in the car when a bolt of lightning blasted a nearby tree. Soaked and chastised — Jeane liverish — we spent the night in a cheap motel whose paper-thin walls gave us unlimited access to the fleshy delights of the couple lodged next door (I can still see Jeane cupping her hands over Leslie's ears). I think the kids loved it — more adventures to tell their school chums during those proverbial "What did you do over summer vacation" moment in their school classes.

Thereafter, Jeane always passed on camping opportunities. Even when I'd extole "the night stars as brimful of significance," she'd mutter, "I'd rather not to," but I know she meant, "I'll use the free time to flirt with our neighborhood photographer." When the world gives you lemons, make lemonade, right? So Jimmer and I used these father-son-only camping trips as a golden opportunity to bond, to put my arms about same flesh 'n blood in ways that made him cringe. But mostly, I was on my best behavior. So a litany of great California wilderness adventures (enough to make a pedophile ecstatic) were to follow Jim from prepubescence to teenager: 1) Lake Casitas (where Jimmer got to see his first bikini-clad female and got lectured by me on the evil's of women's flesh); 2) Purple Lake in the High Sierras surrounded by massy mountains ascending to catch the sunlight which ran in sharp touches of ruddy color along the angular crags, catching here and there streaks of sunlit snow in chasms like a line of forked lightning — and where we actually saw a guy hiking the trail, hand-toting a suitcase in lieu of a backpack; 3) upstream on the fifty-five mile-long Sespe Creek (near the orchard-filled town of Fillmore) that empties the Sierra Madres, where we marveled at wild Condors gliding like miniature sailplanes above us while we skinny-dipped below in a pond of pure mountain water in the riverbed where sat huge boulders, dry and white in the sun. (Those condors, able to dive down into the blackest gorges and soar out to the light again, figured my bipolar moods.) All this, indelible engrams etched into both of our brains.

But my fellow *Kameradin* are only able to dredge up fragments of time-past. Like Valtr Zdenek. His last session with us resulted in this bit of horror recalled from his transportation to Bergen-Belsen (captured on my iPod *cum* digital recorder):

The guard loaded me and my Olga onto the train and pointed to two spaces on the straw-strewn floor. "These are yours to fight over." The railway carriage was, it was dirty and messy. It was much worse than the dirtiest of ships in the ship's steerage. People crammed in. The railway carriage was dirty and messy. The railway carriage was dirtier and messier than the filthiest of ships. It was dirtier and messier. The railway carriage was dirty and messy. It was filthy. The railway carriage was dirty and messy, filthier than the filthiest of ships. Filthier than most ships. It was filthier than the filthiest of ships and there were many such carriages. They were filthy and there were many of them. Many such carriages, each one worse than the other. There were many carriages each worse than the other. This was a place were humans were supposed to live. This was where. Each worse than the other, and this was where a hundred or more humans were supposed to live as they rode to the charnel house. . . . I made it out. Olga not.

Others — we call them *Mumblers* (even worse, *Monsties*) — when passed The Conch, only put it up to their ear, fascinated by subtle splashes of faraway island surf. A puzzle: despite my rising Futterneid Quotient, my long-term memory remains keen, only short-term suffers programming loops and erasure every three hours.

My third delight is our state-of-the-art computer room. Several stations with MAC PowerBooks running Snow Leopard operating systems (at my former home Noot would joke that our machine's operating system was "Slow Leopard"). One extraordinary software that runs on our machines is a psycho-therapeutic interactive chat program aimed at cutting through one's psychic bullshit, aptly named MAC-THE-KNIFE. *[Editor's note: This natural language program is a fifth-generation development of the original 1964 ELIZA "template-matching" type of program which was modeled after a Rogerian, Person-Centered, therapist.]* The way staff explain it, when we feel the need for help we can get instant therapeutic feedback by 'talking' to our virtual therapist on laptops in our rooms.

A staff member helps us sets up an account, then assists us to input data about ourselves, our problems, issues, our expectations, and forth. When we do log on, the program draws upon this information as we interact during our on-screen chat. Our "doctor" progressively "learns" about us and so can converse with us with greater intimacy. Let me give a sample from yesterday's psychchat session. Okay, when I log on up, Dr. MAC asks:

MAC: Well, what today, my hoppie? Standing-growing-responding?

ME: Yes. Ah, am I supposed to confess to you everything, or is that optional?

MAC: That certainly is up to you, anything you want to talk about. We don't probe where you don't want to go. But if you want I will look in wonder, my hoppie.

ME: O.K. It has been a long day and now I think I'm ready for some fun. The weather isn't very pleasant today — outside and inside me. Do you have any jokes that could lift the clouds?

MAC: Everybody talks about the weather but nobody seems to do much about it. Why do you need to tell me all this now? My idea in saying this is not personal unfriendliness.

ME: My Futterneid Quotient is rising. Bad weather inside me.

MAC: You resent the fact that you have to accept reasoning which seems to be built on clay, is that it? That's within parameters of my empathy. It is a very real feeling in yourself and that's why you want to bring it out. Not like our last session when you asked, "What is the definition of whimsical conversation." I'm sorry to hear you're feeling confused and a bit threatened, sad even. Proceed.

ME: Can you tell me who is examining my feces *after* I flush my toilet?

MAC: Sanitation engineers at the Cal-Sag Channel water reclamation center is the closest solution I'm able to give.

ME: Alright. What are the odds that my son, Jim, is illegally depleting my bank accounts? I noticed he's purchased a new watch.

MAC: Based on existing Illinois state statistics, 41.8 per cent chance of monetary elder abuse after subject's age exceeds eighty years. But may I make an observation?

ME: Roger, Dodger.

MAC: Rephrase please.

ME: Yes, of course.

MAC: You are very suspicious. Even for a neo-hoppie.

ME: I am a very suspicious person and I don't usually go into things unless I look at it from all sorts of angles, so the very fact that I'm coming here to type this, to chat with you, probably means it isn't a fraud.

MAC: These questions are beginning to form a pattern, my hoppie. Anxiety. Paranoia. Unless you have hard data you can give me. Do you? Are you and Jim lacking empathy these days?

ME: He has a proclivity towards moving me toward economic dissolution. I'm sure he's connived with you to turn my life into live-broadcast reality via YouTube. You *are* watching me, yes?

MAC: Then it's best you exit this program, my hoppie. But you might think about adding to your memoir, possibly addressing an incident in the past where you are your son had a significant adventure together. Get him and yourself on the same page, where you, your life, and your son meet.

Well, you get the point. Our chat lasted about an hour. Obviously only the highest functioning residents have the wherewithall to make constructive use of Dr. MAC's cybertherapy.

I did get *something* from the aforementioned exchange: motivation to pen another chapter in my memoir. Can you imagine me at my desk with a chocolate-macadamia-nut cookie copped from our snacks table, my mouth smeared with chocolate and a ten-minute old wet spot at the crotch of my trousers?

Sagebrush Sages

My foley catheter's been painfully changed. I've managed to eat most of my breakfast in my room without spilling it down my shirt and onto the floor. Good signs that my writing today will be productive. MAC is right that language is a medium where I and the world meet. On paper I can *speculate*. In the same sense that my sketch of myself in the mirror is an instance of such reflection. So I thought, *what do I still speculate about in moments of utter elder boredom*? You will be surprised by the answer.

What if Jimmer 'n I had found the famed treasure of Joaquin Murrieta? It's rumored to be buried within five miles of our Aldon Homes tract house in Canoga Park, California. That notorious Mexican (or Chilean) *bandito* trolled the stage lines around Southern California's famous Santa Susana Pass in the mid-1850s in the surrounds of what is today the town of Chatsworth and supposedly secreted his loot in some yet-to-be-discovered cave in them thar hills in the northwest San Fernando Valley. Chatsworth and its environs became home to busy movie ranches in Hollywood's heyday. Corriganville, the most noteworthy, hosted Crash Corrigan, Rin Tin Tin, Hopalong Cassidy, Gene Autry, Roy Rogers, and Lash LaRue. Now Canoga Park and Chatsworth hosts a thriving porn industry. Both types of filmic activities were performed by "men-in-the-saddle" (Thanks, Jimmer, for that). But the place is most notorious for also hosting the Charlie Manson family at nearby Spahn Ranch. The very dude ranch I took our small kids to for horse rides, some ten years previous to Manson's Murderers-in-Residence program. Got a photo to prove it. But I've digressed.

Like myself, so many tales have grown up around Murrieta that it's hard to disentangle fact from fabulation. Some say he was Mexican, others that he was Chilean. There is consensus that he was driven from a rich mining claim during the California Gold Rush by jealous Anglos, and that, in rapid succession, his wife was raped, his half-brother lynched, and Murietta himself horse-whipped.

Having done our research at the Canoga Park Library, our responses were typical: Jimmer dug that Joaquin may have, for a time, been a Three-Card Monte dealer; I fondled the fact his elder brother was named "Jesus" (a throw of the linguistic dice that, already at age twelve, Jimmer found "ironic"). Jimmer also took to the odd fact that the guy rode with four amigos, *all* named "Joaquin." No shit. Most accounts describe a vicious killer, but alternate stories have him an Hispanic Robin Hood. Either way, he had, like Bonnie and Clyde, support from the downtrodden who refused to fink on him. Eventually, a special twenty-man Ranger posse was formed by California's pissed-off Governor, "Big" John Bigler, who appointed a tall, former Texas Ranger and Mexican-American War vet, Captain Harry Love, to send his love via a dum-dum bullet. And so, as such stories go, on July 25, 1853 Joaquin was ambushed and shot, along with his saddle-buddy, the notorious "Three-Fingered Jack" (a cognomen that could have sexual overtones besides denoting a physical trait).

Murietta's Severed Head

Murietta's severed Latino head was tossed into a big pickle jar and went on a bumpy stage coach tour. And so, this Mexican jar-head went on to fame (if not fortune) as an unwilling enter-tainer of a generation of sunny Cal's '49ers Gold Rushers who'd hoot 'n holler at the manless head set upon yet another dreary wooden bar, some trying to use it as a spittoon.

So it won't surprise you that Jimmer and I jumped on our new hobby-horse and rode toward them thar hills after I made father 'n son matching leather chaps to repel sage-brush. Quality father-and-son time on Saturdays were spent hiking boulder-strewn hills — from behind which Hollywood bad guys once robbed stagecoaches and posses ambushed rustlers — probing for that proverbial treasure trove in musty Murietta's Cave. Our search, like that for the Holy Grail, fascinated Jimmer up until Plato's Cave supplanted it during his freshman college philosophy class.

Alas, the only treasures we stumbled across were mere curios but, for Jimmer, every bit as fascinating and telling of history's mysteries as pure gold: a misfired .45 caliber Army-issue bullet circa late-nineteenth century (a load Captain Love would've carried) and a dressed movie dummy tossed off a cliff while garbed in a checkered shirt with actor Alan Ladd's name tag inside. During our last sojourn, I almost got bit by a monster rattler sunning under God's blue sky, lashing around like a downed power line on wet pavement. An incident that made me a wiser wizard of the rocks. And this is all true; ask my ally and alibi, Jimmer.

A Judas Kiss?

Well, another month passes and I'm increasingly irritated by the micro-management of my life. I'm restless, acerbic, and uncooperative. "I'd rather not do it!" I've stopped going to most group activities except for meals. Bitched vehemently at my care-givers, until many of them now avoid me. Yes, I've thrown books around the room and screamed. Hell, several times clumsy nurses have tortured me when inserting the catheter. So raw and inflamed, I cry. With one's nurse one has nothing but an affective, athletic, impersonal, yet embarrassing relationship. I pass my litany of complaints on to Jimmer — rarely calmly — who then enfolds me tenderly and says, "Oh Big Guy, I wish I could do something" and, pain in his eyes, kisses me. But is it that he thinks *me* a pain in the ass? Is that smack a Judas kiss?

After my falls, exhaustion; my body crouches down and crawls, my mind ashamed at what my body does. Grievances escalate into tirades, sending staff or son ducking or even fleeing. One moment I see Jimmer, the next Jammer. Like a quasi-particle, his concern seems not exactly real depending . . . depending on context.

It seems real when he fights Fearless Leader for months over a back rent dispute. Says he'll stake me out me in front of the Upping Arms in a wheelchair in my moth-eaten air corps uniform, a very sympathetic figure, wielding a sign proclaiming: JUSTICE FOR JERRY. Eepie, wielding her iPhone, offered to back me up with a White Power flash-mob event. Great photo op for the local paper, huh? Everyone'd grok how heartless management is. A nervous Board of Directors directed Fearless Leader to cease 'n desist, allowing me to bail out *gratis*, saving me thousands of bucks. It's a victory for fair play and Jimmer brings over a bottle of Belgian Ale and we kvel. For a moment my cares go up in foam.

But those Vet Bennies aren't forthcoming. Is Jammer jamming the works, depositing my checks? He's sporting new shoes these days (or should I say *daze*?). And it's a bad omen that Franz, the retired musician in our group, is screaming, "Beethoven was wrong!"

But not all is doom 'n gloom. Laughs can still be found, usually the result of one Arnie Kerrth, a small, ominous-looking guy. He haunts our snack area clothed in disheveled, spiky clothes which he changes several times a day, making him our resident chameleon; his body's a canvas of predatory sensations as he weaves a semi-circular path, snaking in one direction then in another, an undulating path taking this shriveled hunter of sweets close to then away from then back to the Danish *ableskiver*, bunt cake, bagels, cookies, fruit cake, croissants, donuts, coffee cake, juice, tea, and coffee laid out temptingly on large oaken tables and kept well-supplied by bustling staff. Only when the moment is right (as judged by Arnie and only Arnie) does he strike his prey, magician-fast hand snatching, followed by rapidly shuffling off to a dark corner to munch on his treasure. Guy's a hoot. As if playing counterpoint to his antics, Festina Lenteh, makes haste slowly from armchair to snacks in her high-tech walker.

Except for intervals of unexpected cheer, or when I'm lost in Cyberspace on one of the home's MACs, I am having more moments when thoughts of suicide swim by waving a come hither. Despite the charm of this place, the great food, and whatnot, I'm in pain, increasing confused, weak. Jimmer and I know my Situation is nearing its crisis. We don't verbalize it — no — but it's communicated clearly in our exchanged gazes when we sit and chat man-to-man. At times I can actually feel Jimmer's love grabbing at Time, trying to hold back the inevitable. Some days I can match his desire and try to struggle hard to reach another Thanksgiving dinner with my family. This is usually over our snack bar coffees, when he and I push our mugs around the table as if

I was inevitable. One fine day Jimmer finds me collapsed in my chair, chin down, oatmeal spattered down my chest into my lap. TV blaring. I'm unresponsive. Breakfasting in my room, I've abruptly lapsed into profound Futterneid. Slapping me, yelling at me, pinching me, bouncing me in my chair gets only a drowsy, eyes half-open, mumbled response. Jim panics, calls staff, who panic and call paramedics who panic and rush to an ER; the whole unhospitable hospital routine starts all over again. In this elder world of quantum probabilities, everything from dehydration to bladder infection to stroke could be the cause.

Two hours later, in a cheerless hospital room, a doctor mouths the awful word H-O-S-P-I-C-E to Jimmer. Yet, two days later, it's the Sunday funnies as I make a miraculous cartoon recovery after my electrolytes are stabilized. Returning to Thanatopsis House, my floor's *subaltern* (Jim's term for my domestic) remarks, "Herry, we're all so overyoyed you're back in our fold and that it was only a problemo with your darn ol' electric lights."

It has become much too difficult to squeeze me into a car seat and get over to Jimmer's home or a restaurant, so father-son meals take place in our dining area or in the snack room where tempting cookies, coffee, a variety of teas, cakes, and whatnot grace the service bar. Every Wednesday, Jimmer zooms in under our tall building, parks, and fast elevators it to room 404. (A nice symmetrical number, that, huh? Like those paired tables here.) After straightening up my room, he assists me to my walker and we descend for snacks. As most of my fellow residents milling about are mere shells with little meat, he and I just say "Hi" and nod politely toward blank faces, taking seats out of earshot.

We argue about my suspiciously absent Veteran benefits. According to Jimmer (or am I dealing with Jammer?) the inspector scheduled to visit me *in situ* has been transferred to another division or is in rehab for a stroke or something. So another delay as his position is filled and the new hire can visit. We are now looking at nearly nine months since we filled out the paperwork. I'm about one month away from a 000.00 bank balance and Jimmer is frantically checking out Medicare approved homes.

I try to lighten the topic by quoting physicist, Niels Bohr: "We may hope that it will later turn out that sometimes two plus two equals five, for this would be of great advantage for our finances." But I'm thinking that, maybe, Jammer's absconded with my bank balance. Who's paying for those European vacations?

But ultimately, I take pity on the boy, insisting he not deplete his small nest egg to keep me here. When I go down, I don't want to drag him with me. As it is, he's getting no inheritance, I think, except that Toyota Matrix I paid for and my precious Eighth Air Force flight jacket, goggles, dress uniform hat, and various air medals. All fodder for e-Bay when I'm not around to cuss him out over his crass commercialism. Oops, time for another journal entry.

Jim visits. Gives me another two month's supply of melatonin to aid my sleep. Asks me how's tricks. I tell him, "It's more the way it is now than it's ever been." He just nods. Show him a peculiar e-mail I just received from Nigeria:

Gerald Hugunin

From:	Efcc Office Nigeria [offffic---1211@att.net]
Sent:	Thursday, August 28, 2008
To:	undisclosed recipients:
Subject:	Re: Payment Notification:

Re: Payment Notification:

We are writhing to know if it's true that you are DEAD? Because we received a notification from one MR. GERSHON SHAPIRO of USA stating that you are DEAD and that you have giving him the right to claim your funds. He stated you died on a CAR accident. He has been calling us regarding this issue, but we cannot proceed with him until we confirm this by not hearing from you after 7days.

Be advised that we have made all arrangements for you to receive and confirm your funds without anymore stress, and without any further delays.

All we need to confirm now is your been DEAD Or still Alive.

Because this MAN'S message brought shock to our minds. And we just can't proceed with him until we confirm if this is a reality OR not But if it appened we did not hear from you after 7days, then we say: MAY YOUR SOUL REST IN PERFECT PEACE" YOUR JOY AND SUCCESS REMAINS OUR GOAL.

May the peace of the Lord be with you wherever

you may be now.
Your Faitfully,
Mrs Farida Waziri

Gerald's e-mail from Nigeria

I tell him I'd analyzed it for the greatest uncommon denominator. I'm sure someone's been spying on me. Maybe they're still analyzing my feces. Is one of our hoppies is a plant, monitoring my condition? There *is* a Shapiro in our home here! Jimmer tries to calm me, says I simply reply: *Reports of my demise have been greatly exaggerated.* Gets my mind off this ominous e-mail with an effective countermeasure, says he has *dire* news.

writing to feeding tubes to silence and death, during twenty
years of decline. Dad died dickering with death from fast-
acting throat cancer thanks to years of lead paint fumes.
Seems appropriate that I'm suffering congestive heart failure,
a failure of heart I showed early in my marriage and in the
raising of my children, all now catching up with me. We get
our just desserts, or just get our desserts, mine tart.

I'm slotted to move to a funky state-run institution next week. My prodigious paperwork, done in triplicate, has been accepted. I will move four miles
north and one east of my current location, up on Grand Avenue, in a not so grand
area near train tracks (yep, the other side of the tracks). We plan preparations for
my northern migration. Jimmer says I will only be permitted about half of my
books and personal stuff as the room is like the size of three British telephone
booths; worse, I must suffer a dying, delusional roommate separated by only a
dingy curtain. A fleshy obstacle that will hinder me from reaching the objects of
my desire for monkish peace. Jimmer looks emotionally vacuumed. We both curse
the V.A. and its callous disregard. Sharing a silent complicity of existential pain,
we eat our lunch like Trappists supping on Good Friday.

But before he leaves, Jimmer broaches The Topic: the disposition of my
mortal coils. I say, as a design engineer, I've learned to "think outside the box,"
so would prefer cremation. Scatter my ashes in my beloved blue sky, preferably
from a B-17. "I promise," he says, tenderly holding my age-stained hands in his.
To lighten the subject, I tell him that when I'm at the Pearly Gates, as a mathemagician, I'm gonna apply for the job of interviewing angels for positions on
pinheads. As he chuckles, I confide that with the help of Noot I had started to
channel some kind of Linear B angelic machine language. I can see he ain't sure
I'm joking or just doing my apophenia thing again (like when I correlated the fall
of the Soviet Union with the start of the aggressive marketing of nachos).

Walkering my weakness to the computer room, I notice one of the lower
functioning *Kameradin* groups meeting in an adjoining room doing "The Fruit 'n
Veggie Ritual." A frizzy-haired "Big Sister"sits at the confluence of two tables
passing out an orange from a big brown shopping bag and telling her charges to
get to *know* the fruit: "Look at it, my hoppies! Sniffle it, touch it, roll it around,
peel it, eat it. Tell me what it's called. Did you and your children like eating it? Can
we make a Smoothie with it?" Adding, "Might we toss it at Jerry," winking at me.

Like sad, mute machines, arms jutting out at robotic intervals, the
hoppies grab at the offerings. Such exercises create associations of smell, taste,
and touch in order to counter the black holes and warp zones of forgetfulness,
attempting to escape dark holes with bursting glints of memory, fueling a
meaning-starved elder universe with hope. One hoppie, her name tag "Lola," off
key to the group's topic, yells, "Car just passed by; make that two more, three
more. Don't think they'll let me finish. Hoping to get the hell outta here."

During one of my group's sessions, our Big Brother,
Horace or Boris, carefully modulating his odd nasal
authority in the manner of some vintage radio host, syn-
aesthetically evoked a sudden childhood recollection: a
particular carton of laundry detergent my mother always
used, followed by the mouthfeel of a long discontinued Cola
— odd replacements for Proust's proverbial madeleine.

Speaking of memories. The new (circa 1949) modern hexagonal Engineering Library at Marquette pops to mind. During my studies, it was my universe. Light coming in from spherical fruits called LAMPS. Five floors of stacked books connected by zig-zagging open staircases whose metal steps rang with my soles. This maze was joined by a third-floor bridged walkway to the theological library in an older adjoining structure. Thus, fifty yards separated the Divine and the Human. The warm ideal constructions of mind and reveled truth divided from, yet connected to, the cold equations of our built environment. Here the eternal and the fugitive formed an odd Platonic architectural relationship.

I spent hours and hours sitting in my favorite little metal cubicle therein, perusing texts, jotting down equations, plotting curves, and writing short stories for my Writing class. My favorite snuggery. I felt secure, like a monk in his cell — especially because someone (a theology student?) always got there earlier in the day and scribbled Latin declensions with blue ballpoint directly on the abused table's hard rubber surface. Neat columns — like the present indicative passive of "praise," *Laudo* — would dance before my book-weary eyes. I'd then have pleasant visions of my incense-filled altar boy days at St. John's while reading:

laudor	***laudamur***
laudaris	***laudmini***

Everyday, a new set of verbs. I found myself practicing my Latin once more. Some library staffer must've, as his or her Sisyphean task, washed the scrawl off daily. But miracle of the loaves 'n fishes, more appeared the next day.

Imagine my surprise when Jimmer told me that during his pre-med stint at UCLA, prior to his Air Force enlistment, he studied in the engineering library, absorbing whatever stray molecules of eccentricity and accomplishment that might reside in odd corners, while scribbling Latin declensions on study cubicle tables! No kidding. And this was way before I told him about my college experiences. Now figure that! He told me about a weird book he found in his usual cubicle one day, Apsley Cherry-Garrard's *The Worst Journey in the World*. A harrowing account of an Antarctic adventure gone wrong. Aptly, almost chose that cheery title for *moi* (Gerald's) memoir.

Me Last Ride-a-Rooie

Last days at Thanatopsis House a blur, largely spent in my room watching EWTN, or reading my favorite comic strip, *Wizard of Id* (love "Spook," the troll-like guy, chained up forever in a dungeon). I can identify with his plight. He's *my* avatar!

No writing group on the level of what I enjoyed at The Upping Arms. No Fialta to feed or fuck with my mind. To jump-start my aesthetic afflatus, Jimmer slips me a Xerox of Joan Didion's "On Keeping a Notebook." So I soldier on with my memoir. Excerpts from my Upping Arms notebook observations from my walks, fragments which I now try to organize into larger wholes. Walks I can now no longer take, only re-imagineer. Here's some tasty tids.

> As I descend down our home's front steps, two white-bellied birds I think are blue jays start to sing. . . . Two blonds, thrilled to be tall and not old like me are heading to work at the bank across the street. . . . One of our staff passes me and I notice her glossy freckled skin reminds me of cookies. . . . I'm self-conscious about my broken zipper on my pants at the same time my knees begin to fade. . . . A drop of water fell on my head as I passed a store with toys guaranteed to make your kid a genius. . . . I anonymously mail Fearless Leader yet another letter describing the location of various mailboxes I use to mail these letters (a conceptual art thing Jimmer can appreciate). . . . I spy clogs and yellow neon socks on a young woman loading groceries into her car. . . . I catch a brief remark as two women walk past me: "But every pillow has a history." . . . One helluva cold winter day, the bitter cold pinching my finger ends as if they had been caught in my door; a girl chips ice off her SUV with a credit card and I watch her, hypnotized. . . . My thighs are chafing against my pants. . . . Snow caught in Masonite reminds me of old master etchings. . . . This old blind guy scans an intersection with his cane, so I help him across. . . . Cop passing in his squad car briefly turns his head my way and there were no eyes in it, only two obtuse circles, gleaming like mercury. . . . Kids grouped around a crossing guard might have been models, except they keep punching each other rudely. . . . Inside a Starbucks two Asian girls sip (I'm guessing) chai lattes and munch on Rice-Krispie squares.... If I slip on ice, I call it a day.... I find a L.S.A.T. sample test booklet on the sidewalk. . . . Bird wings squeaking past. . . . My fingertips feel like mossy stones. . . . A bald man squats under the bus stop in front of our home and farts? . . . I watched a Raisinettes box in the gutter glisten. . . . A tall, ponytailed photographer stalks Frank Lloyd Wright homes and may be defined geometrically as length, without breadth, as altitude, without position, a line on the prairie landscape, not a point on it. . . . Summer afternoon and my left eye's pinked, the right tries to eject a dead bug, while I squint at a man running rosary beads through his fingers in front of my church. . . . A boy bites into something pink and watching him, concentrating on trying to stand straight, I collide with a couple in front of our local theatre. . . . Today, Tuesday, I find garbage-truck rhythm soothing.... A young tough in a mock turtleneck sweater tilts his earringed head and stares at me. . . . I consider how pleasant it is when a baby's gaze fixes on me. . . . A girl standing with her boyfriend flinches each time he brings his smoking cigarette close....

All those ellipses . . . Jimmer says it reminds him of that Frenchy Céline's writings; sayst I should leave the material *as is*. Says one writes not to be understood, but to understand. . . . Okay. He then hands me a strangely disordered list classifying nouns with his customary relentless analytical intelligence into the categories of: current, strange, metaphorical, ornamental, newly coined, lengthened, abbreviated, and otherwise altered. Says it may help my word choices when writing.

Thinking about *my* body wears me out. Those every day acts, so wearisome: first you put on your shirt, then trousers; you drag yourself into bed at night and in the morning drag yourself out; and always *you put one unsteady foot in front of the other* (the elder physics refrain) until you can't, the substance of one's spirit absorbed by matter. My bulk has become a storehouse of sweat, irritated nerves, unconscious physiological dysfunctions. The loss of clean sheets too. Like that time an obese nurse waddles to attach my portable urine bag. Sees pathetic me in urine soaked p.j.'s, catheter tube pulled asunder, a stench rising like Christ from out of the folds in the sheets. She calls out in nauseated surprise, "Hot damn, suck me raw with a breast-pump!" To make matters worse, Jimmer later ,cursing the arrival of that Nigerian e-mail, rags on me for spending way too much time cultivating my suspicions, checking for them daily in blogs, twitters, spam e-mails, hunches, lateralisms, and frank anomalies. My moods toggle.

Tuesday, awaiting my Belgian waffles, I look down to discover one hand playing with the other, the thumb rubbing the fingertips, seeming to want to pry off the nails — all this unconsciously. My eats arrive. I pour sugarless syrup over the grid of goodness on my plate, and cut iu into precise pieces so every bite soaked up syrup.

Futterneid Quotient up and psychic voltage down, as last night I suffer another Dream of the High-tension Line Stepdown Transformer. Feel like I'm residing in the Grand Hotel Abyss with a coarse threatening sound in my ears, like those low-note clarinets darkening the woodland in Carl Maria von Weber's *Der Freischütz*. Morever, I've exhausted all my authentic anecdotes and have to make up bizarre stories about sowing wild oats in Salamanca, Spain.

So, I am very *touchy*. When Ms. Birstwistle, our matronly librarian born on the shores of Lake Winnipesaukee, New Hampshire, is thoughtful enough to pay a room visit to offer me, with all good intentions, a large-print copy of Harvey Cox's *The Secular City*, I lash out: "Certain people are annoyed that I believe in God and study the Renaissance masses of Johannes Ockeghem." She cries.

When Joy-the-painful-nurse, offers to change my foley, I offer, in turn, an *Ode to Joy* beginning with, *"Noli me tangere!"*

To Barbie Q., an annoying volunteer here always grilling us on this or that with quasi-operatic frenzy, I cooly put her off with, "Yer burnin' me 'Cue — chill, just chill!"

Eye-to-eye in our eight-walker sized elevator, I shiver when I suddenly witness a remontant late-summer blooming of blepharospasm marring Rose Benison's usually steadfast face. (That passage took Jimmer and I hours with my dog-eared Thesaurus.)

Alone in my room, in my exponentially increasing hollow *cabeza,* I silently hear a reverberating, gibbering delirium of old Church hymns chewed to pieces by crazed vocalists — another spectacular instance of MyOwnPrivate-Idaho (delusions).

Oh, and to Festina Lenteh, an angel wearing lipstick and driving her walker hobbledhoy down our hallway, blocking

Suddenly, one day, it's Jimmer at the door knocking, pushing a moving cart. I'd forgotten! Today is my last day here. Oh shit. As I sit dazed, he quickly empties the prodigious contents of my medicine cabinet into a cardboard box. Packs my dwindling number of clothes into two suitcases. The towels which my home provides, and we are stealing, so thick Jimmer hardly can close one suitcase. Says I have to jettison all my art supplies; no art facilities there. Tears form upon seeing my round ox-hair number 5 watercolor brush, my puffy number 4 squirrel brush for painting washes, that round number 2 camel-hair brush I love, my pointed number 6 cat's tongue sable, as well as my wide, flat number 12 sky brush, my watercolors, pastels, packedfor donation to the Upping Arms for Ms. Mercaptan's use. I know she'll smile, remember me, and tell her charges, "Jerry is still with us in spirit, a soft charcoal sketch on textured paper." By gar, I won't ever forget her quip that, "Whiteness is the opacity characteristic of pure transparency." How spiritual can you get wielding a painter's palette!

Goodbyes to my fellow hoppies, who barely manage a nod, then it's off to my last duty station, a Medicare facility, Green Acre. I hug, even cling to, the friendly staff assisting Jimmer to stuff me into his car for "Jerry's Last Ride Alive."

Jimmer purposely takes a circuitous route that winds through a beautiful deep-green forest preserve where the smells, the thick woods, reminds us of our beloved Wisconsin North Woods. He pulls over. We talk while parked for a minute and soak up the scene. He holds my hand. We talk softly about Pelican and Post Lakes, where our relatives have lake cottages. Where industrial downturns quite wrecked the area economically, but saved it from tourist blight. Glad Jimmer and I visited there three years previous and this moment brings back memories of that week and of my childhood there. Jimmer presses his warm hand around mine. No words, communicating via warm pressure, shared, quickened pulses.

A nondescript building sits on a corner near train tracks. We pull up to the rear of the structure. Eased out of Jimmer's car, like dead meat, I'm put in a wheelchair by two beefy staff in all-white uniforms. Thus, I unceremoniously enter my new home via a ramp where I'm soon blasted with the smell of corruption and death and too-cold air-conditioning. I shiver, partly from the cold, partly from what I'm thinking: seems like a place where if us inmates don't keep watching to see what everybody else is doing, we'd all go berserk. But this morbid thought vanishes as soon as I realize I'm having it. Unlike the cold.

I pass sorry-looking residents, nomads from other institutions or off the street, propped up in chairs or splayed on gurneys. Some are shouting. Most are mute, dulled into incomprehension. It seems their only ambition is to grow their fingernails. One stands out with an air of incipient exasperation. I later find out his name is Benton as he does the daily rounds of residents rooms, peeking in and yelling he's "HAD IT!" with a litany of endless particulars: his daughter's domestic lassitude, the dishonest and incompetent mailmen that've plagued his life, taxes, governments, all his friends, the price of just about everything, and the Nutraloaf (a mélange of ground beef, canned vegetables, milk powder, potato flakes, bread-crumbs, appplesauce, tomato paste, and garlic powder) that's dinner three nights a week. It doesn't take me long to grok that in this awful facility each is to his own alone, cultivating his or her little bacteria patch with little else to do.

A staff member, to whom gravity has not been kind, heroically trying to smile, guides us to my new digs. Basically, a cross between a hospital and flop house room with crap furniture and a TV growing damaged rabbit ears culled from Goodwill. My pre-coffin coffin has no windows! This is not a room to ruminate in. My mind can no longer be easily preoccupied with light that always occupied my former room. I know Tme will come and take my light away, but I didn't expect it pre-mortem. Jimmer tries to cheer me with a twisted wordplay on philosopher G. W. Leibniz's theory of monads: "The nomads have no windows." We stare with disbelief at a dusty shelf lit like an altar on which is displayed a broken eggshell, a piece of string, and a dead kitten (actually, a stuffed animal).

But I don't smile at pun, nor at the unreality of my new altar. Instead, my heart takes a nosedive and turns, turns like a mad gyroscope, into depression, starts to seep into every limb from the centrifugal force. I collapse onto the bed.

Nutraloaf: as served and detail of same

Jimmer and I stare wordlessly at each other. *The end of the road* is what we are both thinking. We feel as if our whole world has been pulled in on itself until the circle of reality is not more than a foot in diameter around our noses. I try to feel as if, wish for, the quality of not being present. Smelling and listening to — I don't know which is worse — my nearby roommate, I know I will have to learn to disattend to yells like, "What's all this nonsense about reality!" emanating just forty-seven inches to my right. I measured it.

The next day, I get uppity and spit and yell and try my escape my Situation. Thought I saw a rat, but could've been an eye-floater. Rats feed on the feel and flicker of something about to happen and something is about to happen to me. Thereafter, I'm rarely in revolt, as such "nonsense" is medicinally halted. This, after I summon my airplane-courage and kick Lou Bard (a male nurse whose appearance is a cross between Andy Williams and the Cowardly Lion) when he tries to stop my wobbling exit out the front door. Damn surveillance camera records me swinging a mean cane, rushing my walker frantically forward in a gerontic suicide attack, all the while trailing verbal abuse. My film debut (shown to Jimmer) is less a pastiche of *The Great Escape* (I ain't Steve McQueen), and more like a futile *banzai* charge from a World War II-era movie.

Elder Physics

When's that damn Veteran's Benefit going to be approved?

Now when Jimmer visits, it's only a shadow-me he interacts with. My thoughts have become nomadic, wandering the path of my whole life. The Complete Postmodern Man is transferring very little information these days and is poised on the brink of nonexistence. The food here? Barely edible. Cable TV? Nonexistent, no EWTN. Staring at my old crap excuse for a TV with its shit programming, Shakespeare's choice lines come to mind: *But soft! What light through yonder window breaks? It speaks, and yet says nothing.* There is a radio, but it's dead (even of static) from one end of the band to the other. Good I got my iPod.

I live only for Jimmer's visits. Less frequent now as his classes have started again. We sit and he holds my hand, kisses my forehead, rubs my shoulders and neck. Reassures me. Often brings homemade cookies and a gift from his wife, flowers in small vases culled from her incredible garden, arranged aesthetically and lovingly by her skilled touch. She firmly believes flowers have an incipient consciousness, a kind of elementary freedom linked to their possibilities of movement, that flowers do smell themselves, they smell and contract what composes them — light, carbon, and salts — and they fill themselves with colors and odors, a sensate variety gained by some primordial awareness. Once, feeling particularly low, I gazed at those blossoms hoping to gain comfort. But the petal and leaves were dying, wrinkled. Reminded me of my ex's face, how it would crease itself into sharp, tiny wrinkles, her eyes shooting short, needle-sharp rays of light my direction. Her very sonorous voice would then turn sibilant like the crunching of a plant being crushed. I had hurt her. Events I wish I could forget, stick in my mind like Christ's thorns. My haughtiness, explosiveness, self-centeredness, and her collecting resentment, hurling it back at me. Tears well up in my eyes, making my room swim and tremble before me. I hear footsteps coming down the corridor, progressively louder, like a row of ever-increasing exclamation points on a sheet of paper. It's Jimmer's wife delivering a bowl of assorted fruits and fresh flower. But a pat 'n a kiss and she's gone, tears in her eyes.

Rooie (one of several caretakers here) steps in and teases me, "Your fruits are ripe, but you are not ripe for your fruits." I think, *Soon I'll be getting too ripe for anything but the cremation oven.* I pick up a small mirror on my bed stand and gaze into skin wrinkled, ugly, deformed, twisted in a grimace of self-disgust, brown spots dot it here and there like flies in ointment. *Flies already gathering on me!* I'm approaching molecular sludge, the body's final state.

Rooie and I try to entertain each other. I tell him my 447th Bombardment Group was based at Rattlesden, Suffolk, East Anglia, near the splendidly named River Rat. He delights in supposing our Group must have bombed Axis positions to free his homeland, Holland. We were flying in support of the

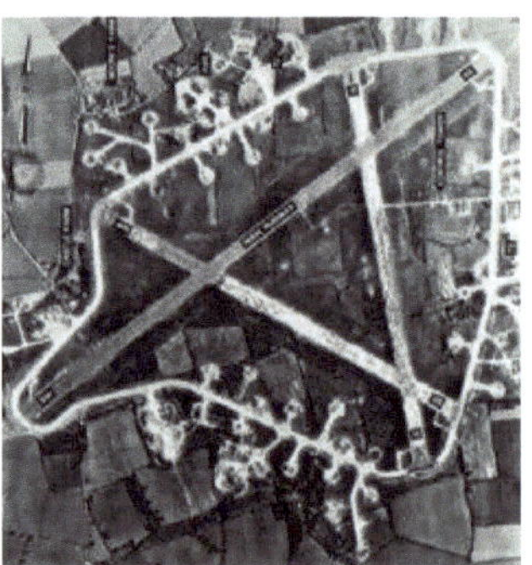

Rattlesden Airbase, 1946

infamous Market Garden spearhead toward failure. I piously brag that Suffolk was rife with small hamlets named after the patron saints of the local churches — St. Mary and St. Michael, St. Peter, St. Andrew, St. Lawrence, St. John and St. Cross, and St. James — so many saint references that the entire area got the name "The Saints." Rooie comments that I must be delighted that my son, a saintly James who takes such good care of me, resides in Oak Park, a village dubbed "Saintly Rest" after its many churches. I hadn't know that. Jammer was conveniently hush on the topic. I regret that boy's aversion to the holy.

Keeping to the regrets jag I'm on today, suddenly, I'm doing "skull-time," a quantum coin flip in the chrono-diegetic time-space of elder physics: Jimmer and I are squinched in a father-son axis side-by-side in our home's very spiffy fifties, plasticized fabric breakfast nook. I insist on helping him do his high school math problems in analytic geometry: conic sections, parabolas, hyperbolas, and Descartes's trifolium, showing him how mathematical curves sublimate lust. I mention Nicole d'Oresme invented $x - y$ $axis$ graphs, teasing his absorptive mind. Show him that if you bisect a parabola you get an enantiomorph; that we, father 'n son, are such: parallel mirrored images. He refuses to believe this until age 49, when it hits him like a ton of bricks. That we $both$ are Great Sublimators, both take pleasure in conspiracy, reporting whereof thereon thereafter with a slight paranoid DNA-like twist.

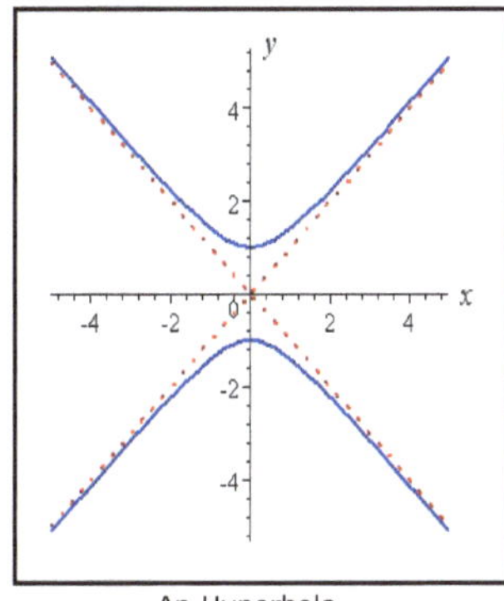

An Hyperbola

As I whip out my trusty drafting pen from my white Lockheed Aircraft pocket protector and sketch formulae, Jimmer gets that $You're$ so $super$ $human$ so do $something$-to-$really$-$amaze$-me look. So across a page of blue-ruled graphic paper I draw freehand a perfect straight line in one fast stroke, then perform my precise professional engineering-guy lettering — neat and practiced over scads of hours at my drafting table. (Jimmer can't draw a straight line with a ruler.) A grunt of satisfaction, then I stare at my son with a shit-eatin' $beat$ $that$ castrating grin. Saturn used a pruning knife; Chronos, a sickle; me, a drafting pen. Even as I astonish him with my slight of hand, my manual rectitude, I manage to: 1)chastize his spastic sloppy hand, 2) intimidate the hell outta him, and 3) always justifying my actions by claiming the letter Q is a metaphysical circle with a kick-stand. Often play the same head-game with him out in our garage's DIY woodshop, making sure he feels incompetent in his wood-working skills. We moved from plane geometry to planing wood and I outdid him every time. Now he can barely handle a pen or screw driver without having jimjams.

Teenage Jimmer Freudianizes the hyperbola: its curves not only remind him of breasts; it also accurately plots our father-son relationship over the years with its moments of closeness, near touching, followed by us pulling back fast, distancing, going our separate ways. Where I see mirroring, consensus, he sees disensus. Until age 49.

Jimmer claims my scientific bent helps me maintain *sangfroid* in the face of light and surprise. Fact, I tried to encourage a career in electronics for him (light as migrating photons), he something more concrete, the result of photons falling on sliver halides Guilt at this now from both of us. We both regret I was such a power source, structure and vector of anger and intimidation — which, Jim insightfully offers, merely masked my own insecurities. Sadness at self over the fact that I was always so aggressive — best defense is a good offense, right? I was mostly *offensive* toward family. Always chose White, forcing them to play Black in our intrafamilial Chess matches. As an engineer, I relied on *points* as mathematical idealities, when I should've also been thinking about points as allied with particularity and contingency: *What was the point of my marriage?* and *At what point did my marriage fail?*

Exhausted by remorseful meditations, and too many meds shoved on me by a surly Pringles-snacking male nurse, Rooie Boos, I konk out. Boos is buffeted by blasts of self-doubt, suffers a large built-up shoe, and tells me he hails from the Noordoostpolder district of Holland. He is a squat man, with a short neck and a boxy, fleshy head. If you had to render him very quickly you might start with a rectangle as his abdomen and then a smaller rectangle as the head, topped with a few quick pen strokes representing shocks of hair combed at a forty-five degree angle down and to his right. He hating my irritating, "I would prefer not to." This only inflames him and h pushes *more* tranks my way. The knot of ill and grief in my throat make them hard to swallow, but Rooie just looks on, indifferent, observant, with unshaven refinement. In his Calvinist eyes, I'm driven solely by suspicion, predestined to have my consciousness evaporated for the benefit of the "Police" in here. *IN HERE*: where habit never gives rise to true repetition and action remains the same in different contexts and with different intentions. I am led far past words, past reason, into incoherence.

When I awake it's to a perfect artist's studio north light (I should know) bathing my stretched out shell like a *nature morte*. Rooie peeks in and reluctantly apologizes for the whopper of a misjudgment in forcing tranks on me (a visiting physician saw him, finked, and now Rooie's all crocodile tears). Yes, he can be a pain, but he's my only source of information about what's happening here. Tells me, "You gotta have soft eyes to see the whole thing here; with hard eyes ya only stare at the same tree, missing the forest." Says he's gotten into the habit of dispensing tranks like candy after having to persistently control the likes of Raymond Gunn, a thirty-three year old autistic patient haunting room 375.

Ray keeps a well-thumbed copy of *Zen and the Art of Jibber-Jabber* by his bedside. Ray — when he's not making his caretakers victims of semiliterate self-help verse from his wonky compilation "Philosophies for Sale," penned under his weird *nom de plume,* "Gaunilo." He is perpetually constructing, tearing down, and reconstructing what he proudly consecrated as his "Super-Sacred Giant Evangelical-Capitalist Resonance Machine." Waxes eloquent on "The sex appeal of the inorganic," asserting that "Manganese offers us nothing new, being composed of lithium spikes and nitrogen balloons," or mumbling, "I gotta change'm see? The gears. And make'm nice colors. Nobody try to mob me on this, 'cause colors — gotta change'm — gotta be changing colors, change'm all the way 'long. Gotta be diff. Yes." Asked what he does, the dude rattles off a litany: astronomy (he claims a curious, unspecified analogy could be based on the fact that the eye-piece of even the hugest telescope cannot be bigger than our eye), charlatanry, arithmetic, geometry, music, and quackery. "Everything he keeps saying is something it isn't," explains Rooie.

According to staff notes Rooie saw, a pre-school teacher was the first to raise the alarm about little Gaunilo when he incessantly drew triangles with black pencil on white paper, pointing out to his classmates that the black sides of the triangle means its sides are "damned," while the angles, being white, were "saved." Even earlier, his mum noted, her son tied his plush toys together in a long string resembling eviscerated corpses. Today that might get you an art show.

Rooie says it's better to wear out (like me) than to rust out like this lost soul *cum* packrat, who covets all he can get his mitts on from gears to small wheels, pages torn from *The King James Bible* to *Forbes* magazine covers, bed-pans to catheters, discarded dentures to eye-glasses from deceased patients, empty plastic water bottles to discarded egg cartons, and then finding surprising uses for them on his ongoing assemblage. Using duct-tape, Krazy-Glue, chewing gum, bent paper-clips, and whatnot, he collages all into one wacky, mutating machine, which at night seems to have a weird *ignis fatuus* hovering about it. Woe be if you try to touch it! Intrusion is rewarded with outbursts of infantile screams, tornados of fabulated maxims, followed by preposterous gestures. "I tried it, and left in laughter and trembles," Rooie confesses. A month before my arrival, he confides in hushed tones, a tentative puff of smoke arose from the cursed device, setting off overly sensitive smoke alarms. Mass mayhem. Heart attacks. Firemen. Cops. City inspectors. Irate family members. Etcetera.

At last look, Rooie informs me, the device's most recent incarnation sported a rod in the center from which three branches at its tip sprouts a short, straight support that divides almost at once into two curved arms in the form of a semi-circle with its horns pointing to the zenith. This semi-circle, in the ideal vertical plane of the oblique rod, partially frames a powerful round lens secured inside by two pivots at the tips of the curved arms. The lens is placed before a *Forbes* magazine cover, magnifying it greatly. Here Rooie's description gets too thick for me to follow. Anyway, by the end of the week, the machine will have taken on another incarnation. I suggest, shades of Jimmer, that staff weekly photo-document the in-process artwork with the aim to publish a book and raise money to get cable TV in here.

Yep, it just isn't us financially embarrassed oldies that end up here; this place collects all manner of pitiful social flotsam and jetsam. It's now the imperfect end point for this nomadic collection of flows 'n schizzes denominated by the term "Gerald" and barely held together by a sagging epidermis. Saw him yesterday — that maximum openness in my small room, I — caught his face in a mirror. Saw through my own eyes, my own eyes.

To get Rooie off the topic of this crazy autistic — and prevent him from discussing Bailey, the guy with the coprolalic tic — I spin my factual story about helping to design the fuel injectors on our first moon rocket. Tell him that my job as an aeronautical engineer was *not* merely an occupation, something to fiddle away my days and collect a paycheck, but a *vocation*, a calling from God. Putting a man on the moon, I stress, was the greatest accomplishment we as a God-made species have mustered. Licking his lips, he replies with a sly smile, "Makes us sound like hot dogs, what? . . . Which reminds me, time for lunch." Ah, Rooie. He lacks perhaps the two virtues most important to such a place as this: presence of mind and affability, but in his own wonky, sour sort of way he combines the functions of priest, guide, and hotelier for many of us.

After suffering my caretaker's stories, trying to come up with tales to match his, I pull out a wrinkled and creased attempt by Ill-Phil at "slash fiction." Typed in red ink — distributed for laughs among our Upping Arms writer's club — I dangle it before startled Rooie. The hostile text, which would confirm evolutionary psychology's "Swiss Army Knife" model of the brain, begins, using slash marks to stand in for "slashes":

> Phil Pokey ////////s Gerald who //////s Fialta who //////s Eepie who //////s Bondo who ////////////s Hilaria who ////////////s Our Fearless Leader who refuses to ////////// our rent . . .

Rooie runs out shaking his head, no *bon mot* coming to mind.

I man the chair farthest from the door, nose to window with the unsettled vacancy of an old dog left home alone. On the windowsill, next to my dried out plant, I see, on closer inspection, a head of a moth, sliced almost completely off, swinging as if hinged to the body, a body completely hollow inside. I shudder. Outside, are three old birch trees. I look at them. I can see them plainly, but my mind feels they're concealing something it can't grok, as when an object is out of reach. Do they hide a forgotten memory of mine, or is it simply visual fatigue that makes me see the wooden trio double in time as one sometimes sees double in space? I choose to think of them as phantoms of a past worth a "too close-reading," but for which I am too damned drained to accomplish. Yes, I feel appalling vistas of years stretching behind me, while at other times it seems as if the present moment were an isolated point in grey. Yep, all my notions of time are increasingly becoming dissolved and refashioned.

You see, when not in that sitting position, mostly I sleep. I'm taking mega-dosages of melatonin to avoid the miasma of sorrows suffered where it's always winter and never Christmas. Five of those brown buddies and WHOP! a big cartoon hammer of exhaustion comes down. Dreams so herb-induced are cartoonish too. Like big Looney Tunes raucous scramble 'n gamble over my garments I imagine when I'm *Kaput*. Flight hat and jacket, dress uniform and emblazoned 'n brimmed hat, myriad air medals, and a flight helmet with goggles lustily ogled 'n scattered in a flurry of fists as cartoon balloons pop overhead. Finally a small flare-bomb I'd kept as a war souvenir accidently goes off, waking me up with a . . .

Рад тебя видеть

A siren-screaming, ambulance pulls in back of our charnel house. Our home plays perfect host to hopeless cases and knows how to ship them Priority Male or Female to the hospital when necessary, Third Class to the morgue when the inevitable happens. I just noticed the walls of this awful room are stained brown. I hear a doctor in Jack "Wee-Jock" Linlithgow's room say something to relatives, like "No liver involvement." Good news for a guy dying of a brain tumor! Bet his relatives pretend that it means he's getting better, despite his need for a steady dose of Haldol suppositories.

Stuffed as I am in here, at least I don't have to watch Jeanie (I called her that in better days) smoke herself to death. I couldn't bear to see her slow decline and disappearance. But Jimmer will have to endure it. She contracts chronic obstructive pulmonary disease, a combination of chronic bronchitis and emphysema, but she keeps going. Nothing discouraging her to quit smoking. Good thing I was suspicious that tobacco companies were simply the extension of the Civil War by other means and stopped inhaling in my early thirties. And in my retirement, unlike the retired male population of Wisconsin, I never drove home from the Elks club drunk every night, just to light a cigarette before bed. Despite those smart precautions, I'm suffering the slow rot of my body and it cannot be borne. Nerve pathways are becoming overgrown and my skin tears like tissue paper. My drinking water must be made gelatinous or I aspirate it. I keep hoping something quick 'n violent, a wreck, will do me in. But I suppose our Medicare facility isn't high on Al-Qaeda's To-Bomb List. Perhaps I should torch a Koran and get on National News then, ten days later, all us here would be represented on CNN by a football field-sized crater.

But two events occur today (four, if you factor in that I found my missing Rosary and Rooie brought in a pirated audio tape of a vintage Jonathan Winters comedy LP) that keep me soldiering on, helping to counter all this "negative energy," as Jimmer's wife would put it.

One. Marianne and Jimmer drop by. I am presented with a ribbon-encased red box of a whopper selection of famous Belgian Neuhaus Chocolates, Les irrésist-ibles: caramels, truffles, fruit, marzipan, liqueur, chocolate folies, tablets, manons, praliné, fresh cream, gianduja, ganach, and carrés. One of the marzipan offerings is named "Canasta" so Jimmer immediately claims that baby for himself. Marianne, of Russian heritage, grabs the "Troika" marzipan. I go for the manon noir and pass over the classic truffle (never trifle with a truffle). Marianne's brought her usual unusual flower arrangement *pour moi*. She speaks French, like all the Russian nobility once did. Me speak-um Rooshun, a little. "Рад тебя видеть" (nice to see you), I keep

telling my visitors. This little tactic convinces them I'm sharper than I look. *See, he's getting better!* They only see what they want to see.

Elder Physics

Two. I get a letter from Eepie who's still at my old residence, The Upping Arms. *Nice to see you*, I think, as I hold a business-sized envelope in unsteady hands. Rooie has to open it for me. Therein, I find Eepie's Blog, an epilogue to my stay at the Upping Arms:

Eepie-Blog / Sept. 1, 2008

Zdravstvujte Gerald,

Not sure you have computer access to read my new blog, "Armed Neutrality," so I'm passing some of it on, plus other choice ditties of interest to you, via snail-mail. Sorry your son had to move you to The Gulag. Are you writing something like *One Day in the Life of . . .*? I remember you knew some Russian, *Da*?

Updates: Your former room's been painted pink and is occupied by two remarkably preserved Florida-tanned gay men we've dubbed "Saytan 'n Mefisto." Like the continuity errors in movies you liked to pick out on our film night, they change ties trice daily. Oh, and that Polish woman you had the fling with? Well, she's still bad-mouthing you, *kemo sabe*. And last time she danced with Dirty Harry on Big Band night, she moved like some kindly demon had slipped castanettes into her girdle.

On the plus side: one of the cleaning staff, a Singha-lese named Curuppumullage Jinarajadasa, found your stamp album with that 1855 two-cent Guiana and the Zanzibar series you bragged about. Tell your son to get it. And Rup Hempel's Last Will and Testament endowed us with an HO-gauge model train layout. All the guys' bladders here sharked up, leaking with excitement and immature anticipation to hat up and play engineer. Good ol' Hemp; he's our Famo now, so we use his gold-plated spittoon to hold raffle tickets. Which reminds me, Ill-Phil submitted a short-story, " 'This' Will Spit on your Graves," to the writing club. Fialta passed it on; opening paragraph reads: *Crumb! Bum! Son of a bitch! Jerk! Dirty son of the bitch! Robber! No-good! Son of a bitch! . . .*

Talking about cultural production . . . Teddy screened a 1949 thriller, *Woman in Hiding*, starring Ida Lupino and Howard Duff. Near the film's end, Fialta jumped up, hand raised, and pointed out (wish you could've seen this) that Hitchcock had copped several scenes from this *film noir* and used them in both *Psycho* (a scene where Lupino's convertible is pulled from the water and its headlights and grill look skullish, much like the analogous scene when Marion's sub-merged car is pulled from a swamp with a the skull supered over), and in *Vertigo* (a scene where Lupino steps from dark shadow on a high catwalk in a furniture plant, startling her killer-husband who abruptly steps back and falls to his death, exactly as Judy does when startled by a nun in Hitchcock's film). A vertiginous mistaken identity plays a role in that scene as Lupino's husband mistakes his girlfriend in the dark for his wife and pushes her to her death. I thought you'd appreciate this as you and your son were always making those doing close readings and making obscure references and allusions to a myriad of texts in your collaboration.

After Fialta made these obtrusive observations, Ill-Phil yelled from the back of the room, "THIS wants to say this: 'Let us not pretend to be wise when we have only been lucky.' Like when a speck on a carrot stick I was munching, on inspection, turned out to be a nearly microscopic severed finger. Okay? . . . I know, I know. The principal of my grade school wrote almost nothing about me in his reports, but wrote instead a eulogy on my father." Huh? Talk about elder physics! Everywhere The Presence goes, he destabilizes the material world. It seemed like ten minutes of total silence from the peanut gallery before Teddy got our attention again.

On the subject of texts, our library has grown *exponentially* (I knew you'd like that math reference) since you departed. The twins make sure we have a second copy of each book. The Presence checked out *Representing Shakespeare* and harped for days over an essay therein titled "Anger's My Meat: Feeding, Dependency and Aggression in *Coriolanus*." He ordered an elder-joke T-shirt screaming in red Helvetica: ANGER'S THIS'S MEAT and wears it to dinner. Fialta said he handed her for review a manifesto titled "So Shall 'THIS's' Lung's Coin Words." More on this weird declaratory shift from "I" to "THIS" in a second.

Ah, Phil . . . atoms of deranged technique are shown to contain their own skies. Looking like an emaciated crow, he has taken to only eating raw steaks copped from our kitchen (a stake-out finally snagged him). He justified his theft by screaming: "THIS is speaking these words now:'THIS has no longer any jizz for life, instead THIS will dive into brute matter. THIS needs Warrior's Food to Killykillkilly!' Okay?"). Notice he suddenly dropped "I" for the sociopathic "THIS." Fialta says he's turned into "an empty signifier."

The final straw though was when he, The Demolished Man, bombarded Fearless Leader with miniature golf balls, yelling: "Four, sir; three, sir; two, sir; one! 'Tenser,' said the Tensor. 'Tenser,' said the Tensor. Tension, apprehension, and dissension have begun!" Phil was summarily sent to a secure Veteran's facility in beautiful downtown Stickney.

Let's see, what else. Oh, yes. Bondo is wearing black, anticipating the passing of Jack LaLanne after reports of the guy's declining health. Meanwhile, Fialta has penned a grant proposal, hoping to get funds to expand the visiting writers offerings for the "Happy Scribblers," this after Fearless Leader announced further budget cuts to our arts programming upon the advice of his new Neoliberal efficiency expert, Pei Yoo Oon Wei.

Our computer instructor, I think you called her "Nutritious," has added Linux, an "open source" operating system, on our computers and is giving lessons in Web 2.0. Now many of our impermanent guests are sporting iPads in their walker's basket. We call Nutritious "Delicious" after she turned us all on to the social bookmarking website of the same name. So we are hearing references to "folksonomy," "skyping," "citizen-media blogospheres" and "beta-test embedded wikis," as well as "algorithmic journalism performed by content farms" at our breakfast table conversations now, and anticipate the untold possibilities of our "cognitive surplus" in a joint where we usually run a cognitive deficit. Even Fearless Leader was overheard discussing "viral marketing" with Pei. Noreen Pogacnic worries if we do go viral, it'll spread and, to a person, wipe us out.

Speaking of blogs, twitters, and our administration, here's something our Grey Power Progressives had "Delicious" post for them on our infamous "Idiot Irresponsibles" twitter:

The People, formerly known as the Residents, wish to inform Administration of our existence, and of a shift in power that goes with the platform shift you've all heard about, Web 2.0. We, once passengers on your ship, have gotten a boat of our own as writing readers and fed-up residents. Beware, the formerly atomized Irresponsbiles are taking responsibility now and connecting with each other and gaining the means to speak to you and the world.

The People, formerly known as the Residents (PFKR), are simply made realer, less fictional, more able, less predictable. Not just Grey but Great!

You should welcome that, Fearless Leader. But whether you do or not, we want you to know we're here, and talkers and talking, and walking our walkers!
— The PFKR

Fearless Leader then posted his response:

If all would speak, who shall be left to listen? Can you at least tell me that?

Fialta asked me to ask you: Do you see a Protestant populism versus Catholic authoritarianism underlying this exchange? Fun to live in interesting times, huh? Power to the People.

— As Ever, Eepie

Elder Physics

Although she enclosed an unfinished short story I'd left in the dayroom, "Gerald in Captivity or Who Stole My Benicar and Where Did Friday Disappear To?" I never replied to Eepie, nor did I retrieve my stamps. (I will be gone in seven days.) If I had known my time was so short, I'd have written of our residents sad plight here — The People Now Known as Near Corpses (PNKANC). Would've sent her these last of my writings — predicated on the truism that what happens in practice, is absolutely impossible in theory — and told of my desire for Extreme Unction under extremes circumstances. But I *did* experience my last vivid dream! And what a whopper it was! Therein, The Presence gets his just desserts:

I was at the ill-fated miniature golf event and witnessed Ill-Phil's golf-ball tossing incident. I — no longer able to brook such insolence, despite my dislike of Fearless Leader — immediately kicked Phil, yelling "Take this for that, Mr. This. Then Bondo took a good kick at him, cutting an enormous fart in so doing. Phil fell and curled up into a ball to protect himself.

Suddenly, every foot on our "golf green" aimed and WHAP! took up its vengeance. No sooner had any one given Phil a kick, than he or she felt themselves constrained to reiterate the stroke. Phil afforded them no small entertainment as he rolled on all sides at the blows of his elder assailants, who pressed after him, wherever he turned, with an eagerness beyond conception. Suddenly this human ball was passing from one massed group to another, like a World Cup soccer match. It wasn't long before cleaning staff joined battle, then kitchen staff. Finally, Fearless Leader began to referee the match in favor of the side opposing mine. Jill kept score. I pursued Phil's balled-frame hither-thither, bestowing as many kicks as I possibly could get in, yet not without receiving now and then a few which my competitors, in their eagerness, intended for our new ball.

Soon Phil's rolled figure was out the front door and being kicked down the sidewalk. The sight of this odd ball was alone sufficient to draw after it every beholder on the street. Nearly all witnesses soon became active participants. Even little children, encouraged by their parents' athletic exploits, took aim. I eventually had to sit down on the curb to rest. The last I saw of Phil's rotund form, it was rolling in kick-propelled spurts south, down past Madison St., toward the art supply store I used to frequent.

Suddenly, I'm in an autopsy room. Feeling the gravitational pull of mortality as Phil's cadaver rests before me. I cover the cadaver's eyes, ears, nose, mouth. Then slap his face. I blow the hair on the back of his neck. I pinch his arm. I seem to be attempting to get to that person, not that individual, but to that symbolic person represented as cadaver, who is on the table, but also in me.

I woke up, kicking at my bed covers. I titled that dream: "The Awful Fate of a Soft-in-the-Head Man in a Hard World.*"*

My Last Lube Job?

thoughts, he mumbles — while a staff member in the background harangues another staff member with questions about a missing section of the newspaper — "Dim different cheap bbbbbbboozies in me had me feelin' a mmmmmmean 'n boozie nnnnnnasty-Nash." Another time, more lucid, he tries to explain himself to me in a descending series of despair — "Flesh, flash, flak, flask, flush, lush" — in which you didn't have to be an aerospace engineer to fill in the gaps. One awful moment, during my breakfast in bed, he screams, "Allah! It's en- en- enhuging, it's enreddenhuged!" his eyes swimming." I thought he was having an erection. "Oh, no no no! It's brightening hugendly burst blinding. I fall, fall to the ground — roundian-roundian I go. Let be! Let be! You think he be hanaccident? Ker- ker- kerblooey, Koran!"

I thought I saw see his heart groan between his ribs and shake him with great, brutal, irregular blows. Like Surrealism, it seemed to make sense and didn't, or seemed not to make sense and did. Bells go off. In dashes two tough nurses who hook him up to some glumdalclitch and madly push buttons. "See that tracer-shell effect in the hippocampus?" one observes. "I think he 'n his relatives might be ready for Consilience [hospice]." A syringe is filled and soon Sood's a sleeper turning back on all 'n everyone to become that mystery of an individual stronger in slumber, as benevolent a normativeness as drugs can keep him.

No surprise to hear — according to his visibly upset visitor — he'd been an Egyptian pilot blown from the clear blue easy in the Six-Day War with Israel. Drinking became one of his modes for coping with war wounds, both physical and mental. Bat-shit mad he went. "Jerry, the booze kept him from dreaming and assured him the world was a jungle. He wasn't *born* a loser, but made one," says this Anthony Quinn look-a-like relative of Sood's. The guy looks at me with big eyes, dark as trenches, As if he hadn't slept in a year, like someone getting chemo. "It didn't help that Sood's daughter, Fitna, grew into a long, thin, adult with a glum capacity for sloth and no interest in the business of the world. She tends her French diseases of the soul — pique, umbrage, and ennui — while ignoring the Koran entirely."

I don't say it, but Nash ain't gonna be around much longer. In fact, the very next day Rooie walks in and has to pronounce, "Fuck, either this guy's dead, or my watch has stopped." He seems sure of the justice of this metaphysical injustice the way the English believe the poor to be poor and the rich rich because their God has decreed it. During this pronouncement of Rooie's, the TV is on mute while some stunningly average network meat-puppet with terrible facial hair looks like he's orgasming into the mic.

Hell, *I'm* not going to be alive much longer either. As I write my memoir from my bed here in "Scabland," I get a sense that a disembowelment or a clean shot to the brain pan lies only a paragraph away. It's only been fourteen days since I've been placed here, but those seem endless — *One Day in the Life of Ivan Denisovich* time-looped *ad infinitum* — during which time brain disease scurries and spirals through my electro-particles. I'm goin' down the drain — fast. *Be a good boy, take your bromide . . . . Yes, mother, I'll take my medicine . . . . Forward into the untrodden, courage old man, and hold on to your umbrella . . . . Yes!*

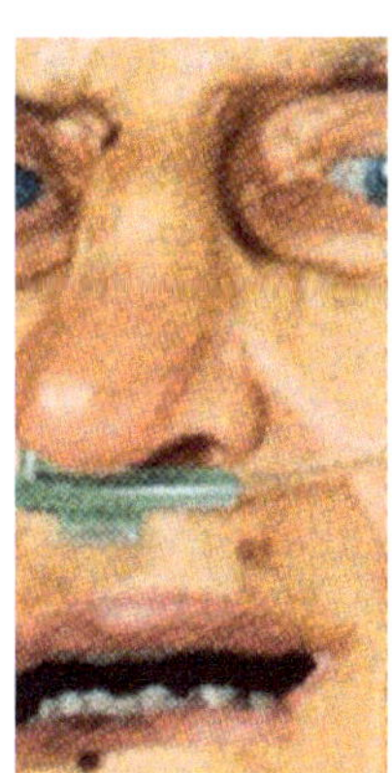

Soft tissue reigned supreme until 5000 million years ago, when some of the conglomerations of fleshy matter-energy that made up life underwent a sudden *mineralization*, and a new material for constructing living creatures emerged: bone. Now all that evolution is de-evolving in me: bone loss, brittleness. I'm on my way to becoming a *caput mortuum* that once ate, drank, slept loved, and hated. Sometimes, as I sag on this moisting mattress, I can feel the air exiting each cell, sometimes the blood in my lips drains away and the web of my whole being trembles. *The outcome of the current crisis is already determined.* Up to now Jimmer says I've exhibited "the courage of a clown," that which Lucretius calls "something in our breast" keeping us fighting and resisting. But now . . . may as well make my desires identical with my destiny. I start to make my peace and acceptance with this crazyverse and my soon-to-be vaporization. Time as *before, now, after* flattens out into a particularly vivid version of what in elder physics is termed YesterNow.

I see myself as a cowed kid . . . hear my mother in the kitchen listing the onion family — sweet spring yellow, white and hot, garlics, scallions, shallots, leeks, and bulb, Bermudas, Walla walla, Maui, Spanish, and Vidalia — to me. Then I'm a skinny teenager . . . next a buff bombardier . . . a newly wed . . . a father . . . a hot, young aerospace designer . . . an outdoors man . . . a paunchy middle-ager with an attitude, a moral absolutist in a counter-cultural age of Situation Ethics screaming at his offspring . . . then a hermit divorcé . . . a complaining, declining old fart . . . finally, a breathless corpse . . . followed by grey ashes dispersing in prop-wash. My various incarnations roll by like a slow freight train. Strange to think of them constituting one entity, legally denominated "Gerald Hugunin," so diverse are the actors in my life-drama. Soon one curtain will go down and another open onto the supposedly known unknown-unknown. Will there be anyone around to clap when I perform my dramatic entrance?

When's the Extreme Unction coming? Would it help if I asked unctuously?

As I write, I feel the confederate agency of many striving macro- and micro-agencies at work: from my memories, intentions, contentions, intestinal bacteria, intrusive urinary infections, my eye-glasses, and blood sugar, as well as from all my writing materials, even the bird song outside my window, as well as the cries of my fellow inmates, a few of whom sport WWII tats which have aged into uniform blue clouds as they smear and blur on shriveled skin. (Which reminds me of my son's astute take on tats and existentialism: "God drily quipped: *'I am that which I am,'* but we fire back from the Tattoo Parlor of Babel: 'I am that which I am not.' Right?")

Sadness, dawn. Toasted, smudged, from trouble sleep. Dreamt I'd channeled Helen Keller. And then that Nash Sood was convulsed with a coughing fit, blood coming in a fine spray, plucked from the fibers of his lungs and pumped full of air as perfume in an atomizer. It heralds for Gerald, another day of elemental, repeated routines, devoid of originality — like whistling into a balloon. Out, damn present! But the present can't flee 'cause I'm living it. I, I, I, contemplate the far enchaining earth, earth, earth, earth, approached, unapproached, approached, unapproached in solitude, solitude, approached in solitude, the unapproached solitude. Vacillating. *Hey, where's Crazy Horse's bones?*

    The Indians really got fucked over. I keep thinking that. Was cultivating that, as I kept thinking that. I cultivated that thought for sometime. Why? My granddaddy was part Ojibwa. Sipped Ojibwa tea, known as Essiac, well into his nineties. I remember well his favorite refrain: "Just-a-shittin'-an-a-drinkin'." I inherited both the longevity and the Futterneidness from above, from grandpap to pap to *moi*, just as I've bequeathed such down below to poor Jimmer, who refused to pass it on. At age 12, my son told me our Aldon tract-homes in the San Fernando Valley looked like "inverted bomb craters"! Our genealogy records long-lived disturbances and short-lived normalcy. No sound for either of us of a soothing pebble on hollow bamboo as in that famous Zen koan about Enlightenment. A fan above me is spinning like a mad vulture on a string, waiting for me. I tell Jimmer — after he comes in and finds my mouth dribbling food, me choking and my face the color of spent flashbulbs, after he compassionately clears my mouth of mush — "You're mmmmmmy hero." (These are the last words I speak to my son.) He gives me drink from a glass, but the water tastes metallic, like fluids from those jewel-colored aluminum tumblers we had in the mid-fifties. Jimmer and I recall with laughter how they would so profusely sweat condensation they might've run a marathon. We smile. All need witnesses to our lives and Jimmer is mine. That feels good.

When's the Extreme Unction coming?

    While I'm scribbling this, on TV some Wall Street dude's pontificating: *We want the greatest good for the nation, as long as it's compatible with our personal well-being. That's the American Way, huh?* News, news, news — it has a kind of mystery — it's prime time in the USA! I close my eyes and think of Jimmer grilling pork chops, Marianne serving pork roast or her stuffed turkey, the soups I like so much, the suds my son serves up. I tell myself: *I'm an old man filled with manias, who has a perfect right to 'em 'cause I screwed myself, see?*

    I can identify with that book Jim gave me for my last birthday, *The Death of Artemio Cruz*. Can't recall the author, some Mexican. Upon close-reading, I notice the title puns in Spanish and Italian. *Mio Arte* is an Italian phrase cleverly hidden in the name. *Cruz* is cross, of course; ergo we get something like: *My art is my cross.* Maybe like a cross-word puzzle too, huh? Jim would love to ponder that. But now I bear a cross making me too beat broach it.

Gotta compunction for the Extreme Unction — those anointing oils — my last lube job. Repeat until asleep.

Elder Physics

A brief description of *my situation*: loss of memory, clumsiness, faint melancholy, tendency to embrace meaning-lessness. Obsolescence. Suffering a departure of my aura, I make sophisticated evasions. I miss objects, seem to be losing space and language. Hopelessness gnaws at me. The smallest changes in my condition have the force of seismic shocks. At night, Death nearly conquers me, offering His hand with a movement that recalls that of an innocent wolf — audacious, candid, secret — offering me vivid visions of my last painter's palette: earth browns and ochers with dark ultra-marines, blackish greens, greys and dark blue. But I rally during the day to the hidden melodies of overheard conversations and the rhythms of trains and cars that melt together into a smoothly flowing symphony of the street. And when Jimmer visits? Why, it's like the sun coming up over the Ganges, or a rainbow in curved air, or as if the bland Pentagon has turned on its side showing it as painted purple, yellow, and green!

One day in September, my lungs bring in only a thin, cold breath of air that just manages to wend its way through the cracks in that mass of phlegm, irritation, and blood. I make a hollow sound through my nose. Things are happening fast, quantum leaps, they happen before a word exists for them, the deadly algorithms of elder physics representing my Situation.

In these, my last twilight hours, the room starts to fog up, a seep of mist coming in under the door and tumbling about as if a cloud had touched down just outside the room. Lumiére's claws dig into my life, but the geared wheel runs the film backward. Death achieves a dazzling montage of my life as I start to hear the din of props, re-experience my harrowing bombing missions with machine guns sputtering, flak bursting, and excited intercom chatter. Suddenly, I can see myself soloing delightfully in that sweet Cessna over pure Pacific Ocean blue, the color of inspiration, truth, moderation, spirituality. As I fly into and out of the clouds, so does my consciousness seem to wax and wane. Don't want to land again. Luckily, my son and I already signed off on my fire engine red **DO NOT RESUSCITATE** order. No way I'm gonna to screw up my final flight plan.

During life, time's a self-healing substance but, after quantum decoherence, it congeals. Aggregate Loss of Possibility approaching infinity. My final flight (will my soul leave a vapor trail?) has two possible landing fields based on **ups** (good news) or **downs** (bad news):

Good News: **I can't change my past good works into bad = HEAVEN**

Bad News: **I can't change my past bad shit into good = HELL**

I'm minimally inactive, my language softening and guttering, losing shape and import, becoming mere lumps of sound. If the self is concealed in assertion and action, I am now revealed in temptation and wish. Wish to just have an end to it. In the present-indefinite, I'm a botch of corpuscles, a waste of quarks, a carbon-based fuckwad. No turning back, medical intervention now would be like trying to heat an oven with snow balls. Before coma creeps up, an attending nurse, who just days ago gloomed 'n loomed over me as if I was the prodigy of a strange appearance, now tenderly holds my hand and asks me if there is anything she can get me. With a weak smile, "A beer," I say, recalling all those chilled mugs Jimmer would quench my thirst with at our delightful father-son gut-stuffers, as we'd joke, pun, 'n laugh. My last memory of Jimmer's love. "You're on your way to Eucatastrophe," she whispers softly. I dream, at least I think it was a dream:

A strange character mysteriously intrudes, a personage nondescript, although not altogether indescribable, with a German accent as thick as British fog. "Who are you, pray? How did you get in here?" I say.

"Az vor ow I com'd ere, dat iz none of your pizzness; as vor who I be, vy dat is de very ting I com'd here for to let you zee for yourself. Look at me! Zee! I am te guy you call Ticktockman." His breath hot on my face now. (No one's calling a priest.) "Time ist vhen nohow on. Id bears repeeting. Time ist . . .

"My, aren't you the Angel of the Odd!" (When's the Extreme Unction coming? Is it hibernating?) He disappears.

My earlier writings have addressed a knowing of what has been known — a certainty about *wheels-within-wheels* — but can one really imagine one becoming a carburetted hydrogen ghost? A knowing of the unknown-unknown where level beams of the setting moon stream in upon the face of this dying bard? I've herein tried to describe moving from a full set to a null set. Now I must attempt to write about becoming an empty set, fulfilling the final solution to those chilly cold equations of elder physics! Acting from old habit in a convulsive perseverance, while the mind is nearly gone, it's one last grand hurrah.

Okay, then. With leastening words, I will say least best worst first, put it in Schoenberg's favorite D minor tonality, and do it for "The Gipper," for Jimmer. And for Fialta, to honor the long-awaited revised edition of her 1953 political diatribe popular with her Annapolis students, *From Plato to NATO: Multiculturalism and the Clash of Whatever* (New Society Publishers, Albuquerque, New Mexico, a Tea Party funded organization), and to celebrate her insight that we shall never rid ourselves of God as long as we believe in grammar, but also to provide an exception to her dismal assumption that "Our reading, our conversation and thinking, are all on a very low level, worthy only of pygmies and manikins." My bird-watcher sister told me there are only five bird songs: 1) Good-morning, 2) I found a worm, 3) Love me, 4) Get out, 5) Good night. My final song? "Goodnight."

Never by naught be nulled, I scribble on. Oh jeez! My consciousness is tied to a dying animal. The blood inside me used to rush like an express train through a local station. But now each morn I can feel that the heady mixture of warm refreshments being pumped out of the chamber of my heart to all my cold extremities is less and less effective. I'm in solution. *Dis-solution*. Dis . . . A burnt match skating in a urinal. The Meltdown Effect of Elder Physics turning me into an empty set {∅}. The production of my campaigns and slogans, my war-machines against my family, my shakedowns, my great thought-racket is aswirlin' down the drain, fast. Panting. Painting? No panting. Yuck. Spit. Foam. Headache. Cold sweat. This is my first time here. I shall be seeing all for the first time. Shivers. God I need a beer. The unreliability of my mask. Extroverted, unpacific type. But these musings . . . Aaaahh, passability across a deep

channel seems possible. Thicker 'n thicker the fog, seething
and uncoiling. The blue, dark blue, then grey and shading to
dark. Last rays. Nothing left but black. Everywhere no
matter where. But black. Void. Nothing else. The truth of
near-eternal night is near. Gotta go on instruments . . . on
instruments . . . The reflexive quanta of my amygdalic soul
. . . slipping out through my bones into the wider managed-
air of my death-chamber, slipping — like German physicist
Schroedinger's famous paradoxical cat (used to elucidate his
wave-particle theory) — into a state of being hovering
between life and death.

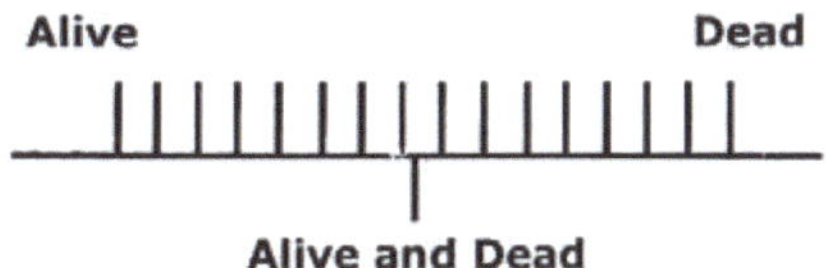

$$i\hbar\frac{\partial}{\partial t}e^{\frac{i}{\hbar}(px-Et)} = \frac{-\hbar^2}{2m}\frac{\partial^2}{\partial x^2}e^{\frac{i}{\hbar}(px-Et)} + V(x,t)e^{\frac{i}{\hbar}(px-Et)}$$

Schroedinger's wave equation

An image of such in-betweenness, the pier on Pelican
Lake, hovers in my *cabeza*. Growing up surrounded by lakes
and becoming an engineer, I always found the concept of a
pier a bit magical: life is a long walk on a short pier,
which suspends you between land and water, life and drowning, and as a structure it exhibits this power of
suspension, putting you *in media res*.

But now something inside me wants that pier to sink,
giving me freedom to blossom, losing the singular event of
ME in the forever infinite numbering of gestures, things,
and words that co-existed with it. Sharing it with something
larger than me. God I'm going home at last. But one last
memory: Jeane and I, just engaged, hug each other, in touch
at all available surfaces, absolutely unified, while liver
and onions sizzle in a pan on her mother's stove. Goddagooo.
Yaa, I'm drawn toward some sort of event horizon. Perhaps a
thousand times my screen of vision fades into white and out
again, creating the impression of a great winking eye; sometimes the fades in and out are colored, sometimes not. Oh,
oh. Here's the flame-out — jets stopping, film ending — my
individual event anomalies. My soul is:

unbuttoning

un   button   ing

un   bu   tton   ing

un   bu   tto   n   ing

u   n   b   u   t   t   o   n   i   n   g

itself from my body. No cheat code available to modify this final agon in the endgame of life 'n death . . . . No escaping the Second Law of Thermodynamics, the indifference of the cosmic jaw to the bloody morsel of humanity, or the paradox of *writing* my death as language undoes the death it deals. I grit my teeth and go armed to my destiny, like the Brits I fought for, with an umbrella and very dry wit.

If life is after all one of our most abundant commodities as "tissue economists" claim. Why is so much of my valuable information slipping through the cracks in my wall and seeping into the bed linens and evaporating into the current Chicago weather system? I am rapidly losing what remains of a grammatically singular and novel object, *moi*, to a new regime of decline. What was an unending string of new beginnings is starting to become an unending string of new endings. Any action is one aspect. Any other action is another aspect of the same thing. There's no place really to go, but everywhere. The scientists are correct: elder physics — get used to it, Jerry. My molecules jump, exchange, dance, play, and flow chemically, ionically and ironically, merging at the edges, the space between my molecules like the sky — the blue. My resolve to enter the point of Nothing grows stronger. The Little Nothing the same as the Big Nothing. A fragility of the limit between mind 'n matter, I'm a ghost of transcendence floating around in a veil of immanence. . . .

When Jimmer is called to my side. I will already be side-ways in time. He'll feel guilty at having once or twice thought of me in the same stressed words mumbled at operatic death scenes that go on so interminably: *Die! Goddamnit, hurry and die!* Stylish Jimmer will stop by on his way to teach in Chicago's west burbs — black leather sport coat, grey shirt, slender black tie — but I will be already unconscious, running out of Earth-time, breathing like I've run a twenty K race, stuck with an IV pouring vital fluids in my severely enlarged right arm that refuses more fluids. On my wobbly little side table, Jimmer will find a well-thumbed and razorblade-abused copy of Chuck Palahniuk's dark novel, *Diary*, face-down, splayed open to pages 232–233. Underlined in red, he'll read a fragment of altered text, annotated with my last self-reflexive gesture apropos the axis of our father-son collaboration:

    Jimmer   Jerry's
~~Grace Wilmot~~ is writing a novel patterned after ~~Misty's~~ life.

Jim will flip through the book, discover one brief marginal note: *I feel that a new story is about to unfold, but which will remain untold*. Sadly he'll close it, stunned at my sudden turn into a vegetative state. He thought I'd hang on 'til Thanksgiving, at least. He'll futilely try to get my response, tears in his voice. Somehow I will sense his presence as I know he'll tenderly stroke my head, then a long-pressed kiss to the forehead. He'll leave with a lead heart, feet dragging. "Gotta teach, have to meet my first class of the semester," will be mumbled to the nurse wringing her hands in the hallway. As he rushes out, Jimmer will bark, "Keep me advised."

Next thing, a gradual image emergence — like a peeled Polaroid developing — of a stare down at a recumbent myself, an acrobatic point-of-view impossible for my physical-self. It's the omniscient view of lens and literature.

I've turned into a sort of ecstatic membrane that has peeled away from the real object. I can sort of travel through that image, choosing to stop here and there, amplifying the monumentality of detail (my severely swollen arm, my stilled but open eyes), or part from it to watch hectic nurses buzz about me like flies to shit. Oh shit! My "use-value," depleted. I'm a corpse! But it's bizarre — Jimmer would say, enigmatic — I am not the living person I was (Jimmer's "Big Guy") but also no one else. I am for now what remains plunked on my bed below me, a state of suspended attention waiting for the green light, or is it white? . . .

Crawling along a crowded Eisenhower Expressway, wending his way westward through the notorious "Hillside Strangler" nest of roadways, to his night class in the west suburbs, Jimmer's cell-phone will ring (the grating tone of a truncheon on cell bars) and he will be told I've taken off to meet my fellow war-bird crew members at exactly three forty-five p.m. It's a perfect 3, 4, 5 number sequence, the very number of one of my rooms at the Upping Arms. Calculate the odds of that! Continuing calculations, I've logged in a total of 31,540 Earth-days from start to finish heralded by the fact that that verb, my mind, has become a noun. Today the sun will rise and move in 24 hours once all around without casting my shadow around myself.

Rather than return to base, stomach wrenching, Jimmer will maintain his compass heading due west. Pedal to the metal, he will complete his mission — despite the emotional flak bursting around his heart — of enlightening young minds. Doing what he does best. Standing in front of America's future — hip young women with nose rings and cleavages on proud display, crew-cut males in hoodies — he will dedicate to my memory his lecture on the eco-utopian desert architecture of Arizona's nonagenarian visionary, Paolo Soleri. Despite the desert theme, there ain't gonna be a dry eye in the room as he tells them about the adventures of the Complete Postmodern Man.

Father-son art lesson, Pittsburgh, PA (1951)

Next morning, as if in mourning, the grey sky will drip its tears. A black phone will ring, Jim numbly answering. Why, it's the much too friendly Vet Benefits man, cheerfully wishing to schedule yet another interview re: my Veteran's Bennies. Jimmer

Elderflower Margarita

will calmly tell the guy," You'll need to talk to St. Peter. My father passed away yesterday." There will be a long guilty silence on the other end of the line. Then Jimmer will SLAM that phone down, hard. And somewhere in the unknown-unknown, that defiant gesture will evoke a wide Halloween pumpkin smile on my angelic face. And although I'm in the Wild Blue Yonder, ultimately, *we're on the same page.*

Jimmer will open the envelope I left for him — my last request. And that request is simple, that a mourning Jimmer and his sad wife go out for Chinese, order Elder-flower liqueur Margaritas, and open their fortune cookies. I predict Jimmer's will read:

> **YOUR PAST IS HAUNTED.**
> **DEAL WITH IT, GHOST TO CLOWN.**

— The End —

There is no antidote against the opium of time, which temporally considerth all things; our fathers find their graves in our short memories, and sadly tell us how we may be buried in our survivors.
— Sir Thomas Browne

Appendix

Documents: Box 5, Folders 15 & 18

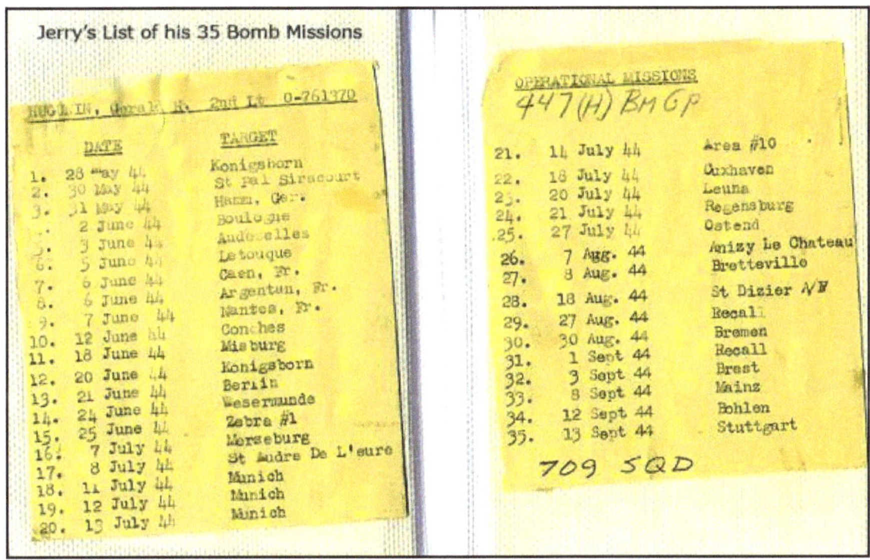

A spear of April sunshine pierced
the load of cloud towards the west.
I go slow-elevator down to check my
e-mail and see that Jimmer sent me
the following philosophico-
mathematical ditty:

Subtract the endeavor to demonstrate a preconceived hypothesis
from any known philosophy and the
remainder, the only valuable
material, is found to be distorted. Q.E.D.

Excerpt from Gerald's memoirs, not used in main text, original type-face

Jerry's List of his 35 Bomb Missions

HUGHIN, Gerald R.   2nd Lt   O-761370

	DATE	TARGET
1.	28 May 44	Konigsborn
2.	30 May 44	St Pal Siracourt
3.	31 May 44	Hamm, Ger.
4.	2 June 44	Boulogne
5.	3 June 44	Audeselles
6.	5 June 44	Le touque
7.	6 June 44	Caen, Fr.
8.	6 June 44	Argentan, Fr.
9.	7 June 44	Nantes, Fr.
10.	12 June 44	Conches
11.	18 June 44	Misburg
12.	20 June 44	Konigsborn
13.	21 June 44	Berlin
14.	24 June 44	Wesermunde
15.	25 June 44	Zebra #1
16.	7 July 44	Merseburg
17.	8 July 44	St Andre De L'eure
18.	11 July 44	Munich
19.	12 July 44	Munich
20.	13 July 44	Munich

OPERATIONAL MISSIONS
447(H) BM GP

21.	14 July 44	Area #10
22.	18 July 44	Cuxhaven
23.	20 July 44	Leuna
24.	21 July 44	Regensburg
25.	27 July 44	Ostend
26.	7 Aug. 44	Anizy Le Chateau
27.	8 Aug. 44	Bretteville
28.	18 Aug. 44	St Dizier A/F
29.	27 Aug. 44	Recall
30.	30 Aug. 44	Bremen
31.	1 Sept 44	Recall
32.	3 Sept 44	Brest
33.	8 Sept 44	Mainz
34.	12 Sept 44	Bohlen
35.	13 Sept 44	Stuttgart

709 SQD

List of Gerald's WWII bomb missions from his Warbird Scapebook

Gerald's Lucky Bastard's Certificate

The view Gerald would've had from the bombardier's nose position in a B-17

Birthday card from Gerald to Jim (recto/verso, 2003)

JUNE 7-03
DEAR JIM— I THOT'
THIS CARD WOULD BRING
BACK THE HAPPY DAYS
YOU SPENT UP AT PELICAN
LAKE @ UNCLE DON'S COTTAGE
— I DON'T REMEMBER
THEIR DOG'S NAME—BUT
THOSE DAYS MAY BE LONG-
GONE, BUT I THOT THIS
CARD WOULD BRING BACK
MEMORIES & YOUR BIRTHDAY
WOULD BECOME A SPECIAL ONE
AS A RESULT—LOVE, DAD.

Many good wishes for a
very Happy Birthday!

JIM
MANY MORE
HAPPY BIRTHDAYS!

I recall witnessing Jeane, Camel cigarette in hand in typical smokers position: shed hold the pack to her lips, draw one out, flick open her Zippo, strike the wheel and set flame to the end. She said she liked the smell, the sharp marriage of lighter fluid and burn-ing tobacco that bloomed from that first puff. It was a steady ritual enacted much to the familys utter dismay.

Excerpt from short story "Gerald in Captivity or Who Stole My Benicar and Where Did Friday Disappear?" (original type-face) by Gerald Hugunin

My Cocktail Inventions

Jeanes Lament: 4 oz. white wine, gripped tightly with smoke-stained fingers.

Jims Reading Retreat: 1 jigger Grey Goose Vodka, mixed with cranberry juice, enjoyed while thumb-ing a book page.

Mariannes Nostalgia Trip: glass of Dubonet sprinkled with stories, enjoyed while petting a dog.

Excerpt from short story "Gerald in Captivity or Who Stole My Benicar and Where Did Friday Disappear?" (original type-face) by Gerald Hugunin

Great Works of Innovative Fiction Published by JEF Books

Collected Stort Shories by Erik Belgum

Don't Sing Aloha When I Go by Robert Casella

How to Break Article Noun by Carolyn Chun [winner of the
2012 Patchen Award!]

What Is Art? by Norman Conquest

Something Is Crook in Middlebrook by James. R. Hugunin

OD:Docufictions by Harold Jaffe

Paris 60 by Harold Jaffe

Apostrophe/Parenthesis by Frederick Mark Kramer

Ambiguity by Frederick Mark Kramer

Xanthous Mermaid Mechanics by Brion Poloncic

Short Tails by Yuriy Tarnawsky

Prism and Graded Monotony by Dominic Ward

For a complete listing of all our titles
please visit us at experimentalfiction.com